"Filled with romance, family s[...] Turansky's dual-time novel, *Th[...]* will stir your faith—and your [...] District!"

—Julie Klassen, author of *The Sisters of Sea View*

"In this enchanting romance, Carrie Turansky opens the door of Longdale Manor and invites readers to explore its vast collection of artwork and the secrets hidden inside. As the characters, both past and present, wrestle to forgive those who've wronged them, the beautiful manor house harbors deep sorrows and the sweetest of joys."

—Melanie Dobson, award-winning author of *Catching the Wind* and *Enchanted Isle*

"Turansky explores building godly relationships while maintaining faith through serious trials and disappointments. Set amid the dramatic beauty of England's Lake District, *The Legacy of Longdale Manor* is a romantic and deeply satisfying love story revealing our Heavenly Father's shepherding grace. A beautiful book to warm and lift the heart."

—Cathy Gohlke, Christy Hall of Fame author of *Ladies of the Lake* and *A Hundred Crickets Singing*

"Once again author Carrie Turansky inspires us in this beautifully written tale! Two broken women living a century apart seek healing and a sense of belonging. Yet only faith, family, and forgiveness have the power to change everything and open the heart to finding love. An unforgettable and uplifting story!"

—Kate Breslin, bestselling author of *In Love's Time*

"*The Legacy of Longdale Manor* is a poignant story of broken family relationships set amidst the lush backdrop of England's Lake District. Author Carrie Turansky weaves together a split-time tale that ties together generations dating back a century. A masterful plot dealing with issues that every reader will relate to."

—Michelle Griep, Christy Award–winning author of
The Bride of Blackfriars Lane

"Two women, one manor house, and a century of family secrets weave together to form a heartfelt journey to redemption and forgiveness. *The Legacy of Longdale Manor* is a beautiful story of faith, with a hint of English charm that will appeal to fans of *All Creatures Great and Small*."

—Gabrielle Meyer, author of *When the Day Comes*
and *In This Moment*

"Carrie Turansky weaves an intriguing tale combining old and new as two couples explore questions concerning family, identity, and what real love truly means. Set in the charming villages and surrounds of England's Lake District, this is a story to savor over a nice cup of tea."

—Carolyn Miller, award-winning author of *Dusk's Darkest Shores* and the MUSKOKA ROMANCE series

The
LEGACY
of
LONGDALE
MANOR

The
LEGACY
of
LONGDALE
MANOR

CARRIE TURANSKY

BETHANYHOUSE
a division of Baker Publishing Group
Minneapolis, Minnesota

Published by Bethany House Publishers
Minneapolis, Minnesota
www.bethanyhouse.com

Bethany House Publishers is a division of
Baker Publishing Group, Grand Rapids, Michigan

Printed in the United States of America

Library of Congress Cataloging-in-Publication Data
Names: Turansky, Carrie, author.
Title: The legacy of Longdale Manor / Carrie Turansky.
Description: Minneapolis, Minnesota : Bethany House, a division of Baker
    Publishing Group, [2023]
Identifiers: LCCN 2023012896 | ISBN 9780764241055 (paper) | ISBN 9780764242199
    (casebound) | ISBN 9781493443710 (ebook)
Subjects: LCGFT: Christian fiction. | Novels.
Classification: LCC PS3620.U7457 L44 2023 | DDC 813/.6—dc23/eng/20230331
LC record available at https://lccn.loc.gov/2023012896

Author is represented by The Steve Laube Agency.

Baker Publishing Group publications use paper produced from sustainable forestry
practices and post-consumer waste whenever possible.

23 24 25 26 27 28 29   7 6 5 4 3 2 1

To my husband, Scott,
who has always supported me in my writing,
and who makes each day brighter
as we walk through this life together.

I'm blessed and grateful for you and your love.

"For this is what the Sovereign LORD says: I myself will search for my sheep and look after them. As a shepherd looks after his scattered flock when he is with them, so will I look after my sheep. I will rescue them from all the places where they were scattered on a day of clouds and darkness. . . . I will search for the lost and bring back the strays. I will bind up the injured and strengthen the weak."

Ezekiel 34:11–12, 16 NIV

One

2012
London, England

The lift door slid open, and Gwen Morris stepped into the third-floor offices of Hill and Morris, one of the most prestigious art and antique auction houses in London. She still felt a thrill each time she walked down the dark paneled hallway toward her new office and took in the beautiful paintings, jewelry, and antiques on display.

The receptionist looked up as Gwen approached. The young woman's eyes widened, and she quickly looked down at her desk and shuffled some papers.

Gwen's steps slowed. "Good morning, MaryAnn."

"Morning." MaryAnn slowly lifted her eyes to meet Gwen's. "Your grandfather—I mean, Mr. Morris—would like you to come to his office right away."

A prickle of unease traveled through Gwen, but she quickly dismissed it. He probably wanted to discuss some new acquisitions, or perhaps give her feedback on her first month as junior specialist for art history and antiques.

"Thank you." She started down the hall and glanced through Charlene's open office doorway. As the older woman met her gaze, her expression hardened, and she turned toward the windows. That was odd. Charlene usually offered a "Good morning," or at least a nod as Gwen passed.

She continued down the hall and received chilly looks from three other colleagues. What was going on? Certainly, the weather was gloomy, and they all had a heavy workload, but she couldn't imagine why everyone seemed to be in such a dark mood this morning.

She approached her grandfather's outer office, and Mrs. Huntington, her grandfather's fiftyish administrative assistant, lifted her head, her face impassive. "Mr. Morris said you are to go right in."

Gwen's stomach tensed. This did not bode well. She straightened her shoulders, stepped into her grandfather's office, and closed the door.

Her grandfather looked up, his gray eyes cool and assessing. He sat behind his large wooden desk, with his back to the tall windows behind him. Dark gray clouds draped the buildings on the opposite side of St. James Street, and rivulets raced down the glass in a dizzy dance. The downpour outside seemed a perfect reflection of her grandfather's shadowed expression.

He nodded to the chair in front of his desk. "Have a seat, Gwen."

A shiver raced down her back as she lowered herself into the chair. She should ask what was wrong, but she couldn't seem to force out the words.

"We have a situation . . . a very serious situation, I might add." His gray eyebrows drew down into a deep *V*. "One of the Impressionist paintings we auctioned last Saturday"—he glanced at his computer—"*Avenue of the Allies*, which you listed as a copy of Childe Hassam's painting by the same name . . ."

Gwen nodded, remembering the painting clearly. Hassam was an American Impressionist who painted in Britain and

France as well as the US. His work was copied by many artists in the late 1800s and early 1900s.

He focused on her again. "It was an original."

A shock wave jolted Gwen, and she sucked in a sharp breath.

"The buyer is thrilled to have purchased an original Hassam at one-tenth of its true value," her grandfather continued. "But the seller, Ivan Saunders, is irate. He's threatening a lawsuit and promising to spread the story of our incompetence far and wide."

She stared at her grandfather and tried to swallow, but her throat seemed blocked by a huge boulder. How could she have made such a terrible mistake?

Her thoughts raced back to the last week of February, when she'd started in her new position. After one year as an intern, stepping into the role of junior specialist had been a huge transition. That same week, she'd gone through a painful breakup with her boyfriend, Oliver St. Charles. She'd lost hours of sleep over that heartache, and her mind had been in a fog. Was that why she'd failed to realize she was evaluating an original Hassam?

"Well, Gwen, what do you have to say for yourself?"

"I . . . I don't know what happened. I checked the painting's provenance. Then I compared it to other paintings by Hassam, looking at the style and brushstroke, the color choice, and size of the work. They all seemed so different from his other paintings, and there was no signature, so I assumed—"

"His signature was revealed when the frame was removed. It's been verified as the original." Her grandfather steepled his fingers, his serious gaze drilling into her. "Why didn't you remove the frame and look for the signature?"

"The frame was beautiful. I thought it might possibly be worth more than the painting, and I didn't want to damage it. And the fact that there was no visible signature made it seem most likely it was a copy."

"Did you check the catalogue raisonné?"

"Yes. It said the original was part of a private collection owned by . . . someone. I don't remember the name, but it wasn't Ivan Saunders."

"If you had any question, you should have spoken to Charlene, or run your findings past others who have more experience before you catalogued it."

The burning sensation in her stomach rose, singeing her throat. "Charlene was unwell that week and not in the office."

He gave a brief nod. "Charlene and a few others are looking at the pieces you've evaluated since then. Nothing else glaring has come up, but that doesn't excuse the mistake you made with the Hassam."

Gwen lowered her chin, wishing she could melt into the floor. She had seriously disappointed her grandfather. Worse than that, she'd confirmed what she'd always suspected: She wasn't good enough. She wasn't ready. She might never be. This position had only been given to her because she was Lionel Morris's granddaughter. And now that she'd made this colossal error, she faced losing the position she'd worked so hard to attain.

She looked across at her grandfather, pain and regret squeezing her heart. "You're right. There's no excuse. I should've done more research and consulted with others, rather than trying to handle it on my own."

"I imagine you were trying to prove yourself, but I'm afraid that was a very costly error in judgment. You've tarnished your reputation in the art community and with your colleagues at Hill and Morris."

He didn't add *and with me*, but she could feel the weight of those silent words. "I'm sorry." Her voice came out a rough whisper.

"This is a very difficult way to start your career."

That went without saying. "What will happen now . . . about the painting?"

"I've spoken to our legal department."

Gwen's heart clenched. Oliver worked in the legal department. Now he had even more reasons to be glad he'd broken up with her. Everyone at Hill and Morris would consider her a foolish upstart who'd proven she didn't deserve the position she'd been given.

"They'll work out a settlement with Ivan Saunders," her grandfather continued, "but it will be costly and not soon forgotten by anyone."

Gwen acknowledged his words with a slow nod. How could she have let this happen? Was it her pride or lack of experience that had taken her down that path . . . or both?

She looked up and met her grandfather's gaze. "What can I do? How can I make this up to you?"

He tapped his index fingers together for a few seconds as he studied the rain-washed windows to his left. "I have an old friend, Lilly Benderly. She wants to sell some of the art and antiques in her home, Longdale Manor, near Keswick. She can't afford our usual fees, but there's the possibility of a future investment there, and I'd like to help her." He shifted his gaze back to Gwen. "I want you to go to Longdale, evaluate the pieces she's interested in selling, and make the arrangements to have them shipped to London and prepared for auction."

Hope surged in her chest. "Of course. I'd be glad to go." She had no idea where Keswick was located, but she didn't want to admit that to her grandfather. She'd look it up later. "Did she say how many pieces she wants evaluated?"

"No, she didn't. But this will give you time away from London until the storm blows over. I think that is the best way to avoid embarrassment."

His embarrassment, or hers? She closed her eyes and suppressed a sigh. Why hadn't she been more careful? Couldn't she do anything right? She pushed those questions down, opened her eyes, and focused on her grandfather again. "When did you want me to go?"

"As soon as we can make the arrangements."

Gwen nodded, but questions swirled in her mind. What type of art and antiques did her grandfather's friend want to sell? If she handled this project well, could she regain her grandfather's trust?

"Take your time, and be sure you evaluate each piece correctly," he said. "Lilly is a recent widow, and a bit eccentric. But I want her to receive the best sale price possible. Can you do that, Gwen?"

She gave a firm nod. "I'll do my best and run all my work by you and Charlene."

"Good. Mrs. Huntington will give you Lilly Benderly's contact information. Let her know you're coming. Stay in Keswick as long as needed to do a thorough job." He paused and looked toward the door, indicating the meeting was over.

She rose on wobbly legs, then willed strength into them and faced her grandfather. "I know my mistake has put you in a difficult position. I'm truly sorry for that. It won't happen again. I promise."

His stern expression softened. "We all make mistakes, Gwen. It's what we learn from those mistakes and how we recover that's important. I hope you'll take this lesson to heart."

His gentle words sent new courage flowing through her. "Yes, sir. I will."

"You've been given a great opportunity at Hill and Morris. I hope you'll do all you can to make the most of it."

Gwen lifted her suitcase onto the bed in her small London flat, pulled the zipper around, and flipped open the top. Her hand stilled, and she looked out her bedroom window as the painful events of the morning replayed through her mind. She'd let her grandfather down in the worst way and made a costly mistake that was going to follow her for years to come.

She blinked and tried to shake off the dazed, disappointed feeling coursing through her. This was not the end of her career. It couldn't be. Somehow, she would find a way to rebuild. She crossed to the dresser and took a shirt from the top drawer.

The front door opened, and footsteps sounded on the wooden floor. Lindsey Winters, her roommate, looked in from the hallway. "Gwen, what are you doing home?" Her gaze darted to the suitcase on the bed. "What's going on?"

Gwen sighed. "It's a long story. You might want to sit down."

Lindsey lowered herself into the chair next to Gwen's bed. "What happened?"

Gwen sank down on her bed. "I made a huge mistake evaluating a painting, and my grandfather is sending me away until the dust settles."

"What kind of mistake?"

Gwen poured out the story, her eyes burning as she repeated what she'd done and the response of her grandfather and coworkers.

"Oh, Gwen, I'm so sorry. It's no wonder you're upset. But he didn't sack you. He's giving you a chance to show him you can do the work." That was just like Lindsey, always looking for the positive side in any hard situation.

Gwen gave a reluctant nod. Lindsey was right. Her grandfather had offered her the opportunity to redeem herself and prove she was worthy of her position at Hill and Morris.

"Where's he sending you?"

"He wants me to evaluate some pieces for an old friend who lives in Keswick, wherever that is."

Lindsey's eyes lit up. "That's in the Lake District."

A distant memory stirred Gwen's mind at those words. "The Lake District?"

"Yes, up north. Oh, it's so lovely this time of year." Lindsey smiled. "Mum and Dad took me to Windermere on holiday when I was sixteen. That's not far from Keswick. We went hiking in the hills. They call them *fells* up there. And we took a boat ride across Lake Windermere and visited Beatrix Potter's Hill Top Farm."

The Lake District . . . Gwen rose and crossed to her closet. Her mum had mentioned painting in the Lake District when she was younger. She reached up to the top shelf, pulled out a large round hatbox, and carried it back to her bed.

"What's in there?" Lindsey asked as Gwen lifted the lid.

"Everything that was in my mum's desk." She glanced at the papers and photographs that nearly filled the box, and her throat tightened. "It's hard to believe she's been gone almost two years."

"I'm sorry, Gwen." Lindsey's voice softened. "I wish I'd known your mum. From what you've told me, she sounds like a very special person."

"She was. I still miss her every day." Gwen blew out a breath and pushed the first few papers aside. "I think my parents met in the Lake District."

"Really?" Lindsey scooted closer. "I've never heard you say much about your father."

Gwen's throat tightened, and she tried to force down the jumbled feelings coursing through her. "That's because I've never met him. He left my mum before I was born."

Lindsey's eyes widened. "Oh, Gwen. I didn't know."

"It was a long time ago." She tried to sound as though it didn't bother her, but that wasn't the truth. She'd asked Mum about her father several times. But Mum only gave brief replies that left Gwen with more questions than answers. Finally, when she was eighteen, she'd begged to know why her father hadn't been a part of their lives. Did he even know she existed? And if he did know, why didn't he care he had a daughter?

Mum said she had her reasons and made Gwen promise she would not go searching for him on her own. Mum said she would explain more when Gwen graduated from university, so Gwen had reluctantly agreed. But Mum had died in a terrible car accident only three weeks before Gwen's graduation, taking the story with her to her grave.

Gwen lifted a stack of photos and sorted through them. A few seconds later, she found the one she'd been looking for. A young couple stood arm in arm on the shore of a lake with high hills in the background. Her mother looked as though she was in her early twenties. Her long brown hair cascaded over her shoulders, and her bright blue eyes shone with a hopeful light. The tall man standing beside her looked ruggedly handsome, with light brown hair, deep-set gray eyes, and a strong, square chin. Gwen guessed he was also in his twenties, but older than Mum. His arms were muscular and suntanned, and he held what looked like a tall wooden stick that curved at the top and had a carved head.

Lindsey leaned closer. "Is that your parents?"

"Yes." Her voice quavered as she stared at the father she'd never met.

Lindsey tipped her head. "It looks like there's something written on the back of the photo."

Gwen turned it over and read, *Jessica and Landon on our wedding day, 10 June 1985, Keswick.* She blinked and stared at the words. Her parents were married in Keswick.

She studied her father's image, considering the possibilities. Did he still live in or near Keswick? The thought of meeting him after all these years sent a shiver down her back. She'd promised her mum she wouldn't search for him, but that was before her mum died. Surely her mum's death released her from that promise.

But doubts rose and clouded her thoughts. Something very painful must have happened to make her mum keep that part of her life a secret. Was she ready to learn the truth about her father and discover why he'd never been a part of their lives?

She'd always longed to know her father and sense that true father-daughter connection. This was her chance. It would take courage to begin her search. But if she did find him, would he welcome her into his life, or would he break her heart as he'd broken Mum's?

❦

David Bradford gripped the sides of the old folding ladder and climbed toward the top. He pushed open Longdale's attic door, and cool musty air rushed out, along with an odd scent he couldn't name. Squinting into the darkness, he pointed his torch toward the eaves and scanned the dusty timbers. Something moved, and he gripped the ladder.

"What do you see?" his grandmother called from the bottom of the ladder.

David scrolled the beam of light over the squirming black mass between the wooden eaves and suppressed a shudder. "I'm afraid you've got bats, Nana."

"Bats! Good heavens!" His grandmother tugged on his pant leg. "Come down at once! Bats carry rabies."

David doubted the bats in Longdale's attic had the disease, but he'd rather not personally test that theory. Gritting his teeth, he backed down the steps. Bats! One more problem to add to the growing list of things he needed to address before they could move ahead with his plan to convert Longdale into a luxury hotel.

"This is dreadful!" His grandmother looked up, her soft gray eyes filled with worry. "We have to be rid of them."

"It won't be easy, Nana." He stepped down beside her and raised the ladder into the ceiling. "Bats are protected. It's against the law to disturb their roosts."

Her silver eyebrows rose. "Protected?" Her stunned expression quickly changed to steely resolve. "They must go! I won't stand for an attic full of bats!"

David kept his voice even, hoping to calm her. "We might be able to get permission to move them. If not, we'll probably have to enclose the area so they can continue living there undisturbed."

"We can't open Longdale to paying guests with bats roosting in the attic!"

He laid his hand on her shoulder. This kind of upsetting news wasn't good for her heart. "Don't worry, Nana. I'll make some calls and take care of it." He guided her down the hallway, away from the soft rustling sounds coming from the attic.

She looked back at him. "Oh, you are a dear. I'm so glad you've come. Arthur always took care of things like this, but now that he's gone . . ." Her voice choked off, and she shook her head. "I need some tea. Let's go down to the kitchen."

He agreed, and they took the back servants' stairs down two flights to the bottom level and followed the long, arched hallway to Longdale's cavernous kitchen.

Mrs. Galloway, or Mrs. G., as his grandmother liked to call her, stood by the stove, stirring a pot of something that smelled delicious. He sniffed again and determined it must be chicken soup.

Mrs. G. greeted them with pink cheeks and a cheery smile. Then she noticed his grandmother's worried look, and her smile melted away.

"We're in need of some tea." Nana crossed to the large worktable in the center of the kitchen. "David has discovered what's making those strange noises in the attic."

Mrs. G. turned from filling the electric teakettle. "What is it?"

"Bats!" Nana's chin quivered. "We've been invaded by a colony of bloodsucking creatures!"

Mrs. G.'s hand flew to cover her heart. "Saints above! They can't get out of the attic, can they?"

"No," David quickly replied. "I'm sure they won't bother us. I faced a similar situation last summer when we converted an estate in Berkshire into a spa." He didn't add it had taken more than a month to get permission to remove the bats, and it had cost several hundred pounds to remedy the problem. His grandmother's income didn't match the needs of maintaining the estate, and he didn't want to add to her financial worries. He'd figure this out. He had to if he was going to help her save Longdale.

A bell buzzed behind him. He turned toward the bell board to see where the summon originated. "Someone is at the front door."

"Nancy is cleaning upstairs," Mrs. G. said. "She'll answer it for you."

David turned to his grandmother. "Are you expecting someone?"

She blinked a few times, then her eyes widened. "I am. We better go up."

He held back a chuckle. His grandmother's memory was not as sharp as it used to be.

His grandmother started toward the kitchen doorway, then looked back. "Mrs. G., will you please bring our tea up to the library, along with some cinnamon biscuits and an extra cup for our guest?"

Mrs. G. nodded. "I'll be up as soon as it's ready."

David followed his grandmother up the stone stairs. "Who's joining us for tea?"

"Gwen Morris. She's the granddaughter of an old friend from London."

He'd never heard his grandmother mention someone by that name. "Is she in the area on holiday?"

"No, dear. She works at Hill and Morris."

His steps stalled. "The auction house?"

"Yes. Her grandfather, Lionel Morris, has been a dear friend for many years."

He stared at his grandmother. "*The* Lionel Morris of Hill and Morris?"

"Yes, dear. That's what I said. His granddaughter is going to look at the paintings and antiques and help us decide what to prepare for auction."

He grinned and shook his head. Lilly Benderly was always full of surprises. He'd mentioned the idea of selling some of the paintings and furnishings a few days ago, as that seemed like a logical way to raise the funds needed for the repairs and renovations. At the time, she hadn't seemed in favor of the idea. He supposed she'd changed her mind and forgotten to tell him. He followed her into the large entrance hall.

Nancy, the middle-aged woman who helped with cleaning twice a week, stood by the front door, blocking his view of the woman waiting there. Nancy turned to his grandmother. "This is Miss Gwen Morris to see you, ma'am." She stepped aside.

"Welcome to Longdale." Nana crossed toward her with an outstretched hand and warm smile. "I'm Lilly Benderly."

Gwen returned his grandmother's greeting and smile, and David did a double take. She was young and attractive, with long golden-brown hair that fell over her shoulders in soft waves. Her eyes were an unusual shade of blue green, like the lake on a summer day. She wore a fashionable green wool coat and brown leather boots and . . . she towed a rolling suitcase.

Had his grandmother invited her to stay at Longdale?

"I'm pleased to meet you." Gwen lifted her gaze, taking in the dark woodwork and elaborately carved staircase and mantel over the marble fireplace. "Longdale is a beautiful home."

"Thank you. We're very fond of it." She motioned toward David. "This is my grandson, David Bradford. He's the one I told you about."

He shot his grandmother a questioning glance. What had she told her?

Gwen looked his way and held out her hand. "It's good to meet you, Mr. Bradford. I'm looking forward to assisting you and Mrs. Benderly."

He took her hand. It was soft and warm, matching the look in her eyes.

"There's no need to be formal." His grandmother looked from Gwen to David. "You must call us Lilly and David."

Gwen nodded. "Thank you. Please, call me Gwen."

David studied her. She couldn't be more than twenty-five, and she looked more like an actress or model than an art and antique appraiser. Why had Lionel Morris sent her instead of someone older and more experienced? "What is your position at Hill and Morris?"

"I'm a junior specialist for art history and antiques."

"A junior specialist . . . as opposed to a senior specialist?"

She lifted her chin and met his challenge with a steady look. "Yes. I have an undergraduate degree in art history and a master's in art business. I finished a one-year internship at Hill and Morris in February. That's when I started my current position."

His grandmother sent him a puzzled look. "David, there's no need to question Gwen's credentials. She traveled all the way from London to help us. We want her to know how much we appreciate her coming."

Chastised, he nodded. "You're right." He turned to Gwen. "We're glad you're here. No offense meant."

"None taken." But her cheeks glowed bright pink, and her words sounded a bit forced. She turned back to his grandmother. "I appreciate your invitation to stay at Longdale, but if that's not convenient, I'd be glad to find accommodations in Keswick."

His grandmother shook her head. "Oh no. You must stay

with us. What would your grandfather think if I sent you off alone?"

Gwen sent David a quick glance before she looked back at his grandmother. "If you're sure it's all right. It would make my job easier."

"We're positive, aren't we, David?" His grandmother turned to him with a lifted brow.

"Yes, of course. It makes sense for you to stay here. We have plenty of room."

His grandmother gave an approving smile. "Good. Now that's settled, let's go into the library. Tea is on the way, and we can have a chat."

Gwen sent an uncertain glance toward her suitcase.

David stepped forward. "I'll take that for you." Without waiting for her reply, he rolled it over to the bottom of the staircase, then he followed Gwen and his grandmother into the library.

He watched Gwen as she took a seat next to his grandmother. Her earlier prickly response to his questions had faded. She seemed more relaxed now, smiling and nodding as his grandmother regaled her with the history of Longdale.

His chest tightened as he watched his grandmother's delighted expression. She loved every beam and window of this crumbling old house. If he was going to save it for her, he would need to build an alliance with Gwen Morris.

But did she have enough experience to appraise his grandmother's treasures for their true value? And even if she did, would the sale provide the funds needed to take care of the repairs and renovations, or would he and his grandmother lose the home that had been in the family for generations—the home that one day should be his?

Two

1912
London

The low murmur of the crowd filling the Fairweather Music Hall drifted past the closed velvet curtain, sending a thrill through Charlotte Harper. She turned to her father with a wide smile. "It sounds like a full house."

Her father nodded, his dark eyes glowing. "I believe you're right. The committee was wise to move the meeting here so we could accommodate a larger audience."

Charlotte's heart lifted. How proud she was of her father and his rise to prominence in the Higher Life Movement. As keynote speaker for this series of four meetings, his messages about pursuing a deeper commitment to God and gaining total victory over sin had captured the hearts and minds of devoted Christians all over London. The church sanctuary had been filled the last three nights, and hundreds of people had to be turned away. That had prompted the committee to change the venue to this new location for the fourth and final meeting.

Her mum, Rose Harper, stepped forward and brushed a piece of lint from the lapel of Father's new black suit, affection shining in her soft brown eyes. "You look quite handsome, Henry."

He sent her a brief glance, then looked away with a slight frown. "I'm sure the audience is more concerned about the content of my message than my appearance."

A flash of hurt crossed Mum's face, and she stepped back. "Of course, dear. I simply meant the new suit was a good choice." The black fabric with the pale gray pinstripe was an unusual choice for her father, but the tailor insisted it was quite appropriate for a speaker of his standing. Charlotte hoped the more conservative members of the audience wouldn't criticize him for his appearance.

Father's gaze darted to the men working backstage, then he grimaced and ran his finger around the inside of his collar.

Mum's brow creased. "You look flushed, Henry. Are you feeling ill?"

"I'm fine. This collar is simply too tight. You'll have to order me a larger one tomorrow."

Mum nodded. "Yes, dear. I'll take care of it."

Charlotte studied her father's glistening forehead and hoped he wasn't coming down with an illness. She pushed that thought away. He was in perfect health. It was probably just the excitement of tonight's events or the warmth of the backstage lights that was making him uncomfortable.

Charlotte's twelve-year-old sister, Alice, pulled the curtain back an inch and peeked out. "Oh, look at all the people!"

Charlotte reached for her sister's arm. "Alice, step back."

"They won't see me." A delighted smile lit up her sister's face. "There must be at least a thousand people out there."

Charlotte stepped behind Alice and looked around the edge of the curtain. Her breath caught, and her heart soared. Almost every seat on the main floor was filled, and the balconies swarmed with more people eager to find a seat . . . and they had all come to hear her father give his message.

She glanced back at her parents, intending to tell them what she'd seen, but Sir Anthony Fitzhugh, the head of the Higher Life Spring Series Committee, approached.

"Good evening." Sir Anthony nodded to Mum, then reached out and shook Father's hand. He was taller than her father and had a silver moustache, full beard, and kind blue eyes that gave him a distinguished appearance. He and her father had been good friends for several years.

Father smiled. "Good to see you, Anthony."

"Glad to be here with you. It's almost seven o'clock. Are you ready?"

Father nodded. "I'm looking forward to it."

Sir Anthony's expression radiated warmth and approval. "So am I, my friend. So am I." He turned to Mum and motioned to the right. "I've reserved seats for you and your daughters in the first row. If you go down those steps and into the hallway, you'll see the side entrance to the auditorium to your left. An usher will help you find your way."

Mum smiled. "Thank you, Sir Anthony. That's very kind."

"You're most welcome." He cocked his eyebrows. "If I hadn't reserved them, I'm afraid you'd be left standing."

Charlotte and Alice exchanged a smile. How wonderful that their father was receiving the respect and acclaim he so well deserved. He spent hours preparing, consulting commentaries and various books to add depth and insight to his messages. In the last few months, invitations had been pouring in from congregations and groups all over England. One had even arrived from New York. Her father's eyes had glowed when he'd read the letter and announced the news to the family. He hadn't accepted the invitation yet, but if he agreed, they would all be sailing to America in a few months, and Charlotte was delighted at the prospect.

Mum rose on tiptoe and kissed Father's cheek. "We'll see you after."

He accepted her kiss but turned away without answering.

Mum hesitated a moment, then she shifted her gaze to Charlotte and Alice. "Come along, girls." She took Alice's hand and started down the backstage steps.

Charlotte squeezed her father's hand. "I'll be praying for you."

He took his handkerchief from his jacket pocket and blotted his forehead. "Thank you." But he didn't meet her gaze. Instead, he glanced toward the curtain, as though he was already engaged with the audience.

Her hand slipped from his, and she turned and followed her mother and Alice into the hallway. Mum gave her name to the usher, and he opened the door to the auditorium and led them to the three reserved seats in the center of the first row.

Charlotte took the third seat. Mum sat in the middle, with Alice on her left. As Charlotte settled in and looked around, the lights came down and the crowd hushed. All around them a sense of excitement and anticipation filled the air.

Sir Anthony stepped from behind the curtain, strode to the pulpit in the center, and faced the audience. "Good evening, ladies and gentlemen. It is my great pleasure to welcome you to the fourth meeting in our Higher Life Spring Series." The audience responded with polite applause.

Charlotte glanced at Mum. Her cheeks were slightly pink and her expression expectant as she looked up at Sir Anthony.

When the applause died down, Sir Anthony's gaze traveled across the audience. "The Lord is doing powerful work among us, calling us all to full surrender and total commitment to Him. Our hope and prayer are that tonight's message will bring deep conviction and holy consecration to each one present. May we all dedicate ourselves fully to pressing on to God's higher calling.

"And now I encourage you to give your full attention to Henry Harper, our dear brother and deeply devoted fellow sojourner on the road to the higher life." Sir Anthony swept his hand to the right.

Her father stepped out from behind the curtain and crossed to center stage as hearty applause filled the auditorium. The two men shook hands, and Sir Anthony walked offstage. Her father placed his Bible on the pulpit and looked out at the audience, his dark eyes bright and intense.

Love for him surged in Charlotte's chest. His dedication to God, his powerful preaching, and his handsome appearance made her proud to call him her father. There was no one she loved and admired more.

He opened his Bible and raised his gaze. "Tonight, we will look at the words of Jesus and His call to enter through the narrow gate. We will ask the question, Are you following the Savior through that narrow gate and down the road that leads to eternal life? Or have you, like so many others, lost your way and wandered to the wide and rocky path that leads to destruction?"

Charlotte clasped her hands in her lap, stirred once again by her father's words. Ever since she was a little girl, she'd heard him speak about that narrow gate. He and Mum had modeled a life of devotion and commitment, and she tried to follow their example. But she had to admit there were times she resisted the Spirit's promptings and stubbornly chose to go her own way. That thought niggled her conscience. She pushed it away and focused on her father's words once more.

He lifted his hand as his gaze swept the audience. "There are many trials . . . and temptations that come our way. The enemy of our soul is always on the prowl, looking for an opportunity to steal, kill, and destroy those who follow the Lord. He tries to . . . pull us off that narrow path." Her father's voice faltered. He looked down and gripped the sides of the pulpit.

Confusion wound through Charlotte. Had he paused for emphasis, or was something wrong? She glanced at her mum, hoping for reassurance. But concern lined her mum's face as she looked up at him.

Her father slowly lifted his head, his eyes searching the crowd. His face had gone deathly pale, and his chin quivered. "I'm sorry. I can't seem . . . to catch my . . ." He swayed, then he slumped and crashed to the floor behind the pulpit.

The crowd gasped. Charlotte's hands flew to cover her mouth, and she sprang from her seat.

"Father!" Alice cried and grabbed hold of Mum's arm.

Mum pulled away and strode toward the stage. Charlotte gripped Alice's hand and hurried after her. Sir Anthony rushed out from the side of the stage. Two other men followed and circled around Father, hiding him from Charlotte's view.

A man pushed through the gathering crowd behind Charlotte. "Let me through! I'm a doctor!" He climbed onto the stage and knelt beside Father.

Charlotte's heart pounded, and fearful thoughts raced through her mind. Voices rose around them, and the crowd pushed in closer. Mum bowed her head and clasped her shaking hands in front of her mouth, her lips moving in silent prayer.

Alice looked up at Charlotte with tear-filled eyes. "What happened? What's wrong with Father?"

"I don't know." Charlotte's voice trembled. She leaned to the left, trying to see past the men surrounding Father, but it was impossible.

"Stand back. Give him air," the doctor commanded, and the men moved back, widening their circle.

All around her, voices rose in prayer, some crying out, others murmuring softly.

Sir Anthony rose and looked their way. "Mrs. Harper, Henry is asking for you."

Mum opened her eyes and started for the side stairs. She looked over her shoulder, pain etched across her pale face. "Come with me, girls."

Charlotte took Alice's hand and followed Mum. When they reached center stage, the men surrounding her father parted and let them through. Charlotte's stomach dropped, and dizziness washed over her. Her father's face had gone pasty white, and his eyes were clouded. They had loosened his collar and unbuttoned his shirt at the neck.

Mum knelt and reached for Father's hand.

"Rose," he whispered.

"Yes, I'm here," she said softly.

"I'm sorry. I . . . never meant . . . this to happen." Anguish twisted his pale, glistening face.

"It's all right, Henry." Tears gathered in Mum's eyes. "Please, be calm. You don't have to speak."

"But . . . I . . ." His gaze shifted to Charlotte, heartbreaking emotion flickering across his face. "Forgive me."

Charlotte's throat swelled, and she knelt next to Mum. "There is nothing to forgive," she said, forcing out her words.

Father shook his head and closed his eyes. "If this is the end . . . know that I am truly sorry. I love you all very much."

"And we love you." Mum raised their clasped hands and kissed his fingers.

A man ran in and leaned toward the doctor. "The ambulance is here."

The doctor laid his hand on Mum's arm. "We're taking him to St. Luke's."

Mum nodded and swiped a tear from her cheek. "We'll follow." Her voice faltered, and her gaze traveled around the circle of men.

Four men strode in, carrying a canvas stretcher. Sir Anthony and the doctor moved everyone back. The men lowered the stretcher and transferred Father into place, then they grabbed the handles and lifted him.

Gasps and voices rose from the crush of people gathered in front of the stage.

"Henry!" a woman's voice cried out.

Charlotte turned and scanned the crowd. A blond woman stood at the edge of the stage, a handkerchief clutched to her mouth and tears flooding her blue eyes. Her gaze connected with Charlotte's, and her features twisted painfully. She spun away, pushed through the crowd, and strode up the aisle.

Sir Anthony turned to Mum. "I can take you and your daughters to the hospital in my motorcar."

"Thank you." Mum's voice barely rose above a whisper. Sir Anthony offered her his arm. Mum slipped her hand through, and they followed the men carrying Father's stretcher offstage.

Charlotte took Alice's hand and hurried after them, her mind spinning in frantic circles. Would Father recover, or was this the last time she would see him? A chill traveled through her, and she closed her eyes against that dreadful thought. She had to hold on to hope.

But hope seemed like a distant dream as more unsettling thoughts filled her mind. She'd always been taught God watched over and protected those who loved Him. Her father was at the height of his ministry and having a profound impact on many people. How could God strike down such a devoted and faithful servant? Her frightened heart couldn't make sense of it.

$$\infty$$

Charlotte carried the tray of used teacups into the kitchen and let the door swing closed behind her. She set the tray on the table, released a deep sigh, and rubbed her gritty eyes. Bone-weary and numb with grief, she could hardly connect one thought to the next, but she had to keep going.

Hundreds of people had come to her father's funeral that morning at the church, and Mum said it was only proper they invite their closest friends back to their home for a reception after. Now, Charlotte was stepping in as hostess to give Mum a short break.

She closed her eyes and leaned against the kitchen counter. If only she didn't have to return to the sitting room where a crowd of guests waited. They'd come to express their condolences and try to offer comfort. But it had been a long, painful day. Surely they would leave soon so the family could grieve in private.

Her eighteen-year-old brother, Daniel, walked into the kitchen. His wavy, dark brown hair was mussed, and his brown eyes shadowed. He looked almost as weary as she felt. He had been away at Oxford when Father collapsed. They'd sent him a telegram, and he'd raced home in time to see Father in the hospital. But Father had been unconscious by the time he arrived. Daniel hadn't been able to say good-bye, and that added to his grief.

He met her gaze. "Where's Mum? Sir Anthony and Mr. Walker want to speak to her before they leave."

Charlotte glanced toward the back stairs. "She went up to her room for a few minutes."

He nodded, lines creasing his forehead. "I'll go up and get her."

"No, I'll go. Could you tell them she'll be down shortly?"

He nodded, then searched her face, and his anxious expression eased. "I know this is hard, Charlotte, but we'll get through it."

She gave a slow nod, but she wasn't sure how. Father had been like the sun, the center of their universe. And they'd been like planets rotating around him, soaking in his powerful energy and light. How could they go on without him?

She forced those painful thoughts aside and climbed the back stairs. She found Mum in her bedroom, standing in front of her dressing table mirror, pressing a washcloth to her face.

Charlotte kept her voice soft, hoping not to add to Mum's pain. "Mr. Walker and Sir Anthony want to speak to you."

Mum turned and looked her way with a dazed expression. "What do they want?"

"I don't know. Daniel said they're preparing to leave and are asking for you."

Mum sighed. She dried her pale face and looked in the mirror once more. Her eyes were red-rimmed from weeping, and gray shadows beneath her eyes gave evidence of her lack of sleep.

Charlotte stepped closer and laid her hand on Mum's back. "I'll go down with you."

Mum met her gaze in the mirror, then turned and touched Charlotte's cheek. "Thank you, my dear. I don't know how I would've survived this week without you and your brother. Even Alice has been a sweet comfort."

Charlotte's eyes stung. She pressed her lips together and nodded. Mum was always gentle and ladylike, qualities Charlotte admired but often lacked. She'd been closer to her father and more like him with her love of reading and spending time outdoors. But Father was gone now. She and Mum would have to look out for each other if they were to survive this great loss.

Mum pulled in a deep breath and lifted her sagging shoulders. "I'm ready."

Charlotte forced a brief smile, then followed her mum down the stairs and into the sitting room.

Sir Anthony and Mr. Walker stood together by the fireplace. They both looked up as Mum and Charlotte crossed the room toward them.

Mum nodded to the men. "Thank you for coming. It's a comfort to have friends with us at a time like this."

Sir Anthony reached into his jacket pocket and pulled out a white envelope. He held it out to Mum. "This is the honorarium we'd planned to give Henry. I wish it were more."

Mum took the envelope and looked down for a moment. When she raised her head, her eyes shimmered. "Thank you."

Sympathy filled Sir Anthony's face. "Please let me know if

there is anything I can do to help. I'd count it a privilege to assist you with any practical matters or spiritual counsel. Just send word, and I'll come."

Mum bit her lip and glanced away. "I appreciate that."

"Very well, then. I'll take my leave." Sir Anthony nodded to her and walked toward the door, where his wife waited for him.

Mr. Walker stepped forward. "I want to echo Sir Anthony's words and offer my assistance as well. I can return to go over your husband's will and his other business affairs whenever you're ready."

Mum's eyebrows lifted. "His will?"

"Yes. As his solicitor, I prepared his will just a few months ago."

"I see." But confusion filled Mum's face.

"I'll help you take care of those matters, Mrs. Harper. That's what Henry would want."

"Yes. Of course." Mum glanced at Charlotte, and then back at Mr. Walker. "Can you come tomorrow?"

His eyes widened for a moment. "That soon?"

"Yes. I think it's best if we understand Henry's wishes."

Mr. Walker shifted his weight to the other foot, looking uncomfortable. "Very well. I can return tomorrow afternoon, if that's agreeable."

"That will be fine. Thank you."

Charlotte's gaze followed Mr. Walker as he left the sitting room. What had Father stated in his will? Her parents owned their home. That would go to Mum, but Charlotte knew little else about their financial situation. Surely Father had made plans to provide for them. He loved them and would've made certain their futures were secure, wouldn't he?

Charlotte stared across the dining room table at Mr. Walker, and her throat constricted. How could what he was saying be true?

Confusion filled Mum's face. "So, Henry left the house and all our belongings to me, but that's all? There is no life insurance?"

Mr. Walker shifted in his chair. "I'm afraid that's correct." He flipped through the papers in the open file on the table. "I spoke to Mr. Harper's banker this morning. He told me there are one hundred forty-two pounds in the account. As soon as I have the death certificate, I can withdraw those funds for you."

Mum gaped at the man. "One hundred forty-two pounds? I don't understand. Is there another account? Where is the money he received from his tutoring and speaking engagements?"

Mr. Walker shifted his gaze away. "I'm not aware of any other account."

"But Henry always led me to believe we had sufficient income and savings. He never mentioned a shortage of funds."

Daniel shot a worried glance at Charlotte, and she returned an uncertain look. Was that truly all that was left to them?

"I suppose Mr. Harper expected to live a long time and continue adding to his savings."

Mum sat back, looking stunned. "I had no idea we had so little money." She focused on Mr. Walker again. "Well, at least we have our home."

Mr. Walker grimaced. "Were you aware the house is mortgaged?"

Mum shook her head. "You must be mistaken. The mortgage on the house has been paid off for several years."

"That may have been the case, but the banker said Mr. Harper took out a loan against the house last year."

Mum blinked. "How much is the loan?"

He gave the amount, and Charlotte stifled a gasp. She shot another quick glance at her brother, trying to make sense of Mr. Walker's words.

Daniel turned to Mum. "Why would Father take out a loan?"

"I have no idea. He always gave me a generous monthly

household allowance, but he took care of everything else. We rarely discussed finances."

Daniel's dark eyebrows dipped. "Do you think he took out the loan to pay my expenses at Oxford?"

Mum looked back at him. "He told me your school expenses were taken care of. Perhaps that is what he meant."

Mr. Walker closed the file and looked across the table at Mum. "I'm sorry, Mrs. Harper. I realize this puts you in a rather difficult position."

She lowered her gaze. "Yes . . . yes it does."

Charlotte clasped her hands in her lap. With no funds coming from life insurance, they would have a difficult time providing for themselves. Daniel might have to quit Oxford and find a position. But who would hire him without a proper education?

Mum pressed her lips together for a few seconds, then looked across at Mr. Walker. "This is all quite overwhelming. I'm not sure what to do."

"I understand. I wish I had better news." Mr. Walker slipped the folder into his leather case. "Is it possible you have some other source of income I'm not aware of?"

Mum sighed. "No, we have no other income."

Mr. Walker leaned forward. "You might want to consider selling the house to pay off the loan and any other outstanding accounts. That would settle your debts, and you'd be free to make a fresh start."

Mum's eyes widened. "Sell the house? Do you really think that's necessary?"

"I'm not sure what other course to suggest."

Charlotte's stomach dropped.

"Do you have family members who would . . . take you in? That would lessen your expenses."

Mum's cheeks flushed. "My mother and brother have both passed away. And my father and I are . . . not closely connected."

Mr. Walker nodded. "I see. Well then, perhaps you have friends who might open their home to you?"

Mum lifted her hand to her forehead, shielding her eyes. "I'm afraid most of our friends live in modest homes. Taking in all four of us would be a great imposition."

Mr. Walker's expression turned grim. "I'm afraid, madam, you may have no other choice."

Mum's chin trembled as she rose. "Thank you for coming. You've given us much to consider."

"Of course. I'll be in touch when I have the death certificate and the funds from the bank." Mr. Walker reached for his leather case and stood. "I'll let myself out."

Charlotte's stunned gaze followed him as he passed under the archway and left the room. This was the only home she'd ever known. Where would they live if it had to be sold?

Mum turned toward Charlotte and Daniel, new resolve in her expression. "Well, my dears, it seems we have only one course of action. I'll have to write to my father at Longdale and try to repair the breach."

Three

2012

Gwen stepped out onto Longdale's stone terrace and quietly closed the French doors behind her. A light morning breeze drifted past, carrying the scent of moist earth and rain-washed garden. On the hillside below the terrace, brilliant daffodils brightened the view. A stone path wove through the flower bed and led down to the dock at the edge of the quiet lake. A light mist hovered over the water, giving it a touch of mystery. The only sounds she heard were the wind in the trees and the call of a large white bird as it rose from the water's edge and flew toward the mountains on the opposite side of the lake.

She pulled in a deep breath, soaking in the beauty and tranquility of the scene.

"Good morning." The voice came from behind her, and she turned. David walked toward her, carrying two steaming mugs and offering a half smile. "Coffee?"

"Thank you." She accepted the mug, and the fragrant steam rose and tickled her nose. "Black?"

He nodded and took a sip from his mug, then he shifted his gaze toward the lake. "Quite a view, isn't it?"

"Yes, very peaceful."

"I've been coming here since I was ten, when my grandmother married Grandfather Benderly, and I still can't get over it." He lifted his mug as though toasting the lake and all the beauty around them.

"So, she married again, later in life?"

"Yes, she was a widow. It was a second marriage for them both."

Gwen nodded, noting his grandmother had inherited Longdale from her second husband, not her parents or grandparents. That might make his grandmother less attached to some of the pieces Gwen would be appraising. She tucked that information away to consider later. "I can see why so many people want to come to the Lake District on holiday. It's lovely."

His gaze scanned the lake again, his eyes reflecting pleasure. "There's nowhere else like it in all of England."

She studied him, noting his unique silver-gray eyes, thick brown hair, and the dark scruff covering the lower part of his masculine face. She guessed he was about thirty, but she couldn't be certain. He was quite handsome, but she quickly dismissed that thought. She was here on business, and she'd best keep her mind set in that direction.

"Have you lived here long?" she asked.

He shook his head. "My home is in Manchester. I'm just here to . . . help my grandmother settle some estate matters since my grandfather's passing."

That was evasive. Their first meeting had been uncomfortable, and his questions had put her on guard. But she needed to set aside her first impression and try to bridge the gap. Building positive rapport with David and his grandmother would make her job easier, and doing her work well was the only way she could regain her grandfather's trust.

He looked her way. "Have you been to the Lake District before?"

"No, but my mother came here to paint when she was in her

twenties." She glanced down, debating her next words. Was it possible he knew of her father? It was worth testing the water. "I think my father is from this area."

He cocked his eyebrow. "You're not sure?"

Her face warmed, and she shifted her gaze away. "He and my mother divorced before I was born. And no matter how often I asked, she refused to talk about him."

A slight frown creased his forehead. "You're an adult now. It seems you have a right to know."

"She intended to tell me when I finished my university studies, but she passed away before that could happen."

His serious expression softened. "I'm sorry."

She steeled herself and took a sip of coffee. Why had she told him something so personal? It was time to shift the conversation. "So, what about your parents? Do they live nearby?"

"My mother and her husband live in Italy, near Siena. He's a wine dealer. My father died when I was seventeen. Cancer."

She tightened her hold on the mug. "I'm sorry." It seemed she was moving from one difficult subject to the next. There had to be something they could safely discuss. "And your grandmother . . . is she your mother's mother, or your father's?"

"My father's." His half smile returned. "Nana was born in the late thirties and lived through World War Two as a child. Her first husband died in a boating accident after they'd been married twenty years. She met Grandfather Benderly a few years later through mutual friends. He passed away in February. That's when Nana had to take responsibility for Longdale, and she asked me to come."

Learning Lilly had lost two husbands tugged at Gwen's heart. Even though she had only known his grandmother for a day, she'd been impressed by her kindness and spritely personality.

"I admire her strength," David continued. "She's really quite amazing . . . but managing Longdale on her own is more than she can handle, especially with the repairs that need to be made and the debts my grandfather left behind." His expression grew somber. "That's why she asked you to come."

She straightened her shoulders. "Right. I'm here to evaluate some of her paintings and furnishings and prepare them for auction."

"And we need an accurate appraisal to receive as much as possible."

Gwen bristled. Why did he seem to think she was incapable of doing her job? "I may be new to my position, but I've spent years studying art and antiques at university and with my grandfather. He's one of the founders of Hill and Morris."

"I understand that. But your grandfather is not here. You are. I need to know you'll give us the best appraisal possible."

She held his gaze. "I will do my best for your grandmother and for Hill and Morris. That's my commitment."

His intense expression eased. "Good." He looked out at the lake again.

"In fact, I'd like to get started. Is your grandmother up? I didn't see her as I came through the house."

"She comes down for breakfast at eight." He checked his watch. "It's about that time. Shall we go in?"

Gwen nodded and turned toward the house. She shouldn't have reacted so strongly to David's questions. But it was hard not to feel defensive when the memory of her grandfather's disappointment was so fresh in her mind.

An hour later, Lilly led Gwen up the winding staircase in Longdale's tower. David followed close behind.

Lilly stopped on the landing and placed her hand over her heart. "Goodness, I haven't been up here for several months. It's quite a climb." She pulled in a deep breath and sent Gwen a weak smile.

David quickly stepped past Gwen and reached for his grand-mother's arm. "Nana, are you feeling okay? Do you want to sit down?"

"No, dear. I'll be fine. I just need to catch my breath."

David shot Gwen a fierce look, as though his grandmother's winded condition was her fault.

Lilly glanced up the stairway. "I forgot these stairs were so steep."

Gwen leaned to the right to look around David and see Lilly. "Perhaps David should help you down, and then he and I can go up together."

Lilly glanced up the staircase. "No, we're almost to the top. There are things I want to show you—things he knows noth-ing about."

David frowned. "Nana, you can give me a list. Gwen and I can take care of it."

"There's no need. I'm ready." Lilly held on to David's arm and started up the stairs again.

As Gwen passed the window, she glanced out at the gardens and lake. Her breath caught at the sparkling beauty.

Her thoughts shifted back to breakfast as she continued up the stairs. Lilly had laid out the plan for the day. She wanted to start on the uppermost floor and work their way down through the house. Gwen had been surprised to learn Longdale had fourteen bedrooms, as well as servants' quarters on the top floor. Those servants' rooms hadn't been used for many years, but Lilly thought there might be a few items there that could be sold.

After breakfast, Lilly had given Gwen a quick tour of the main floor, showing her the library, music room, drawing room, morning room, and gallery leading to the terrace. She said the lowest level housed the kitchen, stillroom, butler's pantry, housekeeper's sitting room, storage rooms, and laundry room. It sounded as though Lilly wanted Gwen to evaluate pieces in almost every room. She also mentioned an old groundskeeper's cottage she wanted to show Gwen later that day, saying there were some unique furniture pieces stored there.

This job was going to require more time and effort than Gwen had imagined, but what an opportunity!

They reached the top floor, and Lilly opened the first door on the left. "This is our archives room."

Gwen and David followed Lilly inside. A dry, dusty scent filled the dimly lit room. Lilly crossed to the window and raised the shade. "We keep these lowered to protect the photographs and documents."

Gwen scanned the wooden cabinets and bookshelves lining the room. "What kind of documents do you keep here?"

Lilly pulled open the nearest cabinet and lifted out a box. "There are so many interesting items—estate maps, architectural drawings of the original house and the additions, tax records, letters, journals, and, of course, family photographs." She lifted a small book from the box and laid it on the table in the center of the room. From the look of the dark blue leather cover, the book appeared to be from the late 1800s or early 1900s.

"This journal will give you a taste of what life was like a century ago." Lilly reached in a drawer, took out a pair of white gloves, and slipped them on. "We must be very careful."

White gloves were old school in Gwen's opinion. Today's archivists simply washed and dried their hands and avoided lotion when looking at documents, though it was true that oil and the pH of the skin could affect photographs. Gwen usually wore tight-fitting latex gloves when she examined those.

"Come closer so you can see." Lilly carefully opened the journal.

Gwen stepped up beside Lilly, and David stood on the other side.

"Look at this entry."

8 April 1912. We visited Longdale today. It is the most beautiful house I've ever seen, but we were not welcomed as we had hoped. Grandfather was quite fierce and unforgiving. Angry words were exchanged, and Mum left in tears. I have no idea what we will do now. The Storey family have been very kind, but we can't stay with them forever. Oh, my heart is so heavy. How long must I carry this painful secret?

Lilly looked up, her eyes bright. "Doesn't that sound like an intriguing mystery?"

Gwen nodded. "Who's the author of the journal?"

"I believe it belonged to my husband's great-great-aunt, Charlotte Harper."

Gwen smiled. "Very interesting."

"Yes, it is. I think she would've been about your age when she penned those lines."

David shifted his weight to the other foot. "Nana, is there something here you want Gwen to evaluate for the auction?"

Lilly blinked and turned to him. "I don't think the items in this room would be valuable to anyone outside our family."

"Then shall we move on to another room?" He nodded toward the door.

Lilly sent David a puzzled look. "Gwen needs to understand a bit about our family and Longdale's history so she can know the true value of the items we're going to show her."

David sent Gwen a look that said, *Can you help me out here?*

Gwen gave David a slight nod, then turned to Lilly. "I adore history, and I especially love family stories, but I think David wants us to move on so we can make the best use of our time."

Lilly sighed. "Very well, but feel free to come back and read the journal or look at anything else you'd like. I've spent months assembling our family tree. As they say, people without knowledge of their personal history are like trees without roots!"

Gwen smiled. "Thank you. I'd love to learn more about your

family." She noted David's frown, then added, "In my free time, of course."

Lilly patted her hand. "Good. I'm sure you'll appreciate all the wonderful things we have stored here."

Three hours later, after they'd walked through the mostly empty servants' quarters and prepared a list of items for auction in the first bedroom, Gwen, David, and Lilly strolled out to the terrace. A small round table, covered with a flower-patterned cloth, had been set for lunch. Gwen saved her notes on her iPad and closed the cover.

"Why don't you sit here, Gwen." Lilly indicated the nearest chair. Gwen took a seat, and David sat opposite her.

Lilly glanced around the table and smiled. "It looks as though Mrs. G. has prepared a delicious lunch for us." She held out one hand to Gwen and extended the other to her grandson. "Will you pray for us, David?"

Without hesitation, he nodded and reached for Gwen's hand. Her fingers clasped his, and warmth traveled up her arm. She mentally shook off the sensation and lowered her head.

"Father, thank You for this day and for what we've been able to accomplish. We pray You'll continue to lead and guide us as we move forward with our plans. Thank You for our food and bless the one who prepared it. In Jesus's name, Amen."

Surprise rippled through Gwen as she lifted her head. His prayer sounded sincere. Did his faith match his words, or did he only pray that way to please his grandmother? Conviction stirred her heart. Who was she to question the sincerity of his prayer?

In the two years since she'd lost her mum, she'd drifted away from the faith that had seen her through her years at university. But hearing David's prayer reminded her of the comfort she had received when she'd allowed the Lord to guide her daily thoughts and actions.

She glanced at David. It had been years since she'd met a man who was comfortable praying aloud and acknowledging his belief in God. She couldn't help admiring him. She squelched that thought and shifted her gaze to her plate. One glance at the sandwich, fresh strawberries, cucumbers, and potato crisps made her mouth water.

Lilly picked up her sandwich. "Oh, good. Mrs. G. made Coronation chicken salad. That's one of my favorites."

"Mine too," Gwen added, then bit into her sandwich and enjoyed the zing of the curry and chutney dressing mixed with chicken, crunchy almonds, and sweet grapes. She hadn't realized how hungry she was until she'd sat down to enjoy this lovely meal.

Lilly nibbled on a strawberry, then asked, "Has David told you about our plans for Longdale?"

Gwen darted a glance at David. "Not yet."

"We're going to use the funds from the auction to renovate the bedrooms and add bathrooms so we can open Longdale to paying guests." Lilly sent David a proud smile.

Gwen's eyebrows rose. "Oh, that sounds . . . interesting."

"Yes, it's going to be quite a change for me, but David has assured me we can keep some of the rooms in the east wing for my private living quarters."

Gwen shifted her gaze to David. "So, you're going to open Longdale as a bed and breakfast?" She couldn't keep a note of concern from her voice.

"No, Longdale will be a luxury hotel for people who are looking for an exceptional holiday experience in the Lakes. We'll also host small weddings, parties, and corporate events."

"That sounds like a lot of work. Who is going to manage it all?"

Lilly looked hesitant. "That is a good question. I do enjoy entertaining, but I've never had more than three or four houseguests at a time, and those were family or friends—not strangers."

David leaned forward slightly. "Don't worry, Nana." He shot a heated look at Gwen. "We'll hire an experienced hotel-and-event manager to oversee everything and give our guests the service they expect at a top-rated hotel. I hope to see us listed in the Michelin Guide one day."

Gwen scanned Longdale's stone façade. "That's going to require a lot of changes to the house."

"I'm meeting with an architect tomorrow to discuss the plans."

"I hope your architect is a specialist in preserving historic buildings."

"He comes highly recommended."

"But is he qualified in historic preservation?"

David narrowed his eyes. "I'm sure he's more than qualified to oversee the work needed."

Lilly patted David's hand. "I'm so glad you're handling everything." She shifted her gaze to Gwen. "David says the repairs and renovations are essential to preserve the house, and the changes will be minimal."

Gwen's stomach tightened. They didn't sound like minimal changes to her.

David nodded. "Updating the bedrooms and adding adjoining bathrooms will be good improvements for Longdale."

Gwen could not let this pass. Lilly seemed to have no idea all that would be involved in a project this size. "In order to open your home to guests, won't you have to address fire, safety, and accessibility issues, as well as expand the dining room and provide additional parking?"

David lowered his eyebrows, obviously not pleased with her comments.

Lilly shifted her gaze from Gwen to David and blinked a few times. "Oh dear. That does sound daunting. I do wonder what your grandfather would say about all of this."

David touched his grandmother's arm. "I'm sure he'd approve. We'll make the transition as quickly as possible, then you can relax and enjoy your home for years to come."

"Well, I'm not sure how many years I have ahead of me, but we must preserve Longdale. It will all be yours one day, so it's only right you should lead the way."

Gwen's stomach churned. Lilly was eighty-four, and she seemed to have some health and cognitive issues. Was it fair to put her through all the drastic changes necessary to turn her home into a hotel? Did David truly have his grandmother's best interests at heart, or had he come up with this plan for his own benefit?

Four

1912

Charlotte climbed the stepladder and pulled three leather-bound books from the top shelf in her father's study. A sudden thought struck, and she clutched the books to her chest. This wasn't Father's study anymore. Soon this wouldn't even be their home. She slowly climbed down, trying not to let the wave of grief overwhelm her.

Daniel pushed a crate of books to the far wall. "Shall I leave these here or put them out in the hall?"

Mum glanced at the growing stack of crates. "They're fine there. Would you mind taking this to Mr. Montgomery?" She held out a small wooden box. "I'm sure your father would want him to have these mementos of their travels on the Continent."

"Of course." Daniel sent her an understanding look as he took the box and then left the room.

Charlotte glanced down at the books she'd retrieved from the shelf and released a soft sigh. All the reference books and commentaries Father had used to prepare his messages would have to be sold, along with most of their furniture and belongings. She placed the books in a wooden crate and turned to Mum. "I'm glad Sir Anthony is willing to buy Father's books."

"Yes, it was very kind of him to offer." Mum tucked a strand of brown hair behind her ear and pulled another book from the lowest shelf. "That's certainly a much better option than sending them off to a bookseller for a fraction of their value."

Alice looked up from where she lay on the rug, a few feet away. "Well, I don't think we should sell this atlas. I'm sure Father would want us to keep it." She carefully turned the page of the large book filled with colorful maps, one she and Father had often enjoyed looking at together.

Mum's eyes glistened, and she sent Alice a tender smile. "If it means that much to you, then you may keep it."

"Thank you." Alice returned Mum's smile, then looked down at the map of South America and ran her finger along the Amazon River.

Charlotte glanced at two books she'd set aside on Father's desk. One focused on native birds of England, and the other featured beautiful color plates of British wildflowers. "I'd like to keep these two."

Mum gave a thoughtful nod. "You and your father shared a great love for nature. Keeping those will be a good way for you to remember him." Her eyes filled, and she quickly turned back to the bookshelf.

Charlotte's throat tightened, and she swallowed hard. Three weeks had passed since her father's death, but the pain was still fresh for them all. Mum seemed to be in a fog much of the time. But this past week, she'd pressed on, packing up the house as they prepared it to be sold.

Mum had written to Grandfather Benderly and to her friend Jenny Storey, who lived on a farm not far from Longdale, her grandfather's estate. But no replies had come . . . at least not yet.

A tremor passed through Charlotte as she placed two more books in the crate. What would they do if neither was able to take them in? There was the possibility Sir Anthony Fitzhugh's daughter would allow them to stay with her temporarily, but they were barely acquainted.

She ought to pray, but the pain of her father's passing had squelched her prayer life to next to nothing. If God didn't care enough to keep Father alive when they needed him so much, how could she count on Him to hear her prayers and help them now?

A wave of guilt washed over her heart. Her father always said they must trust God in good times and bad and never stop praying. She could almost hear him now, reminding them that facing challenging circumstances did not mean God was not in control, overseeing everything, and working circumstances out for the best. But it was hard to hold on to that teaching when her heart was so sore, and there seemed to be no answers for her painful questions.

Mum sighed and lifted her hand to her forehead.

Charlotte studied Mum's sagging shoulders, and a shaft of fear shot through her. Mum had little appetite since Father's death, and she wasn't sleeping well. Her clothes seemed to hang on her thin frame. Would Charlotte lose Mum as well?

Charlotte scanned the room. Most of the books were packed. All that was left was cleaning out Father's desk. It was probably best if she did that rather than Mum. She crossed to stand beside Mum and laid her hand on her shoulder. "Why don't you go up and lie down for a while? We're almost done here. I can finish up."

Mum massaged her forehead. "I do have a bit of a headache. Perhaps that would be best." She gently touched Alice's head as she passed, then walked out and closed the door of the study.

Alice looked up. "What do they serve for tea in Brazil?"

Charlotte blinked. "I don't know. Why do you ask?"

"Because I'm hungry, and I was just thinking it might be nice to have tea like the Brazilians do." Alice closed the atlas and rose.

A slight smile tugged at the corner of Charlotte's mouth. "I'm not sure what they serve in Brazil, but there are some ginger biscuits in the kitchen cabinet."

Alice's eyes lit up. "I love ginger biscuits!" She dashed out of the study, leaving her book on the floor.

Oh, to be young like Alice and not feel the weight of concern for Mum and their unsettled future. Charlotte picked up the atlas and placed it on top of her two books. Memories of conversations she'd shared with Father about traveling to see the world came rushing back. When that letter had come from New York, inviting her father to speak at the Higher Life Conference in August, they'd all been excited about the possibility of sailing across the Atlantic and seeing some of the United States.

Was that letter still in his desk? Had he answered them, or were they still waiting for his reply? She ought to write and let them know they'd need to find another speaker.

She pulled open the top center drawer, searching for the letter, but it only contained fountain pens, a letter opener, a few stamps, and a ruler. No letter from New York. She checked the left drawer and found files with articles, sermon illustrations, and notes from her father's past messages.

Where did he keep his correspondence?

She pulled out the right drawer and found several letters and a few files with information about the students he tutored. She sorted through the pile of envelopes and found the one from New York. She pushed in the drawer, but it stopped a few inches short. Had something fallen behind, preventing it from closing?

With a weary sigh, she pulled open the drawer, took out the files, and tried to push it closed. Once again, the drawer stuck. Frowning, she bent down and peeked in. She couldn't see anything blocking the way, but when she reached in and felt around the back of the drawer, her fingers closed around what felt like a small bundle of papers. She pulled out a stack of envelopes tied with a blue ribbon. Who were they from?

There was no address on the top envelope, only the name *Henry* written in elegant script. She untied the ribbon, and uneasiness prickled through her. Were these letters Mum had written to Father while they were courting? Had he kept them all these years to remind himself of those early days of their love?

She considered asking Mum about them, but Gwen didn't want to cause her more pain. She slid the folded stationery from the envelope, turned toward the window, and let the light shine on the words.

Dearest Henry,

How I miss you and long to see you again. When can you come? It seems like ages since we had those few stolen days together in Cornwall.

Charlotte frowned. When had her mum been in Cornwall?

How I wish our circumstances were different and we could let the world know of our love. The lonely days and nights only serve to remind me of all those blissful days we spent together. Oh, my darling, I count the hours until we can be together again. Please know that you fill my mind and heart.

With all my love,
E. M.

Charlotte froze, staring at the initials. Who was E. M.—someone her father loved before he met and married Mum? Her eyes darted to the date written at the top of the page.

8 January 1910.

Charlotte gasped, and a wave of dizziness flooded her. She sank down in the desk chair and lifted her hands to cover her eyes. This couldn't have been written to her father only two years ago. That would mean . . . No! He couldn't have betrayed her mum!

She dropped her hand and scanned the letter once more. The passionate words could hold only one meaning. Heat surged into her face, and angry tears flooded her eyes. How could her father stand in the pulpit night after night and exhort others to gain total victory over temptation and sin when he had been involved with another woman? How could he be such a hypocrite?

Was this why he'd asked them to forgive him after he collapsed?

Was this why the Lord had struck him down and ended his ministry?

Her hands shook as she pulled out the next letter. But halfway down the page, she closed her eyes and crumpled the paper. She couldn't read anymore. It was too painful, too dreadful to think of her father caught in sin and living a lie.

The door opened, and Alice walked in, carrying a cup and saucer.

Charlotte quickly shuttered her emotions. She must never let her sister know of their father's secret sin. Alice adored him. It would shatter her heart.

"I brought you some tea and biscuits." Her sister crossed the room and set the teacup on the desk.

Charlotte shoved the letters into the drawer and pushed it closed.

Alice's smile faded. "What's wrong?"

Charlotte looked away. "Nothing." She picked up the stack of files from the desk and placed them in an empty crate, then she reached for the correspondence.

"Aren't you going to have your tea?"

Charlotte blinked, her thoughts spinning. "Yes. Thank you. I just want to clear off the desk."

"Do you think I should take a cup to Mum?"

Charlotte forced her shaking hands to still. Mum might be resting. But sending Alice off with this task would get her out of the room and give Charlotte time to decide what to do. "Yes. That's a good idea. A cup of tea might be just what she needs." She forced a smile, and Alice hurried off toward the kitchen.

As soon as her sister disappeared, Charlotte pulled open the drawer and took out the letters. Her stomach roiled as she stared at the stack clutched in her hand. Mum must never see these letters. She was already so deeply grieved by Father's death. Learning he had been unfaithful would break her heart. And in her weakened condition, that painful revelation might kill her.

Charlotte strode toward the fireplace. No one else must ever know her father's teaching had only been a cover for his sin. She tossed the letters into the fire. The flames leaped up and singed the edges of the envelopes. A fiery red line burned across the face of the envelope, turning it brown until all that remained was gray ash. Ashes to ashes, dust to dust.

The fire might have destroyed proof of his guilt, but the words were branded in Charlotte's mind, searing her soul and burning the truth of his betrayal deep into her heart.

Charlotte shifted in her seat as the railway car rocked and swayed past rolling hills, peaceful farms, and quiet villages. Seated across from her, Alice leaned against Mum's arm, with her eyes closed and her lips slightly parted. A peaceful, relaxed expression filled her sister's face. Charlotte glanced away, thankful her sister didn't have to carry the same heartache Charlotte hid from her and everyone else.

Charlotte studied Mum's pale face. Weary lines crossed her forehead and fanned out from the corners of her closed eyes as she rested her head against the train window. Even the roar of the engine and vibrations of the train hadn't kept her awake.

It had been a long, exhausting day of travel for them all. They'd arrived at the station just past seven that morning to see Daniel off on his return trip to Oxford. He'd insisted he should go with them, find work in Keswick, and help support what remained of the family. But Mum had refused. His fees at Oxford had been paid, and there was no use wasting those funds. He was to finish the term and join them later. Daniel finally agreed, and the four of them shared a tearful good-bye on the platform as the cool morning mist surrounded them.

Thirty minutes later, Charlotte, Alice, and Mum had boarded the train to Manchester, where they transferred to a second train and continued north to Kendal. The final leg of the journey would deliver them to Keswick, where Mum's friend Jenny Storey had promised to meet them and take them to her farm.

Charlotte's stomach tensed as she pondered their uncertain future. Why hadn't Grandfather Benderly replied to Mum's letter? Did he have a heart of stone? Any man with an ounce of compassion would've welcomed his widowed daughter and her family while they grieved and recovered from all the changes brought on by the untimely death of their husband and father.

When Charlotte had voiced that thought to her mother, her mum quietly explained that perhaps Grandfather Benderly had never forgiven her for eloping against his wishes and marrying Henry Harper twenty-one years earlier.

A new thought jolted Charlotte, and she sat up straight. Had her grandfather realized her father's weaknesses and seen his true character? Was that why he had opposed their marriage? A new wave of pain flooded in, and she closed her eyes.

The sense that she ought to pray filled her mind again, but she resisted. Praying wouldn't clear her confusion or ease the ache in her heart—not when she refused to release the hurt and the bitterness.

The conductor stepped into the car and started down the aisle. When he reached their row, Charlotte held out their tickets. He accepted them with a brief smile. "Headed to the Lakes on holiday?"

Charlotte hesitated. "We're going to visit friends."

He nodded, looking pleased. "You're blessed to have friends in the area." He punched the tickets and passed them back to her. "How long are you staying?"

"I'm not sure."

"Well, I hope you enjoy your visit."

"Thank you."

The conductor continued down the aisle, and Charlotte's thoughts shifted to the Storey family. Mum told her she and Jenny had grown up together at Longdale Manor, where Jenny's mother had worked as the cook and her father as the head gardener. After Rose eloped with Henry Harper and moved to London, Jenny had stayed in the area and married a local sheep farmer, Leland Storey. Jenny and Mum had exchanged letters and maintained their friendship through the years.

Jenny's latest letter welcomed them to stay at their farm, but Mum didn't want to impose on them for long. She planned to go to Longdale, appeal to Grandfather, and explain how much they needed his help. She hoped he would be willing to listen and forgive. If not, they would have to rely on Jenny until they could sort out some other place to live.

Charlotte released a tired sigh. How could their lives have come to this—no home and no way to provide for their basic needs? It was too humbling, too painful. And this predicament was all her father's fault. If he had cared about them at all, he would've made plans to provide for them. Instead, he'd followed his wayward passions, mismanaged the family's finances, and betrayed them all!

A wave of shame heated Charlotte's cheeks. How could he do it? Why had he thrown away everything for the passing pleasures of sin? She would never understand his choices. Never!

"Keswick," the conductor called as he walked back up the aisle. "The next stop is Keswick."

Charlotte reached across and touched her mum's arm. "This is our stop."

Her mum stirred and opened her eyes, then blinked and looked around. "Oh dear." She woke Alice, then quickly gathered her traveling bag and Alice's sweater.

Charlotte lifted their lunch basket from the floor, grabbed her bag, and stood as the train slowed and the station came into view. She clenched her jaw and straightened. She had no choice now but to move forward and hope that somehow they could make a new life for themselves in the Lake District.

Five

1912

A stiff breeze blew up from the lake and ruffled Ian Storey's hair beneath the brim of his cap as he guided the horses through the village of Keswick. He hunched his shoulders and tucked his chin into the wool scarf wrapped around his neck. The calendar might have turned to April, but the weather had not caught up with the knowledge it was spring. Gray clouds hid the sun, and it looked as though it might rain before they could bring their guests home from the station.

His mum leaned to the left, glancing down the village street past the shops and St. John's stone church. "I hope their train wasn't early. I'd hate to keep them waiting out in the cold."

Ian took out his pocket watch. "We're on time. Hopefully the train will be too." He clicked to the horses, urging them on. "Did Mrs. Harper say how long she and her daughters wanted to stay with us?"

Mum shook her head. "No, she didn't. And I'm not sure what your father will say about that, especially if their visit lasts more than a few days."

Ian shifted on the wooden wagon bench. They'd added two

guest rooms to their home so they could accommodate people who came each summer to attend the Keswick Convention, but those were paying guests. And from what his mum had told him, Rose Harper was a recent widow who had little money and two daughters and a son to support.

Mum sighed. "It's a shame Rose's husband made no plans to provide for his family."

He glanced her way. "No life insurance?"

Mum shook her head. "They had to sell their home in London to cover the funeral expenses and pay off the mortgage."

"What will she do now?"

"She hopes to convince her father to let them live at Longdale Manor."

He nodded, pondering Mrs. Harper's connection to Longdale and the Benderly family. Longdale was an impressive estate perched on a hill above Derwentwater, with expansive grounds and flourishing gardens. His grandparents on his mother's side had worked there years ago, and his mum had spent her girlhood at Longdale. That was where she'd first met Rose Harper, although she'd been Rose Benderly then.

"Why don't they go straight to Longdale, rather than staying with us?"

"I'm afraid there has been a rift between Rose and her father ever since she and her husband married. Mr. Benderly didn't approve of the man."

Ian cocked his eyebrow. "Maybe Mr. Benderly was concerned for a good reason."

"Perhaps." Mum gave a thoughtful nod. "Henry Harper came to Longdale as a humble tutor for Rose's brother John, but he became a well-known religious speaker. He made quite a name for himself. Remember, we heard him speak at the Keswick Convention two years ago."

Ian nodded, vaguely recalling Henry Harper's message. He wasn't impressed then, and the current situation didn't change his opinion. Harper might have become a well-known speaker, but he seemed to lack practical wisdom when it came to looking after his family.

Scripture said a man who didn't care for his family was worse than an unbeliever. Still, Ian shouldn't judge him. He didn't know the man, and it seemed he had died unexpectedly.

Ian pulled the wagon to a stop at the side of the station and glanced down the tracks. A cloud of gray smoke rose above the trees in the distance. Soon, the rumbling of the engine grew louder. "Looks like we're just in time." He climbed down and assisted his mum.

They crossed the platform as the train rolled into the station, pulling three passenger cars and a baggage car. The brakes squealed, and a cloud of steam hissed out around them. The conductor stepped down, followed by a line of passengers. A few people moved forward to greet travelers and help them with their bags.

A middle-aged woman in a black suit and hat took the conductor's hand and stepped down to the platform. A young woman in an equally somber black dress, who looked to be around twenty, followed her, carrying a cloth-covered basket and holding the hand of girl who looked about twelve.

"There they are." His mum lifted her hand and waved. "Rose!"

The other woman's eyes lit up, and she started toward them, carrying a small suitcase.

His mum met her friend with a warm smile and gentle hug. "I'm so glad you've come." She stepped back and looked them over. "It's such a long trip from London. You must be tired."

"We are a bit travel weary, but we're glad to be here." Rose turned toward the young woman and the girl. "These are my daughters, Charlotte and Alice. Girls, this is Mrs. Jenny Storey, and this is . . ." She looked up at Ian with a question in her eyes.

Jenny chuckled. "You don't recognize my son Ian?"

Rose smiled. "Why, yes, of course. It's good to see you, Ian. It's just that you were much younger the last time we met."

Ian nodded to her. "I supposed I have changed a bit since then. Welcome to Keswick." He turned to Charlotte and Alice. "Hello, Miss Harper, Alice. We're glad you've come."

Charlotte slipped her arm around Alice's shoulders and sent him a hesitant smile. Her large brown eyes seemed to reflect curiosity and caution as she studied him. "Thank you."

He returned a warm smile, hoping to put her at ease. Had he met her when her parents attended the convention? He didn't think so. "Have you been to the Lakes before, Miss Harper?"

"No. This will be my first visit." She pushed a loose tendril of wavy brown hair away from her pink cheek and glanced at her mother.

"Thank you for allowing us to come." Rose turned to his mum. "I hope it won't be an imposition. You must tell us if it's not convenient for us to stay with you."

"Nonsense. We're delighted you're here."

His mum looked toward the train. "Do you have other luggage?"

"Yes." Rose took three claim tickets from her pocket. "Two trunks and a suitcase."

"I'll get those for you." Ian took the tickets and collected their luggage. A porter carted the trunks and suitcase to their wagon, and he and Ian lifted them into the back, while his mum and Rose climbed up front.

He turned to Charlotte. "I hope you don't mind riding in the back. It's probably not what you're used to, but it's the only way to get all of us and your trunks home to the farm."

"I'm sure it will be fine." But a line creased the area between her eyebrows as she looked toward the wagon.

"I'll help you up." He held out his hand.

She slowly reached out, took hold, and climbed in the back without too much trouble.

"I put a blanket over those hay bales." He pointed to the old quilt he'd taken from the barn, hoping it didn't smell too much like the sheep.

"Thank you." Charlotte settled on the blanket and arranged her skirt, still looking a bit uncertain about riding in the back of the wagon.

He turned to Alice. "Shall I give you a lift?"

She grinned. "Yes, please." He easily boosted her up. Alice landed on her feet with a thump and sent him a bright smile. "You're strong."

He cocked one eyebrow. "That comes from wrestling the sheep at shearing time."

Her eyes widened. "You actually wrestle with them?"

"Only if they're ornery."

"Come and sit down, Alice." Charlotte patted the blanket next to her, and her sister wiggled between the trunks and joined her.

Ian caught Alice's eye as he walked forward and winked at her.

She sent him a delighted smile. "I like him," she announced.

Ian stifled a grin and climbed into the driver's seat. At least he'd made a good impression on one of Rose Harper's daughters.

Charlotte sent Alice a warning glance as the wagon jolted into motion. Her impertinent sister had forgotten her manners and was embarrassing them all.

Alice shrugged. "What?"

"You shouldn't say things like that," Charlotte whispered.

"Why not? He's nice," Alice whispered back.

Charlotte firmed her lips and shook her head.

Alice huffed, crossed her arms, and leaned against the side of the wagon.

Charlotte adjusted her hat and tried to calm her ruffled spirit. What would Ian think of them? He seemed good-natured and might even be considered handsome with his light blue eyes, square jaw, and light brown hair. But a handsome appearance did not guarantee noble character. She had considered her father handsome and charming, but those qualities had only been a mask for a deceitful heart. She would not be so easily fooled again.

Tears stung her eyes, and she turned her face away from Alice. When would the pain of her father's betrayal fade? Would she ever go through one day without remembering those dreadful love letters and her father's web of lies?

The wagon picked up speed as it rolled down a hill and listed to the left. Charlotte gasped and gripped the blanket. She'd seen many wagons in London, but she'd never ridden in one like this. What kind of life was she headed for?

Ian looked over his shoulder. "Sorry about the rough ride. We've had a lot of rain this month, and it washed out the road in some places."

Charlotte nodded. "It's all right." But her words carried a slight tremor, betraying her true feelings about the jostling journey.

"Just hold tight. We should be home to Valley View in about twenty minutes." He probably meant to encourage her with those words, but it only stirred more questions in her heart.

How long would they have to stay at Valley View Farm with the Storey family? She hoped her grandfather would have a change of heart and allow them to come to Longdale. But what would they do if Mum couldn't repair that broken relationship?

She closed her eyes, her thoughts spinning. A cry rose from her heart, but she quickly extinguished it. She was on her own now. God didn't seem to care what happened to them. Not anymore.

Ian settled the horses in their stalls and hung the harnesses on the barn wall. He needed to feed and water them before he returned to the house and joined the family and their guests for dinner. Grabbing a pail from the wall, he started for the pump.

His father walked through the open barn doorway. "How was the road? Did they repair that section by the bridge?"

"Not yet. I'm afraid I gave the ladies quite a wild ride."

Father grunted and rubbed his bristly jaw. "Can't say I'm glad to have three more mouths to feed."

Ian shifted the pail to the other hand. He didn't want to argue with his father, but he could not let that comment stand. "Mum couldn't turn away one of her oldest friends. It wouldn't be right."

Father shook his head. "We have enough trouble of our own without taking on theirs."

Ian sighed and glanced out the barn door, toward the house. They'd lost Granddad Storey only a few weeks ago, after he had suffered a series of strokes. Ian had left Oxford midterm and returned home to be with the family and help carry the workload his grandfather had handled for so many years.

Losing the beloved patriarch of the family had been painful and impacted them all, but that shouldn't stop them from helping Rose Harper and her daughters.

He met his father's gaze. "If Mum and Milly were in the same situation, I hope someone would offer them a place to stay and give them time to recover."

His father studied him with weary eyes. "Well, I hope they won't stay long. We'll be busy with lambing. Your mum will be too busy to coddle them."

"I don't think they expect coddling."

He scoffed. "You saw how they were dressed. I doubt they're

65

used to taking care of themselves, or that they're interested in helping us."

"I wouldn't expect them to do farm chores."

"Why not? They expect to eat at my table. They should at least help your mum and do what they can."

"They're our guests, Dad."

"Guests or not, they better do their share, or they'll not be welcome here."

Ian straightened his shoulders. "The woman just lost her husband and her home. They've little money and no other options."

"She's George Benderly's daughter! She ought to go to Longdale. Coming here doesn't make sense."

An angry retort rose in Ian's throat, but he swallowed his reply and strode past his father. It wouldn't help to continue defending Rose Harper. Once his father set his mind against someone, there was no changing it. Ian would have to look for another way to ease the situation and shield them from his father's inhospitable attitude.

Charlotte crossed the guest room and lifted the lid of the larger trunk. Their neatly folded dresses, petticoats, and assorted undergarments lay inside. She scanned the room, and a sinking feeling hit her stomach. Where was she going to put their clothes? Their home in London might not have been luxurious, but each bedroom had a dresser and wardrobe. This room contained neither. The walls were plain, whitewashed plaster, and the two small windows were framed with unfinished wood. Gray wool blankets covered a double bed and the smaller single bed. A nightstand with a glass oil lamp and a rag rug were the only other furnishings in the room.

She turned to Mum. "How am I going to unpack when there's nowhere to put our clothes?"

Mum stood in front of the window, staring outside. She blinked as she turned to Charlotte. "What?"

"There's no wardrobe. Where am I going to hang our dresses?"

Mum looked around the room with a dazed expression. "I suppose we can hang some on those pegs." She motioned toward the row of wooden knobs fastened to the wall opposite the bed.

Charlotte took the top dress from the trunk and shook it out. She tried to smooth out the wrinkles, but it was useless. "This looks dreadful. I can't wear it like this." She swung around and faced Mum. "Do you think they own an iron?"

Shadows clouded Mum's eyes. "I'm sure they do. We'll ask Jenny later."

Mum's weary expression pierced Charlotte's heart. She must learn to hold her tongue and not complain about their situation. The weight of grief and their uncertain future was draining the life from her mother, and voicing her own frustration was not helping. She pressed her lips tight, determined to shift her focus. They had one another and a roof over their heads for the time being. Helping Mum get through this dark valley was what mattered most.

She laid her hand on Mum's shoulder. "I'm sorry. The room is fine, and the Storeys seem kind."

"Yes, very kind, although I can tell Jenny's husband is not too pleased we're here."

Charlotte tensed as she recalled Leland Storey's curt greeting and brooding expression, but she didn't want to confirm her mum's worries. "That's probably just his way. Jenny and her son and daughter gave us a warm welcome."

"Yes, I'm grateful. I don't know where we'd be if they hadn't opened their home." Mum pulled in a deep breath and straightened her shoulders. She crossed to the trunk and pulled out one of Alice's dresses. "Let's make a pile of those we want to press, then we can organize the rest and use the trunk as storage."

The courage and acceptance Mum showed despite her pain and loss smote Charlotte's heart. Someone with weaker character might have been driven to despair and given up, but not Rose Harper. She kept moving forward, making the best of their difficult situation.

Charlotte's throat tightened as she watched Mum separate their clothing. She wanted to follow Mum's example, hold on to courage, and make a new life, but the secret heartache she carried made it all seem almost too much to bear.

Six

1912

Ian held out his hand toward the flickering flames in the kitchen fireplace. Warmth spread through his work-roughened fingers while the fire hissed and popped. The savory scent of lamb stew filled the kitchen, and his empty stomach rumbled. "That sure smells good."

His sister, Milly, stood in front of the stove, stirring the large pot. "It should give our friends a fine dinner."

Milly's dark brown hair was pulled back in a loose bun, and her cheeks were rosy from the heat of the stove. She was twenty-four, three years older than Ian, and taller than most girls. She could almost look him directly in the eyes. Others might consider her plain, but Ian thought she had her own kind of natural beauty. Her quick wit, skills in the kitchen, and the special way she had with the sheep had won his admiration years ago. Dad's sour moods never seemed to ruffle her spirit, proving she had the patience of a saint. Milly believed the best about Dad and everyone else, and that made Ian appreciate her even more.

Milly looked his way. "What do you think of Mrs. Harper

and her daughters?" She kept her voice low and glanced toward the hall leading to the guest rooms.

He stepped closer. "They seem like good people."

"Mum said they had to sell almost everything they owned." She shook her head. "I can't imagine how terrible it must have been for Mrs. Harper to see her husband collapse onstage like that."

"I'm sure it wasn't easy for the daughters either."

Milly lifted a hand to her mouth. "They were there too?"

"Yes. Mum said all three were with him that day."

Milly placed a loaf of bread on the cutting board and made the first slice. "I'm glad they've come to Valley View. Spending time here will give them a chance to get their feet under them."

"I hope so, but it won't be easy."

Milly nodded. "We must do all we can to make them feel at home."

"Yes." Ian's thoughts shifted to his father's comment in the barn. "Dad's not in favor of them staying very long."

"I hope he keeps his opinion to himself." She handed him the plate of bread.

Ian sent her a doubtful look. "That would be a miracle." He set the bread plate on the table, then turned back to Milly. "What else can I do to help?"

"Would you get two more chairs? I think they're in Granddad's room. Or maybe out in the shed?"

Ian nodded and set off down the hall toward Granddad's room. He stopped at the doorway and swallowed hard. Seeing the empty room still cut him to the heart. His granddad had lived a long and meaningful life, but Valley View just wasn't the same without him.

He crossed to the bedside table and picked up the framed photograph that sat next to his granddad's black leather Bible. The image showed his grandparents standing arm in arm with Derwentwater in the background. Though their expressions were serious, he could see the peaceful contentment in their eyes.

When Ian was younger, he'd grumbled about having to stay up half the night out in the barn with his granddad during lambing season. But as he grew older, he'd come to appreciate those times and the lessons his granddad had passed on about caring for the sheep and trusting God through good times and bad.

His thoughts drifted back to a conversation he'd had with his granddad a few months ago, before the final stroke had taken his life.

Light from a golden sunset had flowed in on Granddad as he sat in the overstuffed chair by the window. His black-and-white border collie, Bryn, lay at his feet. She lifted her head and wagged her tail as Ian entered the room.

"I was thinking about the ewes." Granddad looked up at Ian with a fading smile. "I'll go out to the barn and check on them after dinner."

Ian laid his hand on Granddad's shoulder. "You've done enough today. I'll take care of them tonight."

"You're a good lad, Ian. They'll be safe with you watching over them."

Ian's throat had tightened. The years of hard work overseeing Valley View had taken a toll on his granddad's health and physical strength, but they hadn't diminished his love for his farm or his family.

Granddad had turned and met his gaze. "I'm too old, not much good to anyone anymore."

"No, that's not true." Ian squeezed his granddad's shoulder, willing him to accept his words. "You're the cornerstone of the family. We need you. We always will."

Granddad shook his head. "Maybe before, but not now."

An ache had lodged in Ian's chest. So much had been lost with the strokes, but their bond of love remained, and that was enough.

Footsteps sounded in the hall, and the memories faded like wisps of smoke.

Charlotte Harper stopped in the open doorway. Her brown eyes widened, and her lips parted. "Oh, hello, Ian. Milly sent me down here to get two chairs."

His face warmed. His sister must've known he'd gotten distracted. "I'll bring them."

"Of course." She stepped back, then stopped. "I wanted you to know that we're very grateful to you and your family for opening your home to us."

"I'm glad you're here—I mean, I'm glad you all could come."

Her cheeks turned pink, and she dipped her head, but it didn't hide her soft smile. "Thank you. We're glad to be here." She turned and strode down the hall.

Ian watched her go. She reminded him of someone. He thought for a moment, then glanced at the photograph on the bedside table. His grandmother had dark hair and eyes like Charlotte.

What had made him compare the two?

Maybe it was the way his granddad always talked about "my Ellie," as he liked to call her. He'd often told Ian about their early years together and how happy they'd been. Those memories of their courtship and marriage seemed to have the power to reach across time and comfort his granddad like nothing else. Was that kind of love something you found or something you built with time and intention? Would he ever find someone who would inspire love like that?

He'd been attracted to a few women he'd met at Oxford. One in particular came to mind—Genevieve Montrose, the daughter of his favorite professor, Giles Montrose. Her father had invited him to their home for dinner a few times, and Genevieve was always attentive as well as attractive. He'd considered calling on her, but then his granddad's health had turned, and he'd left Oxford before he could take that step.

He glanced at the photo of his grandparents once more. Could he find a woman who would stir him to the devotion his granddad described? He wasn't sure, but that didn't mean he wasn't intent on finding out.

Charlotte clutched her shawl more tightly around her shoulders, slipped outside, and quietly closed the kitchen door behind her. The cool night air washed over her, sending a shiver down her back, but it wasn't an unpleasant sensation. The air felt fresh and clean, so different from the air of London that was often rain-soaked or heavy with coal smoke.

The moon shone bright, spreading silver light over the farmyard, fields, and mountains beyond. Past the barn, a small section of the lake shimmered in the moonlight. Milly said earlier it was called Derwentwater. That seemed strange, but so many things were different here.

She lifted her gaze and studied the glittering path of stars trailing across the sky. Was that the Milky Way? She'd never seen it so clearly before. In London, the cloudy skies and glow of city lights often hid all but the brightest stars.

Tipping her head, she listened. Wind whispered in the trees, a few insects buzzed, and a lonely bird called—such peaceful sounds. Nothing like the sounds in London at night, where she usually fell asleep to the rattle of carriage wheels over cobblestone streets or a train whistle in the distance.

She glanced at the long, low stone building to the right. Lantern light glowed in a few windows. Was that the barn where the lambs were born?

At dinner, Ian, Milly, and Mr. Storey had talked about the ewes who were expected to give birth soon and the need to take turns checking on them throughout the night. Were they out there now? She considered looking in, but she decided against it. She knew nothing about sheep, except that they produced wool that was spun and woven to make clothing.

Her fingers slid over her shawl, feeling the soft weave of the wool fabric. Her mum had given her this shawl last Christmas, and she treasured the gift. It not only provided comforting warmth, it also reminded her of happier days.

The barn door slid open, and a lantern bobbed as Ian trudged up the path, his gaze on the ground, seemingly unaware of her.

She pulled in a sharp breath. If she turned and hurried back into the house, he would see her and probably think she was strange for coming outside in the middle of the night. It would be better to wait for him and explain herself.

Striding up the path, he came to a halt as he spotted her. "Charlotte. Is everything all right?"

"Yes. Everything is fine. I just couldn't sleep. It's so . . . quiet here." That was true, but her restless spirit was more to blame for keeping her awake than the quiet countryside.

He gave a slow nod, silver moonlight reflected in his eyes.

She glanced past his shoulder toward the barn. "Were some new lambs born tonight?"

"Yes. Two of the shearlings gave birth."

"Shearlings?"

"First-time mothers. We like as many ewes as possible to lamb out in the fields. But we bring in the oldest, the shearlings, and those we suspect carry twins to keep an eye on them and help if needed."

She liked the lilt of his voice and the way he spoke about caring for the sheep. "That's kind of you."

"The lambs are the future of the farm. We do all we can to see that as many as possible survive."

"You're headed back to the house?"

"Yes. I need to wake Milly. I've got two ewes who are close to giving birth, and one is having trouble."

"Oh, I don't want to keep you." She stepped aside so he could pass.

He nodded to her and started toward the house, but then he looked back. "Would you like to see the lambs?"

Her heart did a funny little leap. "Yes, I would."

He smiled. "Wait here. I'll get Milly and be back in minute." He strode off at a brisk pace, looking like a man on a mission.

Her cheeks warmed as she watched him go. What would Mum say about a midnight visit to the barn with Ian, especially since her hair was down and she was wearing her nightgown under her coat? Well, she was completely covered, and Milly would be with them.

Ian soon strode back up the path. "Milly will be along as soon as she's dressed." He led the way to the barn and slid open the door. They walked inside, and he pointed to the first stall on the right. "One of the new lambs is in here." He smiled as he lifted his lantern, and the golden light spread into the stall. "He's a fine one."

Charlotte stepped closer, and her breath caught. A large, woolly ewe with a dark gray face hovered over a little lamb with a damp, black body and quivering legs. The lamb toddled around his mother, nosing her underside, looking for a meal. Charlotte smiled as she watched him.

Leaning on the stall's half door, she studied the lamb's face. What was it about baby animals that pulled at her heartstrings? There was such sweetness and vulnerability about them.

She looked up at Ian. "He's lovely."

Ian straightened, a proud light shining in his eyes. "That he is. And she's taking good care of him."

Another ewe bleated, and Ian turned toward the sound. "I better check on that one. She's the one having trouble." He set off down the center aisle of the barn, following the pitiful sound.

Milly hurried in through the doorway. Her hair was tied

75

back with a ribbon, and she wore a long apron over her brown dress. Her eyes went wide when she saw Charlotte. "Goodness, I didn't expect to see you out here."

"I couldn't sleep, so I went outside to get some air and saw Ian coming out of the barn. He invited me to see the lambs."

Milly sent her a quick smile. "Then see them you must." She motioned for Charlotte to follow her, then strode down the aisle, lifting her lantern and checking in each stall.

Charlotte followed close behind until they reached the fifth stall. Inside, Ian knelt on the straw beside the ewe.

"There now, don't be afraid. It won't be long. You're doing a fine job." His gentle tone seemed to ease the sheep's heavy panting.

Milly glanced at Charlotte, then nodded toward the sheep. "This one's a shearling. Lambing is all new to her." She pushed open the half door, stepped inside, and knelt next to her brother. "Has she been struggling long?"

"About an hour." He pressed his lips tight as he continued examining the ewe.

"Can you tell what's wrong?"

"I'm not sure." He ran his hand over her woolly side and bent closer. The ewe bleated again, and Ian's face lit up. "I see the hooves!"

Milly moved closer, and Charlotte rose on tiptoes, trying to see what was happening, but the brother and sister blocked her view. Working together, Ian and Milly coaxed and calmed the ewe until the newborn lamb plopped down on the straw.

Ian's grin spread wide. "Good work! That looks like a fine lamb." He quickly rubbed the lamb with straw, then stepped back a few feet.

Milly moved back as the ewe slowly turned toward her lamb. The ewe took a few tentative steps closer, but rather than nuzzle or lick her offspring, as Charlotte expected, she sniffed it a few times, bleated loudly, and backed away.

"Come on now." Milly gently lifted the lamb and placed it in front of the ewe. "This is your young one. She needs your care." But once again, the ewe bleated and stepped back.

Ian grabbed another handful of straw, rubbed the lamb again, and coaxed it to stand. "Go on. Your mum has a meal for you." He nudged the lamb toward the ewe. The little one took a few wobbly steps toward her mother, but the ewe lowered her head and butted the lamb away.

Charlotte gasped. "Why is she doing that?"

Ian shook his head. "Sometimes a mother rejects her young." He sent a worried glance toward his sister.

"Let's try again." Milly joined Ian and slowly moved the wobbly lamb closer to its mother. This time, the ewe stamped her foot and lowered her head in warning.

"That's enough." Ian scooped up the lamb and held it to his chest. He frowned and studied the ewe with a disappointed expression. "Seems she won't accept this one as her own."

Charlotte watched the quivering lamb in Ian's arms. What would happen to it now? How could the lamb survive without the mother's care?

"Shall we try one more time?" Milly asked.

"I don't want to risk it," Ian said. "I'm afraid she's a bummer lamb."

"A what?" Charlotte looked from Ian to Milly.

"That means she's rejected by her mum," Milly said with a sad look. "We'll have to take her inside and feed her."

"In the house?" Charlotte asked.

Milly nodded. "We'll pen her up in the kitchen where we can keep her safe and warm. She'll need a bottle every two to three hours. If not, she won't survive."

Charlotte's throat grew tight. The poor lamb, cast off by her mother and likely to die if someone didn't take on the role the mother had refused.

77

"I'll get a blanket." Milly left the stall and soon returned. "We can wrap her up in this."

Ian held out the lamb, and Milly tucked the old blanket around her. "Check on the ewe across the way. She'll be delivering soon." He nodded to the opposite stall. "I'll take this one in and give her a bottle."

"I can help." Charlotte spoke the words before she'd thought them through.

Ian turned toward her and raised his eyebrows. "You want to feed her?"

"Yes. I'd be glad to. Then you can finish out here."

Ian and Milly exchanged a glance, and something passed between them that Charlotte couldn't read.

Ian turned back toward Charlotte. "Come along, then. Take the lantern, and I'll show you what's needed."

She followed him out of the barn into the cool, quiet night. Her breath puffed out in a faint cloud as they walked up the path toward the house. Doubts rose and swirled through her mind. Could she really take care of the lamb that was only a few minutes old? If she didn't handle the job correctly, the lamb might die.

She reached for Ian's arm. "I've never done anything like this before."

A smile tugged at the corner of his mouth. "You mean watching a lamb being born in the middle of the night, or feeding a bummer lamb its first meal?"

She sighed. "Neither one. I've always lived in the city. I've never even had a pet."

His smile spread wider. "I'm sure with a bit of training you'll do just fine. I can tell you've a heart for this lamb. That's really all that's needed."

Ian carried the lamb into the kitchen and settled her on the floor, still nestled in the blanket, not far from the stove. He turned to Charlotte. "Set the lantern on the table. I'll warm up some milk."

He should get back out to the barn and help Milly, but his sister could manage for a little while. She often took a night watch on her own. Getting started feeding a newborn lamb could be a challenge, and as Charlotte said, she'd never done anything like that before.

She placed the lantern on the table and turned toward him. "What can I do to help?"

"Just speak softly to her and keep her calm while I get the bottle ready."

Charlotte knelt on the floor and rested her hand on the lamb's back while Ian stoked the fire in the stove, then pumped water into a pan. He took the glass bottle from the icebox and carried it back to the stove.

"Is that sheep milk?" Charlotte asked.

Ian nodded. "During lambing, we always keep some on hand in case we need to feed a bummer."

The little lamb bleated and squirmed, as though she knew what was coming. He placed the glass bottle in the water, then glanced at Charlotte.

She ran her hand gently down the lamb's back. "There now. Your milk is coming soon." Her gentle words and touch calmed the lamb, and she settled into the old blanket once more.

Ian smiled. Charlotte wasn't put off by the idea of sitting on the cold kitchen floor to comfort the newborn lamb. In fact, she looked quite taken with her little charge.

"How many bummer lambs do you have each year?" She looked up at him, and though the hour was late, her brown eyes shone bright. She made quite a nice picture with her long brown hair falling over her shoulders, her pink cheeks, and full lips.

He quickly dampened that thought and cleared his throat.

"We had three bummers last year. Sometimes we don't have any. But when we do, they become quite attached to whoever feeds them."

Her slender eyebrows rose. "You mean if I feed her, she'll become attached to me?"

"That's right. But we'll take turns. It's quite a job to feed her every few hours."

The water in the pan began to simmer, and Ian swirled the bottle around. He took it out and tested a drop of milk on his hand. Then he squatted on the other side of the lamb and held out the bottle to Charlotte. "Here you go."

She sent him a hesitant smile and questioning look.

"Just hold it to her mouth. She'll know what to do."

Charlotte bit her lip, tipped the bottle down, and touched it to the lamb's pink mouth. The little one licked the rubber tip a few times.

"That's right," Charlotte said softly.

The lamb took one more lick, then pulled the rubber nipple into her mouth and began vigorously sucking.

Charlotte looked across at Ian with a smile. "I think she's got it."

He grinned. "Yes, she's a smart one."

Charlotte laughed. "And strong." She adjusted her grip on the bottle and tipped it up to keep the milk flowing.

Ian's heart warmed as he watched Charlotte. Her willingness to feed the lamb seemed to speak of a gentle, kindhearted spirit. "That's the way. You're doing a fine job."

Charlotte's cheeks flushed pink. "She seems to like the milk."

"And the one who's feeding her." He spoke the words without thinking, and his neck warmed.

She looked down at the lamb, her dark eyelashes fanning out to shade her eyes. "Have you always wanted to be a . . . shepherd?"

Ian considered her question for a moment. "We're shepherds

and farmers. We use both terms." He rubbed his jaw. "But the answer to your question is complicated."

She lifted her gaze to meet his. "Why is that?"

He blew out a deep breath. "This farm has been in our family for years. My great-granddad, my granddad, and my father all raised sheep on this land. Soon I'll have to decide if I'm going follow in their footsteps. It's what my father wants, but I'm not sure it's the right life for me."

"If you don't run the farm, what would you do?"

"I'm studying archaeology at Oxford."

Her eyes rounded. "Archaeology . . . at Oxford?"

He lifted his chin. "That's right. But we lost my granddad to a stroke not long ago. Spring is our busiest season, and my father couldn't handle the work alone. So I took off this term to come home to help my family through the spring and summer."

She continued to study him with a puzzled expression. "Does that surprise you?"

"I just never imagined you'd studied at Oxford."

He huffed. "I've a brain as well as a knowledge of sheep and farming."

Her cheeks flushed. "Of course. I didn't mean to offend."

Her words had stung, but he shook them off. "No offense taken." He sat on the floor and looked across at her. "All my father ever wanted was to run this farm. He has a hard time accepting I might want a different life."

"I see." She tilted the bottle so the lamb could get the last of the milk. "Pleasing your father and living up to his expectations can be a difficult task."

"Did you and your father see eye to eye?"

She stilled, and a shadow seemed to pass over her face. "I thought we did, but after he passed, I realized we didn't really know each other at all." The sorrow in her voice surprised him.

"I'm sorry for your loss." He gentled his tone, hoping that would ease her pain.

"Thank you." Her words came out as a choked whisper, and she seemed on the verge of tears.

He clenched his hands and looked away. What was a man supposed to do when a woman cried? He never knew if he should try to comfort her or leave her alone to cry in private. Milly and Mum rarely let their tears flow. When they did, he usually fled to the barn. But avoiding painful situations felt cowardly, and he didn't want to desert Charlotte in her time of need. It wouldn't be right.

He steeled himself and looked her way. "What happened that made you change your mind . . . about your father?"

She let out a shuddering breath. "I can't . . . It's too dreadful to say."

He straightened. What had Henry Harper done?

He recalled his mum saying Charlotte's mother and father had eloped and married without the consent of her mother's family, causing a rift that had lasted more than twenty years. Was that what caused Charlotte's distress? Or was it because her father had made no plans to care for his wife and children in the event of his death, leaving them homeless and in need of charity? That was hurtful, but it didn't seem to match the level of Charlotte's pain.

Whatever had happened, Henry Harper had deeply grieved his daughter's heart, and that bothered Ian more than he would've expected.

A knock sounded at Charlotte's bedroom door the next morning just after eight. Mum and Alice had already gone to help with breakfast, and she was just finishing making her bed. "Come in," she called.

The door opened and Milly looked in from the doorway. "Good morning, Charlotte."

She returned the greeting before asking, "How is the lamb?"

"She's fine." Milly smiled. "You sister is feeding her now, and she's having a jolly time."

"I'm sorry I overslept. I meant to be up by seven to help with breakfast and feed the lamb."

Milly lifted her hand. "Don't worry. We all catch whatever sleep we can this time of year, and that lamb has had more attention than most of our other bummers." She held out a slim, navy-blue book. "I thought you might like this."

Charlotte hesitated before taking it. Milly and her family had already done so much for them.

Milly's expression softened. "When my granddad had his first stroke, it was a terrible blow. I didn't want to burden others with my worries, so I started writing in a journal. I thought it might be a comfort to you to have a place to put your thoughts."

Charlotte's eyes burned, and she blinked back her tears. "You're very kind . . . you and your family. Coming here has been like finding a safe harbor in a storm."

"We're all very sorry for the loss of your father and the challenges that has brought to your family." Milly's brown eyes glowed with sincerity. "Now, come to the kitchen. Mum has made us a fine breakfast."

Charlotte sent her a tremulous smile. "I'll be along as soon as I finish making the bed."

Milly nodded, then turned to go.

"Milly, wait."

She looked over her shoulder. "Yes?"

"I appreciate the gift . . . very much." Charlotte wanted to say more, but her voice choked off.

Milly waved away her words. "No trouble at all. See you in a few minutes." She disappeared down the hall.

Charlotte ran her hand over the cover of the journal, then looked inside. Creamy white pages with faint lines waited to be filled. Was this the place she could pour out her heart with all the conflicting thoughts that had kept her awake for hours last night?

Memories of the previous night came flooding back, and she pulled in a quick breath. She'd almost told Ian about her father's betrayal. Was it the late hour or his kindness that had broken through her defenses and tempted her to reveal that dark secret? What if she had told him? What would he think of her and her family?

She closed her eyes and shook her head. It was too shameful. She couldn't ever tell him or anyone else.

Seven

2012

David strode into the library, his mind on the meeting he'd just completed with the architect. He clenched his jaw as he recalled the architect's final comments. The budget would have to be increased to meet the expectation of guests looking for luxury accommodations.

He spotted Gwen sitting at his grandfather's desk and stopped midway across the room.

She looked up and seemed to read his mood. "Your grandmother suggested I work in here."

He grimaced. "I need a file from the desk."

Gwen snapped her laptop closed, shuffled her papers together, and rose from the chair. "I don't mind moving." But it was obvious from her tone and stiff posture that she did.

He stifled a growl. Why was she so easily irritated? Why was he?

She crossed to the chair in the corner, without looking his way, and took a seat with her laptop.

He pulled open the lower desk drawer and scanned the files. He didn't want to be at odds with Gwen. But ever since lunch yesterday, she'd avoided eye contact and said little. He pulled out the file he needed, closed the drawer, and turned toward her. "Have I offended you?"

She sent him a cool look. "Why do you ask?"

"Because you're giving the impression I have."

Gwen's expression remained unchanged, but her cheeks flushed.

He shifted his weight to the other foot. "Look—we have to work together, and that's going to be difficult if you're harboring a grudge against me."

Her eyes flashed. "I am not harboring a grudge."

"Really? Then what's bothering you?"

She looked toward the windows for a moment, then returned her gaze to him. "I do have some concerns."

He frowned. "And they are?"

"Longdale is a beautiful home with unique architecture and a rich history. I'm not sure your plans to turn it into a hotel are going to honor that history and preserve what is precious to your grandmother."

"I thought I made it clear yesterday. I'm doing this to *save* my grandmother's home. I'll preserve as much of Longdale's unique character as possible."

"What does that mean?"

He huffed. Why did she seem to think he knew nothing about historic preservation? "For the past six years, my work has focused on converting historic estates into hotels, spas, and multi-unit flats. I own the company. That's what I do."

Her eyes widened for a split second, then she masked her surprise. "Okay, but are you sure this plan is what's best for your grandmother?"

"What my grandmother needs is for Longdale to bring in an income."

"I would think you'd want her to enjoy her remaining years, rather than burdening her with a construction project and seeing the home she loves turned into a hotel."

Heat rushed into his face. "You've been here two days! You know next to nothing about our family or the challenges we're facing."

She lifted her chin. "I may not know you or your grandmother well, but I have the advantage of seeing the situation with fresh eyes."

"And you think I'm not seeing things clearly?"

"I didn't say that!"

"Well, that's what you're implying."

"What I'm saying is, I think it's important to preserve homes that have architectural significance and honor their history."

"How do your preferences about preservation outweigh my experience turning crumbling estates into profitable businesses?"

"Well . . . I simply mean—"

He held up his hand, cutting her off. "Nothing you've said gives you the right to find fault with my plans or question my commitment to doing what's best for my grandmother."

Emotion flashed across her face, then she pressed her lips in a tight line. Closing her eyes, she pulled in a deep breath. "You're right. I apologize." She rose and strode out of the library, leaving her laptop and papers behind.

David groaned and sank into the desk chair. Why did he let her get under his skin? Was the stress of managing this project making him rude and short-tempered? Or did Gwen's response to his plan trigger him for another reason?

Memories of his father's critical attitude and harsh words floated through his mind. All his life, he'd tried to do well at school and in athletics to gain his father's approval, but it was never enough. When he turned eighteen, he'd left home determined to break away from his family and stop trying to please his father. But then his father was diagnosed with cancer and died two months later, before they had a chance to reconcile.

He squeezed his eyes tight, wishing he could go back and

make different choices, but that was impossible. He'd waited too long. Time had run out. And he'd carried a load of grief and regret ever since.

He laid his head back against the chair and replayed his conversation with Gwen. He didn't like the way she'd questioned his competence with the project or his concern for his grandmother. If he was honest, he had to admit she had wounded his pride.

Still, she had a valid point. He had downplayed the extent of the changes needed when he'd discussed the renovations with his grandmother. He'd done that so she wouldn't worry, but now he wasn't sure that was the best approach. Maybe he needed to have another conversation with his grandmother and explain the plans in detail.

He was determined to save Longdale and find a way to bring in an income for his grandmother, but how could he live with himself if his plans stole his grandmother's happiness from her final years?

☙

Gwen hurried up the stairs, intending to go to her room and take some time to calm down, but as she approached her door, she changed her mind and continued down the hall. She needed a distraction—something to take her mind off her conversation with David.

She climbed the circular stairs in the tower to the top floor and slipped into the archive room. Her head throbbed as David's heated words replayed through her mind. She leaned back against the door and released a shuddering breath.

What was she thinking? David was going to send her packing if she didn't stop criticizing his plans. How would she explain that to her grandfather? She had to put aside her concerns and do the job she'd been assigned. That was the only way she could rebuild her grandfather's trust and hold on to her position at Hill and Morris.

But what about Lilly? Was David truly doing what was best for her?

"Am I seeing things clearly, Lord, or am I wrong?" She whispered the prayer, knowing she needed wisdom, because on her own, she had just about ruined her working relationship with David. No clear answer came, but her heartbeat slowed to a steady pace. Times of prayer had been an anchor in the past, and she needed that connection to the Lord now more than ever.

She turned toward the wooden cabinets. Maybe if she took a few minutes to look through one of the boxes, it would give her some mental space and help her feel more settled.

She pulled out a box and opened the lid. On top lay the journal Lilly had read aloud the day before. Questions popped into Gwen's mind as she lifted the journal from the box.

She opened the cover and scanned the first words written in graceful script: *This is the private journal of Charlotte Harper, begun the 4th day of April 1912. Please don't read these entries unless I've gone home to heaven.*

Gwen smiled. What an interesting prologue. It made her even more eager to discover what Charlotte had written in her journal, and she turned the page.

I can barely see to write as tears fill my eyes. My heart is so heavy, I hardly know how to put it into words. I thought I knew my father, but now I realize I did not. How could he teach one thing at meeting after meeting and then live in the totally opposite way, betraying us all . . .

Eight

1912

Charlotte lifted her gaze, taking in the view of the large three-story stone house with a tall round turret on the left, two balconies, and mullioned windows all around. Manicured lawns spread out around the house, bordered by flower beds filled with colorful early spring blooms.

She turned to her mum as they walked up the gravel drive. "This is where you grew up?" She kept her voice low and glanced around, half expecting a troop of gardeners or servants to appear.

"Yes, this was where I was born and lived until I was eighteen and married your father." Mum led the way up the steps to the double front door carved of dark wood. "Longdale Manor has been in our family since my grandfather purchased it in the 1860s."

"It's lovely." Charlotte could hardly believe this was where her mum had spent her childhood. What would it have been like to grow up surrounded by such luxury?

"It is one of the grandest houses in the district. I have some very happy memories of my time here." Mum glanced over her shoulder toward the hillside gardens that sloped down to

Derwentwater. Along the pathway, yellow and white primrose and daffodils waved in the breeze flowing up from the lake.

A bittersweet look filled Mum's eyes. Finally, she turned toward the door and straightened her shoulders. "It's time I introduced you to your grandfather." She lifted her hand and rapped three times.

A few seconds later, the door opened, and a tall, thin butler looked out. "May I help you?"

"Yes, would you please tell Mr. Benderly that his daughter is here to see him?"

The butler faltered for a second, but he quickly recovered. "Of course. Please, come in." He opened the door wider, and they stepped inside.

Charlotte's breath caught as she glanced around. The large entrance hall was open to the third story and paneled in dark wood all around. To their right, a beautifully carved staircase led to the upper floors. In the center of the opposite wall, a marble mantel surrounded a large fireplace, where a cozy fire burned. Comfortable furniture was grouped around the fireplace, and sculptures of hunting dogs stood on each side of the hearth. Several landscape paintings and formal portraits of men and women hung on the walls. The elaborate furnishings confirmed her grandfather's wealth. Did he have compassion to match?

"Please wait here." The butler turned and left the hall, disappearing through a doorway to the right of the fireplace.

Mum's face had gone pale, and she clasped her gloved hands tightly.

Charlotte touched her mum's arm and forced confidence into her voice. "I'm sure all will be well."

Mum glanced her way. "I hope so. I've prayed for strength to forgive and make a fresh start. I hope your grandfather is of the same mind."

Charlotte swallowed and nodded.

Moments later, the butler returned. "Please follow me."

Mum sent Charlotte a quick glance, then they crossed the hall after the butler and entered another room that appeared to be a library. Bookshelves filled two walls, and tall windows on the opposite wall looked out to the lake. At the far end of the room, a distinguished man with silver hair, beard, and moustache sat behind a large wooden desk. He was dressed in a well-cut charcoal suit and black tie.

He looked up as they entered, but he didn't rise from his chair. His expression remained firm and unwelcoming. "Well, Rose, this is unexpected."

"Hello, Father." She hesitated. "You didn't receive my letter?"

His steady gaze remained fixed on her. "Not that I recall."

"Oh . . . well, this is your granddaughter, Charlotte." She glanced at Charlotte. "This is your grandfather, George Benderly."

Charlotte forced a brief smile and nodded to him. "Hello, sir."

Grandfather studied her with a frown. "She looks like her father."

Charlotte pulled in a sharp breath, too stunned to reply.

Grandfather narrowed his gaze. "He didn't have the courage to come himself, did he?" When Mum didn't answer, he crossed his arms. "Why are you here? What do you want? Money?"

Mum's eyes filled with tears, which she quickly blinked away. "I explained everything in my letter. Henry is . . . no longer with us. He passed away last month."

Grandfather didn't flinch. "He's dead?"

Mum nodded. "It was quite unexpected." Her voice wobbled as she continued, "He was speaking in London for the final night of the Higher Life Spring Conference, and he just . . . collapsed. The doctors said it was a heart attack."

Grandfather huffed. "Well, I can't say I'm sorry to hear it. I never liked the man, nor did I trust him after I found out he'd been carrying on a secret affair with you."

Pink splotches bloomed on Mum's cheeks. "Father, please. It wasn't like that. We kept our feelings private, but I'm not ashamed of that. We truly cared for each other."

"Well, you ought to be ashamed! Carrying on for months behind my back!"

"We did nothing wrong. Henry's intentions were honorable. You know that. He came to you and asked for my hand."

Grandfather's glare deepened. "He did no such thing!"

Mum's lips parted. "But Henry said he asked your permission for us to marry, and you refused. Then you threatened to send me away to prevent us from seeing each other. That's why we eloped."

Grandfather's face reddened. "That is a lie! I found out he was meeting you in secret, and I dismissed him. The nerve of that man! You were barely eighteen, and he was ten years older! Even if he had asked to marry you, I never would've given my permission."

Mum clenched her hands. "You're saying he never asked you for my hand?"

"That's exactly what I'm saying. And if that's what he told you, then he was a liar!"

Mum stiffened, and her eyes flashed. "Don't speak of Henry that way. We were married for more than twenty years, and I loved him."

Charlotte's throat burned, and she pressed her lips tight. Her father hadn't been worthy of that love, but this wasn't the time to reveal her father's betrayal. It would only reinforce her grandfather's poor opinion of her father and devastate Mum.

Her grandfather rose from his chair. "You listen to me, Rose. Henry Harper might have come to Longdale to be your brother's tutor, but as soon as he met you, he decided to worm his way into your affection to get his hands on your inheritance."

"Father, that is not true! Henry didn't marry me for my money."

"He thought he was clever and could fool us all, but his plan failed. When you ran away with him, I washed my hands of you! He never got one penny from me, and neither will you!"

Mum's chin trembled, and she looked close to breaking down.

Charlotte gulped in a breath. "Please, Grandfather, all that happened a long time ago. No matter what you think of my father, there's nothing we can do about his choices or the way he lived his life."

Grandfather shifted his steely gaze to Charlotte. "So, you want to defend your father?"

Charlotte's heart hammered, but she kept her voice steady. "My father is gone now. But you have a daughter, a grandson, and two granddaughters who have suffered a great loss and need your help."

He lifted his silver eyebrows and shifted his gaze to Rose. "You need my help?"

Mum pulled in a deep breath and gave a slight nod. "We couldn't stay in London. We sold our home, and I thought we might come to Longdale to . . . stay with you."

Grandfather leaned forward and placed both hands on his desk. "So . . . now that he's gone, you want to come back." He shook his head. "You've been a great disappointment to me, Rose, staying away all these years."

Mum blinked back her tears, obviously trying to keep her emotions under control with little success. "I've written to you a few times each year. Mother always replied, but after she died, you never answered my letters. Did you even read them?"

Grandfather seemed unmoved by the hurt in her voice. "I saw no need to read letters from someone who had turned her back on me and run off with a scoundrel."

Mum's back went ramrod straight, and her eyes glittered

with anger. "That is enough! I will not stand here and listen to you berate a man who can no longer defend himself." She jerked her chin to the side. "Come along, Charlotte. We're done here."

"But, Mother, we haven't—"

"I am finished listening to his insults. We're leaving." Mum swung around and marched out of the library.

Grandfather's eyes flickered with emotion, but he quickly schooled his features. "Go on then, girl. I've nothing more to say to you."

Charlotte pressed her hand to her stomach. "I'm sorry we've upset you. That wasn't our intention. Good day." She walked out of the library and passed through the hall. The front door stood open. Through the doorway she caught sight of Mum standing off the far side of the gravel drive, her head down and a handkerchief clutched to her mouth.

What a disaster! The painful wounds of the past had been ripped open. Rather than help her mum heal, this visit had brought more pain. What were they going to do now?

Ian walked into the kitchen and heaved a tired sigh. He'd spent hours out in the fields, checking on the ewes and their new lambs, then taking his turn in the barn, helping with lambing there.

His mum looked up from the sink where she stood washing dishes. "You look weary, son. Sit down and I'll pour you a cup of tea."

"Thanks. That sounds good." He pulled off his jacket and hung it on a hook by the door, then took a seat at the table. The heat from the kitchen fireplace warmed his back, and his tense muscles began to relax.

"A letter arrived for you from Professor Montrose." She handed the envelope to him.

"Thanks." He tore it open, scanned the first few lines, and smiled.

"Good news?" Mum asked.

"He received the funding he needs to begin planning his next trip to Egypt." He skimmed the page. How he wished he could go along on that trip, but the expense made it impossible. Even if he did have the funds, his father needed his help through the summer. Still, he couldn't help wishing he could join the professor. He shook his head and slid the letter back into the envelope. The dream of traveling to Egypt and taking part in his first archaeological dig would have to wait.

Mum watched him with a concerned look. "Everything all right?"

He nodded, hiding his disappointment. "Everything's fine."

She glanced toward the window and fields beyond. "How many more lambs today?"

"Eleven out in the fields, and two more in the barn so far. Dad's out there now."

Mum lifted the steaming kettle from the back of the stove. "That's a good number."

Milly came in the side door, carrying a wicker basket of clean laundry she'd taken from the line. "How are the lambs?"

Ian gave a soft chuckle. That was the main topic of conversation this time of year. "Eleven more born outside, and two in the barn. All seem healthy."

"Good." Milly set down the basket and looked at the sleeping bummer lamb they'd penned in the corner of the kitchen. "This one's doing well. Alice has been feeding her every few hours and having a grand time." She glanced around the kitchen. "Where is she?"

"The lamb fell asleep after the last feeding, so I sent her outside to explore the farm a bit." Mum carried the steaming mug toward the table. "That young one can't be cooped up too long."

The main door flew open, and Rose walked through. Her face looked flushed, and her eyes were red, as though she'd been crying. She stopped just inside the kitchen doorway when she saw them.

"Hello, Rose. Would you like a cup of tea?" Mum lifted the mug.

"No, thank you. Excuse me." Rose lowered her gaze, strode past them, and hurried down the hallway toward the guest rooms. As she disappeared, Charlotte entered the kitchen, wearing a guarded expression.

His mum placed the mug of tea on the table and turned to Charlotte. "How was your visit?"

"I'm afraid it didn't go well."

Milly joined Ian at the table. "I'm sorry, Charlotte. Tell us what happened."

Mum frowned at Milly. "Perhaps she'd rather not."

"I don't mind." Charlotte clasped her hands. "I'm afraid my grandfather has a long-standing grievance against my father, and he doesn't seem willing to let it go, even though my father is . . ." Her voice cracked, and she crossed her arms and looked away.

Ian's chest tightened. He hated to see Charlotte so upset. Grief was a hard road, and troubled family relationships didn't make it easier.

"There now." His mum laid her hand on Charlotte's arm and guided her toward the table. "Sit down, and I'll make you some tea."

Charlotte looked toward the hallway. "I should go check on Mum."

"Why don't you give her some time to collect herself?" his mum continued. "She'll come out when she's ready."

Charlotte hesitated, then slowly removed her hat. "If you think that's best." She took a seat opposite Ian, placed the hat in her lap, and accepted a mug of tea.

Ian studied Charlotte as she took a slow sip. Her cheeks and nose were pink from the cold walk back from Longdale. A few tendrils of her dark brown hair had come loose when she removed her hat. She brushed them from the side of her face and took another sip.

Milly settled in the chair next to her. "I'm sorry about your grandfather, but I'm not surprised. I've heard he doesn't welcome anyone into his home. And he rarely goes into the village, not even to attend church."

Mum released a sigh as she sat next to Ian. "It's sad. He used to attend St. John's with your grandmother when she was alive. Since she died, he hardly leaves his estate."

Charlotte placed her mug on the table. "I don't understand him. It's been more than twenty years since my parents married, but he's still angry about it. He said some dreadful things to Mum. She's very hurt."

Milly sent her an understanding smile. "I'm sure they'll work it out in time."

Charlotte wrapped her hands around the steaming mug. "I don't know if we'll ever be welcome at Longdale." She glanced around the table at them. "I'm sorry. We thought he would've been ready to receive us. But that's not the case."

"Don't worry about it," Ian quickly added. "You can stay with us as long as you'd like."

Milly and Mum exchanged surprised glances, and Ian hoped Charlotte didn't notice.

"I'm not sure your father would agree to that," Charlotte said slowly.

Ian clenched his jaw. Why couldn't his father at least pretend to be hospitable? He'd have to speak to him again, explain the situation, and make sure he didn't add to Charlotte's burden. "My father may be gruff, but he'll not turn away friends in need."

Charlotte took a sip of tea and cradled the mug in her hands.

"Perhaps I should try to find a position. Then I could contribute toward the cost of staying with you."

"You mustn't worry about that," his mum said, her voice soft with compassion. "At least not yet."

Milly's face brightened. "Maybe we shouldn't dismiss the idea too quickly."

"What do you mean?" Ian frowned at his sister. "You want Charlotte to go into service?"

"Service isn't the only option for a young woman. She might find a position in one of the shops in Keswick."

He crossed his arms, taking in that thought. He didn't like the idea of sending Charlotte off to earn a wage just to appease his father.

Charlotte's gaze shifted from Ian to Milly. "I've no experience working in a shop. Do you think anyone would hire me?"

"Why not? You're intelligent and well-mannered," Milly said. "I'm sure you'd be an asset to any shopkeeper and sure to increase his business."

Charlotte's eyes glowed at Milly's compliment. "I've never sought a position. How does one go about it?"

Milly thought for a moment, then smiled. "You must come with us to Sunday services at St. John's. Several shopkeepers attend our church. We'll introduce you to folks and help you make the right connections."

Charlotte's expression brightened. "Thank you. That's very kind."

Ian sat back and considered Milly's plan. Helping Charlotte find a position in a shop might be the first step toward her family eventually having a home of their own. But if she worked in a shop several hours a day, he'd rarely see her. That thought didn't sit well. He'd enjoyed showing her around the farm, introducing her to country life, and sharing conversations. But he had to think about what was best for Charlotte and her family.

That was most important, not his wish that she might spend her days at their farm with him.

Charlotte rose from the church pew and straightened her jacket. She hadn't attended a church service since her father's funeral, and she'd been hesitant to come that day. But Milly's promise to introduce her to potential employers had made the decision for her—that, and Mum's insistence it would be rude not to attend church with the Storeys.

The worship service at St. John's was quite different from those she usually attended in London. Sitting in this small stone chapel with its simple wooden pews, single stained-glass window, and rows of glowing candles had given her a sense of peace. The people seemed well acquainted, and several had welcomed her when she'd come in. They sang the hymns with strength and conviction and listened attentively to the sermon. The Reverend Matthew Donovan seemed to be a sincere and humble man whose attitude matched the beauty and simplicity of the building and the warmth of the congregation.

Ian closed the hymnal they'd shared for the final song and looked her way. "I hope you enjoyed the service."

Charlotte nodded. "I did."

"Reverend Donovan has only been here about six months, but he's won the hearts of the people with his clear messages and caring ways." He grinned. "And his sermons are much shorter than our previous vicar, who usually went on for more than an hour."

She smiled. "I liked his message. He even included a bit of humor."

Ian nodded, his eyes shining. "A little humor helps the solid truth go down well."

Charlotte and Ian stepped into the aisle. Alice, Mum, Jenny, and Milly followed them. Mr. Storey had stayed home to keep an eye on the ewes and newborn lambs.

A slow-moving line of parishioners waited their turn to speak to Reverend Donovan, who stood at the rear door.

Milly stepped up beside Charlotte. "I see a few of the shop owners. As soon as we go outside, we'll make the rounds, and I'll introduce you."

Charlotte's stomach fluttered, and she smoothed her hand down her skirt. "Thank you, Milly. I appreciate it."

When they reached Mr. Donovan at the doorway, Ian introduced them.

Mr. Donovan smiled. "Welcome to St. John's. We're glad you could join us today." His soft gray eyes seemed to radiate kindness and welcome.

Mum held out her hand. "That was a wonderful message. Your explanation of suffering as a gift was quite enlightening. I've read that passage in Philippians many times, but it never struck me as it did today."

His eyebrows rose slightly, and he searched her face as he held her hand. "I'm glad it was meaningful to you. Those of us who have experienced suffering look at things a bit differently, don't we?"

Mum gave a brief nod. "Yes, I suppose we do." She paused a moment, then said, "My husband passed away a short time ago, and Jenny and Leland have been kind enough to allow us to stay with them until we can make other arrangements."

"I'm very sorry for your loss." His gentle tone seemed to suggest he understood the pain of losing someone dear to him.

"Thank you," Mum said softly.

He released her hand and turned to Jenny. "Perhaps I could stop by the farm this week for a brief visit. Would Tuesday afternoon around three be agreeable?"

Jenny glanced at Charlotte's mum, who nodded. She turned back to Mr. Donovan. "We'd welcome your visit."

Charlotte replayed the reverend's interaction with them as she descended the church steps. He seemed to be a caring man who took shepherding his flock seriously. She hoped his visit would be a comfort to her mum and help her through her time of grief. They'd faced so many losses and changes since her father's death.

Her brow furrowed as she thought of her father. He was a brilliant, charismatic speaker, but looking back, she realized he seemed more concerned about delivering a powerful message than caring for his family or the people who listened. Gaining the admiration of his peers and gathering a following were more important to him than humbly serving those who needed to understand the truth of the Gospel and love of God.

She glanced at Mr. Donovan, standing in the doorway at the top of the stairs. He held the hand of a stooped, silver-haired woman in a ragged brown coat. He offered a caring smile as he patiently listened to what she had to say. Mr. Donovan would probably be just as happy preaching to ten simple country folks as he would five hundred influential people in London.

The truth struck her heart, and sadness draped over her like a heavy blanket. Her father never would have been satisfied to lead a small country parish like St. John's. He was not a caring shepherd like Mr. Donovan.

"Charlotte." Milly slipped her arm through Charlotte's and lowered her voice. "Do you see that tall woman dressed in the blue suit and matching feathered hat?"

Charlotte glanced across the churchyard to a small circle of women standing in the shade of an oak tree. "I see her."

"That is Mrs. Clifton. She owns one of the best dress shops in Keswick." Milly smiled. "Ready to meet her?"

Charlotte nodded. It was time to put away thoughts of her father and focus on finding a position to help provide for her family. That had to be her focus now. But as she crossed the churchyard, she couldn't ignore her aching heart. If it weren't for her father's choices, she and her mum wouldn't be facing these painful circumstances.

Charlotte carried a stack of dishes from the table after the Sunday afternoon meal, and her thoughts returned to meeting the shop owners following the church service. Milly had made three introductions, but no one needed a young, inexperienced assistant. Her throat tightened as she placed the dishes by the sink.

She ought to pray and ask the Lord to help her find a position, but guilt pricked her conscience. That morning's worship service had stirred her in ways she hadn't expected. Since discovering her father's betrayal, she had ignored the promptings to pray. How could she ask the Lord for help when she had closed her heart to Him for so long?

Ian rose from his place at the table and stretched. "That was a fine meal, Mum."

"Glad you enjoyed it." Jenny returned his smile and set the kettle on the stove to heat.

Mr. Storey pushed back his chair. "We better go out and check on the sheep."

"I'll check the western pasture." Ian crossed the kitchen and took his jacket from the hook on the wall.

Mr. Storey gave a nod, then strode out the door.

Alice rose from where she'd been sitting on the floor, feeding the bummer lamb. "May I come with you?"

Ian glanced her way with a smile. "You're all done there?"

"Yes." Alice held up the empty bottle. "She finished all the milk."

Ian shifted his gaze to Charlotte. "Anyone else want to go along?"

She didn't want to appear too eager, but it was a lovely spring day. A walk around the farm to see the new lambs might lift her spirits, especially if she could spend time in Ian's company. "I'll come with you and keep an eye on Alice."

Her sister scowled. "I don't need anyone to keep an eye on me."

Mum sent Alice a pointed look. "It's good to go together."

Milly turned from the sink, where she was helping her mother with washing up. "You'll need to wear boots if you're going to tramp around the fields."

Charlotte looked down at her shoes. "These won't do?"

"I'm afraid the mud will spoil them."

"Not to worry." Jenny held up a finger. "I have an extra pair that look about your size. I'll bring them down."

A few minutes later, Charlotte slipped her feet into the dark green, knee-high rubber boots. They felt cold and heavy, but everyone in the Storey family wore the same type of boots when they worked outdoors, so she was glad to don a pair.

Ian grinned. "They look like a good fit."

She returned a smile and wiggled her toes. "Yes, they're surprisingly comfortable."

"They'll keep your feet dry, and that's what's important." Ian picked up a long wooden staff with a carved handle.

As they waited for Alice to put on her coat, Charlotte studied the staff. The carved head featured a black-and-white border collie crouching toward a black-faced sheep with curled horns. The carving was surprisingly lifelike and made of different material than the long wooden section. "That's a beautiful staff."

A proud light lit Ian's eyes as he held it out for her inspection. "That it is."

She ran her hand gently over the top. "The carving is so intricate."

"The handle is carved from a sheep's horn, and the bottom is sturdy oak." A hint of sadness clouded his eyes. "My grand-dad carved this staff before he had his stroke."

"He was a wonderful artist," she said softly.

"Yes. He had many talents, and carving was one of his favorite pastimes during the winter months."

"Did he sell his carvings?"

Ian shook his head. "He made them as gifts for family and friends."

Alice closed her top button. "I'm ready."

"All right, then. Let's check on those sheep." Ian pushed open the door, and Alice and Charlotte passed through.

They walked down the lane, where moss-covered stone walls outlined green fields dotted with sheep. On the far side of the valley, steep hills covered with rocks and heather rose to the sky. In the distance, Derwentwater sparkled deep blue. The scene was breathtakingly beautiful, and a fresh wave of hope rose in Charlotte's soul.

"Look at all the lambs!" Alice ran ahead and unlatched the wooden gate leading into the pasture.

Charlotte spotted several young lambs among the flock as she and Ian followed Alice through the gate. The grass was soft and springy beneath her feet, and the air smelled fresh and clean. Clumps of creamy primrose dotted the field, brightening the view.

Ian latched the gate behind them. "I saw Milly introducing you to some of the shop owners after church. Any good prospects for a position?"

Charlotte brushed a strand of hair from her face, wishing she could give him a different answer. "Mrs. Clifton is looking for an assistant at the dress shop to make alterations and help customers choose patterns and fabrics."

"Would that suit you?"

She hesitated, disappointment dampening her spirit. "I can turn up a hem or sew on a button, but I've never done more than that. We always bought our clothing from a small shop near our home in London. The dressmaker was a friend of my mother.

She offered simple, modest clothing at a reasonable price." She plucked at the skirt of her black dress, one they'd purchased after her father's death. "They were not always to my taste."

He grinned. "I don't know much about women's clothing, but you look lovely to me."

She glanced his way, pleased by his comment. "Thank you."

His smile eased. "I'm sorry the dressmaker's position isn't an option. What about the others?"

"I met Mr. Jenkins, the owner of the butcher shop, and Mr. Langston from the apothecary, but neither was looking to hire anyone." She bent and plucked a primrose from the grass to avoid looking him in the eye.

"I hope you won't be discouraged." His understanding tone surprised her, and she looked up. "There are other shops. Milly can take you around the village this week, if you like."

She didn't want to admit she didn't have the practical skills needed and that she doubted anyone would hire her, so she kept quiet and continued across the field.

"More positions will become available as the weather warms. Lots of people come here on holiday in the spring and summer, especially as it gets closer to the convention."

She glanced at him. "I remember my parents discussing the Keswick Convention, but I don't know much about it."

He sent her a half smile. "It's the highlight of the year around here. People come from all over England to hear the teaching and strengthen their faith and commitment to the Lord." He stopped to check on a young lamb.

"I've heard it's been going on for years."

He nodded, and when he seemed confident all was well with the lamb, he continued. "The convention started back in the 1870s with just a few hundred people. Last year, more than three thousand attended. There's a strong emphasis on prayer and consecration. I've heard some inspiring messages from missionaries serving around the world."

Ian's enthusiasm made it obvious he was a committed Christian. What would he think of her if he knew how her father's death and betrayal had shaken her faith? She swallowed and looked away, dreading the thought.

"I remember hearing your father speak at the convention two years ago," Ian said. "But you and your mum weren't with him."

Her stomach tensed as she recalled why she'd remained in London. "My mother was ill, and I stayed home to help care for Alice."

"Your mum mentioned he'd spoken a few other times in the past. I'm surprised you never came with him."

"That was when I was younger. I suppose he didn't feel it was appropriate for me to attend."

Confusion lit Ian's eyes. "The convention is a family affair. People bring children of all ages."

"Then I'm sure he wanted to focus on his messages and not be distracted by us." She couldn't keep a touch of hurt from her voice. Was that truly why he'd left her at home? What else was he doing while he was in Keswick and his family was in London? Was that where he'd met E. M.? Pain pierced her heart. She clenched her jaw and looked away.

"Charlotte? What is it?"

She pressed her lips together and shook her head.

Concern filled his expression.

"Ian!" Across the field, Alice waved her arms. "A lamb is stuck down there!" She pointed toward an area where the ground dropped away into a rocky ravine.

Ian set off at a jog, and Charlotte hurried after him. When they reached Alice, Charlotte scanned the area. They stood at the edge of a cliff overlooking a small waterfall pouring into a rushing stream about twenty feet below. A little lamb lay motionless at the edge of the water on the opposite side.

"Oh, the poor thing. Do you think he's still alive?" Charlotte leaned forward.

Ian stretched out his arm, holding her back. "Stay away from the edge. It's slippery. I'm going down." He squatted and quickly lowered himself over the side.

Charlotte and Alice hovered together on the bank, watching Ian as he descended the wet, moss-covered rocks. He jumped the last few feet, then sloshed across the fast-flowing stream, with the water rising almost to the top of his rubber boots. Within seconds, he knelt by the motionless lamb and lifted it from the rocks. He looked it over, then bent his head close. Turning toward them, he lifted his face. "He's alive!"

"Wonderful!" Charlotte called, slipping her arm around Alice's shoulders.

Ian strode back across the stream and looked up at Charlotte. "We've got to get him back to the barn soon or he won't survive." He started the climb, holding the lamb close to his chest with one arm and gripping the rocks with the other.

Charlotte bit her lip as she watched him haul himself up.

Ian set his mouth in a determined line and climbed one careful step, and then another. When his head was just a few feet from the top, he stopped and looked around. "I need two hands the rest of the way. Can you take him?"

Charlotte's heart lurched. "I'll try," she said, then lay down on the grass and reached over the side.

Ian slowly lifted the lamb toward her, but inches separated them.

She scooted forward, hanging her upper body over the ledge.

"Charlotte!" Alice grabbed her legs and held on.

"Careful," Ian called. His face looked flushed, and drops of sweat glistened on his forehead.

She reached down, extending her arms toward the lamb.

Ian hoisted the lamb up once more, and she grasped a handful of cold, wet wool. Struggling forward another inch, she adjusted her hold. "I've got him!"

She tried to scoot back but the weight of the lamb held her

in place. Ian heaved himself up over the bank and pulled her back across the grass. She held tight to the lamb as she sat up. Mud streaked the front of her dress, but the lamb was safe.

"Are you all right?" Ian knelt next to her and searched her face.

"Yes. I'm fine." She passed him the cold, limp lamb and tried to brush mud and grass from her shirtfront, but it smeared across her hands.

"I'm sorry about your dress." He reached out his hand to her. "Let me help you up."

She took hold and rose. "This is one time I'm glad I'm wearing black." A smile pulled at her lips.

He responded with a grin. "Yes. Good choice for a task like this."

Alice sent him a worried look as she reached out and touched the lamb. "Do you think he'll live?"

"I hope so. Let's take him back and see if we can revive him." They set off at a quick pace across the field.

Charlotte glanced at Ian as he walked up the hill, carrying the lamb against his chest. The determined set of his jaw contrasted the softness around his eyes. The combination perfectly reflected his role as a caring shepherd. Without hesitation, he'd put himself in danger to rescue the lamb that had wandered off into a dangerous place. And now he would bring the lamb safely home to give him the very best chance for recovery.

Her chest expanded, and a smile rose from her heart. When she'd first met Ian, his confident manner, handsome appearance, and charming smile had made her uncomfortable and even a little suspicious. But his thoughtfulness and the gentle way he took care of the sheep made it clear he was a good man—nothing like her father. She was glad to have such a kind and caring friend.

Nine

2012

Gwen clicked through to another art website and scrolled down. She glanced at the photo she'd taken of the Impressionist painting hanging in one of the upstairs bedrooms, then compared it to the image online. There it was, *Thatched Cottage in Normandy*, by Berthe Morisot, painted in 1865, oil on canvas, private collection—yes, Lilly Benderly's collection!

She squinted at the image on the website, wanting to be sure, and rubbed her eyes. It was after ten, but she'd wanted to finish her research on this painting before she went to bed. She reached up and stretched her arms, trying to relieve the ache in her neck and shoulders. Hunching over a computer for hours on end was not good for her posture or her health. She'd have to make sure to take a walk tomorrow morning and more breaks during the day or she was going to turn into a hunchback.

The library door opened, and David looked in.

She dropped her arms, and heat filled her face. She hadn't seen him since their argument that afternoon. He'd been absent at dinner. When Gwen asked about him, Lilly said he'd gone into the village to meet with someone about the bats in the attic. That comment had sent a shiver down Gwen's back.

"Do you mind if I come in?" His tone was soft, almost apologetic.

"Not at all. It's your library . . . or it will be one day."

He approached the desk and tucked his hands in his pants pockets. "I'd like to apologize for the way I responded earlier."

Surprise rippled through her.

"I have a hard time accepting criticism. It's something I'm working on, but I should've listened to what you had to say without becoming defensive."

She blinked. "Wow, I didn't expect that."

He cocked an eyebrow.

"I mean, thank you for the apology. It takes humility to acknowledge you're working on something like that."

His mouth quirked up at the corner. "That doesn't mean I won't do it again, but at least you know I'm aware of the issue and I'm trying to change."

She swallowed, knowing the ball was in her court. "I should also apologize. I didn't handle myself well in that conversation. I've had some . . . difficulties in personal relationships and at work, and that tends to make it hard for me to trust people and believe the best about them."

His gaze traveled over her face as though he was looking past her words to the hurt she carried inside. "I'm sorry to hear that." His tone was gentle, so unlike the way he'd spoken to her that afternoon. What had happened to make him change his mind? Whatever it was, she was grateful.

"Maybe we should start over." He extended his hand. "I'm David Bradford of Bradford Consulting in Manchester."

She took his hand, and pleasant warmth wove around her heart. "I'm glad to meet you, David. I'm Gwen Morris from the London office of Hill and Morris. I'm looking forward to working with you on this project."

His smile spread wider, and a teasing light flickered in his eyes. "Thanks. I appreciate your willingness to come to Longdale and evaluate our art and antiques for auction."

"Your grandmother has a wonderful collection of paintings. There are some valuable pieces that should auction for a good price."

"Can you give me an estimate on what we might receive?"

"Not yet, but several of the paintings are by English and French Impressionists, and museums are always looking for those, as well as private collectors."

David nodded, looking pleased. "That's encouraging." But then his smile faded. "I could use some good news after my meetings with the architect and the bat removal company."

"Those meetings didn't go well?"

"Not especially."

"Do you want to tell me about it? I'm a pretty good listener."

"Sure." He motioned toward the couch by the fireplace. They sat down and he told her the changes the architect believed needed to be made to the renovation plans—changes that would result in the project costing much more than he'd first imagined.

As she listened, a sense of connection and empathy grew in her heart. David's apology and this honest conversation revealed a different side of him. Her doubts about his intentions toward his grandmother seemed silly now.

She and David might see some things from different perspectives, but that didn't mean they couldn't be friends—maybe even good friends. Working together, they could find a way to do what was best for Lilly and Longdale . . . as well as for Hill and Morris.

Gwen stifled a yawn and tied her shoes. She slipped her phone in her jacket pocket and trotted down the main stairs.

A brisk walk was just what she needed to get the day off to a good start.

No one else seemed to be up yet, so she walked out to the terrace and took the steps to the garden path. Setting off at an easy pace, she let her gaze travel over the dew-covered lawn and misty lake. The cool air flowed past her cheeks, carrying a fresh, clean scent. Clouds covered much of the sky, but the sun peeked through in the east.

She'd only walked a short distance when her phone buzzed. She pulled it out, read the caller's name, and tapped it on. "Good morning, Grandfather."

"Hello, Gwen. I'm phoning to see how the work is progressing."

She hesitated. He hadn't called to see how she was feeling or apologize for sending her off in such a brusque manner. He was checking up on her, making sure she was doing her job.

Her spirit deflated. She should be used to the way he put work ahead of relationships, but it still stung. She adjusted her hold on the phone, determined to rise to the occasion and sound professional. "The work is going well. Longdale is a beautiful home. Mrs. Benderly has some amazing art and valuable antiques."

"How many pieces are you evaluating?"

"I've listed thirty-two so far, but there are several more rooms we haven't looked through yet. It's going to take quite a while to do the research."

"That's not a problem. Take all the time you need."

"I could photograph the pieces and create the list, then come back to London to do the research and analysis there."

"No, no. We're handling everything here. It's best if you stay there and see the job through."

"That could take a few weeks."

"That's fine. We've got everything covered here. You're not needed."

She winced and tried not to let his words cut too deep.

"Gwen?"

She cleared her throat. "Yes, I'm here."

"I expect you to do a thorough job. Make sure you evaluate each piece correctly. You must do your best for Lilly and for Hill and Morris."

"Of course."

"We can't have any more mistakes like the one you made with the Hassam."

"I understand."

"I hope so." He paused for a moment, then said, "Lilly told me she is converting Longdale into a hotel. That's going to take a big investment. I hope she knows what she's doing."

"Her grandson is helping her."

"Well . . . keep me informed."

"I will." She swallowed. "While I'm here, I'm going to see what I can learn about my father."

"What did you say?" Disbelief and irritation edged his words.

She pushed on. "I know my mum and dad were married in Keswick. I have a photo taken on their wedding day. But I don't know his full name. Can you tell me—"

"That chapter is closed, and it should stay closed."

"But I'm an adult now. Why won't you—"

"You know how your mother felt about this, and she had good reasons. That's all I intend to say."

Pain ricocheted through her chest. Why didn't he respect her and realize she was mature enough to handle whatever she would learn about her father?

"You're at Longdale to do a job. That should be your focus." He cleared his throat. "I have a meeting. Give my regards to Lilly."

"All right." She waited, still hoping he might at least end the call on an encouraging note.

"Good-bye, Gwen."

"Good-bye." Her eyes stung, and as she clicked off the call, her vision blurred. Why did his abrupt manner hurt so much? She knew he rarely spoke of anything other than his work or the weather. Even after Gwen's mother died, he'd only taken off the day of the funeral, then he'd gone back to work. He didn't often speak about his daughter, and he'd never volunteered any information about her father.

She lifted her gaze to the sky, trying to ease the ache in her chest. How she longed for a more meaningful connection and to be seen and loved despite her mistakes and weaknesses.

The gravel on the path crunched, and she looked over her shoulder.

David approached. "Good morning." As he came closer, his smile faded. "Everything okay?"

She swiped a tear from her cheek. "Yes. Everything is fine."

He cocked his eyebrow.

She held up the phone. "Bad call."

"Did someone die?"

Her strangled laugh escaped. "No, it was my grandfather checking up on me."

"That doesn't sound too bad."

Should she explain and admit her mistake? What would he say if she told him she would've lost her position at Hill and Morris if she wasn't Lionel Morris's granddaughter? She shook her head. "It doesn't matter. I'm fine."

"Would you like to walk with me?" He motioned down the path with a winsome half smile.

His suggestion loosened the knot in her throat, and she nodded. "I'd like that."

His gaze rested on her for an extra beat, then he looked away. They set off down the hill, weaving their way through the garden and onto a path that led through a wooden stile into a pasture.

Gwen scanned the green meadow dotted with wildflowers. "Where does this path take us?"

"Through our fields and around the lake."

"How far is that? I haven't had breakfast yet."

He grinned. "We can walk for a while and then turn around whenever you'd like."

"Sure." She released a deep breath and matched her pace to his.

"I appreciated our conversation last night. I took some of your suggestions and made a new list to discuss with the architect."

A wave of pleasure passed through her. "Please, tell me more."

For the next few minutes, she listened as he listed the changes he wanted to make to the renovation plan. Most were ideas she had suggested.

"While they're working outside, enlarging the parking area, I want to focus on my grandmother's living quarters. That will involve removing some walls to combine the last four bedrooms in the east wing into a private living quarters."

Gwen nodded, visualizing the rooms. One was his grandmother's current bedroom.

"I want her well settled before we start adding bathrooms to the other guest rooms." They came to the next wooden stile, and he offered her his hand as she stepped up and over. When he let go, she missed the strength of his hand and comforting touch.

"I'm wondering," he continued, "if you could focus on evaluating the furniture and paintings in those four rooms, and then send those items off to London to help clear out that area."

Gwen glanced his way. "We usually ship the entire group together. It's an added expense to have the team come twice to pack and transport the pieces to London."

"Could you make an exception—send part now, and the rest later?"

She took a few more steps before answering. "I'll have to check on that."

"I'd like to sell some of the pieces as soon as possible."

"I understand, but it takes time to research and evaluate each piece. Then we have to create the catalogue pages and set up the online auction as well as the live auction."

"Assuming we can send an early shipment, will you be able to tell me the value of those items?"

She hesitated. "I can give you an estimate, but I can't guarantee the sale price."

He studied her with a serious look. "On average, how close is your estimate to the actual sale price?"

She wanted to tell him she had everything under control, and her estimates were always on target, but that wouldn't be the truth. "We always suggest a range for the expected sale price. And I'll be consulting with others on our team to be sure I'm giving you and your grandmother the best appraisal possible. But the buyer is the one to determine the final price."

A shadow crossed his face. "I see."

She hated to disappoint him, but she had to be honest. There was no guarantee how much he would receive from the auction. She wished she could provide a solid answer for his dilemma . . . but she wasn't a miracle worker.

David spread out the blueprints on his grandfather's desk and scanned the design. Combining the four bedrooms at the end of the east wing and adding a new bathroom and small kitchen for his grandmother's use was going to be a costly project. But seeing that she was comfortable and had everything she needed was his top priority.

Gwen walked in, carrying her laptop. "Have you seen Lilly? I want to ask her about a painting in the second bedroom."

"She went into the village for an appointment."

"When do you expect her back?"

He checked his watch. "She said around three, so any time now."

Gwen glanced at the desk. "Are those the renovation blueprints?"

"Yes. Would you like to take a look?"

She nodded and seemed pleased that he'd asked.

"The architect says we can remove this wall in the east wing, but this one is load bearing. It has to stay. We'll build Nana's new bathroom and kitchen where her bedroom is now."

"That's a big change, but you'll save money on plumbing with the kitchen and bathroom back-to-back."

He nodded. "It wasn't my first choice, but it makes sense." He pointed to a window. "This is her favorite view of the gardens and lake, so we're making this area her sitting room and shifting her bedroom to the other side."

"That is a lovely view, and now she'll be able to enjoy it all day." She ran her finger over the blueprints. "What about the fireplace on this wall? Can you save it?"

He grimaced, knowing she wouldn't like his answer. "I'm afraid it has to go in order to create the new doorway to the kitchen."

She bit her lip and scanned the blueprint again. "What if you saved the marble mantel and surround, then added them here as a decorative feature?" She pointed to the new sitting room wall. "You might be able to add an electric or gas fireplace for warmth and atmosphere."

He mentally calculated the cost of moving the fireplace. "I'm not sure that's feasible on our budget."

"That carved marble mantel is remarkable. Think how much comfort it would give your grandmother to save it and have a cozy fire in her sitting room."

He rubbed his chin. "We might be able to move it. Have you done the appraisal on it?"

"Not yet, but if I'm not mistaken, it's French, from the early nineteenth century. Quite valuable."

"Really? I thought it was original to the house."

"No. It was common for builders to use an antique piece like that to add value and beauty to a home."

David crossed his arms, considering Gwen's words. Should they sell the fireplace mantel and surround, or could they afford to keep it? Gwen seemed to think it would help his grandmother feel more at home in her new private living quarters. He could image her sitting by the fireplace, enjoying a cup of tea and reading a book. He turned back to Gwen. "I'll speak to my grandmother. If the fireplace is important to her, I'll find a way to keep it in her sitting room."

Gwen's eyes lit up, and she sent him a dazzling smile. "That's wonderful. You're going to make your grandmother very happy."

He shrugged it off, but he couldn't help smiling. "It's not a big deal."

"But it is. You'll be saving an important piece of Longdale's history, but most of all, it shows how much you care about your grandmother. That says a lot about you."

His chest expanded, and energy flowed through him. He hadn't realized how much he wanted to win Gwen's admiration. Knowing she appreciated his decision made him even more determined to look for ways to save the important features of Longdale's design, and most of all to keep his grandmother's comfort and wishes at the forefront of his mind.

Gwen rolled over and released a deep sigh. She'd been lying there for well over an hour, but sleep wouldn't come. Her thoughts kept jumping from the stack of research waiting for her to the mistake she'd made with the Hassam to the frustrating call from her grandfather.

She pulled the sheet up to her chin and closed her eyes, but her grandfather's disapproving words ran through her mind again. He certainly didn't want her coming back to London anytime soon. In his mind, she was an embarrassment, and she needed to stay at Longdale for the indefinite future. Not only was he unhappy with her for undervaluing that Hassam, but he also definitely didn't want her looking for her father—and he wouldn't tell her why.

She huffed out a breath and tossed the blankets aside. She might as well get out of bed and find something to do until she felt sleepy. She put on her slippers and grabbed her robe from the end of the bed. Maybe reading some more entries from that old journal would distract her from her own troubles.

She tiptoed up the stairs and turned on the lights in the archive room. The air was cold, and she clutched her robe more tightly around herself. Perhaps Lilly wouldn't mind if she took the journal to her room. She pulled open the top center drawer and retrieved the journal from the box.

Three minutes later, she was back in her bedroom. Grabbing a throw blanket, she settled in the overstuffed chair in the corner and laid the blanket over her lap.

She'd been at Longdale five days, and she'd visited the archive room three times on her own. She'd looked through two boxes of photos and read a few entries in Charlotte's journal that stirred up several questions. Piecing someone's life together through journal entries was like solving an intricate puzzle.

So far, she'd learned Charlotte's father had died unexpectedly and left the family with little money and no way to support themselves. They'd left London and come to Keswick to stay with the Storey family. Charlotte's grandfather lived at Longdale, but something had caused a rift between him and Charlotte's mother, leaving them dependent on their friends.

Gwen shivered and tugged the blanket tighter. When her mum died, her grandfather had given her a home while she completed her master's program and internship, then he'd offered her the position at Hill and Morris. He might not be openly affectionate, but at least he hadn't left her to fend for herself.

How would Charlotte survive? And what was the terrible secret she felt she must hide?

She turned the page and read the next entry.

Today, Ian saved a lamb that had fallen down a rocky hillside near a stream. My heart was in my throat as I watched him climb down those slippery rocks, retrieve the lamb, and then start the climb back up. He only made it partway, then he needed my help to grab the lamb so he could climb the last few feet. I had to hang over the side, and I nearly fell. But Alice held on to me, and then Ian pulled me back across the muddy grass. My dress will need a good scrubbing, but I don't care. It was thrilling to partner with Ian to save that lamb. It drew my heart toward his and made me see him in a different light. His handsome features and outgoing personality remind me of my father, but now I realize they are not as much alike as I first suspected. That is a blessing and a relief.

Ten

1912

Charlotte swallowed hard and blinked back hot tears. For the last few minutes, she'd held her tongue while Mum told Mr. Donovan about Charlotte's father's ministry. She shifted in her chair and stared toward the sitting room fireplace. She could not break down—not in front of Mr. Donovan, Jenny, and Ian, as well as Mum and Alice. But how much longer could she sit there and not say a word?

Mum dabbed at her eyes with her handkerchief. "I wish you had known Henry. His ministry had a powerful impact on many people."

Mr. Donovan nodded, his expression reflecting compassion. "I'm sure he was equally devoted to his family and loved you all very much."

Bile rose and singed Charlotte's throat. Her gaze darted around the room, looking for some way to escape.

Mum said nothing. Instead, she lifted the handkerchief and blotted her cheeks.

Anguish twisted Charlotte's heart, and a heated denial rose in her throat. She sprang from her chair and strode toward the door.

"Charlotte?" Surprise filled Mum's voice, but Charlotte didn't turn around.

She grabbed her shawl from the hook without answering, stepped outside, and started down the path. Cool air rushed past her face, but it couldn't cool her bubbling anger or calm her racing heart.

How could she let them go on believing Henry Harper was a saint when nothing could be further from the truth? But if she told them what he'd done and shattered that image, it would surely break her mum's heart and damage her faith, as it had Charlotte's. She shuddered and continued down the hill toward the pasture.

"Charlotte!"

She looked over her shoulder. Mr. Donovan followed her on the path. She considered ignoring him, but she already looked foolish for rushing out of the house without explanation. She slowed, and he quickly caught up.

"I'm sorry," he said. "I meant to bring you comfort, but it seems I've done the opposite."

She brushed a strand of hair from her face. "No, it's not your fault."

"I am truly sorry for your loss. You must have loved your father very much."

Those words pierced her heart like a burning arrow. "Yes, I did . . . love him . . . but he—" Her voice broke off, and she swallowed a broken sob. The crushing weight of her father's sin and her effort to hide what he had done almost drove her to her knees. She folded her arms across her stomach, trying to hold back her tears, but it was no use.

Mr. Donovan gently touched her arm. "Charlotte?"

"He betrayed us!" The words burst past the painful knot in her throat. She gasped and raised her hand to cover her mouth.

Mr. Donovan's eyes rounded. "He betrayed you?"

Like water poured from a pail, there was no way to take it

back. But if she told him the rest, would he understand and help her find a way past all this pain, or would he condemn her along with her father? She summoned her strength and lowered her hand. "After my father died, I discovered letters that made it very clear he was . . . involved with another woman."

Mr. Donovan studied her in silence, grief lining his face. "I'm so sorry." He glanced toward the house. "And your mother . . ."

"She doesn't know—neither do Alice or Daniel I couldn't tell them."

He gave a slow nod. "So you've kept this information to yourself?"

Tears filled her eyes. "It's so dreadful. I didn't want to hurt them."

"The way you've been hurt?"

"Yes." Her voice came out a rough whisper. She looked away, feeling as though a dark cloud had descended over her again. "How could he preach devotion to God and striving for sinless perfection day after day when he was sneaking off for more than two years to meet that woman? I don't understand it. I never will."

Mr. Donovan looked out across the fields. "It is painful and difficult to comprehend, but your father was human and prone to give in to temptation just like the rest of us. He's not the first man to fall in similar circumstances. Remember what happened to King David?"

Hurt pierced Charlotte. "You're not excusing him, are you?"

"No, not at all. What he did was wrong and hurtful to you and your family, and to that woman. Most of all, what he did is offensive to God, but that is why Christ came—to pay for our sins and make a way for us to be forgiven."

Charlotte's thoughts spun as she tried to apply Mr. Donovan's words to her situation.

"Temptation is a powerful force, Charlotte. Our enemy, the devil, is always looking for an area of weakness where he can attack and try to destroy us. And he often targets those who are in leadership because he knows if he can cause them to fall, it will have a ripple effect and harm many more."

"You think I should blame the devil and just accept that my father was living a lie?" She couldn't keep the bitterness from her voice.

"No, but for your own sake you must find a way to forgive him."

Her heartbeat pounded in her ears, and her thoughts swam. "How can I? I adored him, but he broke his most sacred vow and shattered my trust forever. Then his reckless choices left us without a home or provision." She shook her head. "It's too much."

"He never confessed or repented?"

A denial formed on her tongue as her thoughts rushed back to the day of his heart attack. "After he collapsed on stage in London, he called us to him and said he was sorry. Of course, we had no idea what he meant."

"Did he say anything else?"

She hesitated, replaying the scene in her mind. "He said that he loved us." Her voice caught. "But how can I believe it? If he truly loved us, he never would've done what he did."

Mr. Donovan clasped his hands behind his back as they continued slowly down the path. "Whether you believe him or not is your choice. But as you consider it, I'd encourage you to remember all your experiences with your father, not only what you discovered after his death."

Memories came rushing back. Walks in the park, conversations about nature and God's amazing creatures, books they'd read and discussed, times they'd debated the mysteries of life, faith, and heaven.

Should she let those memories override the revelation of his betrayal? How could she make sense of it all? Who was her father—the inspiring, well-read Christian leader, or a two-faced sinner?

She sighed and rubbed her aching forehead.

They reached the drystone wall surrounding the western pasture. Mr. Donovan rested his arms on top and gazed out across the valley. "When we choose to forgive others, we are not excusing what they did or saying it was right. We're releasing them into God's hands and allowing Him to deal out justice as He sees fit."

She ran her hand over the moss on top of the stones. "I've never heard forgiveness described in that way. I've always thought it meant letting someone off the hook after they said they were sorry."

"That is the common perception, but God has a different idea. He knows we are not designed to carry the justice of the world on our shoulders. That would be too great a burden. He wants us to release offenses and offer forgiveness for our benefit as well as the offender's."

Charlotte leaned against the wall. "Do you think the Lord took him when He did because of . . . what he was doing?"

Several seconds ticked by before Mr. Donovan answered. "I don't know. I think that's something best left in God's hands."

Charlotte gazed out across the pasture. Forgiving her father seemed impossible. The hurt and pain of his betrayal cut too deep. Just saying the words wouldn't make it true. She needed more time to consider Mr. Donovan's words before she could take that step.

Another question burned in her heart, and she looked his way. "Is it right for me to keep this from my mother, or should I tell her the truth?"

Mr. Donovan clasped his hands. "I don't know the answer to that question either. But I'll pray for you and ask the Lord to make it clear."

Disappointment clogged her throat. If only someone would tell her what was best and take that burden from her shoulders.

"To help with that decision, I would encourage you to ask yourself, Would it heal or cause more harm?"

Charlotte sighed. "It would hurt her deeply, but doesn't she have a right to know? In the end, isn't it better to know the truth? Oh . . . I just don't know!"

"Then wait and pray. He'll show you the best path."

Waiting wouldn't be a problem. But praying and acting on the answer . . . that was another story.

Ian stood on the path a short distance from the barn, watching Charlotte and Mr. Donovan at the bottom of the hill by the drystone wall. They were obviously deep in conversation. He'd followed them out of the house, intending to join them, then thought better of it, considering how upset Charlotte seemed to be.

He felt certain it was more than grief over her father's death that had sent her running from the house. The heartache in her anguished expression as she'd fled confirmed it.

What had her father done? He kicked at a small stone and sent it flying. Why wouldn't she confide in him? He might not have the seminary training Matthew Donovan possessed, but he was a good listener, and he cared about her. She had become more than a houseguest. She had become his friend.

He looked up toward the sky, released a deep breath, and received the warmth of the sunshine on his face. "Lord, You know I've little experience understanding women or comforting broken hearts. How can I ease her burden? What can I do?" It was a simple prayer softly spoken, but it came from a sincere heart, ready to listen and obey.

He waited, pondering his questions a few more seconds. A thought came to him, easing his frustration. He didn't need to know the details of her heartache to lend his support. He might not be the one Charlotte had chosen to confide in first, but he could look for ways to lift her spirit and give her hope. He wasn't sure what he might do, but he would wait, watch, and listen. And when the time was right, the Lord would make it clear.

It was well past midnight when Charlotte rose from her bed, lit the lamp, and turned the flame down low. Mum and Alice slept peacefully nearby in their beds.

Being as quiet as possible, she slipped her hand under her mattress and slowly pulled out her journal. The pale light of a half-moon shone through the window and spread across the hardwood floor. Taking her shawl from the hook on the wall, she wrapped it around her shoulders and sat on the rag rug. The light of the moon fell over her shoulders and onto her lap.

With her pen in hand, she opened her journal and poured her thoughts onto the page. Crossing out words and rewriting phrases, she scribbled on, then turned the page and wrote a few more sentences. Mr. Donovan's words about forgiveness and God's commitment to handle the justice for wrongs done stirred her thoughts and spilled onto the page.

She stopped and held up the pen. If she wrote that she forgave her father, would it take away the pain? Would she be released from carrying the shame of his betrayal? Even if forgiveness had that power, she still didn't know if she should tell her mum the truth.

She released a weary sigh and settled back against the bed. Lowering her pen, she continued writing. But this time it wasn't simply thoughts and questions. It became a plea.

I'm sorry, Lord. I shouldn't have waited so long to bring these hard questions to You. It's just been such a difficult time, and I've felt so hurt by all that has happened.

Tears slipped down her cheeks like a silent offering, carrying away some of the pain, but a lump remained in her throat.

This is too hard a load for me to carry alone. Telling Mr. Donovan the truth helped, but I need more . . . more answers . . . more direction. Will You show me what to do and how to move forward? I need to hear from You.

She waited, not knowing exactly what she expected. No voice came from heaven, but a small flame of hope lit in her spirit.

Ian scooped up his last bite of chicken pie, savoring the tasty mixture of tender meat, garden vegetables, and flaky pastry—a good reward at the end of a long workday. He wiped his mouth with his napkin. "That was a fine meal, Mum."

The others gathered around the table added their compliments.

"No need to thank me," Mum said with a brief smile. "I wasn't the cook tonight."

Ian's brows rose. "Who was?"

Mum nodded across the table. "Charlotte prepared the meal."

Charlotte's mother smiled, looking pleased. "That's wonderful, dear."

"I certainly needed her help today," his mum continued. "Milly was busy with the lambs, and I had to go over to Mary Tate's. Little Abe was under the weather, and after his long illness last year, Mary was beside herself. He'll be fine, but it took quite a while to calm Mary's fears."

"That's understandable." Ian shifted his gaze to Charlotte. "Thank you for the fine dinner. The chicken pie was the best I've tasted in a long while."

Charlotte met his gaze with a sweet smile. "I'm glad you liked it."

Mum huffed out a breath. "Are you saying her chicken pie is better than mine?"

Ian gulped, and his gaze darted back to Mum. "No, I mean . . . it's different, but just as good as yours."

Mum's eyes twinkled, and she laughed. "I'm teasing you, Ian!"

His neck heated. He rose from the chair and took his plate from the table. He'd only meant to compliment Charlotte, but he'd ended up embarrassing them both. As he turned from the table, the bummer lamb bleated, knocked over the barricade in the corner of the kitchen, and scampered across the floor.

"Whoa!" Ian set aside his plate and hustled after the lamb. "Where do you think you're going?" He scooped up the squirming lamb. She bleated again, obviously not happy about being captured. "I think this one is getting too rambunctious to stay in the house."

"I agree," Mum said, rising from the table. "That's the third time she's broken loose today. You need to take her outside."

Charlotte crossed to Ian's side. "But who will feed and care for her?"

He held the lamb close to his chest and ran his hand over her woolly back, trying to calm her squirming. "She's done well with bottle feeding. I think it's time to try something else."

"What?" Charlotte asked.

"Come with me. You'll see."

Her eyes lit up. She turned toward his mum as if asking her permission to be relieved from cleanup duties.

His mum waved toward the door. "Go on, then. The cook shouldn't have to wash the dishes as well."

"Thank you." Charlotte sent Ian a quick smile, took her shawl from the hook by the door, and walked out of the house with him. "Where are we taking her?"

"To the barn." He hoped his idea would work, but there was no guarantee. This lamb needed a new mother if she was going to survive.

The sun hung low in the western sky as they followed the path toward the barn, but there was still enough light for them to see without a lantern.

He pushed open the barn door and walked to the fourth stall. "This shearling gave birth this afternoon, but her lamb was stillborn." The memory of helping deliver the lifeless lamb replayed through his mind and sent a painful twist through his gut.

She looked up at him. "I'm sorry. Why did that happen?"

"I'm not sure. Sometimes they labor too long, but I don't think that was the case this time. It might have been a defect or an illness." He opened the half door and slowly entered the stall. "Sometimes a shearling will accept another lamb in the place of the one she lost." He lowered the lamb to the floor and stepped back to the doorway.

Charlotte stepped up next to Ian and peered into the stall. "Oh, I hope she'll accept her." Her soft words whispered across his face, and the faint scent of lavender teased his nose.

He pulled in a slow deep breath, savoring the sweet scent and her nearness. He swallowed and forced his thoughts back to the scene before them. "It would be good for both of them if she does."

The ewe turned toward the lamb as she toddled closer. The little one bleated and nosed her way under the ewe, looking for a meal. The ewe stepped to the side, sniffed the lamb's back, and tossed her head.

Ian leaned on the half door, watching the scene unfold. "My granddad had another method for a situation like this."

"What did he do?"

"He'd skin the stillborn lamb and place the coat over a bummer to convince the ewe the bummer was her own."

Charlotte grimaced and rubbed her upper arms. "That sounds rather gruesome."

Ian nodded. "I've seen it done, but I didn't have the heart to do it this time."

"It reminds me of the Bible story about Jacob tricking his father into giving him the blessing by putting on a goat's skin to appear hairy like his brother Esau."

Ian smiled. "Yes, it does sound a bit like that, although my grandfather's motives were better than Jacob's."

Charlotte smiled, then watched as the ewe walked around the lamb and continued sniffing and nudging her gently, looking undecided. The little one nosed under the ewe once more, clearly determined to find a meal. Finally, the ewe lifted her head and stood fast as the lamb tucked her head under the ewe.

Charlotte clasped her hands in front of her mouth. "Oh, she's letting her feed!"

Ian's chest swelled, and his smile spread wide. "Yes. It seems we've made a match."

Charlotte looked up at him, her eyes shining. "I'm so glad."

He stilled and searched her face. Charlotte's large brown eyes were surrounded by thick dark lashes, with slim eyebrows arching above.

Her winsome smile widened, and a matching pair of dimples appeared in her softly rounded cheeks. "What is it?"

His breath snagged in his throat, and his heart hammered. A strong sense of connection surged through him, bringing with it a jolt of joy. He'd never met anyone like Charlotte, and he couldn't deny his growing attraction. She was nothing like Genevieve or the other women he'd met in Oxford. There was a sweetness and sincerity about her that drew him to her. Warmth flooded through him as he took a step closer. Would she welcome his kiss?

Her full pink lips parted slightly as she looked up at him with trusting eyes.

The barn door hinges creaked, and they both turned toward the sound.

The door swung wide, and his father walked down the aisle toward them. "What did you do with that bummer?"

Ian and Charlotte exchanged a quick smile, then he focused on his father. "She's in here with the shearling. They seem to have taken to each other."

His father stepped up beside them and frowned. "Didn't expect that."

Charlotte looked at Ian with an approving smile. "She's not a bummer anymore. Ian knew what to do. He has a shepherd's heart."

His father huffed. "If that were true, he'd have no trouble leaving his Oxford studies behind and taking up his responsibilities here."

Heat surged into Ian's face. "Dad!"

"What?" His father crossed his arms. "She ought to know you're the kind of man who'd rather dig up old bones than carry on the work this family has been doing for generations."

"You know there's more to archaeology than digging up bones."

"Here's what I know—running this farm is a worthy occupation, nothing to be scorned or tossed aside so easily. The men in our family have always raised sheep, and we've been proud of Valley View and our life here."

Ian pulled in a calming breath. "I respect what you and Granddad have done—the sacrifices you've made and the life you've built. But I don't know if it's the life for me."

His father shook his head. "Your time at Oxford has puffed you up. You think you're too good for us."

"Dad, that's not true!"

His father waved off Ian's words. "Go on. I'll see to the ewes tonight." He turned and strode down the aisle before Ian could answer.

Ian's stomach clenched tight, and he shook his head. Why couldn't his father appreciate that he had put aside his archaeology studies and come home to help the family through the spring and summer? Why wasn't that enough?

Charlotte laid her hand on his arm. "You're doing so much to help your family. Don't let him discourage you." Her soft words and comforting touch eased some of his frustration, but they couldn't erase the sting of his father's harsh words.

They walked outside, and Charlotte's steps stalled. Above them, glowing bands of purple, pink, and orange filled the evening sky. The golden sun had dipped behind the mountains, leaving the blazing colors and scattering reflections of fairy-tale-pink clouds in the deep blue lake.

"Oh my, it's so lovely." She breathed out the words with soft reverence.

Ian stopped beside her and looked up. "He's painted a fine sky for us tonight."

"Yes, and beauty like this is a balm."

He glanced her way, his look inviting her to tell him more.

She scanned the sky again. "When I see a sunset like this, it reminds me God's creativity and goodness are always with us . . . even in hard times."

Ian gave a thoughtful nod. "Yes, that's important to remember." The golden glow from the sunset shone on his face, high-lighting his long straight nose, intent blue eyes, firm square jaw, and fine mouth.

Had he been about to kiss her in the barn, or was that only wishful thinking on her part? What would it be like to kiss Ian? She bit her lip and looked away.

She'd sensed a growing closeness between them and had noticed his lingering looks. The reservations she'd had when they first met had faded as she'd gotten to know him. It was true he had a vibrant personality and was handsome like her father, but that was where the similarities ended.

Ian's kindness toward his family and thoughtful care of the sheep showed his good character ran deep and true. The restraint he maintained in the face of his father's criticism increased her admiration.

Family relationships were never simple or easy to understand. She'd experienced that herself, and she could tell Ian struggled to balance his love for his family with his independence.

Ian released a deep breath, his expression calm as he watched the sunset's fading colors.

She smiled, glad they could enjoy the peaceful moment together.

He looked her way. "I suppose we should go in."

She met his gaze, wishing they could recapture that special moment of closeness they'd shared in the barn. She had no experience with romance and had never so much as held a man's hand. How could she let him know how she felt without being too forward?

His eyes clouded, and his expression grew more serious. He shifted his gaze away and kicked at a small stone, sending it flying across the farmyard. "Good night, Charlotte." He turned away and started up the path toward the house.

She swallowed hard, pushing down her disappointment. What a fool she was to think Ian might have special feelings for her. That wasn't true. To him she was only a houseguest, or the daughter of his mother's friend. She needed to guard her heart and banish her romantic daydreams before she embarrassed herself and him. If she didn't, it would only lead to heartache.

Confusion flooded Ian as he continued up the path toward the house. He'd seen the questions in Charlotte's eyes and knew she had been waiting for him to speak and make his feelings known. When he hadn't, a look of hurt had crossed her face. That had cut him to the heart. Even as he walked away, he'd almost turned around to explain himself, but he didn't seem to have the courage.

Was that the real problem—a lack of courage?

He shook his head, knowing full well that was not the real reason he'd shut down his feelings and kept silent. He recalled his father's scathing remarks, and he knew the truth. Charlotte would never want a man who couldn't gain his father's approval, or at least convince his father he was man enough to choose his own path.

He couldn't pursue Charlotte, at least not now. That would only complicate matters with his family and add more uncertainty to his future. He must treat her like a sister, just as he would Milly or Alice. He could not allow her to hold a special place in his heart—no matter how strong the pull toward her or how much he wished he could make her his own.

Eleven

2012

Gwen took a sip of tea and returned her gaze to her laptop screen. It was already past three, and she had several more items from Lilly's bedroom she wanted to finish researching that afternoon. Her grandfather had approved David's request to send an early shipment to London. David was grateful, but that meant she needed to finish her appraisals and catalogue those pieces as soon as possible.

She studied the photo she'd taken of the sterling silver dresser set with a hairbrush, comb, and mirror. Each piece had a swirling floral design, and the hairbrush had natural boar bristles set in a rosewood base. The glass in the mirror was clear and free of any cloudy distortion.

Lilly told Gwen the set belonged to her mother and had been passed down to her many years ago. Gwen had encouraged her to keep them since they were family heirlooms, but Lilly had assured her she was ready to let them go.

Gwen clicked through other similar listings, comparing them to Lilly's set, and decided they probably dated from the 1920s. She estimated their value would be between three hundred and three hundred fifty pounds.

"Here you are." Lilly walked into the dining room carrying two shopping bags and wearing a cheery smile. "I had a lovely afternoon in Ambleside."

Gwen glanced up. "It looks like you did some shopping."

"Yes, and I had lunch with a dear friend." She reached into one of the bags and took out a small square parcel wrapped in white paper. "I brought you a treat."

"That was thoughtful. What is it?"

Lilly passed her the parcel. "Open it and see."

Gwen scanned the blue-and-white label. "Sarah Norton's Grasmere Gingerbread." She looked up at Lilly. "Thank you. I haven't had gingerbread in years."

"It's not your typical gingerbread. It's more like a cross between a sweet biscuit and spice cake."

Gwen opened the paper and sniffed. "It smells good."

"The little shop where they make it is quite a tourist attraction. People wait in a long queue for their turn to go in. I always stop by whenever I'm in Ambleside." Lilly nodded toward the gingerbread. "Try it."

Gwen took a bite and found it was sweet and spicy with a chewy texture. She felt the zing of ginger on her tongue and smelled a whiff of nutmeg. "Mmm, it's delicious."

Lilly laughed softly. "I agree. That's why I don't mind waiting my turn."

Gwen held out the package. "Please, join me."

"No, dear. Those are for you. Enjoy them." Lilly's eyes twinkled, and she pointed to her bag. "I have my own supply."

"Hello, ladies." David walked in, and as he crossed to the table, he cocked one eyebrow. "Is that Grasmere gingerbread?"

Gwen brushed a crumb from the corner of her mouth. "Yes, your grandmother just introduced me to it."

"It's good, isn't it?"

"Yes. I'd be glad to share." Gwen held out her package.

"Don't take Gwen's." Lilly pulled another parcel from her bag and held it out to David. "I brought some just for you."

"Thank you, Nana." David smiled, looking pleased as he unwrapped his package and sampled a piece. "Just as delicious as I remember." He brushed off his hand. "Now, I have some good news."

Lilly smiled. "I love good news."

"Let's sit down." He took a seat across from Gwen, and Lilly sat next to him.

"I got the final permission to have the bats removed from the attic, and the company said they can do the job next week."

"Oh, that's wonderful!" Lilly clasped her hands. "What an answer to prayer!"

David nodded. "They plan to come next Tuesday, and they said it should only take three to four hours."

Lilly patted his hand. "Thank you, David. I'm so pleased."

"That's not all. I made a call and found an investor who wants to team up with us."

Lilly's smile faded. "An investor? I didn't know we were looking for one."

"I wanted to see if he was interested before I brought the idea to you."

That didn't seem to reassure Lilly. "Who is this investor?"

"His name is Max Henderson. I've worked with him on four projects when we turned estates into hotels or spas. Most of those were closer to London, but he likes the idea of investing in the Lake District." David leaned forward. "His idea will bring us some income right away, and that will help us finance the renovations."

Lilly glanced from Gwen to David. "What is his idea?"

"He suggests we bring in four luxury houseboats that we can rent out."

Gwen tensed. Would houseboats be a good fit for Longdale?

"He has connections with a distributor and can get a good

price," David continued. "And he's willing to cover most of the cost if we'll handle the rentals and allow the boats to tie up at our dock. We'd split the rental revenue fifty-fifty."

Lilly blinked a few times, looking from Gwen to David. "I'm not sure our neighbors or the parish council would approve of houseboats on Derwentwater."

"Why not? There are all kinds of boats on the lake. They wouldn't bother anyone. Renters could park their cars here, board the boats from our dock, and then they'd be self-sufficient. I think it's a great idea. And best of all, Max says he can get the houseboats here within a month, in time for the summer season." He turned to Gwen. "What do you think?"

She hesitated, trying to come up with something positive to say. David was obviously excited about the idea. "It's an . . . interesting idea, but Lilly has a point. I'm not sure your neighbors or the local authorities would welcome houseboats on the lake. There may be rules against that sort of thing."

David tipped his head, acknowledging her point, but he didn't seem daunted. "I'll check into it. But I can't imagine it would be a problem."

"If it is allowed," Gwen continued, hoping to slow him down, "it might be a challenge to find renters."

"That won't be a problem. We can register with vacation rental websites, and when we open the hotel, we'll add the houseboats as one of the options on our own website."

Gwen looked out the window to the view of the lake and mountains, and doubts swirled through her mind. People came to the Lake District to enjoy the natural beauty of the area. Filling the lake with houseboats wouldn't be her first choice, but this was Lilly and David's home and their decision. She was here to do her job and restore her grandfather's trust. Still, she couldn't ignore the nagging feeling David's new plan just might lead to trouble.

"They're here!" Gwen called as she hurried down the main stairs. She'd heard the lorry coming up the drive, then confirmed the team's arrival when she looked out her bedroom window. She was eager to greet the men who would pack and transport the first shipment of antiques, furniture, and paintings to London for auction.

David stepped out of the library. "The movers are here?"

Gwen met him at the bottom of the steps. "Yes, but please don't call them movers. They're specially trained fine art and antique shipping specialists."

He grinned. "I see."

"Is Lilly up yet?"

"I haven't seen her, but I'm sure she'll be down soon."

As if his words had conjured her, Lilly descended the stairs. "Good morning, my dears."

"Morning, Nana." David held out his hand to her as she reached the bottom step. "The moving team from Hill and Morris is here. Are you ready for this?"

Lilly lifted her chin. "Of course. This is an important step forward for Longdale's future."

Gwen admired Lilly's spirit. It had to be daunting to let go of so many well-loved items from her home and face all the changes David was proposing. It made Gwen even more determined to manage her part of the job well and make the process as easy as possible for Lilly.

They crossed the entry hall, and David pulled open the front door. Outside, a large white lorry and a small black car had parked near the front steps. Two men hopped down from the cab, and two more climbed out of the car.

Gwen stepped forward, introduced herself, and shook hands with the leader of the team. Her grandfather had called last night to give her his name and explain the process again. She had listened patiently and assured him she was prepared.

Within minutes, the metal ramp had been put in place and

the team dispatched to the east wing to begin packing the items on Gwen's list. She followed the men upstairs to show them the way and make sure they packed the correct pieces. When two of the men carried out the first painting, Gwen followed them down the steps and watched as they carefully loaded it into the lorry and secured it on the racks.

When she returned to the house, David met her in the entry hall. "Everything going well?"

"Yes. I'm keeping a close watch to make sure they're handling it all properly."

"Thank you. I appreciate it." He watched the two men as they crossed the entry hall and started up the stairs again.

Gwen followed his gaze, but out of the corner of her eye she caught sight of something, and her breath caught. In a brass canister between the stairway wall and arched entry, a wooden staff with a carved head rested next to a cane and two umbrellas. She hadn't noticed it before, probably because the shadow from the stairwell and the umbrellas had blocked her view.

She stepped closer and pulled the staff from the canister. "What is this?"

David joined her. "It looks like a shepherd's staff."

"Where did it come from?"

"I'm not sure."

"Do you think Lilly knows?" Her serious tone seemed to catch him by surprise.

"Is it valuable?"

She shook her head, trying to make sense of seeing it there. "I don't know. . . . It's not that. It's just . . . I've seen this staff before in a photo of my mother and father." She looked from the staff to David.

His eyebrows rose. "Really?"

"Yes. I only have one photo of my father, and in it, he is holding this staff . . . or one exactly like it."

"A lot of people raise sheep in the Lake District. I'm not

sure why my grandmother has this. It may be more decorative than practical."

Gwen lifted the staff to take a closer look. The top was beautifully carved and featured a black-and-white border collie crouching in front of a black-faced sheep with curled horns. The rest of the staff was made of sturdy wood that had been stained dark brown. A chill raced down her arms. It couldn't be her father's staff, could it? She turned to David. "Where's Lilly?"

"In the library." He motioned that way.

Gwen's thoughts spun as she started toward the library. She knew her father and mother were married in Keswick. She'd even brought the photograph with her on this trip. But her grandfather's warnings and the lingering memory of her mum's refusal to tell her about her father had left her feeling torn about looking for him.

Finding the staff had to be a sign—a sign that she should move ahead and see what she could learn. Did Lilly know him? If so, then there would be nothing stopping her from finding her father. Her heart thudded hard, and she pressed her lips tight. Was she ready for that?

Lilly looked up as Gwen and David entered the library. "I thought it was best if I stayed out of the way." She glanced toward the door. "I can hear them going up and down the stairs, but I didn't want to watch them moving everything out to the lorry."

Gwen nodded, then held out the staff. "I just noticed this in the entryway."

Lilly smiled. "It's a lovely staff, isn't it?"

"Yes. The carving is quite detailed. Do you know who it belongs to?"

Lilly's silver eyebrows rose. "It was Arthur's."

Gwen's spirits deflated. "Of course."

"What is it, dear?" Lilly rose from her chair. "I don't want to auction it, if that's what you're asking."

"No, no. . . . I asked because I've seen it before, or one just like it, in the only photo I have of my father."

"Oh. I see." But Lilly's confused gaze darted from Gwen to David.

"He and my mother separated before I was born. I've never met him." She told Lilly and David the few things she knew about him. "You don't happen to know anyone named Landon from this area, do you? He would probably be in in his early fifties now."

"You don't know his last name?"

Gwen shook her head.

"Hmmm." Lilly tapped her chin. "I don't recall anyone by that name, but I could ask some of my friends who've lived here longer than I have. They might know about him or his family."

"Thank you. I'd appreciate that." She glanced at the staff again. It looked so much like the one in the photo. Was it the same staff that had belonged to her father? How could it have come to Longdale?

A loud bump sounded in the entry hall, and they all turned in that direction.

"I'll go check on that." Gwen hurried from the library, but she couldn't dismiss thoughts about the staff or her father. Could this staff be the link that would lead her to her father? And if it did, would that connection bring healing or more pain?

David crossed his arms as he watched the men roll the blanket-wrapped highboy down the ramp and guide it toward the lorry. Gwen stood beside him, her gaze fastened on the chest of drawers. With grunts and a few muttered words, the men finally maneuvered the heavy piece of furniture into place near the back of the lorry's cargo space. The rest of the lorry was filled with his grandmother's valuable furnishings and artwork from the four rooms in the east wing. They'd all been carefully wrapped and packed for the journey to London.

Gwen sent him a quick smile, and he couldn't help noticing how pretty she looked with her hair pulled back, her eyes bright, and her cheeks flushed pink. And it wasn't just her appearance that drew him to her. It was her intelligence, her diligence with this job, and her commitment to doing all she could for him and his grandmother.

"That's the last piece." She descended the steps and spoke to the team leader while the other three men detached the ramp, then slowly slid it in on the far side of the lorry's cargo space.

Gwen shook hands with the men and thanked them. They climbed into the car and lorry, and she rejoined David by the front door. "They did a good job packing everything. I think it should all reach London without any problem."

He crossed his arms. "I'm glad they finished in one day."

"Yes. I thought it might take two."

He watched the lorry and car start down the drive. "When will the online auction go live?"

Gwen looked down, then glanced toward the lake. "It will take at least three weeks, maybe four."

He frowned. "That long?"

"I'm afraid so. One of the other art specialists has to review my appraisals, then they take photos, set up the web pages, and enter all the information into our computer system. My grandfather mentioned sending out a special email to our list of antique dealers and collectors. We want to put your grand-mother's pieces in front of our top buyers so you can get the best price possible." She looked his way. "The online auction is usually live for two weeks. The in-person auction is scheduled right after that."

"When will we receive the funds from the sales?"

"They should be available thirty days after the auction."

Disappointment tightened his chest. "So, it will be at least sixty days, maybe longer."

She nodded. "That's the soonest you'll receive the proceeds."

"Wow. I had no idea it would take two months."

"This is an exceptionally fast schedule, and it's only possible because your grandmother and my grandfather are friends."

He acknowledged her words with a slight nod. "I understand, and I'm grateful. But it's difficult for me to move ahead with the renovations without knowing how much we'll receive from the auction."

Gwen's expression softened. "I'm sorry, David. This is the best I can do."

He wished there was a quicker solution, but she had gone out of her way to send this first load to London ahead of the rest. He needed to accept that and be grateful. He motioned toward the door, and they walked inside.

She turned to him. "Were you able to speak to the local authorities about the possibility of bringing in houseboats?"

He shoved his hands into his pants pockets as he recalled the heated discussion he'd had with a councilwoman that afternoon. "Let's just say the woman I spoke with wasn't too happy about the idea."

Concern shadowed Gwen's eyes. "What did she say?"

"There's no official rule against houseboats, but she is going to bring it up at the next council meeting and suggest they adopt one."

"Oh no. What will you do now?"

"I need to speak to Max. There has to be a way we can still do this."

"Even with opposition from the council?"

"She's only one person. The others might not object."

"But what if they do?"

He lifted his eyes to the dark beams arching across the ceiling. Water stains marked the plaster between a few of the beams. The roof needed to be repaired before there was more damage. And that was only one of the costly repairs they had to make before they could open Longdale to guests. Uneasiness tightened his shoulders. Every day expenses were mounting, and that didn't include the projected costs of the renovations.

"David?"

"I'll work it out somehow. I have to."

Gwen passed the photo of her parents to Lilly. "This is my mother and father. It was taken in Keswick on their wedding day, the tenth of June, 1985."

Lilly studied the image. "My, they are a handsome couple." She looked at Gwen. "I can see the resemblance. You have your father's eyes."

A surge of pleasure flowed through Gwen. "People have always said I look like my mother. No one ever mentioned I resemble my father."

Lilly sent her an understanding smile, then glanced around the archive room. "People in the Lake District take a great interest in their heritage. If your father is from this area, I'm sure there is someone who knows him or his family."

"I'm not positive he's from the area."

"But the fact they were married here makes it a strong possibility."

Gwen glanced at the photo again, wishing it were true. "Without his last name, I'm not sure who to ask or how to find him."

Lilly pondered that a moment, and her expression brightened. "Marriages are recorded in church records. You have your mother's name and the wedding date. That might be enough to find out your father's full name." Lilly's excitement grew as she continued. "I can name five or six churches in Keswick that were active at the time of their marriage. I'd suggest a personal visit rather than a call. You'd probably be taken more seriously."

"That's a helpful idea, but I shouldn't take time away from my work here at Longdale to search for my father."

Lilly waved away Gwen's words. "Nonsense! You've worked at least twelve hours every day you've been here. I see nothing wrong with you taking an afternoon to visit a few churches. And while you're out, you might also check with the town clerk. Your parents could've had a civil ceremony rather than a church wedding."

Gwen nodded as her thoughts rushed ahead. "Is there somewhere I can rent a car for the day?"

"There's no need. David can drive you."

Gwen shook her head. "He's too busy. I couldn't ask him."

"I'm sure he'd be happy to help."

Gwen considered Lilly's idea. She had sensed a more positive connection with David the last few days, and their conversations had been more comfortable, even friendly.

She turned to Lilly. "I'll ask him at breakfast tomorrow and see if he has time."

"Good. That's the spirit." Lilly unrolled a large sheet of paper and spread it out on the table. "Now, let me show you what I've been working on."

Gwen scanned the chart and then glanced at Lilly.

"This is my husband's family tree—the line of all the people who lived at Longdale," Lilly announced with a delighted smile. "Let's start near the top with Charlotte Harper. She is the author of the journal I showed you."

Gwen leaned closer, scanning the names. "Charlotte lived here?"

"Yes, but I don't believe for very long." Lilly traced her finger down the center line and then branched off to the left. "Here she is." She tapped the words written under Charlotte's name. "She was born 1893 and died 1980."

Gwen studied the dates, glad Charlotte had lived a long life.

"I don't know much about that side of the family." Lilly moved her hand back to the top of the chart and then to the right. "This is my husband's line. Charlotte's brother, Daniel Harper, inherited Longdale and took his grandfather's surname, Benderly."

"I'm guessing there is a story behind that name change."

Lilly smiled. "I suppose there must be, although I've never heard it." She traced Daniel's line. "He married Anna Hitchcock, and they had a son named Joseph. And Joseph married Jane Miller. They had a son named Andrew. He was my husband's father."

Gwen nodded. "How did you collect this information?"

"My husband's first wife, Amelia, started working on this family tree. I think she spoke to relatives and looked in local records. I added other names and dates as I found them."

Gwen's gaze traveled over the Benderly family tree and emotion swelled her throat. What would it be like to know who your relatives were and how you fit into the family? Would she ever learn the truth about her father and feel she belonged? "If I do find a record of my parents' wedding, and I learn my father's name . . ."

Lilly turned to Gwen. "Then you can look for him online."

Gwen's eyebrows rose.

Lilly grinned. "I may not be young, but I know how to do a Google search."

"Of course you do." Gwen bit her lip and glanced away.

"What is it, dear?"

How could she explain her emotional tug-of-war? On one hand, she longed to find her father, but on the other, she feared what she'd learn if she did. "My mum told me next to nothing about him, and what she did say were not kind remarks. I think he broke her heart, and I'm not sure I'm ready to step into all of that . . . especially now that she's gone."

Lilly slipped her arm around Gwen's shoulders. "Oh dear. I imagine it is painful to process both those losses."

Gwen swallowed. "Yes, it is."

Lilly gave her shoulder a squeeze. "I think the Lord brought you here for a reason—and we need to pay attention to what He's saying to us." She closed her eyes and released a slow, deep breath.

Gwen watched her and waited. Was she praying?

A few seconds later, Lilly opened her eyes and smiled. "I believe He wants to help you work through these losses and find the answers you're seeking. Restoration and healing may be just around the corner where your father is concerned. I think you should step up the search and keep on praying."

Goose bumps raced up Gwen's arms. Had Lilly truly heard from the Lord? She certainly spoke with confidence.

A new wave of courage flowed through Gwen. She was not alone in her quest. It was possible her father or his family might live in or around Keswick. She would take Lilly's words to heart—keep praying and start the search. Maybe, after all these years, her prayers would finally lead her to her father.

Twelve

1912

Charlotte shifted on the church pew, smoothed her hand over her skirt, and tried to focus on Mr. Donovan's message, but the words seemed to float out of her thoughts as quickly as they came in. She glanced down the row at Ian. He was seated between his mum and Milly, with his intent gaze fixed on Mr. Donovan. He obviously had no trouble focusing.

She released a soft sigh. Ian . . . that was why she couldn't keep her mind on the service.

For the last three days, ever since they'd taken the bummer lamb to the barn, he'd kept to himself and rarely spoken to her. Why didn't he want to spend time with her as he had before? What had she done or said to make him pull away? She'd begun to think he might have feelings for her, but that all seemed like a foolish dream now.

She silently scolded herself and pulled her gaze away from Ian. There was no way to make sense of his apparent change of heart. It would not be easy, but she had to stop thinking about him in that way. She tugged at a loose thread on the edge of her cuff, wrapped it around her finger and unwrapped it, then blew out a deep breath.

Her mum leaned toward her. "What's wrong?" she whispered.

"Nothing." She kept her voice low, but the lie still burned her throat.

Mum sent her a sympathetic look and laid her hand over Charlotte's, stilling her tugging at the thread. "I miss him too," she said softly.

Charlotte pressed her lips tight and turned her face away. Mum had mistaken her restless thoughts of Ian for grief over her father. She closed her eyes, fighting tears. Both men troubled her heart, but in such different ways.

Mr. Donovan's voice caught her attention. She opened her eyes and forced her thoughts back in line.

"These were some of Jesus's final words to His disciples, and a person's last words carry added significance. But these truths are not only for the disciples. They are for all of us who love and follow Him." He paused and looked out across the congregation, then his gaze seemed to rest on Charlotte.

A tingle traveled up her back, and she sat a little straighter. "'Peace I leave with you, my peace I give unto you: not as the world giveth, give I unto you. Let not your heart be troubled, neither let it be afraid.'" His tone was confident yet compassionate, and the message flew straight to her heart. She leaned forward slightly, eager to hear his next words.

"Jesus lays this choice before us. We can give our burdens and troubles into His care and live each day with the peace of Christ ruling in our hearts. Or we can hold on to the pain and wrongs done to us and harbor a troubled heart that hardens and grows bitter over time, stealing our joy and draining our days of the full life He wants us to enjoy."

Mr. Donovan's words echoed through Charlotte's heart. She needed God's peace for so many reasons. She bowed her head and closed her eyes. Mr. Donovan's words faded, and a silent prayer rose from her heart. *Lord, I've held on to my hurt and*

*anger and let them burden my heart too long. I've cried out to
You with my grief, but I haven't asked for Your peace. I've been
impatient and upset about so many things.*

Images of her father and grandfather dashed through her
mind, along with the memory of Mum and Alice in tears as
they left the only home they'd ever known.

*Help me give all these painful things to You. Help me re-
ceive Your peace even while I wait for circumstances to change.
Thank You that You offer true peace of heart and mind, a
peace much better than what the world can give.* She released
a slow deep breath, and her spirit lifted as a sense of calm
returned.

Around her, people rose to their feet. She'd been so caught
up in her prayer she hadn't realized the service was ending. She
rose, and a shaft of sunlight shone through the side window and
warmed her shoulder as she listened to the familiar, comforting
words of the benediction.

"The Lord bless thee, and keep thee: The Lord make His
face shine upon thee, and be gracious unto thee: The Lord lift
up His countenance upon thee, and give thee peace."

Peace . . . peace of heart and mind. That's what she needed,
and it seemed the choice was up to her. It would not be as simple
as saying one prayer. She would need to continually release her
cares to the Lord and wait for His peace. But His peace was
promised, and she would take hold of it.

Charlotte slipped her arm through Milly's as they walked
out of the nave and into the sunny churchyard. The rain clouds
had cleared, leaving a bright blue sky with only a few clouds.
The air smelled fresh and clean and carried the scent of new
grass and spring flowers.

"My, this is a lovely day."

Milly scanned the sky. "I hope the weather holds for the May Day Festival on Wednesday."

Charlotte turned to her. "You attend the May Day Festival?"

Milly smiled. "Oh yes. We have a grand time. The men set up a tall Maypole in the center of the village green, and the school children practice for weeks so they can perform the Maypole dance. I remember how excited we were to dance at the festival. And there's a troupe of Morris dancers who perform accompanied by drums and accordions. Everyone brings a picnic, and we spend the afternoon visiting with friends."

"It sounds wonderful . . . but does everyone attend?"

She nodded. "Most everyone from the village and surrounding farms will come."

Charlotte gave a slow nod, trying to match what she'd been told about May Day festivals with Milly's description.

Milly tipped her head. "How is May Day celebrated in London?"

Charlotte hesitated. "I've heard about it, but we never attended. My father didn't approve of May Day celebrations."

"Really? Why not?"

Charlotte didn't want to embarrass her friend, but she was curious to know her perspective. "He said the holiday had pagan origins, and the Maypole dance was like idol worship."

Milly's eyebrow rose. "Well, it is a very old holiday, so there may have been some connection to pagan rituals in the past, but I don't believe that's true anymore. Mr. Donovan always takes part. He even offers a prayer to open the festival, thanking the Lord for bringing us through the winter and asking Him to bless our crops and herds in the coming season."

Charlotte was about to reply when two young men approached.

The taller man, with bright blue eyes and red hair, doffed his hat. "Good day, Miss Storey."

Milly smiled and nodded. "Good day to you, Mr. Washburn."

He returned a warm smile. "Please, call me Paul."

"Very well. You may call me Milly."

Paul motioned to his companion. "This is my cousin, James Fenton. He's come from Egremont to help us on the farm."

Milly nodded to him. "I'm happy to meet you, Mr. Fenton."

"Mr. Fenton is my father." He grinned. "Please, call me James." He was a bit shorter than Paul, with a tanned face, stocky build, and broad shoulders.

Milly turned to Charlotte. "This is my friend, Miss Charlotte Harper."

Both men nodded to Charlotte with appreciative smiles.

"I've not seen you before, Miss Harper. What brings you to Keswick?" James asked.

Uneasiness rippled through her. How much should she explain? She forced a slight smile. "My mother is from this area, and we've come back to reconnect with family and friends."

James nodded. "There is a lot of natural beauty here as well as good people." He put a hand on his cousin's shoulder. "I'm glad I came."

Paul turned his hat in his hand and glanced at Milly. "Are you planning to attend the May Day Festival?"

Milly's eyes lit up. "We were just talking about that, weren't we, Charlotte?"

Milly's description of the festival replayed through Charlotte's mind. "Yes, we were."

A relieved expression crossed Paul's face. "James and I plan to come." He glanced at his cousin and then back at Milly. "Perhaps we could meet you and Miss Harper and enjoy the festival together?"

Milly's smile bloomed. "I'd like that. Wouldn't you, Charlotte?" Milly sent her a silent plea, urging her to agree.

Charlotte wasn't certain she should accept, but she didn't want to disappoint her friend. She forced a smile. "Yes, we'd be happy to join you."

Milly squeezed her hand and turned to Paul. "Why don't I prepare a picnic lunch for the four of us?"

Paul beamed. "Thank you, Milly. I've heard good reports about your cooking. I'll look forward to tasting it myself."

James grinned and tucked his hands into his pockets. "Spending the afternoon with you ladies should make it a very fine day indeed."

Ian walked out of the church, crossed the grass, and headed for the wagon to wait for the others. Many of the congregation gathered in the churchyard in small groups. Ian nodded to a few people as he passed, but he didn't stop to visit. His thoughts were on Mr. Donovan's sermon.

Jesus's final teaching to His disciples, especially His reminder that those who loved Him would obey Him, stirred Ian's thoughts. It had been a busy lambing season, and as he considered his daily routine, he had to admit he'd made little time to read his Bible or pray. Had he even considered how the Lord wanted him to respond to the challenges he faced?

The image of his father's hardened expression flashed across his thoughts. Then Charlotte's image appeared, with questions and wariness in her eyes.

He had been relying on his own wisdom rather than seeking the Lord's direction in both relationships. Where had that gotten him? Avoiding his father and Charlotte the last few days had only made him feel uncomfortable and burdened. He leaned against the side of the wagon, closed his eyes. *What shall I do, Lord? How do You want me to respond to them?*

He waited, his mind open to sense the Lord's direction. He could speak to his father when he got home and try to resolve the issues between them. But what could he say that he hadn't already said? He'd have to keep praying and wait for more clarity in that situation.

But there was nothing stopping him from clearing the air with Charlotte. He lifted his gaze and scanned the churchyard, searching for her. Perhaps he could speak to her before the ride home. They had begun a friendship, and he sensed he should not turn away from her simply because he was uncertain about the future.

He spotted his mum in conversation with the mayor's wife near the church door. Then he saw Rose and Alice talking with Mr. Donovan in the shade of the tall oak tree, but Charlotte wasn't with them.

He finally spotted her standing at the far end of the churchyard with Milly. Two men stood nearby. One was Paul Washburn, a young farmer who lived a few miles north of the village. He was smiling and motioning toward another man Ian didn't recognize.

He tensed as he watched the two men interact with Charlotte and Milly. Both men seemed jovial, and the shorter man seemed focused on Charlotte. She nodded to him and returned his smiles, apparently enjoying the conversation. Even at a distance, he could tell she was impressed by the man.

He set off across the grass and reached them in a few seconds. "Milly, Charlotte, it's time for us to go."

Milly turned to him with wide eyes, then she cleared her throat. "Ian, you remember Paul Washburn? This is his cousin, James Fenton." Her tone hinted at another question—*Where are your manners?*

Ian offered a stiff nod, but he didn't extend his hand to either young man.

Paul removed his hat. "Good to see you again, Ian. How was your lambing?"

"It went well." He turned to Charlotte. "Are you ready?"

Her lips parted, and uncertainty appeared in her eyes. "Is everything all right?"

"Yes. Everything's fine. I just . . . want to get home and

check on . . . the sheep." He swallowed, knowing he sounded foolish.

Milly's gaze darted from Charlotte to Ian, then understanding seemed to dawn in her expression. "I'm sure Dad has the sheep well in hand." She kept her voice even, but he could hear her underlying frustration.

Ian returned her gaze, meeting the challenge in her eyes.

Milly turned to Paul. "Thank you for inviting us to join you at the festival. We'll look forward to it, and we'll pack a nice lunch for the four of us to enjoy."

Paul smiled and appeared relieved. "Thank you, Milly. We'll look for you on the village green around noon."

The other man turned to Charlotte with a satisfied smile and touched the brim of his hat. "Nice to meet you, Miss Harper. See you on Wednesday."

Charlotte nodded and returned a smile.

As the two men walked away, Milly turned to Ian. "What is the matter with you?" she whispered. "Why were you so rude to them?"

"I wasn't rude."

"Well, you certainly weren't friendly."

"What would Mum and Dad say about you making plans to meet Paul Washburn at the festival without talking to them first?"

"For goodness' sake, Ian. That was the first invitation I've had in a very long while, and I wasn't about to turn him down." Milly took Charlotte's arm. "Let's go, Charlotte."

As the two women crossed the churchyard, Charlotte looked over her shoulder, questions reflected in her eyes.

Ian swallowed a groan. Why had he acted like that? He might not know Paul Washburn well, but he hadn't heard anything negative about him. In truth, it was the other man who made him more uncomfortable. He didn't like the way he was looking at Charlotte.

A thought struck, and he frowned. He wasn't jealous, was he? No! He huffed and blew out a breath. That wasn't it, not at all.

Charlotte carried the lamp into the bedroom and quietly closed the door. Her mum sat on the wooden chair in the corner. She held a flat board on her lap and appeared to be writing a letter. Alice slept in the nearest bed, snuggled down under the covers.

Mum looked up, her gaze soft and more at peace than she'd seemed in some time. "Are you ready for bed? I can put this letter aside and continue tomorrow."

"No, please, go ahead and finish. Who are you writing to?" Charlotte reached back to untie the apron she'd worn over her dress while she and Milly washed the dishes after dinner.

"I'm writing to my father."

Charlotte's hands stilled, and she glanced at her mum.

A calm assurance filled Mum's eyes. "I spoke to Mr. Donovan after the service today. He gave me some good advice."

"What did he say?"

Mum glanced down at the letter. "He encouraged me to apologize for my unkind words and ask for his forgiveness."

Charlotte tugged off her apron. "But what about all the things Grandfather said to you? He was so—"

Mum lifted her hand. "I can't do anything about that. But if I want a clear conscience and peace in my heart, then I must take responsibility for my words and actions. I want to do all I can to be at peace with everyone. Your grandfather may respond well, or he may not, but at least I will have done my part."

Charlotte gave a slow nod. She recalled reading verses in the Bible about forgiveness and living at peace with everyone, but it seemed that principle had rarely been practiced in her family.

Hurts had been hidden. Secrets had been kept. Resentments had quietly built, and forgiveness had never been sought.

She sank down on the bed, pondering her mum's willingness to seek reconciliation with Grandfather, even after all the years of hurt and estrangement. That took a great deal of courage and humility.

Was there some way she could apply those same ideas to her broken relationship with her father? There was no way to send him a letter and explain her hurt and anger or tell him about the resentment she'd allowed to grow in her heart after his betrayal. How could she make things right between them now that he was gone? What could she do to seek peace?

"Charlotte?"

She looked up. The tenderness in her mum's eyes shot a pang through Charlotte's heart. If only she could be as gentle and forgiving as her mum.

"I have no idea if this letter will make any difference to my father, but writing it has already released me from a great deal of hurt and pain."

Charlotte gave a thoughtful nod.

Mum lowered her gaze to the letter and continued writing.

Charlotte lay back on the bed and looked up at the ceiling. If she could write a letter to her father, what would she say? Tears burned her eyes as she recalled the love letters she had discovered and the heartache that followed. She might not be able to mail a letter to her father, but she could write in her journal. Perhaps in the writing she would find some resolution and peace.

Thirteen

2012

Gwen knocked on the office door at St. John's Church and glanced at David. He sent her a brief encouraging smile.

She pulled in a deep breath, thankful he was with her. This was the fourth church they'd visited that afternoon, but so far they hadn't found any record of her parents' marriage.

The arched wooden door opened, and a middle-aged man wearing a clerical collar looked out at them. "Hello, I'm Father Scott. How can I help you?"

Gwen introduced herself and David, then said, "I'm looking for information about my parents. I believe they were married in Keswick in June 1985. But I'm not sure where the ceremony took place."

He lifted one eyebrow. "That sounds rather curious. They don't recall where they were married?"

"My mother passed away two years ago, and . . . I've never met my father."

His expression softened. "I'm sorry for your loss."

She swallowed. "Thank you."

He pulled the door open wider. "Please come in, and I'll take a look and see if I can find that information for you."

She thanked him, and they followed him down the hall and into the second room on the right.

He flipped on the light. "Please, have a seat."

Gwen thanked him as she glanced around the room. A long table and chairs filled the middle of the room, and bookshelves lined two walls.

She took a seat in the closest wooden chair, and David sat beside her.

"Every couple who is married at St. John's signs our register after the ceremony." The reverend crossed to a bookshelf on the far wall and ran his finger down the row of leather-bound books.

Gwen pulled in a shaky breath as she watched him. St. John's was one of the oldest churches in Keswick. With its pink sandstone exterior and tall spire, it seemed like the kind of place her mother would choose for her wedding.

"Here we are." Father Scott pulled a large book from the shelf and laid it on the table next to Gwen. "Let's take a look." He opened the book and flipped through the pages. "What is your father's name?"

Gwen hesitated. "That's what I'm hoping to learn."

He looked up and met her gaze.

"His first name is Landon, and my mother's name is Jessica Morris."

He studied her for a moment, then lowered his gaze to the book once more and ran his finger down the page. He frowned and turned the page. Finally, he sighed and looked up. "I'm sorry. There were only two couples married at St. John's in June that year. I checked May and July as well. Your parents are not listed."

Gwen's shoulders sagged. She glanced at David and back at Father Scott. "We've been to Crosthwaite Church, Lake Road Chapel, and the Methodist church. Are there other churches in Keswick we could check?"

"There are two others, but they are newer congregations that started after 1985."

Gwen slowly rose from her chair, trying to push away her disappointment. "Thank you."

"We appreciate you taking time to look." David stepped forward and shook his hand.

"I wish I could've been more help." He followed them out of the room. "Have you tried the town clerk? Perhaps they were married before a judge rather than in a church."

Gwen released a deep breath. "Yes, we checked there first." She bid him good-bye, and they walked down the hall and out the door.

David sent her a concerned glance as they stepped into the sunlit street. "Want to stop for coffee before we head back to the house?"

She steeled herself. "No, I should get back to work."

He reached for her arm. "Don't be discouraged. This is just a roadblock, not the end of the journey."

Her throat tightened. "But I don't have any other leads to follow. How will I find him?"

"I'm not sure, but we'll find a way."

Her heart lifted, and a wave of gratitude flowed through her. She was not alone in this journey. "Thank you, David."

"You're welcome. Now let's stop and get coffee to go. I could use a shot of espresso to keep me moving today."

The next afternoon, David crossed the entry hall and followed Gwen's voice. He stopped in the open doorway of the sitting room and looked in. His grandmother and Gwen stood together in front of the fireplace with their backs to him.

His grandmother pointed to the painting hanging over the mantel. "This has always been one of my favorites, but we have

163

so many paintings in this room. I suppose we should add it to the list and let someone else enjoy it."

Gwen nodded and tapped something into her iPad.

The painting featured two girls dressed in green standing close together. One of the girls held a white bird with a small twig in its mouth. The other girl was leaning down, kissing the bird's head. He'd never really paid much attention to the painting before.

"I believe the artist is John Millais." Gwen stepped forward to take a closer look. "Yes, I see his signature." She quickly tapped something else into her iPad, swiped a few times, then looked up with a triumphant smile. "It's titled *The Return of the Dove to the Ark*."

"That's right!" His grandmother beamed her an equally bright smile. "I remember the title now. Arthur bought it just after we were married. Isn't it lovely?"

"Beautiful." Gwen's voice sounded soft and wistful.

David crossed the room toward them. "How is it going?"

His grandmother turned to him. "We're making good progress. Gwen is so clever. I've never met anyone who knows more about paintings and artists."

Gwen looked down with a shy smile. "All those hours I spent poring over my art history textbooks are finally paying off."

"It's more than that, dear. You have a keen eye as well as excellent training."

"Thank you, Lilly. You're very kind."

His grandmother's phone rang, and she pulled it from her skirt pocket. "Excuse me." She stepped aside to take the call.

David lowered his voice. "I just had a call from the head of the parish council."

"About the houseboats?"

He nodded. "They met last night, but the issue didn't come up until near the end of the meeting. There was some opposition, but they put off making a ruling until the next meeting."

"When is that?"

"Not until next month. I called Max to explain the situation and ask him to give us some more time, but he didn't answer."

"Did you leave a message?"

"Yes, but I didn't go into detail. I don't want to discourage him." Frustration coursed through David. Why did he seem to hit a wall at every turn? He shifted his thoughts to the upcoming auction. Maybe, by some miracle, those funds would become available sooner than expected. He turned to Gwen. "Did you hear if our shipment arrived safely in London?"

"Yes. I called this morning. They've unpacked everything, and there was no damage. They'll start taking photos and checking the appraisals today."

"Good." He nodded to her iPad. "How many more rooms do you need to go through to get the next shipment ready?"

Gwen swiped her iPad and checked the screen. "We have two more bedrooms, the dining room, the library, the music room, the gallery, and this room. Your grandmother said there is some furniture stored downstairs that she'd like to clear out. We may not be able to accept all those pieces, but at least I can help her sort through them and find someone to take away what she doesn't want to keep."

He blew out a breath. "And we have to wait until you finish all of that to send the next shipment?"

"Yes. It all needs to go together."

He rubbed his forehead. "This is taking longer than I expected."

A look of hurt came across her face.

"I'm not criticizing you. I'm sure you're working as quickly as you can."

"I would think you'd understand how long this kind of work takes after all the renovation projects you've handled."

"Those places were already vacant. I've never worked with an auction house to clear out a property."

She checked her iPad again, her frustration obvious in her stance and tone. "We sent fifty-two pieces to London. Your grandmother and I have discussed about thirty more. This is a big job, David. It takes time to do it right."

"I'm sure it does, and I don't want to pressure you, but I have to make some decisions and—"

His grandmother crossed the room toward them. Her smile faded as she looked from him to Gwen. "What is it? What's wrong?"

Gwen shifted her weight to the other foot and looked toward the windows.

"David, have you said something to upset Gwen?"

His face heated, and he felt like a schoolboy who had been called into the headmaster's office. "I was just saying that this process is taking longer than I expected."

His grandmother's forehead creased. "David, this is a very large house, and we are evaluating paintings and furnishings in every room. I think Gwen is doing an excellent job. She has been very patient and let me share my memories as we look at each piece. We're talking about my life and my home. I wouldn't want to do this with anyone else."

Regret rolled over him. He'd hurt his grandmother and Gwen with his impatience. He lowered his head, shot off a quick prayer, then looked up. "You're right." He shifted his gaze to Gwen. "I apologize."

His grandmother turned to Gwen and lifted her silver eyebrows.

A hint of a smile tucked in the corner of Gwen's mouth. "Apology accepted."

"Good." His grandmother looked from Gwen to David. "We've all been working very hard. Mrs. G. has the evening off, so we are on our own for dinner. Why don't we go into the village? After dinner, we could walk over to the green. I believe there's a musical group playing there this evening."

Gwen glanced his way, waiting for him to speak.

Dinner and a concert sounded good, especially if it would help make up for his impatient remarks. "Let's do it."

Gwen's smile spread wide. "I'll go up and change."

Thirty minutes later, Gwen looked in the full-length mirror in her bedroom and smoothed her hand down her dress. The mossy-green color drew attention to her eyes, but she hoped it wasn't too dressy. This was the only dress she'd packed, so it would have to do.

She glanced at her watch, then grabbed her sweater and purse and started down the hall. David stepped out of his room and walked toward her. As he came closer, her heart did a funny little flip. He had changed into neatly pressed khaki trousers, a white dress shirt, and navy blazer. She met him in front of his grandmother's bedroom door.

He looked at her, his smile slowly spreading wider. "You look very nice."

"Thank you. So do you."

He nodded with a twinkle in his eyes, then knocked on his grandmother's door.

"Come in," she called.

David opened the door, and they both looked in.

His grandmother was seated in an overstuffed chair, with her feet up on an ottoman, a blanket over her legs, and a book on her lap. "I'm feeling a bit tired. I think I'll stay home this evening."

Concern crossed David's face. "Are you feeling ill?"

"No, I'm fine, dear. I think I'd just rather read my book and enjoy a quiet evening."

"Shall I go down and make you some dinner?"

She lifted her hand. "Don't worry about me. The fridge is

full of food. I'll go down and find something after I finish this chapter. I'm at the best part." A hint of mischief lit her eyes as she looked from David to Gwen. "You two go ahead and enjoy the evening."

Lilly's excuses didn't fool Gwen. She wanted to arrange a romantic evening for two. Gwen leaned toward David and lowered her voice. "We don't have to go if you'd rather not."

He sent her a crooked half smile. "I'm okay with it if you are." From the look in his eyes and the warm tone of voice, she could tell he was more than okay with the idea.

She nodded, and a surge of happiness rose from her heart as they set off down the hall together.

Outside, he opened the car door for her, and she slid in. He circled the car and climbed in on his side. They drove past the village to a charming inn on the far side of the lake. The host seated them at a table with a view of the water, and they watched boats sail past as the sun dipped lower and spread a golden glow over the scene.

After they placed their order, Gwen took a sip of her water and relaxed back in her chair. "This is just what I needed. Thank you."

David cocked his eyebrow. "I believe my grandmother is the one we ought to thank."

Gwen laughed softly. "Yes, this was her idea, wasn't it?"

His eyes danced. "She always could read my mind."

The server returned and placed a basket of rolls on the table, along with their salads.

David reached across the table. "Shall we pray?"

She took hold of his hand and lowered her head, pleased that he wasn't embarrassed to offer a prayer in public.

"Thank You, Lord, for this day and time to get away and enjoy dinner together. We're grateful. Guide our conversation and renew our energy for the work ahead. And thank You for our food. In Jesus's name. Amen."

His simple prayer warmed her heart. She lifted her head and smiled across at him. "Thank you."

He nodded and reached for a roll. "I was thinking about that photo you showed me of your parents. Maybe they were married in Ambleside or Windermere or one of the other villages nearby. We could look online and make a list, then go and check the church and village records."

She hesitated, considering his idea. She wanted to find her father, but their last efforts had been discouraging. "That's a kind offer, but I should probably focus on the work at Longdale."

"You don't have to work all day, every day. You can take some time for yourself."

"But the only information I have is my father's first name and the date of my parents' marriage, and that doesn't seem to be getting us very far."

"What about the staff? It must be significant since he held it in the photo."

She gave a slow nod. "I could photograph it and do a Google image search. Maybe that would tell us if there are other staffs like it."

"We could check the local gift shops and see if they have any or know anyone who carves them."

"That's a good idea." The work at Longdale was important to David, but he wanted her to continue the search—and he was willing to help. That was a gift.

"How about tomorrow afternoon, say, four o'clock?"

She agreed, and a wave of relief flowed through her. "Thank you, David."

He grinned. "No problem. I love solving a good mystery."

After dinner, they drove back to Keswick and parked on a side street. The sound of smooth jazz floated in the air as they crossed the street and walked toward the village green. A jazz trio played on a low wooden stage under the lights. All around the green, couples and families had spread blankets on the grass and were enjoying the music.

David scanned the scene with a slight frown. "I should've brought a blanket."

"That's all right. I don't mind sitting on the grass."

He took off his blazer. "The ground is a little damp. You can sit on this."

She smiled. "You're very gallant. What about you?"

He grinned as he spread out his sports coat. "I was hoping there was room for two."

She laughed softly as she settled on her side of the coat. "Please, join me."

He sat next to her, leaning his shoulder against hers. The music floated around them, setting the perfect mood for a romantic, relaxing evening. She asked him about his childhood, and he filled her in on his early years. She learned he was an only child, but he grew up in a neighborhood where there were several boys his age who became like brothers. They were still friends and stayed in touch via texts, since he claimed he wasn't much of a phone person. And each year they got together to watch at least one football match.

He shifted the conversation back to her and asked about her growing-up years. She told him she was also an only child. But unlike him, she'd been somewhat of a loner until she went to university, where she finally formed some deeper relationships.

He listened thoughtfully. "Were those deeper relationships with girls or guys?"

"I had some wonderful roommates, and I dated a few guys, but none of those dating relationships lasted very long. My only serious relationship was last year while I was interning at Hill and Morris." She looked down. "That did not end well."

"I'm sorry."

She waved his words away. "It's probably for the best. But it does make me wonder if not having a father in my life impacted my choices and dating relationships."

"Hmm, I suppose it could. What about your mum? Did she offer advice on relationships?"

Gwen tipped her head and fiddled with a piece of grass. "Not too much. I think she was hesitant because her marriage lasted less than a year. She never dated or talked about wanting to marry again."

An older couple crossed the grass toward them. The man carried a cane and walked with a slight limp. "Mind if we sit here?" He motioned to the open grass area next to them.

David extended his hand. "Not at all."

The woman spread out a small plaid blanket, and the couple took a seat. The man removed his hat and laid his cane on the grass beside them.

David nudged Gwen's shoulder. "Look." He lowered his gaze to the cane.

She glanced that way and froze. It wasn't a cane. It was a staff—a shepherd's staff with a carved head. She sat up straight. "Excuse me."

The man and woman looked her way.

"I noticed your staff. The design is quite unique."

"Yes, it is." He smiled as he lifted it from the grass. "Would you like to take a closer look?"

"I would." She held out her hand, and he passed the staff to her. The curved head included a carved sheep, but the black-and-white dog facing the sheep was painted on rather than carved. The size and scale of the animals was different from the staff her father held in the photo. Still, it might be a lead. "It's very nice. Do you know who made it?"

"Yes, it was given to me on my sixtieth birthday and carved by my good friend John Monroe."

Gwen nodded. "Do you know if he still makes or sells staffs like this?"

Sadness clouded his eyes. "John passed away not too long ago."

Her heart sank. "Oh, I'm sorry to hear that." She darted a glance at David, then pressed on. "Do you know if any of his family members still live in the area?"

He nodded. "His wife, Elizabeth, and his daughter, Carol, are up at their family farm, about three kilometers west of the village."

Gwen studied the staff once more. If the carver of the staff had passed away, would it be worth their time to visit the farm? It might just be another wild-goose chase.

David leaned forward. "Could you give us directions to their farm? We'd like to talk to his family about the staffs."

"I suppose I can draw you a map." He turned to his wife. "Mary, do you have a piece of paper?"

His wife looked in her purse and pulled out a pen and small notebook, and the man began explaining the directions to David.

The woman sent Gwen a kind smile. "Are you hoping to buy a staff like the one Jim was given?"

Gwen hesitated, then said, "No, I've seen a staff similar to yours in a photo I have of my father . . . and I'm searching for him."

The woman tilted her head. "Oh?"

"Yes. His first name is Landon, but I'm not sure of his last name. He's probably in his late forties or early fifties."

The woman sent her husband an apprehensive glance. He stopped speaking and shot Gwen a questioning look. "You're looking for Landon?"

Her heartbeat sped up. "Do you know someone by that name?"

He shifted on the blanket and looked away with a slight frown. "Yes, but I haven't seen him for a number of years."

"So . . . he doesn't still live in the area?"

"No. He doesn't." His tone was clipped, and he looked as though he didn't want to say anything else.

"Please, can you tell me his last name?"

The older man frowned. "The man I'm talking about is Landon Monroe, John's son. But I don't believe he has a daughter." He turned away.

She swallowed hard. Could Landon Monroe be her father? The fact that John Monroe carved shepherds' staffs made it seem like a possibility, but she wouldn't know unless she visited the farm and spoke to the family. She leaned toward David and lowered her voice. "Did he finish giving you directions?"

"Yes. I have what I need. We can go there tomorrow if you'd like."

She nodded, though her stomach took a dive at the thought. The change in the man's tone when she'd told them she was looking for someone named Landon didn't bode well.

Fourteen

1912

Ian yawned and rubbed his cold hands together as he started down the path to the barn. He pulled in a deep breath of brisk air and scanned the clear sky. Lambing season was going well. There had been no need to be up with the ewes for the last three nights. The barn still held two shearlings that had given birth the day before. He would check on them, then head back to the house for breakfast.

Thoughts of Charlotte filtered through his mind as he continued down the path. He missed their conversations and time together. There was so much he'd taken for granted about life on the farm—whether it was the appeal of a newborn lamb, or the beauty of the primrose scattered across the pasture. She saw it all, brought it to his attention, and had brightened his days with her unique perspective and winsome ways.

Tomorrow, she'd be going to the May Day Festival with James Fenton . . . and there was nothing he could do about it. He clenched his jaw, fighting off his frustration. He pushed open the barn door and stalked inside. The scent of hay and animals filled the air.

Milly stepped out of the first stall. "Morning, Ian." She wore a long brown apron over her blue dress and toted a pail of frothy milk fresh from their cow.

"Morning." He looked in the second stall, where one of the shearlings and her newborn lamb rested in the hay.

Milly stepped up next to him and set down the pail. "These two seem to be doing well."

Ian nodded but didn't reply.

Milly turned toward him. "What's bothering you?"

He shook his head. "Nothing."

Milly lifted her eyebrows. "You don't fool me, brother. I can tell you've not been yourself these past few days—especially on Sunday, when you nearly cost me my first invitation from a young man in a very long while."

Another round of frustration coursed through him, and he huffed out a breath. "What did Dad say about going to the festival with Paul Washburn?"

"I'm twenty-four, and old enough to decide something like that for myself."

"You didn't ask him?"

She looked away. "I spoke to Mum, and she said it was fine, as long as Charlotte goes with me."

Ian rolled his eyes. "Who's going to watch out for her with Paul's cousin? I didn't like the way he was looking at her."

Milly chuckled. "You didn't?"

Ian scowled. "No, I didn't. And what is so funny?"

Milly gave his arm a shove. "You are! It's obvious you're fond of Charlotte. Anyone could see that by the way you've been acting, and your behavior on Sunday confirmed it."

Heat rushed up Ian's neck. Had Charlotte come to the same conclusion? Had he made a fool of himself in her eyes? He rubbed his forehead, regretting his words and actions. But the thought of someone else winning Charlotte's affection had made him lose sight of his manners and good sense.

Milly placed her hand on his shoulder. "Don't worry. She just met James. You've the advantage of more time with her."

"But she's going to the festival with him."

Milly sighed and looked at him as though he were thick-headed. "If you'll make an effort and stop acting like you don't care, I think you might still have a chance."

He turned to Milly. "You think so?"

"Yes. Haven't you noticed the way she lights up when you speak to her?"

He leaned on the stall's half door, recalling their interactions. "Do you think it's fair to pursue her when I'm not sure how my future will unfold?"

Milly met his gaze with an understanding expression. "We make our plans, but the future is in God's hands."

He ran his hand through his hair. "I want to return to Oxford in the autumn and finish my archaeology studies, but Dad expects me to stay here now that Grandfather is gone."

Milly laid her hand on his arm. "Those are details that need to be worked out, but none of them should prevent you from pursuing Charlotte—if you truly care for her."

His sister's words sent energy pulsing through him. He *did* care for Charlotte, very much. "You don't think I've ruined my chances?"

"Not at all."

"Has she spoken to you about me?"

Milly grinned. "No, but there's definitely a spark. Now it's up to you to fan that spark into a flame."

He gave a firm nod. "Right. Fan the flame." His thoughts swirled. If he were in Oxford, he could take her to a fine restaurant or the theater, but how did one woo a woman in the country? "What exactly would you recommend?"

She thought for a moment, then smiled. "Why not take her on a boat ride across the lake? I think she'd enjoy that. And it would give you time to talk and see where the conversation leads."

He pictured them together in a boat, skimming across the lake, and his chest expanded. "I like that idea."

"If I were you, I'd do it today, before she goes to the festival and spends time with James Fenton."

"Right." Ian rubbed his hands together, his thoughts racing ahead. He could borrow a boat from one of their friends in the village. Maybe he would ask her to make a lunch to take along. No, he ought to make the lunch himself. That would impress her.

Milly gave him a pat on the back. "You're a good man, Ian. A fine catch. James Fenton has nothing over you."

His spirit rose, and he gave his sister a side hug. He had one day to convince Charlotte he was a more worthy suitor than James Fenton. It was time to get to work and put his plan into motion.

Charlotte quietly closed the bedroom door and carried the broom and dustpan down the hall toward the kitchen. Mum had a headache and had gone to the bedroom to lie down and rest. Milly had taken Alice outside with her to weed the garden. As Charlotte rounded the corner, she stopped in the doorway. Ian stood at the kitchen counter, slicing a loaf of bread.

He looked up and smiled. "Hello, Charlotte."

"Hello." She glanced at the bread, and then back at him. "Are you making lunch?"

A mischievous twinkle lit his eyes. "Yes . . . and no."

"What do you mean?" She took a few steps forward.

"I'm not making lunch for the family. I'm making a picnic lunch."

"Oh . . . you are?"

He nodded. "I am."

She opened the closet and hung the broom and dustpan on a peg on the wall. Why was Ian going on a picnic in the middle of a workday?

He pulled out a small cutting board and sliced some cheese. He slipped the cheese between the bread and added slices of ham. He was obviously packing a picnic for two.

She crossed the kitchen and stood by the sink, a few feet from Ian. She wanted to ask him who was going with him, but she didn't have the nerve. She hadn't heard any of his family mention he had a sweetheart, nor had she seen him talking to any young women at church. But he was handsome, well respected, and at the age when he might want to court a young woman. He must have his eye on someone. A wave of disappointment washed over her, and she brushed some crumbs from the counter.

"It's a nice day for a picnic," she said.

"Yes. The sun is out, and there's a bit of a breeze."

She watched him, dying to ask who was going with him.

He wrapped the two sandwiches in a cloth. "What else should I take?"

She thought for a moment, imagining what she'd like with the sandwiches. "There are a few slices of your mum's apple pie left from last night."

He grinned. "Perfect." He placed the wrapped sandwiches in a basket on the kitchen table, along with two cloth napkins, a jug of water, and two mugs.

She blew out a sigh, fighting off another wave of disappointment. "I'll get the pie for you."

"Thanks." He watched her with a slight smile.

Charlotte took the pie from the cupboard and removed the cloth covering, revealing four slices. "Will two pieces be enough?" She looked over her shoulder.

"I don't know. Will it?"

She stilled. "What do you mean?"

"One is enough for me. How many would you like?"

"Me?"

His smile spread wide. "Yes, you."

She glanced around the kitchen, trying to sort out her thoughts. For days he'd been so withdrawn and avoided conversations. What had changed?

"Are you sure you can take time away from the farm to go off on a picnic?"

"Well, lambing is almost done, and the weather is ideal. I thought you might enjoy a boat ride across the lake and lunch with me."

She blinked, still trying to overcome the surprise. "Oh . . . that sounds wonderful."

He stepped closer. His expression softened, and a hint of vulnerability flickered in his eyes. "I know I've been rather distant lately, and I'm sorry about that. I've enjoyed getting to know you, and I'd like to spend more time with you . . . if you're open to that."

Her heart fluttered. "I'd like that very much."

His smile returned. "Then I suggest we finish packing our lunch and walk down to the lake."

Happiness spiraled through her, making her steps light as she crossed the kitchen with the pan of apple pie. Ian wanted to spend more time with her, and they were going on a picnic, just the two of them . . . alone . . . together! It seemed too wonderful to believe.

Charlotte took Ian's hand and stepped from the dock into a small rowboat. It rocked and swayed, and she grasped his hand more tightly.

"You can sit right here." He guided her toward the rear

wooden bench. Then he took a seat facing her on the other bench and sent her an encouraging smile.

She pulled in a deep breath to calm her jitters and looked around. Across the lake, trees lined the shore, and green and brown hills rose beyond. Sunlight sparkled on the surface of the water, blinking like little diamonds. A few other people were out in small boats, and in the distance, a larger boat chugged north.

She turned to Ian. "I've ridden on a ferry a few times, but I've never been in a small boat like this."

He picked up the oars and attached them to the oarlocks. "I've been rowing across this lake since I was a boy. You're safe with me."

She relaxed her grip on the bench and sent him a smile.

He untied the boat and pushed away from the dock. Then he dipped the oars in the water and pulled back with smooth, strong strokes. The boat picked up speed and was soon gliding across the lake.

He obviously knew how to handle the boat. She was in strong and capable hands. Her shoulders relaxed, and she lifted her hand to shade her eyes and take in the view. The village receded behind them, and a pleasant breeze cooled her face. She turned to Ian. "Where will we have our picnic?"

He nodded to the left as he continued rowing. "We're headed for Rampshome Island. It has a gravel spit on the north side where we can land the boat."

She leaned to the side to look around him, and the boat dipped. She gasped, gripped the bench, and shot him a startled look.

He chuckled and lifted the dripping oars, slowing their progress. "It's best to stay centered, unless you plan to take a swim."

"No, thank you." She sat up straight, balancing herself in the center of the boat. The last thing she wanted to do was to take an unexpected dip in the lake.

Ian glanced over his shoulder, adjusted the angle of the oars, and steered the boat toward a small tree-covered island. "That's our destination."

Charlotte scanned the small island as the gravel spit came into view. He turned the boat, came around, and headed in. The boat scraped the shore and slowed to a stop.

He brought the oars in and rose. "Let me get out first, then I'll help you." He grabbed the basket and blanket and set them on the gravel. Then he held out his hand to her.

She rose and took his hand. Grabbing her skirt with the other hand, she managed to climb out without getting wet or muddy.

He scooped up the basket and blanket, then took hold of her hand again, as if it were the most natural thing to do. Pleasant warmth traveled from his hand and up her arm. His fingers were a little rough, but they felt just right in hers.

"There's a nice spot just up ahead." They ducked into the shade of the tall trees and followed a path through the woods. The trees parted, and they stepped out onto a grassy slope overlooking the water. Ian dropped her hand and spread out the blanket.

"This is perfect. How did you find this place?" She bent and helped him straighten the blanket.

"My friends and I used to come here when we were young. We thought it was our secret spot, but as you can see by the path, we're not the only ones who like to come to the island."

He sat down, and she settled on the blanket beside him. He uncovered the basket and took out their sandwiches. She poured water into the mugs and passed one to him.

"Shall we say a blessing?" He held out his hand.

She nodded and placed her hand in his again. Bowing her head, she listened while he offered a short prayer. Her heart lifted as he thanked the Lord for the beauty of the day and time to enjoy the lake, the island, and the food. His prayer was simple, almost conversational, and so unlike the formal prayers her father had always prayed.

When they finished praying, she bit into her sandwich. The bread was soft and fresh, and a perfect match to the creamy cheese and salty ham. She watched Ian enjoying a few bites of sandwich and tried to picture him at Oxford. "What stirred your interest in studying archaeology?"

"When I was twelve, my grandfather gave me a book of adventure stories about a boy who explored the ancient sights in the Holy Land. I've always been intrigued by the story of Joseph and his life in Egypt."

The thought that a book had sparked his interest in archaeology made her smile. She loved reading, and she had gone on many adventures through the books she'd read.

He took a sip of water and continued. "During my first term at Oxford, I took a class from Professor Giles Montrose. He'd been to Egypt several times, and his lectures were fascinating. His digs have been focused on searching for evidence that will prove Joseph's existence."

Her eyebrows rose. "I didn't know his existence was in question."

"I'm afraid it is. Some critics think his life is just a legend passed down through the generations. And since there are no extrabiblical texts that mention him, Professor Montrose believes archaeology will find the proof."

"What is he looking for?"

"Inscriptions with Joseph's Egyptian name, or his tomb—anything that could tell us more about his life and which pharaoh he served. There's debate about that too."

She pondered that for a moment. "I didn't know there were people who doubted the existence of characters in the Bible."

"Neither did I until I went to Oxford. They discuss and debate everything there." He finished his last bite of sandwich. "That's one reason the study of archaeology is so important. Not only can it provide proof of Joseph's life, it can also establish the existence of other characters and events in the Bible."

She nodded. "I see what you mean."

He gazed out across the lake. "Professor Montrose invited me to go with him to Egypt this summer, but I couldn't accept. After Granddad's stroke, I had to come home."

She could hear the disappointment in his voice, and it tugged at her heart. "Isn't there someone else who could work with your father?"

He shook his head. "It's not just the workload. The cost of traveling to Egypt is out of reach for me, especially on top of the cost of attending Oxford."

"My brother also attends. I understand it's quite an investment."

"I'd never have been able to afford it without my granddad's help."

She tipped her head, curious to know more.

"When I told my father I wanted to go to university, he said he couldn't afford to send me, but I think it was more a matter of him not wanting to me go. Granddad heard us arguing, and he stood up for me and said we should find a way. When Father refused, Granddad called me aside and offered to help pay my way."

"That was very generous."

"Yes, he said he always wished he could've gone to university, but it wasn't possible when he was young." His expression deflated. "My father doesn't understand. I'm sure you remember what he said about it that night we took the bummer lamb to the barn."

She nodded as she recalled his father's critical words.

"He never had a desire for more education," Ian continued. "The only thing he ever wanted is to run this farm. It's an ongoing source of contention between us, especially since my granddad's passing."

Her heart ached for him, and she wished there was some way she could ease the situation. "I'm sorry. That sounds difficult."

He reached for her hand. "No, I'm the one who is sorry. I shouldn't be putting a damper on our day by telling you my gloomy tale."

She squeezed his hand. "I don't mind. I want to know what's important to you."

His gaze rested on hers. "Thank you, Charlotte. It's a relief to talk to you about it, rather than just mulling it over myself."

"I'm always glad to listen."

"I know you are, and I appreciate it very much."

His honest words and gentle touch reached straight into her heart. He had been open with her and told her his troubles. Perhaps it was time she did the same. Could she trust him to understand?

She summoned her courage and met his gaze. "Thank you for telling me more about the situation with your father. It makes me feel I can tell you about my family and why we truly had to leave London."

His focus remained steady. "I'm listening."

Her throat tightened, but she didn't look away. "I always loved and admired my father. He was handsome and intelligent and well respected by ministry leaders. My mum adored him, and so did my brother and sister. But after his death, when I was cleaning out his desk . . . I found letters from a woman he had been secretly meeting."

Surprise flashed across Ian's face.

"I was stunned and heartbroken. In public, he preached the pursuit of a higher life and gave everyone the impression he was a devoted husband and father. But all the time he was carrying on a shameful secret love affair."

"I'm so sorry." His voice came out as a rough whisper.

She swallowed. "My mum doesn't know. Neither do Daniel or Alice."

"You never showed your mother the letters?"

"No. At first, I thought they were letters my parents exchanged while they were courting, but then I saw they were signed with the initials E. M. I only read two of them, then I burned them all that very day." She lifted a shaky hand to her forehead. "I couldn't bring myself to tell Mum. She was already deeply grieving, and I knew it would bring her so much pain."

He rested his arms on his raised knees and shifted his serious gaze toward the lake.

She watched him, waiting for his reply. Now that he knew her father was a hypocrite who had deceived so many, what would he think of her? Would her father's sins taint her in his eyes and destroy their friendship before they had a chance to see if it could become something more?

He looked her way again. "I'm glad you told me. No one should have to carry such a heavy burden alone."

Her breath caught. "You don't think less of me, knowing what he did?"

"Why would I think less of you? You've done nothing to be ashamed of."

"But if it comes out, people will associate me and my family with my father's sins."

"You shouldn't have to carry any guilt or shame because of your father's bad choices."

Uncertainty still gripped her heart. "I wish that were true, but will you still feel the same if it becomes public?"

He took her hand in his. "In my eyes, you're an honest, courageous, and compassionate woman. Your character speaks for itself, and nothing your father has done can change that."

Her heart lifted, and tears flooded her eyes. "That's . . . very kind of you."

He slipped his arm around her shoulders, drawing her close. She closed her eyes and rested against him. What a relief to find such a caring and understanding friend. A man she could trust. A man whose life matched his words.

Fifteen

2012

Gwen scanned the list of names on the computer screen and sighed. As soon as she'd returned home from her evening out with David, she'd opened her laptop and searched online to see what she could learn about Landon Monroe.

David walked into the library, carrying two glasses. "Did you find anything?"

"There are several listings for Landon Monroe." She scrolled to the top of the page again. "One is a soccer player in his twenties. Another is a choreographer in London, but he's almost seventy-five." She focused on the list again. "I can't find much information about the others unless I want to pay a fee."

"It might be helpful."

She looked up at him, debating what to do next. "I think I'll wait until tomorrow and see what we learn at the farm. If that's a dead end, then my father's last name is not Monroe, and we're back to where we started."

He nodded. "That makes sense." He passed her one of the glasses.

Bubbles rose and fizzed in the clear liquid, and a citrus scent tickled her nose. "And this is?"

"Sparkling water with some lemon and lime."

"That sounds good." She took a sip of the cool drink. "Thank you."

He sat on the couch next to her. "Did you look up Elizabeth Monroe?"

"Not yet." She slid her cursor to the search bar and typed in the name. A long list of websites and several images popped up. None of the women looked old enough to be her grandmother. "I'm sure that's a more common name." She quickly scanned the list, then shook her head. "There are so many of them. I suppose it's best to just wait until tomorrow and see if she truly is my grandmother."

He nodded, then studied her with a hint of a smile. "I enjoyed tonight."

Her heart fluttered. "So did I. Thank you for dinner. I would've been glad to split the bill." She smiled, remembering how he'd flagged down the waiter and insisted on paying.

"That's what a gentleman does on a date."

She sent him a teasing grin. "So this was a date?"

He chuckled. "Yes, I believe it was."

She met his gaze. "Well, it was the nicest date I've had in a very long time."

"I'm glad to hear it." He took a sip, looked toward the fireplace, and his expression sobered. "I have a meeting with the architect at one tomorrow, but I should be back by three. We can head out to the Monroe farm any time after that."

She closed her laptop. "I'll be ready."

He checked his watch. "It's late. I suppose we should call it a night."

"Yes." She rose and turned to him. "I'm glad you were with me tonight when we met that couple and saw that man's staff."

David gave a slight nod as he rose.

She wanted to say more but wasn't sure how to phrase it without saying too much. "It's good to have a friend who knows the story and understands."

"I'm glad I could be there tonight, and I'm happy to go with you tomorrow."

Their gazes met and held, and she sensed a stronger connection flowing between them. It felt right, and it made her very glad she'd said yes to the evening out with him.

They climbed the stairs together and said good night in front of her bedroom door. He reached for her and gave her a gentle hug. She sighed into his shoulder, comforted by his strength and nearness.

"See you in the morning." He turned and walked down the hall.

She slipped into her room and closed the door, pondering that hug. David had gone out of his way to make the evening special. Was he simply being a supportive friend, or was he showing her that he wanted more from their relationship?

What did she want? David was a great guy—kind and caring as well as handsome. He was a true visionary who wasn't afraid to take risks to see his ideas become reality. She admired his commitment to his grandmother and his efforts to save Longdale in the face of so many challenges. His faith was important to him, and he seemed to live it out in his words and actions.

With a sigh, she curled up in the chair. *Lord, You know I don't have a good track record where men and relationships are concerned. I like David, but I don't want to get involved with him or anyone unless he is the one You have for me. If David is that man, then please make it clear. If he isn't, please protect me and shut that door. Help me trust You with my future and find the best path forward.*

She slowly exhaled, and a renewed sense of calm settled over her heart. She took Charlotte's journal from the nightstand and gently ran her hand over the cover. When she had first started reading the journal entries, it had simply been a way to pass the time when she couldn't fall asleep. But as she read on, Charlotte's words had struck a deeper chord. She almost felt as if Charlotte was stepping back across time to share wisdom and insight from all she was experiencing.

It was surprising how much they had in common, even though they lived a century apart. Charlotte's father had betrayed his wife, and then left his family without a home or income. Gwen's father had left her and her mum to struggle on their own before she was even born. Grandfather had helped them, but it had not been easy to make a life for themselves in London.

She frowned, pondering the similarities. What had driven her father to desert his wife and daughter? She might learn the answer to that question tomorrow. A shiver traveled down her arms, and she closed her eyes tight. Was she ready to face the answers and finally learn the truth?

David adjusted his grip on the steering wheel and glanced across at Gwen. He could read the tension on her face as she stared out the windshield and clasped her hands in her lap. They were on their way to the Monroes' farm to meet the women who could be Gwen's grandmother and aunt, and hopefully find out how to contact Gwen's father.

He slowed as he approached a crossroad and looked both ways. He passed her the piece of paper with the written directions. "What's next?"

Gwen scanned down the page and read aloud. "Cross the stone bridge, then look for the Valley View Farm sign on the left."

David drove on. "Have you thought of what you're going to say when you meet them?"

"I've run through several scenarios, but I'm not sure what's best. What do you think?"

"When I'm preparing to make a presentation, I always

memorize my opening and closing. If I have those down, the rest seems to flow."

Up ahead, he spotted the narrow bridge that arched over a small stream.

"Wow, I'm glad there are no cars coming our way," she said.

"Right." He drove over, and they passed a large field, where a herd of sheep grazed on the lush grass.

Gwen leaned forward. "Is that the sign?"

David slowed and spotted a wooden sign on the gate next to the drive. "That's it." He turned in and drove up the hill and around a bend.

A whitewashed farmhouse came into view. Gwen pressed her hand to her stomach. "I'm so nervous."

"It will be okay. I'll be right there with you."

She sent him a grateful look. "Thank you."

David pulled to a stop in front of the house, then he hopped out, circled the car, and opened Gwen's door.

She looked up at him with shimmering blue-green eyes. "Here we go."

He took her hand and gave it a gentle squeeze, then they walked toward the front door.

Gwen straightened her shoulders and knocked on the dark green wooden door. The farmhouse looked like it had been built in the mid-to-late-1800s, but it was well kept. The white plaster walls and green trim appeared to be recently painted. A rosebush with bright red blossoms shaded the small front porch and climbed toward the dark slate roof.

The door opened, and an older woman with shoulder-length silver hair looked out. She had rosy cheeks and gray-green eyes that were bright and inquisitive. "May I help you?"

Gwen forced a smile. "I hope so. Are you Elizabeth Monroe?"

"I am."

"We met a man in Keswick last night named Jim, and he showed us his beautifully carved shepherd's staff. He said it was made by your husband, John Monroe."

Emotion flickered across Elizabeth's face. "Yes. My husband was an excellent carver."

"I've seen another staff that is very similar in a photo of my father."

"Your father?"

"Yes. . . . My mother's name is Jessica Morris, and my father's first name is Landon. I'm not certain of his last name, but I think it may be Monroe."

Elizabeth's eyes went wide. "You're Jessica and Landon's daughter?"

"Yes, I am."

The woman's brows dipped. "I know Landon was married to Jessica for a brief time, but he never told us they had a daughter."

"He and my mother separated before I was born. She might not have told him she was pregnant." Gwen didn't know if that was true, but she'd always wondered if that might be why he had never tried to contact her.

Elizabeth shook her head. "I'm sorry. This is very hard to believe."

"I have a photo that was taken on their wedding day." Gwen quickly pulled the photo from her purse and passed it to Elizabeth. "I was born ten months later."

"That is my son."

Gwen pulled in a sharp breath, and her heartbeat surged.

Elizabeth looked up and searched Gwen's face. "I do see a family resemblance." She stepped back and opened the door wider. "Please come in. I shouldn't have left you standing on the doorstep, but this is so . . . unexpected."

"Thank you." Relief flowed through Gwen. She walked inside

and hesitated as her eyes adjusted to the dim light. David gently touched her back and guided her toward the kitchen, following Elizabeth.

"Have a seat." Elizabeth motioned toward the kitchen table. "I'll put the kettle on. This calls for a good cup of tea."

Gwen sat down and glanced around the room. Ivory curtains fluttered at the open window above the sink. Bunches of dried herbs and flowers hung from one of the dark beams overhead. A large stone fireplace with a rough-hewn mantel filled the opposite wall. Hand-painted tiles decorated the broad hearth, and a large cast-iron pot sat on a metal grate inside the fireplace.

Elizabeth set the teakettle on the stove and turned on the gas burner. "I suppose we should start with introductions. You know my name, but I don't know yours."

"I'm sorry. I'm Gwen Morris."

"And I'm David Bradford."

Elizabeth nodded to David, then shifted her gaze back to Gwen. "So, you've come to Valley View to learn more about your father?"

"Yes. We've never met, and I was hoping you could tell me how to contact him."

Elizabeth placed three teacups on a wooden tray. "Your mother didn't stay in touch with him after the divorce?"

"No, she didn't."

"Why was that?"

"I'm not sure."

Elizabeth's hands stilled, and she looked at Gwen. "I have an idea why."

Gwen shot a quick glance at David, debating her next words. "My mother never told me much about my father or why they divorced. She promised to explain what happened when I finished university, but she died in a car accident a few months before that."

Elizabeth's expression softened. "I'm very sorry. That must have been a terrible heartache for you."

Unexpected tears stung Gwen's eyes. "It's been two years, but it's still hard."

"I'm sure it is."

Gwen cleared her throat. "I'd like to get in touch with my father. Can you tell me how to contact him?"

A shadow crossed Elizabeth's face. "I wish I could, but I don't know where he's living at the moment."

Gwen's heart sank, and she had to force out her next words. "How long has it been since you've seen him?"

"About five years. He was living in Glasgow at the time." Elizabeth poured steaming water into the teacups. "He wasn't well."

A bolt of fear shot through Gwen. "But he recovered, didn't he?"

"Yes. I stayed in Glasgow until he was out of the hospital." She carried the tray to the table and served the tea.

Gwen took a sip, hoping to steady her nerves. "You haven't seen him since then?"

"No, he doesn't stay in touch." She slowly lowered herself into the chair and met Gwen's gaze. Sorrow and empathy shimmered in her eyes. "I'm afraid Landon has a drinking problem. It ruined his second marriage, and I suspect it may have destroyed his first as well. He's been in and out of treatment for years."

Gwen stared at Elizabeth. "He's an alcoholic?"

Her grandmother grimaced and nodded. "It's taken a terrible toll on him, physically and emotionally."

Tears burned Gwen's eyes as she tried to absorb Elizabeth's words.

David watched her with a concerned expression. "Mrs. Monroe, are there any other relatives or friends who might know how to contact your son?"

"I don't believe so. We tried to find him when John died last year. But his phone number was disconnected, and our letters were returned. His sister, Connie, drove up to his flat in Glasgow. They told her he'd moved out months before and left no forwarding address."

A dizzying sensation flooded Gwen. How could this be true? She'd always pictured her father as the strong, handsome man in the photo. Of course, he would be older now, but she'd imagined he had a meaningful career and a good life, and the only reason he never reached out to her was because he didn't know she existed. She thought when she found him and told him who she was, he'd be thrilled to claim her as his own beloved daughter.

But none of that was true. Her father was nothing like she'd imagined. She might have learned his full name, but it seemed she was no closer to finding him than she had been before she came to Keswick. Her throat clogged, and a wave of sorrow crashed over her heart.

Elizabeth sighed. "After Jessica left, he fell into a deep depression."

Gwen blinked and stared at Elizabeth. "She left him?"

Elizabeth lifted her hand. "I don't blame her, not at all. I'm sure she had her reasons."

Gwen's stomach contracted. How could that be true? She'd never considered her mum might have been the one who left.

David studied Gwen and seemed to read her distress. He turned to Elizabeth. "How long has your family lived at Valley View Farm?"

"We're the sixth generation to oversee this land." Pride glowed in her eyes, then seemed to dim. "Now it's just me and my daughter Carol left to tend to the farm. But we hold on. It's our family's legacy."

David nodded. "I understand. My grandmother, Lilly Benderly, has a similar devotion to her home, Longdale Manor."

Elizabeth's eyebrows rose. "Longdale Manor? I believe there's a family connection between our family and yours."

Gwen straightened. "What kind of connection?"

"My husband told me some of his relatives worked there a long time ago. Then, a generation later, a man from my husband's family married a woman who lived at Longdale."

Gwen and David exchanged a surprised glance.

"My grandmother loves family history," David said. "She has quite a detailed family tree. We'll have to look and see if there is a Monroe branch."

Gwen sucked in a breath. "I think there is! I was curious about the author of an old journal we found at Longdale, and Lilly showed me the family tree to explain how she fit into the family."

"Who is the author?"

"Charlotte Harper. Does that name sound familiar?"

Elizabeth squinted toward the window. "I don't recall a Charlotte Harper, but my husband knew more about his family's genealogy than I do. Tell me more about the journal."

"It begins in 1912, the year Charlotte left London and came to stay in the Lake District. Her grandfather owned Longdale at the time."

Elizabeth smiled and shook her head. "Can you imagine that?"

"She went through some very difficult times, but she had a remarkable faith and a deep love for her family."

Elizabeth's eyes shone. "I'd like to see that journal." She turned to David. "If your grandmother would allow it."

"I'm sure she'd be glad to show it to you. I'll let her know you're interested." David wrote down his grandmother's phone number and passed it to Elizabeth. "Call her anytime."

Elizabeth nodded, then wrote down her number for David. "Thank you, David. Please give your grandmother my greetings and tell her I'll call soon."

Elizabeth told them more about the farm and her husband. When the tea grew cold, she turned to Gwen. "I'm so glad you came. I hope you'll visit us again. I'm sure my daughter Carol would love to meet you. She's usually here, but she's off to see the dentist today."

"Thank you. I'd be glad to meet her. Does she have other family?"

"No, she's single. Connie is married, and she and Walter have three children. They live in Hawkshead, not too far away. I know they'd enjoy meeting you. How long will you be at Longdale?"

"I'm not sure, but a little while longer."

Elizabeth nodded. "Very good. Perhaps we can plan a family gathering."

Gwen pushed aside her disappointment and forced a smile. "I'd like that." She might not have learned how to contact her father, but she had found her grandmother and learned she had two aunts, an uncle, and three cousins. That was an important discovery.

Gwen rose from the table, and Elizabeth offered her a warm hug. "I'm so happy to know I have another granddaughter. Thank you for coming, Gwen."

"Thank you for your kindness." Gwen took her business card from her purse. "This is my number. I hope you'll let me know if you hear anything about my father."

"Of course, dear." She nodded to the paper David held. "You have my number. I hope you'll stay in touch."

"I will." Gwen smiled and squeezed Elizabeth's hand, then she walked out the door of her father's childhood home with a bittersweet pang in her heart.

David replayed what they'd learned about Gwen's father as he and Gwen left the farmhouse and walked toward the car.

None of it was good news. He glanced at Gwen. She wore a stoic expression, but he could read the pain in her eyes, and his gut clenched.

He opened the car door for her, and she slid in without a word. He strode around and climbed in on his side. What could he say to help her process such devastating news? She'd come with such high hopes of finding her father, but even his own mother didn't know how to contact him.

He clenched his jaw, fighting off a surge of resentment toward the man. It wasn't fair. Gwen was a wonderful woman with a tender heart who needed to be protected and treasured. She deserved to have a father who loved and cherished her.

He turned the key, and the car roared to life. As he drove down the hill and passed through the gate, a thought struck. She did have a Father who loved her—her Heavenly Father. He watched over her and treasured her more than any earthly father ever could.

Did she know Him in that close personal way? She'd always bowed her head and prayed with them at meals, but they hadn't talked about their faith or what it meant to them. He shot off a quick prayer, asking for an opportunity to connect on that level and to have the right words when the time came.

His phone vibrated in his pocket. He clicked it into the magnetic holder on the dash and pushed the speaker button. "Hello, Nana."

"Oh, David, you must come home at once!" Her voice sounded high and frantic.

Fear sliced through him. "What's wrong?"

"There's a mob on the drive!"

He gripped the steering wheel. "What?"

Gwen sent him a startled look.

"Nana, what do you mean?"

"There are people—lots of people—marching up and down

the drive. They're carrying signs and shouting. One man even has a bullhorn!"

"What are they saying?"

"Save the lakes! Ban the houseboats!"

Anger surged in David's chest, and he stifled a growl. How dare they take their protest to Longdale and upset his grand-mother. He could understand people might disagree with him, but sending a mob to his grandmother's home was no way to resolve their differences.

"Mrs. G. is here, and we've locked the door."

"We'll be there in less than fifteen minutes."

"Do hurry, dear. I hate to think of all these people being angry with me."

"I'll handle it. We're on our way." He clicked off the phone and pressed on the gas.

Gwen looked his way. "Poor Lilly."

He careened around a corner and raced down the hill. "I knew that woman on the council was against the houseboats, but I didn't think she would take it this far."

Gwen gripped the door handle. "It sounds like she's not the only one against the plan."

Sixteen

1912

Ian held out his hand and helped Charlotte down from the front seat of the wagon. They shared a smile, and his chest expanded. Ever since their picnic on the island, he sensed a growing closeness between him and Charlotte. It made his steps lighter and filled him with hope.

He turned and helped his sister, who had ridden into the village in the back of the wagon. Milly brushed off her skirt, adjusted her small straw hat, and glanced up the street with an expectant look.

Alice jumped to the ground. "What a crowd of people!"

Ian scanned the scene. Men, women, and children dressed in their finest spring clothing walked toward Keswick's village green. Many carried picnic baskets and blankets folded over their arms.

Milly lifted their basket from the wagon bed and glanced at Ian. "What time is it?"

He took his watch from his pocket. "Ten minutes to twelve."

"Good." Her gaze darted over the people walking past. "I don't want to keep Paul and James waiting."

Ian held out his hand. "I can carry that basket for you."

"No, thank you. I'll carry it."

Charlotte glanced at him with shining eyes. They knew Milly had spent most of the morning preparing special food for the picnic, hoping to impress Paul. When their father came in and questioned her about her plans, he said Ian should go along to watch out for her and Charlotte.

Milly insisted she did not need a chaperone, and there was nothing improper about them attending the May Day Festival with Paul and James. But Father would not be moved—Ian would go with them, or she could stay home. Milly was not happy with Dad's decision, but she eventually gave in, rather than miss spending the afternoon with Paul.

Ian grinned, recalling the conversation. He'd been relieved and glad he could escort Charlotte as well as Milly. When Alice heard them talking about the May Day Festival, she'd begged to join them, and the picnic for four became an outing for six.

Milly and Alice led the way as they strolled with the crowd toward the green. He was pleased Charlotte walked by his side. He nodded to a few neighbors and exchanged brief greetings. Soon they arrived in the center of the village. He glanced around and estimated at least two hundred people had gathered for the celebration. The tall Maypole stood in the middle of the green, topped with a large bunch of flowers and colorful streamers.

Milly stood on tiptoe and scanned the crowd. "Charlotte, do you see them?"

Charlotte glanced around the green. "Not yet."

Ian did his own search. On the far side of the green, he spotted the two young farmers walking through the crowd toward them. Both wore eager smiles until they noticed him. They shot each other questioning glances before continuing across the grass.

Paul stepped forward and lifted his cap. "Good day . . . friends." His gaze darted from Ian to Milly.

Milly returned a warm smile. "Hello, Paul. James."

"We're glad to see you," James added, his smile focused on Charlotte. "It looks like a fine day for the festival."

Milly and Charlotte agreed, then Charlotte introduced Alice. The little girl sent them each a smile, and James shook her hand.

Paul turned to Ian, a challenge in his eyes. "I didn't expect to see you today, but . . . it's good you could join us."

Ian nodded and met the man's gaze, making it clear he was there to watch over his sister and Charlotte.

Across the green, a drummer tapped out a beat, and two accordion players joined him in a lively song. The villagers spread out, opening a large circle as the children came forward and gathered around the Maypole.

Mr. Donovan crossed the green and met the man who led their village council. When the song concluded, the man raised his hands, and the crowd quieted. "Friends and neighbors, we want to welcome you to our annual May Day Festival."

The villagers clapped, and a few whistles and hoots rose from the excited children.

Charlotte looked up at Ian with a bright smile and glowing eyes, and Ian returned the same. She had turned to share her excitement with him rather than James. Surely that was a good sign.

"And now, the Reverend Matthew Donovan of St. John's Church will ask a blessing on the festival."

Mr. Donovan stepped forward. "Let us pray." All heads bowed and he continued, "Father in heaven, we thank You for bringing us through the winter season. We are grateful for this beautiful spring day that is a picture of rebirth and the new life in Christ that You desire everyone to experience. We ask You to watch over us this spring and bless each individual and family with health, provision, good crops, and strong herds, as we seek to honor You, love our neighbors, and serve one another. Please give us a blessed time of celebration with our neighbors and friends today. We pray all these things in the name of our Lord and Savior, Jesus Christ. Amen."

Amens echoed across the green. The children grabbed their ribbons and took their places in the circle for the Maypole dance. Paul spread a blanket on the grass and waited until Milly took a seat, then he sat next to her. Alice plopped down on the other side of Milly, and Charlotte sat next to her. Ian stepped forward, intending to sit next to Charlotte, but James edged around him and quickly took that place.

Frustration coursed through Ian, but then Charlotte sent him an apologetic look. He sent her a slight nod and half smile, acknowledging her look. He would not let James spoil the day for him or Charlotte. He took a seat on the other side of James, sitting at an angle so he could see Charlotte. She smiled again, reassurance and affection in her eyes.

The drummer tapped out the beat, and the two accordion players and a fiddler joined in. The children circled the pole, first one way and then the other, dancing to the music and weaving the ribbons over and under each other.

Alice rose to her knees and pointed toward the top of the pole. "Look at the ribbons!"

They lifted their gazes, taking in the woven ribbons criss-crossing and creating a brightly colored pattern coming down the pole.

Ian studied Charlotte's face as she watched the children. Her smile and dancing eyes made it clear she was enjoying their performance.

The villagers clapped, and some stamped their feet in time with the music. Ian tapped his foot, enjoying the lively song. Delighted smiles filled the children's faces as they skipped, hopped, and wove their way around the pole and back in the time-honored dance, the same steps he had danced when he was young.

When the last notes of the song faded, the children bowed

and let go of the ribbons, which fluttered back to the pole. Everyone applauded, and the children melted into the crowd and rejoined their families.

"That was wonderful!" Charlotte's gaze darted around the group of friends, then rested on Ian.

He nodded. "Aye. It was a fine performance."

A troupe of Morris dancers jogged forward and formed two lines in the center of the green. Dressed in white shirts and trousers, black hats, and green suspenders crossing their chests, the men wore bells strapped around their calves and carried white handkerchiefs in their hands.

The leader called to his troupe, the musicians began the song, and the dancers stepped out in time to the music, waving their handkerchiefs and hopping from foot to foot. The bells jingled with each step, and soon the crowd was clapping and singing along as the dancers paraded across the green to the lively music.

They performed two more traditional dances, and the villagers responded with applause and cheers, then the Morris dancers marched off the green. The councilman thanked the performers, concluded the program, and invited everyone to stay and enjoy the afternoon.

Milly took the cloth napkin off the basket and began laying out the food she had prepared—roasted chicken, sausage rolls, Scotch eggs, sliced cheese, scones, jam, and gingerbread.

Paul's eyes widened. "My goodness, this looks like a feast!" He turned to Milly. "Did you make all of this?"

Milly's cheeks flushed. "Yes, but it was no trouble. I enjoy cooking."

Paul sent her an approving smile. "I'll be glad to taste it all."

Charlotte passed out the plates, and they helped themselves to the amazing array of food. Ian filled his plate and settled back on the blanket. Charlotte waited until the men had served themselves, then she helped Alice and filled her own plate.

While they ate, they all shared memories of past May Day festivals. Milly told about the time she and Ian had set up their own Maypole to practice the dance steps at home. Ian laughed as she recalled how the pole had come crashing down during their first session, barely missing them.

"I've never been to a May Day Festival," Charlotte added. "But I can see why everyone looks forward to it."

"So you're glad you came?" James asked.

Charlotte nodded, her gaze traveling past James and connecting with Ian. "Yes, very glad."

Paul wiped his mouth with his napkin. "I'm glad as well. This is one of the finest meals I've had in a long while. My compliments to you, Milly."

She sent him a pleased smile. "I'm glad you enjoyed it."

Mr. Donovan approached with a bald, middle-aged man Ian didn't recognize. "Good day, friends." Mr. Donovan glanced at their meal. "I'm sorry to interrupt your picnic, but I wanted to ask Charlotte if we could speak to her for a moment."

"Yes. Of course." Charlotte laid her napkin aside and rose.

Mr. Donovan motioned to the other man. "Charlotte, I'd like to introduce Mr. Harlow Matterly. He has recently come to Keswick to reopen his uncle's bookshop."

Charlotte held out her hand. "Mr. Matterly, I'm pleased to meet you."

Matterly pushed his spectacles up his nose, took her hand, and bowed slightly. "I'm glad to meet you as well. Mr. Donovan tells me you're looking for a position in a shop."

"Yes, sir, I am."

Matterly studied her. "He recommends you and says you're well-spoken and you have a good education."

She darted a glance at Mr. Donovan. "That's kind of him to say."

"Would you be able to come to the shop tomorrow and discuss the position?"

Charlotte glanced at Milly and Ian.

Before he could speak, his sister said, "I need to go to the village tomorrow. I'd be glad to take you."

Ian stifled a groan, wishing he'd been the one to offer her a ride.

Charlotte smiled at Milly, then returned her focus to Matterly. "What time would you like me to come?"

"Shall we say nine thirty?" He handed her a small card.

She accepted it. "Yes, that would be fine. I'll see you tomorrow."

"I'll look forward to it." Matterly bowed again and thanked Mr. Donovan. "Good day."

Charlotte resumed her seat on the blanket, looking a bit dazed.

Milly reached for Charlotte's hand. "See, I knew a position would open up for you! And a bookshop sounds ideal."

"I haven't been hired yet, Milly."

She beamed a smile at Charlotte. "I'm sure you will be."

A hopeful light glowed in Charlotte's eyes. "It would be a blessing."

Milly agreed, then passed around the plate of gingerbread. Ian took a slice and bit into the spicy treat. Working in a bookshop sounded like a good opportunity for Charlotte. He should be glad for her, but he couldn't help feeling a bit uneasy. If Charlotte earned a good salary, she and her mother and sister might leave the farm and move into the village. Then he'd probably only see her once a week on Sunday.

The gingerbread lodged in his throat, and he coughed.

Charlotte looked his way. "Are you all right?"

He coughed again. "Yes, I'm fine." But his voice croaked like a frog.

She passed him a jug of water. "Maybe this will help."

He took a long gulp. "Thanks." The water cooled his throat and calmed his cough, but it couldn't wash away his uneasy feelings.

The wind rushed past Charlotte's ears as she ran up the hill in search of Ian. Overhead, heavy clouds scuttled across the sky, carrying the threat of rain, but that wouldn't stop her. She clutched her shawl around her shoulder, brushed strands of hair from her face, and scanned the field above. Several sheep grazed on the rocky hillside, but she didn't see Ian. She ran on, determined to find him.

A few minutes later, she stopped and raised her hand over her eyes, searching the rugged pasture once more. Farther up, past an outcropping of large rocks, she spotted him moving a group of sheep. He carried his staff and called commands to his dog. The black-and-white border collie raced ahead and circled the sheep, rounding up two strays and herding them toward the rest of the flock.

"Ian!" she called, but her voice was swept away by the wind. She pressed on and called his name again. This time he stopped and looked in her direction, then lifted his hand and started down the hill toward her.

She continued up the steep hillside and met him halfway. "Hello!" she called, her breath catching on her words.

"Hello to you!" He searched her face. "Is everything okay?"

"Yes!" She couldn't hold back her smile. "I got the position!"

He smiled. "I knew you would. Matterly would be a fool not to hire you."

She laughed. "I'm not sure about that, but he needs an assistant, and I seem to fit what he's looking for."

"I'm happy for you, Charlotte." He spoke with conviction, but a hint of some other emotion flickered in his eyes. "When do you start?"

A ripple of unease passed through her, but she pushed it away. She needed this job, and she was grateful for it. "Tomorrow. He wants me to come in three or four days a week while he's setting up the shop, and when he opens in June, he'll give me more days and longer hours, especially around the convention."

"And what about the pay? Is it fair?"

"I think so." She told him the hourly rate Mr. Matterly had offered, and he nodded. "The shop has been closed for quite a while. Everything needs to be cleaned and organized before we can open."

"You'll do well with that. I'm sure he'll be glad he hired you."

His kind words warmed her heart. "As soon as he pays me, I want to give your family some money to cover our room and board."

He lifted his hand. "You don't need to do that."

"You've let us stay with you for more than a month. We're grateful, and we want to pay our way."

He shook his head slightly. "I suppose my father would appreciate it, but you must keep some back for yourselves." He looked across the field. "You'll need it in the future if you want to move to the village."

She looked down, trying to hide her disappointment. She thought he was growing to care for her and they might share a future together.

The wind picked up and whipped her skirts around her legs.

Ian glanced at the darkening sky. "We should go down. It's going to rain." As soon as the words left his mouth, raindrops began pelting their heads and shoulders.

A rush of wind blew past, and the sky opened. Charlotte gasped and tried to shield her face from the downpour.

He grabbed her hand. "Come on!" But rather than heading down the hill, he dashed across the field.

"Where are we going?" she called, her words almost blown away by the wind.

"Out of this rain!" He held tight to her hand as they ran past sodden clumps of heather and over the rough ground. The dog barked and raced along at their heels.

A large rock outcropping rose ahead of them at the edge of the field. He led her around the side and then ducked into an indentation in the rocks.

Panting, dripping, and laughing, they stood shoulder to shoulder and leaned back against the dry rock wall. Outside the overhanging rocks, the rain poured down and splashed on the ground.

"This is perfect," she said, raising her gaze to meet his. "How did you know about this place?"

He smiled at her with shining eyes. "I've been watching over our sheep since I was a boy. I know every inch of this land." Water dripped from his hair and ran down the side of his face, but he'd never looked more handsome. "I've ridden out a few storms here."

"I'm glad you found it." She swiped her damp hair from her forehead with the back of her hand and tried to quell her shivers.

"You must be cold." He took off his jacket and placed it around her shoulders. "This will help a little."

"Thank you." His jacket was warm and smelled like the fields and sunshine, a delightful scent that was uniquely Ian. "I must look like a drowned cat."

"Not at all." He gently ran his finger down the side of her cheek, brushing away the moisture. "I'm sorry we got caught in this storm."

"Don't be sorry." She lifted her hand and covered his, pressing it to her cheek. "I'm not."

A flash of surprise lit his eyes, then his gaze softened and traveled over her face. He seemed to be taking in each feature and treasuring them in his memory. His gaze dropped to her lips and then back to her eyes.

Her breath caught, and her heartbeat increased. Did he want to kiss her? Should she let him? The silent question lingered between them for another heartbeat, then a surge of tenderness for him filled her heart, and the answer was clear. She looked into his eyes, inviting him closer.

He whispered her name as he leaned down, then gently brushed his lips over hers. She rose on tiptoe, closed her eyes, and leaned into his kiss. His lips were warm, and his strong arms encircled her, holding her close. The powerful, sweet message flew straight to her heart. He cherished her, as she did him, and she'd gladly given him her first kiss.

He loosened his hold and stepped back with a look of awe and pleasure in his eyes. "That was . . ." He gave his head a slight shake.

"Yes . . . I'm not sure what to say." Her words sounded almost breathless.

He leaned in again and gently kissed her forehead. "There's no need to say anything more. Sometimes actions speak louder than words." His warm smile and glowing eyes seemed to say the kiss had been as meaningful to him as it had been to her.

Hope flooded her soul, washing away some of the pain of past betrayals. Finally, she'd met a man she could trust, someone who was honest and worthy of her love, and with that kiss, she had given her heart into his care.

Charlotte turned the lamp down low, quietly climbed into bed, and snuggled down in the blankets. She leaned back against her pillow, careful not to disturb Alice, who slept peacefully beside her. Opening her journal, she poured out her thoughts and described her interview with Mr. Matterly at the bookshop. Relief had filled her when he'd offered her the position and quoted the salary. Those funds would enable her to pay the Storey family for room and board and have some money left over for necessities. The rest she would save to provide security for herself, Mum, and Alice.

She turned the page, and her pen hovered over the top line. Should she write about meeting Ian on the hillside and describe the kiss they had shared? A thrill raced through her as she replayed the moment and recalled the tender look in his eyes. He'd been gentle, but she'd sensed the passion he'd held in check when he'd kissed her. He truly cared for her. It seemed too wonderful to believe.

Yet he hadn't made any promise about the future or said he loved her. But surely that was what he'd meant by that kiss. A small cloud of doubt rose and cast a shadow over her happy thoughts. Kissing him had seemed like the right thing to do at the time, but had she let her longing for love overrule her common sense? Should she have waited until they'd known each other longer and made sure of his commitment before she'd given him that kiss?

She lowered her pen to the page. *I kissed Ian today. . . . My first kiss, and it was wonderful. He is wonderful.*

The door opened, and Mum walked in.

Heat rushed in Charlotte's face, and she snapped the journal closed.

Questions appeared in Mum's eyes, and she dropped her gaze to the journal. "Is everything good?"

"Yes, of course." But Charlotte couldn't banish her discomfort. What would Mum say if she admitted she'd kissed Ian?

Mum studied her a moment more, then crossed the room and sat in the chair beside Charlotte's bed. A slight frown appeared on her face, and she clasped her hands in her lap. "I'm glad you're still awake. There is something important we need to discuss."

A jolt of panic shot through Charlotte. Had her mum somehow found out about the kiss?

"I know you're happy you've been offered the position at the bookshop." Mum kept her voice low, but Charlotte couldn't miss the concern in her tone. "But I'm not sure you should accept."

Charlotte released a shaky breath. "Why do you say that?"

"We don't really know Mr. Matterly."

"Mr. Donovan introduced us. I'm sure he wouldn't recommend me for the position if he had any concerns about Mr. Matterly's character."

"Mr. Donovan's introduction is the reason I consented to you going for the interview. But now that you've told me you'll be working alone with Mr. Matterly before the shop opens, I don't think it's wise for you to put yourself in a position that could damage your reputation."

Charlotte frowned. "How could it damage my reputation? Mr. Matterly is at least fifty! I can't imagine anyone thinking there would be anything improper between us."

"It doesn't have to make sense to start tongues wagging."

"But I've already accepted." Charlotte shifted to sit up straighter. "Why should I give up a perfectly good position just because some people might not approve?"

Mum sighed and rubbed her forehead. "I hear what you're saying, and we do need the income." Her shoulders sagged, and her voice sounded strained as she continued. "I suppose you may go ahead with it. We'll just have to pray and ask the Lord to watch over you and preserve your reputation."

Charlotte released a deep breath. "I'm sure He will."

Mum lowered her hand and met Charlotte's gaze. "Just promise me you will be very careful."

Charlotte nodded. "Of course."

"Your actions must always be above reproach. Don't give anyone a reason to spread gossip about you. And if you ever feel Mr. Matterly acts in a way that is . . . unbecoming, then you must end your association with him immediately. Do you understand?"

Charlotte gripped the pen, fighting the urge to argue with her mum. "I understand. I'll be careful."

Mum's serious expression eased into a weary smile. "Thank

you, Charlotte. I know I can trust you to honor your word and guard your actions. We may not have wealth or even a home of our own, but we have good reputations, and we wouldn't want to lose those."

A guilty wave flooded Charlotte, and a lump rose in her throat. Her mum trusted her to be discreet and honorable. Had she already broken that trust by kissing Ian?

Knowing how her mum felt about her position at the bookshop and the potential for gossip, she couldn't imagine telling her she'd given Ian her first kiss without any commitment or promise for the future.

Now another secret separated them. She'd kept the first to protect her mum from learning about her father's devastating betrayal. She would keep the second to protect herself from the embarrassment of letting her emotions overrule her common sense.

Seventeen

2012

David made it back to Longdale's gate in twelve minutes and raced up the drive, but halfway to the top he hit the brakes. A crowd of people carrying signs blocked his way and flooded out onto the front lawn.

Gwen gasped. "Look at all the people. What are we going to do?"

"I'll tell you what—I'm going to shut this down." He shoved open the door and climbed out.

"David, be careful." Gwen exited on her side.

He marched up the drive, parting the crowd as he headed toward the house. He scanned the signs as he passed. *Save the Lakes for Our Children. Preserve Our Fragile Ecosystem. Protect Our Lakes, Ban the Houseboats.* He shook his head and marched on.

As he came closer to the house, a man with a bullhorn lifted his hand and turned toward the crowd. "We must make our voices heard! We won't let them ruin this beautiful lake with a flotilla of tourist yachts!"

"That's right!" someone yelled from the crowd.

"Ban the houseboats!" a woman called.

His gut churned as he scanned the scene. Of all the nerve! The man with the bullhorn climbed his grandmother's front steps.

David strode forward and faced the man. "This is private property. You have no right to be here."

The man regarded him with a haughty glare, pointed at David, and announced, "There he is, Mr. David Bradford, the man behind the scheme to bring the houseboats to Derwent-water."

The crowd booed, and someone called out, "Shame on you! Don't you care about the environment?"

David mounted the steps and turned toward the crowd, lifting his hands to quiet them. "This is not the time or place to air your complaints. You're trespassing on private property, and you've frightened my grandmother, who has been an honored member of this community for more than twenty years."

Some people exchanged looks with each other and lowered their signs.

David straightened his shoulders. "We are willing to listen to your concerns at the next council meeting and discuss them there." He motioned toward the gate. "Now, I'm asking you to leave our property."

Voices passed through the crowd, and a few people on the edge turned to go.

The man with the bullhorn lifted it to his mouth. "We'll take our petition to the next council meeting and make sure they understand our opposition to the houseboats. I urge you all to join me there that night." With an angry huff, the man stalked down the steps, ignoring David. The crowd followed their leader across the grass and walked through the flower beds as they made their way down the hill.

Gwen felt like a fish swimming upstream as she passed through the crowd flowing down the drive. She scanned the group and guessed there were at least sixty protestors. Most had lowered their signs and were talking amongst themselves as they passed. She read a few of the signs' hand-lettered messages, and her heart sank.

With such strong opposition, how would David ever gain the council's approval? She hurried forward and spotted David standing in front of the double doors with his arms crossed. He watched the receding crowd with a fierce expression.

No one was going to get past him.

She had to smile. He'd spoken with authority but kept his cool when he confronted the protestors—and he'd convinced them to leave peacefully.

She climbed the front steps and met him by the door. "I think you handled that well."

His expression remained tense. "I might have convinced them to leave, but I'll have to face them again at the next council meeting."

"True, but at least you have time to prepare so you can answer their concerns."

His expression eased, and he shook his head. "I had no idea so many people would oppose the idea."

Gwen glanced down the drive. "Whoever is behind this has a great deal of influence in the community."

The door creaked open, and Lilly and Mrs. G. peeked out.

"Are they gone?" Lilly asked.

David turned. "Yes, Nana. I persuaded them to take their complaints to the council meeting."

Lilly stepped outside, pursed her lips, and scowled at the last few protestors trailing down the drive. "The gall of them coming to my home, waving their signs, and shouting their slogans!"

Concern filled David's eyes. "I'm sorry they frightened you, Nana."

"Frightened me?" She lifted her chin. "I was more angry than frightened. They had no right to bring their protest to Longdale."

Gwen suppressed a smile. Lilly certainly had spunk.

David slipped his arm around his grandmother's shoulders. "It's over now. Let's go inside and put it behind us." He guided her through the door and into the entry hall.

Mrs. G. stepped forward as they entered. "That was quite a ruckus out there. I'm glad you convinced them to leave."

David grimaced and shook his head. "I'm sorry they came here."

Mrs. G. lifted her finger. "Not to worry. Your grandmother and I took up brooms and canes. We were ready to defend the house."

Lilly nodded, then she rubbed her arms, as though trying to banish a chill. "Let's go in the library." She turned to Mrs. G. "Would you please bring us some tea?"

"I'll go put on the kettle."

"Thank you." Lilly lowered herself into a chair by the fireplace and turned to Gwen. "How was your visit, dear? Did you learn anything helpful?"

Gwen took a seat, wishing she had better news to share. "I showed Elizabeth the photo of my parents. She remembered my mother and confirmed the man in the photo is her son, Landon Monroe."

Lilly's eyes lit up. "That's wonderful. Did she tell you how to contact him?"

Gwen averted her gaze. "No, she hasn't seen him for a few years. She doesn't have his phone number or address."

"Oh dear. I'm sorry. I felt certain you were close to finding him."

"So did I." She glanced at David and then returned her gaze to Lilly, determined to focus on the good that had come from her visit. "But I found my grandmother, and she invited me to come back and meet my two aunts and some others in the family."

"That's very kind of her."

David settled back on the couch next to Gwen. "Elizabeth Monroe would like to visit Longdale to meet you and take a look at the journal."

"Charlotte Harper's journal?"

"Yes. She said one of her husband's relatives worked here a long time ago, and another married someone who lived here."

Lilly clasped her hands. "Oh, that's amazing. We'll have to look at the family tree and see if we can discover the connection. I'd welcome her visit."

A few minutes later, Mrs. G. walked in carrying a tea tray and placed it on the low table in front of the fireplace. "Thank you, Mrs. G. I'll pour."

"Very good." She nodded to Lilly and walked out.

Lilly filled teacups and passed them to David and Gwen. "David, I'm afraid this houseboat idea of yours is not going to float."

David coughed and almost spilled his tea. "I thought we were going to put that issue aside for now."

Lilly shook her head. "No, I think it's best if we talk it through."

David set his teacup aside. "Go on."

"I've lived at Longdale for more than twenty years, and it has taken me a long time to build friendships and find my place in the community. I don't want to see that destroyed because we're in a rush to repair the house."

"I'm afraid it's more complicated than that, Nana."

"I don't think it is. This is my home, and I want to preserve it, but I'm also part of the community. We can't forge ahead with our plans without considering the impact it will have on those who live around us. Our good standing with our friends is more important than quickly finishing the remodeling."

David released a deep breath. "So, you want me to drop the idea of bringing in the houseboats?"

Lilly nodded and offered a gentle smile. "You know I love you, and I appreciate all you're doing, but I don't want to make enemies of my neighbors." She motioned toward Gwen. "We'll have the funds from the auction in a few months. Surely that should be enough to pay for the renovations."

David focused on his grandmother with a serious expression. "As you wish. We'll cancel our plans for the houseboats and wait for the funds from the auction."

A queasy feeling rose in Gwen's stomach. Would the proceeds from the auction cover the renovation costs? She wished she could promise the income was certain . . . but there was no guarantee.

∽

David leaned on the terrace balustrade and looked toward the dark lake. A three-quarter moon hung low over the mountains, spreading a faint silver light on the quiet scene. In the shadowy gardens, glowworms winked their faint green lights. A cool breeze flowed past, and he crossed his arms. He should've grabbed his fleece.

It was almost eleven, but he hadn't been able to fall asleep. Too many thoughts had been cycling through his mind. It made more sense to get up and think things through than continue wrestling with his blankets and staring at the ceiling. He'd dressed, then quietly slipped downstairs and out to the terrace.

The quiet serenade of the crickets and peaceful setting usually calmed his mind, but tonight it only offered a dark backdrop as he replayed the afternoon's events. Facing those angry protestors and realizing he'd misjudged the situation stirred up all kinds of emotions.

He'd have to call Max in the morning and cancel the purchase of the houseboats. Closing his eyes, he pinched the bridge of his nose. He would look like a fool in Max's eyes for rushing ahead before he'd secured permission from the council. It would probably kill any hope of teaming up with him on future projects.

Why hadn't he seen this coming? His father had always said he was a dreamer who rushed ahead without considering the consequences.

Maybe he was right.

David blew out a deep breath. Those protestors had taught him a painful lesson. From now on, he would seek more advice and take time to consider the impact on others before he moved forward with his plans.

Soft footsteps sounded behind him, and he turned.

Gwen crossed the terrace toward him. She wore a long jersey over dark pants and a white shirt.

He swallowed and looked away. He didn't want to know what she thought of him after his royal blunder.

"Everything okay?" Her tone was gentle and caring.

"I couldn't sleep."

She stepped up beside him. "I'm sorry about the protest. I'm sure it's hard to let go of that idea."

"Yeah, it is."

She touched his arm, sending a wave of comfort flowing through him. "I admire how you looked for a creative way to finance your project."

He huffed. "Look where that took us."

She stepped closer, leaning her shoulder against his. "Sometimes a setback is simply a redirection."

Her words and touch eased some of his disappointment, but they didn't erase the consequences of his action. "Trying to bring in those houseboats was a crazy idea, and it put my grandmother in a difficult position. My plan failed, and we're no closer to financing the renovations than we were before."

"It wasn't a crazy idea. It's just not the right fit for this community. Don't be so hard on yourself. You're a good man, David."

He looked down, a bit embarrassed by her praise, but grateful she'd sensed his need for encouragement. It was time he stopped swimming in a pool of regret and let it go. He'd faced setbacks before, learned from them, and moved on. He could do it again, especially with someone like Gwen in his corner.

He turned to her, remembering he wasn't the only one who had faced a disappointing setback that day. "Why are you up so late?"

A faint smile lifted her lips. "I couldn't sleep either. I was reading more of Charlotte's journal."

He studied her, noting how the soft light from the gallery window highlighted the gentle contours of her face. He'd thought she was an attractive woman the first time they'd met, but as he'd gotten to know her, it was her inner qualities—her kindness, intelligence, and strong work ethic—that attracted him even more. They drew him toward her and made him want to know her better . . . and for all those reasons he might be falling in love with her.

He straightened, surprised by that thought, and cleared his throat. "Find anything interesting in the journal?

"Charlotte usually writes about simple things—what she's learning and doing at the farm with Ian—but . . . I don't know how to explain it. She thinks deeply about life and faith and comes to conclusions I hadn't considered."

His heart pinged, and he sensed the importance of her words. Was this the open door he'd been praying for? He shot off a prayer for wisdom. "What do you mean?"

"Charlotte's father betrayed his wife, and that almost destroyed Charlotte's faith. But during her time with the Storey family, she seemed to resolve those issues and find her way back to God."

"How did it happen?"

"I think talking to Ian helped, but it was more than that. I need to keep reading. I think it might help me resolve some of the things I've been wrestling with."

He sent her a soft smile. "I'd like to hear what you learn."

Her lips tipped up at the corners, and she looked at him with trust and moonlight in her eyes.

His throat tightened, and he gently ran his fingers down the side of her face. "You are a good woman, Gwen."

She smiled, obviously touched he was repeating what she'd said to him.

He looked into her eyes. "I appreciate your honesty and so much more."

"Thank you."

She was close enough that he could lean down and kiss her, and the look in her eyes seemed to invite him closer. The thought kicked his heartbeat to a faster pace. There was nothing he'd like more, but he sensed this wasn't the right time. He could wait. A day was coming when he would kiss her, and it would be a promise of much more.

A gust of wind blew past, and a sudden chill filled the air. He looked up and scanned the sky. Clouds rushed by, hiding the moon and stars. "It feels like rain is on the way."

He frowned toward the darkening sky. A few hours of wind and rain could mean more trouble for the already-leaking roof. Another gust of wind swirled around them, and large drops splashed around them. He grabbed her hand. "Come on."

They dashed inside, and the wind slammed the French doors behind them.

Eighteen

1912

Ian clicked to the horses, urging them over the bridge on the road to Keswick. He glanced at Charlotte, seated next to him, and his gut clenched. She hadn't said more than ten words to him that morning. When she'd climbed aboard the wagon for the ride to the village, she'd clutched her lunch basket in her lap and sat as far away from him as possible. Now, she gazed steadily off to the left, the silence between them growing more uncomfortable by the moment.

He fingered the reins, trying to make sense of her actions. Was she upset with him for some reason, or was she simply nervous about starting her new position at the bookshop?

She'd seemed so happy yesterday when she'd run up the hill and met him in the pasture. Then they'd been caught in the rain and dashed for shelter among the rocks. With the raindrops glistening in her eyelashes, and the sweet and trusting expression on her face, he'd wanted her to know how much he cared. He'd been thrilled when she'd lifted her face and invited his kiss. Her warm response made him believe her feelings matched his.

But today she seemed distant and enveloped by a cloud of worry, treating him more like a stranger than a beau.

Remaining silent wasn't going to solve the matter. He straightened his shoulders. "Charlotte, are you upset with me?"

She darted a glance at him, then quickly looked away. "Why do you ask?"

"Because yesterday I thought . . . you felt . . ." He huffed out a frustrated breath. Why couldn't he just tell her exactly what was on his mind?

Her cheeks flushed pink, and she stared straight ahead.

It was time to put aside his hesitation and settle matters between them. He directed the horses to the side of the road and stopped the wagon in the shade of a tall tree.

Charlotte sat still and silent, her gaze on the pasture to the left.

He shifted on the seat and turned toward her. "I care for you, Charlotte . . . very much. If I've done something to hurt or offend you, then you must tell me, so I can make it right."

She slowly looked his way, and he saw her eyes were misty. "I'm sorry, Ian. I shouldn't have kissed you."

Her words hit him hard, and he sucked in a breath. "I don't understand. I thought you felt the same way I do."

"We shouldn't let our feelings lead us." Pain flickered in her eyes, but she spoke with conviction. "We've only known each other a short time. A kiss should be an expression of a commitment. A promise."

He frowned as confusing thoughts battled in his mind. He did truly care for Charlotte. When they were together, he could be himself, and he sensed freedom and joy. But was he ready to make a lifetime commitment? How could he consider it when he still needed to finish his degree at Oxford and decide what path he would take in the future?

He searched her face, and his heart clenched. One thing was certain—he didn't just care for Charlotte. He loved her, and he couldn't imagine spending the rest of his life with anyone else.

He reached for her hand. "You're right, Charlotte. A kiss is special and should only be shared by those who love each other. That's why I kissed you. That's what I wanted you to know. I love you, and you are the only one I ever want to kiss."

She blinked, and her lips rose in a wobbly smile. "Really?"

He gave a firm nod. "And if you want to wait to share any more kisses, I can abide by that." He squeezed her hand. "I want you to be happy and feel safe with me. I won't let you down or mislead you. As soon as I'm able, we'll talk again and make plans for our future."

Her eyes widened. "Truly? You want us to . . . have a future together?"

"Yes, I do, and I hope that's what you want too."

Her gentle smile returned, and her eyes reflected a new level of openness and trust. "It is."

Relief washed over him, and he smiled. "Good. I'm glad that's settled."

She scooted toward him and tucked her arm through his. "So am I."

A rush of happiness flowed through him. He lifted the reins, and the horses trotted forward. "I want you to know you can always talk to me about anything that concerns you. We must never let misunderstandings separate us."

She nodded, but he sensed her hesitation.

"You can ask me anything, Charlotte. I'll always be honest with you."

She nodded again. "Honesty is important."

"Very important. Like good soil, water, and sunshine are for crops and flocks."

She laughed softly. "I should've known you would think of it that way."

He grinned. "I suppose I'll always think of life in those terms. Valley View is in my blood."

"I love that about you. And whether you decide to take over

the farm or become a world-famous archaeologist, this land and your family's heritage will always be a part of you."

He sat up straighter, and his grin spread wide. "Yes, they will."

It meant a great deal that Charlotte appreciated his family's way of life. Most of his friends at Oxford poked fun at his country upbringing. To them, farming was far less worthy than an archaeological career. But not Charlotte, and that made her even more dear to him.

As they rounded the bend and the first few houses in the village came into view, she slipped her arm out of his and shifted a few inches away. He glanced at her.

"I don't want to cause any gossip, for your sake or mine."

"I understand." He wanted to guard her reputation and would do his part.

Two more turns, and they arrived at Matterly's Bookshop. Ian pulled the horses to a stop and hopped down. He hustled around the wagon, then reached for Charlotte and helped her climb down. Rather than letting go, he held her hand tight.

She smiled up at him. "Thank you for the ride."

"I'm glad to do it." He glanced past her shoulder at the darkened bookshop. A *Closed* sign hung in the window. "Do you think Mr. Matterly is here?"

She turned. "He should be. He said to come at nine and use the rear door."

"Why don't I go in with you?"

She lifted her eyebrows. "If you like."

"I would. I think it would be good to let Mr. Matterly know you have someone watching out for you."

She looked down, but that didn't hide her smile. They walked around the building and entered through the back door.

"Hello, Mr. Matterly," Charlotte called.

"I'm up front," he replied.

Ian followed her through the back storeroom and out into the main sales room.

Mr. Matterly stood on a step stool, holding a stack of books. "Good morning!" His cheerful greeting reached them before they crossed the room.

Charlotte motioned to Ian. "This is Mr. Ian Storey. We're staying with his family on their farm west of the village. He gave me a ride in this morning."

"That was very kind." Mr. Matterly shifted his gaze to Ian. "I'm glad to meet you, Mr. Storey."

Ian nodded to him. "I'm happy to meet you as well. Please, call me Ian." He glanced around the shop. "It looks like you have a good selection of books."

"That we do, and more are on order from London." He climbed down and crossed to the counter.

Ian skimmed a few titles on the closest shelf. "Do you have any books on archaeology or Egyptian history?"

Mr. Matterly's eyebrows rose. "Well now, those are certainly interesting subjects."

"That's the focus of my studies at Oxford. I've taken some time off to help my family on the farm, but I'd like to continue my studies while I'm at home."

Mr. Matterly looked down at the boxes of books at his feet. "I haven't come across any books on those topics yet, but I've just started sorting and rearranging our inventory."

"I can look for books about Egypt and archaeology while I'm working," Charlotte added.

"Thank you. I'd be grateful." Ian turned to Mr. Matterly. "What time shall I come back for Charlotte?"

"Oh, there's no need. I can give her a ride home. I'll be headed out that way to have dinner with the Langley family around five. I don't mind dropping Charlotte off."

Ian hesitated, wishing he could return for Charlotte and share the ride home, but that didn't seem reasonable with Mr. Matterly's offer. "Very well." He touched his cap and turned to Charlotte. "I'll see you this evening."

She sent him a sweet smile and thanked him again for bringing her to the bookshop.

Ian glanced back at the shop as he stepped outside. Mr. Matterly seemed like a decent fellow, but he still felt a bit uneasy about leaving Charlotte there with him. He supposed he was feeling protective. But more than that, he'd made a commitment to her. She had an important place in his life, and he didn't like to be apart from her.

Charlotte settled on her bed and unfolded the note Ian had slipped into her hand after dinner. The room was quiet now. Mum was out in the sitting room with Jenny and Milly, working on a knitting project, and Alice slept beside her.

A smile formed on her lips as she focused on Ian's note and read it silently.

Dear Charlotte,

In the last three weeks, ever since you began working at the bookshop, I've realized in a deeper way how important you are to me. Before that, I'd grown accustomed to walking in from farm chores and finding you busy in the kitchen. You always greeted me with a cheerful smile and words of encouragement that brightened my day. When we took walks around the farm, you often exclaimed over things I'd seen all my life and taken for granted. You opened my eyes to appreciate what is all around me. When you're gone, you are constantly in my thoughts, and I miss you very much.

But I am proud of you for taking on this new position at the bookshop. I'm not surprised that Mr. Matterly appreciates your diligent work and positive attitude. He is blessed to have you there, as I am blessed to have you here when you're not working.

I look forward to our rides into the village and picking you up each day. Knowing I have that time with you keeps me looking forward with hope for the future.

> *With sincere affection,*
> *Ian*

She read the note again, savoring each thoughtful word. He had been very caring and attentive since she'd started working at the bookshop. They hadn't shared any more kisses, but there had been several secret smiles and loving looks. He'd shown her in many ways that his feelings for her were sincere, and she felt her heart knitted to his more each day.

He hadn't said anything more about returning to Oxford in the fall, and she'd begun to think he might postpone it indefinitely . . . or perhaps she was just hoping he would. She would miss him terribly if he did leave. She pushed that painful thought away, folded the note, and slipped it into her journal.

Her thoughts shifted to the bookshop and all she'd learned since she'd started working for Mr. Matterly. She'd spent several days dusting and labeling every shelf, then cataloguing and pricing hundreds of books. Two shipments had arrived from London, which filled in some of the categories that were not well represented.

She loved opening those crates and looking through the books as she shelved them. She could easily be tempted to spend all her earnings on books if she didn't need to save for essentials and pay the Storeys for their room and board.

Mr. Matterly had proven to be a kind employer. He loved books even more than she did, and he often stopped to read one that interested him. When she noticed he had become lost in a book, she would ask him a question. Then he would usually laugh and say, "Well, then, I must get back to work!" It had almost become a game between them.

The first day at the bookshop, he'd asked about her family and what brought them to Keswick. She'd given a brief explanation. As they became better acquainted, she'd told him more about their situation, but she hadn't revealed the truth about her father. She kept that shameful secret locked in her heart. The only people she'd told were Mr. Donovan and Ian, and both times had been painful and difficult.

She opened her journal. This was a safe place to pour out her thoughts and wrestle through the emotions that still troubled her. On these pages she could be honest and share her deepest feelings. She took up her pen and let the words flow.

Charlotte checked the clock on the bookshop wall once more, and a growing sense of unease filled her. Ian had promised to come for her at four thirty, and it was ten minutes past five. She ran the dust cloth over the nearest shelf, then glanced at Mr. Matterly. "I don't know what's become of Ian. He should be here by now."

Mr. Matterly looked up from his book. "You told him you'd be finished at four thirty?"

"Yes, I did."

"I could give you a ride home if you'd like."

She glanced at the clock again, debating her answer.

Mr. Matterly stepped out from behind the counter. "He probably just got busy with a task at the farm and didn't realize how much time had passed. I wouldn't worry."

Charlotte clutched the dust cloth. How could she not worry? It wasn't like Ian to leave her waiting. In fact, he usually came early and seemed eager to share the ride home with her. But not today.

She released a sigh. "I hate to ask you to drive me all the way out to Valley View."

"I don't mind at all. It's a lovely day for a drive." He took his hat and jacket from the hook on the wall.

"Thank you." Charlotte pinned on her straw hat, then followed Mr. Matterly out the back door. Questions flowed through her mind as she climbed into his one-horse carriage. Had Ian just been busy and forgotten to come for her? That certainly didn't seem like a very caring way to treat her. Had something happened to his parents or sister . . . or Mum, or Alice? She hoped he hadn't become ill or had an accident out in the fields.

Please, Lord, don't let that be the reason!

She gripped the edge of the carriage seat and leaned forward, wishing Mr. Matterly would drive faster.

The ride to the farm seemed to take twice as long as usual. They crossed the stone bridge and rounded the bend in the road, and the farmhouse came into view in the distance. She quickly scanned the farmyard and lower pasture, but she didn't see Ian or anyone else. As they drove closer to the house, she spotted a shiny black motorcar parked by the front walk.

"It looks like the Storeys have a visitor." Mr. Matterly nodded to the motorcar. "Perhaps that's the reason Ian was delayed."

"He didn't mention they were expecting guests, but they do rent their guest rooms to people on holiday." Even if that were the case, why would unexpected guests prevent Ian from coming for her?

"Well, you'll know soon enough." Mr. Matterly pulled the carriage to a stop behind the motorcar.

Charlotte hopped down. "Thank you for the ride."

"You're welcome. I'll see you on Monday." He touched the brim of his hat, lifted the reins, and headed off.

She turned and hurried up the path toward the house. As she came closer, voices drifted out the open window—a deep, hearty voice, followed by soft, feminine laughter. She pushed open the front door, stepped inside, and took a quick glance around the sitting room.

Mr. and Mrs. Storey, Milly, Alice, and Mum were all gathered there. Ian stood by the fireplace and to his left sat a young blond woman in a stylish light green traveling suit and an elaborate matching hat covered with feathers and flowers. She looked up at him with an admiring smile, and he returned an equally warm look.

A warning shot through Charlotte.

Beside the young woman sat a distinguished, middle-aged man with a black moustache and beard. He wore an expensive-looking black suit.

They all turned toward Charlotte, and the conversation stalled.

Ian's eyes flashed, and he straightened. "Charlotte!" He pulled out his pocket watch and then looked up at her. "I didn't realize the time. How did you get home?"

He offered no explanation or apology? She fixed her gaze on Ian. "Mr. Matterly gave me a ride."

Ian's face went ruddy, and he motioned to the middle-aged man. "This is Professor Giles Montrose, from Oxford, and his daughter, Genevieve Montrose."

Charlotte recalled Ian telling her about the professor, but he hadn't mentioned his attractive daughter. She nodded to them. "How do you do."

Genevieve Montrose's gaze swept over Charlotte. "And you are?"

"Oh, I'm sorry." Ian stumbled over his words. "This is Charlotte Harper. . . . She . . . she and her mother and sister are staying with us."

Charlotte's heart twisted. That was all she was to him—a houseguest?

"I see." Genevieve met Charlotte's gaze for only an instant, then with a dismissive lift of her chin, she turned back to Ian.

"We're so looking forward to our trip. You really must come with us. Father needs your assistance, and it would give you the hands-on experience you need for your thesis."

Mr. Storey huffed and crossed his arms. Jenny's worried gaze flitted from her husband to Ian. Milly shot Charlotte an anxious glance.

"Your expenses would all be covered," the professor added, "since you'd be working as my assistant in Egypt."

Charlotte gasped. *Egypt*!

Ian locked gazes with the professor. "All my expenses?"

The professor nodded. "Your passage, food, and lodging would be provided. Of course, any extra outings would be at your own expense."

A look of wonder filled Ian's face. He looked from Genevieve to the professor. "When would we set sail?"

Charlotte's heart plummeted.

"We depart on the twenty-first of June and return in late August." The professor's voice filled with enthusiasm. "Just think of it! You'll not only see the wonders of Egypt, you'll also be part of the dig that could lead to some very important discoveries."

Ian's smile lit up his face. "That would be amazing."

Charlotte stared at him. How could he agree to go to Egypt when his family still needed his help? And what about his promises to her? Didn't they mean anything to him?

Genevieve sent him a fetching smile and reached for his hand. "This is the chance of a lifetime, Ian. Say you'll come."

Charlotte's gaze darted to their clasped hands, and pain pierced her heart. No well-bred young woman would be so bold and familiar without there being an understanding between them. What promises had he made to Genevieve? Had he kissed her as well?

A burning sensation rose in Charlotte's throat, and she swallowed hard. Ian had wooed her and told her he loved her. He'd kissed her and talked about them having a future together. When all the while he had a sweetheart waiting for him at Oxford.

She'd believed him and given him her heart. How could she have been such a fool?

Ian walked with the professor and Genevieve down the path toward the professor's motorcar. His father glared at him as he hustled past and headed for the barn.

Ian clenched his jaw. This was not going to be an easy decision. Someone—or most likely several people—would be upset with him whichever choice he made.

When they reached the motorcar, Genevieve turned to him. "We've already booked our passage on the ship. If you're going to have a room near us, then we must reserve it soon."

"Genevieve is right," the professor added in a serious tone. "Summer voyages fill up quickly. We need to finalize our plans." He took a step, then turned back. "If you can't go, I'll have to find someone else to fill that position. Jonathan Abbington would be my second choice."

Genevieve rolled her eyes and sighed. "Really, Father?"

"He's not Ian's equal," the professor continued, "but he could do an adequate job. This is an important endeavor," the professor continued. "I hope you'll consider all the ramifications for your future before you make a decision."

Ian reached out and shook the professor's hand. "I'll give it careful thought and let you know soon."

The professor nodded. "I'll be waiting to hear from you." He walked around the motorcar to the driver's side.

Ian's thoughts spun as he opened the passenger door for Genevieve. For years he'd longed to see those ancient ruins and take part in a real dig, and this one might even prove the existence of Joseph. Taking part would give him respect in the archaeology community and help launch his career.

But what would Charlotte think of the idea? And how could he leave for the entire summer when he'd promised his father he'd stay at Valley View to help with the work?

Rather than climbing in, Genevieve stepped toward him and laid her hand on his chest. "This will be a wonderful experience for us to share. Can't you just see us dancing on the deck in the moonlight?"

The breeze carried her perfume toward him, and his heartbeat quickened.

She sent him a teasing smile. "Don't disappoint me, Ian. I'd hate to go to Egypt without you. . . ." She rose on tiptoe and placed a kiss on his cheek.

He blinked, surprised by her familiarity. She'd always been friendly when they'd spent time together at Oxford, but never forward. Perhaps she hoped her feminine charms would persuade him to join them. Their gazes met and held a moment more, then she slid into the seat.

Conflicting thoughts rushed through his mind. He had considered calling on Genevieve when he returned to Oxford, but now that he'd met Charlotte, he'd put that idea out of his mind. He watched Genevieve as the motorcar's engine roared to life. She waved and sent him a coy smile.

Ian lifted his hand as the motorcar pulled away. Going to Egypt with the professor didn't mean he had to become involved with Genevieve. He could keep his commitment to Charlotte . . . couldn't he?

Charlotte crossed to the sitting room window as Ian walked the professor and Genevieve out the door. She shouldn't watch them, but she had to see how they would end the visit. Perhaps she'd misread the situation and had no reason to doubt Ian's promises to her.

When they reached the motorcar, Ian and Genevieve stood together, talking. Charlotte strained to hear their conversation through the open window, but they were too far away.

The professor looked intent, and he was likely again urging Ian to join the expedition. His daughter's eyes never left Ian. Her hopeful expression and nearness to Ian made her feelings for him clear. Every smile and gesture seemed designed to lure him toward her.

Charlotte's stomach twisted into a tight knot.

Ian didn't step back or seem put off by Genevieve's actions. His gaze remained on her or the professor, looking as if he was soaking in their words.

Was he even now agreeing to go with them? The offer of an expense-paid trip to Egypt and the opportunity to advance his archaeology studies would be difficult to refuse.

But his family needed him here. She needed him.

Genevieve stepped closer to Ian and placed her hand on his chest. Charlotte had to stifle the urge to call out to Ian. Then Genevieve rose on tiptoes and kissed Ian's cheek.

Charlotte gasped and covered her mouth. That confirmed the truth. Ian had never loved her. He'd lied to her and betrayed her . . . just like her father had betrayed her mother.

Heartsick, she stepped back from the window and fled to her room.

Nineteen

1912

Ian stomped off his boots outside the door and walked into the house. The savory scent of bacon and toast greeted him as he glanced around the kitchen. Everyone except Charlotte was seated at the breakfast table.

His stomach contracted as he crossed to the sink and washed his hands. Where was she? Why hadn't she come out to do morning chores with him as she always did? It wasn't like her to sleep in, even though she wasn't scheduled to work at the bookshop that day. He walked over to the table and took a seat.

"Morning, brother." Milly's tone made it clear she was not happy with him.

"Morning." He bowed his head, praying silently for an answer to his dilemma, but there seemed to be no way around disappointing his family.

What am I to do, Lord?

He waited while his stomach rumbled, then ended the prayer feeling just as uneasy as when he'd begun. Stifling a groan, he buttered a piece of toast, then scooped up a bite of eggs.

Mum passed Mrs. Harper the platter of bacon. "I hope Charlotte is feeling better this morning."

The eggs lodged in Ian's throat. He coughed and looked up. "Charlotte is still unwell?"

Her mother glanced toward the hall leading to their room. "She is up and dressed. I think she'll join us soon."

He hadn't seen Charlotte since the professor and Genevieve left yesterday. When she didn't come to dinner last night, he'd been concerned and asked about her. Mrs. Harper said Charlotte had a headache and was resting in her room. Milly had taken her a tray, but she brought it back a short time later, untouched.

He took a bite of toast and chewed, but it tasted like sawdust in his mouth. If only she would come out and talk to him, he could explain how this trip would strengthen his ties in the archaeology community and open doors for him—doors that could make it possible for him to support a wife and a family in the future.

Footsteps sounded on the plank floor in the hall. He looked up, and Charlotte appeared in the doorway to the kitchen. She stopped on the threshold, then crossed to the open seat across from him.

Her face looked pale, and gray shadows hung in half circles beneath her eyes.

His chest tightened, and determination coursed through him. As soon as she finished eating, he would ask to speak to her and make things right between them.

He held out the plate of toast to her. "How are you feeling this morning?"

She slowly lifted her gaze to meet his. "I'll be all right." Her words sounded cool and aloof, and distrust glittered in her eyes.

Pain shot through him like a burning arrow. Charlotte was not simply unwell—she was hurt and angry.

He swallowed hard, returning Charlotte's gaze, imploring her to understand, but she looked away. A sense of urgency, verging on panic, flooded through him. They had to talk. He had to make her understand.

The sound of horses and carriage wheels came through the open window. Ian lifted his head and exchanged glances with his family.

"Who could that be?" his mum asked.

"I'll see to it." His father crossed the room and pulled the door open. Outside, a carriage fit for royalty rolled into view and stopped in front of the house. The driver in a black cape and tall black hat climbed down and slowly made his way up the walk.

Mrs. Harper gasped. "That's Mr. Green, my father's driver." She rose from her chair and hurried to the door.

The gray-haired driver stopped just outside the door, removed his hat, and held out an envelope. "Mrs. Harper, this is a message from your father's physician."

She took the envelope with trembling hands and ripped it open.

Charlotte crossed to stand by her mother and took her arm.

Alice hurried to join them. "What does it say, Mum?"

Mrs. Harper's gaze darted over the message, then she looked up. "Your grandfather has been injured in a bad fall, and he asks us to come."

Charlotte gasped. "He wants us to call on him?"

"No, he wants us to come and stay at Longdale." An amazed expression filled Mrs. Harper's face as she glanced at the message again. "He has reconsidered my request for us to live at Longdale."

"Oh my goodness." Ian's mum lifted her hand to her heart. "I'm sorry he's been injured, but perhaps it has softened his heart."

Mrs. Harper lowered the letter. "Yes, I think this invitation is an answer to our prayers." Tears filled her eyes, and she turned to Charlotte. "We must pack at once."

Charlotte's forehead creased. "Do you think he's truly put aside his hard feelings about the past, or does he simply need our help?"

"He has a house full of servants who can care for him. But even if he's asking us to come because he needs our help, I still want to go."

Charlotte's gaze swept the room, uncertainty in her eyes.

Ian clenched his jaw. What could he say? They needed a permanent home, and Charlotte's grandfather seemed willing to provide that for them.

"I've asked the Lord to help us reconcile," Charlotte's mum continued. "I shouldn't be so surprised when He answers those prayers."

Mr. Green nodded, a slight smile on his wrinkled face. "I've been instructed to wait for you, ma'am, if you're willing to come."

Mrs. Harper wiped her eyes. "Yes, please wait. It will only take us a short time to pack."

"Very good, ma'am." Mr. Green replaced his hat and walked down the path toward the carriage.

Alice wrapped her arms around her mother. "Oh, Mum, I'll finally get to meet my grandfather!"

Mrs. Harper laughed and pulled Alice closer. "Yes, my dear, you will." She glanced at Charlotte. "I hope his injuries are not too serious, but whatever the case, we'll do all we can to speed his recovery."

Charlotte nodded, but her worried gaze darted to Milly and Ian once more.

He rose from his chair, his breakfast barely touched, and crossed to the sink. The plan had always been for Charlotte, her mum, and sister to eventually leave Valley View. But how could he let her go with everything so unsettled between them?

Charlotte slipped her journal into the folds of her shawl and placed them both in the bottom of the trunk. She straightened and rested her hand over her uneasy stomach. With the arrival of the letter from her grandfather's physician and the surprising invitation to move to Longdale, she hadn't even touched her breakfast. Everything about her life had changed so quickly, it made her feel strangely off balance, especially after discovering Ian's duplicity and involvement with Genevieve.

Alice took her dresses from the pegs on the wall, while Mum folded a petticoat and placed it in the trunk. She glanced at Charlotte. "I hung a few items out on the line earlier this morning. Would you bring those in?"

"Do you think they'll be dry?"

"Probably not, but we can hang them up at Longdale." A hopeful light shone in Mum's eyes, and she seemed eager to be on their way to her childhood home.

Charlotte left the bedroom, pondering the optimism in Mum's voice. She couldn't share those same feelings, not after what had happened with Ian. Maybe moving to Longdale would help ease the pain. At least she wouldn't have to see Ian every day and be reminded of how he'd broken her heart.

She pushed open the back door, and a fresh breeze greeted her. She stopped and scanned the view. Sheep dotted the valley pasture, peacefully feeding on the lush green grass. The steep mountains rose beyond, rugged and majestic, reaching up to the cloudless sky. Her throat tightened, and her vision misted.

She'd grown to love their life at Valley View. Closing her eyes, she scolded herself. She was only a guest, not family. Staying with the Storeys had always been a temporary solution. Today they would leave Valley View behind, and she would have to adjust to another new situation.

She walked toward the clothesline, the weight of worries slowing her steps. What would life be like at Longdale? How would they spend their days? Her grandfather's lakeside estate was certainly more luxurious than Valley View. He had a large staff of servants to care for the house and gardens.

But would there be honest laughter and warm conversation around the table? Would she be able to continue working at the bookshop, or would she have to resign before the shop opened?

Her grandfather had been so stern and unyielding when they'd visited before. He would certainly have an opinion and want her to comply since she would be living in his home and under his rules.

Doubts shadowed her thoughts as she plucked the first blouse off the line. Then she recalled their prayers and the way they'd asked God to intercede for them and give them a permanent home. Mum had humbled herself and taken responsibility for her past choices. She hoped her grandfather would do the same.

If only she could talk it through with Ian. Pain ricocheted through her, and bitterness singed her throat. She would never discuss this move or anything else with him. He had hidden his relationship with Genevieve and misled her about his intentions. She had believed every word he'd said and told him her deepest secrets—and she'd kissed him!

That kiss wasn't entirely his fault. She had to share part of the blame for her bruised heart. She was the one who had dreamed of finding a faithful man who could live up to the image she had created of her father before she discovered his betrayal.

Ian wasn't that man. She swallowed hard, trying to dislodge a lump in her throat as she jerked her dress from the clothesline.

"Charlotte."

She froze, then steeled herself and slowly turned to face Ian.

He walked toward her. "I'm glad I found you. I wanted to speak to you in private before you go."

She clutched the damp dress to her chest and remained silent.

He scanned her face, questions reflected in his eyes. "I wanted to ask your thoughts about the trip to Egypt."

"Why would you ask me?"

He blinked in surprise. "Because . . . I want to know what

you think . . . how you feel about the idea of me accepting the position."

She pulled in a deep breath, trying to steady her roiling emotions. "Where you go and what you do doesn't matter to me." She turned away and plucked the next dress from the line.

"Charlotte, why would you say that? I thought we had an understanding."

"Did you?" She swung around. "Well, you have an unusual way of showing it."

His jaw dropped, and his expression looked so incredulous he almost fooled her, but then the memory of him holding Genevieve's hand and accepting her kiss replayed through her mind.

He stepped toward her. "I understand why you might be upset, but you haven't given me a chance to explain why I want to go."

She stepped back. "I know very well why you want to go and who would be traveling with you."

His face turned ruddy, and his voice matched her intensity. "Is that right?"

She glared at him, silently daring him to explain his way out of the choices he had made.

"Since we haven't spoken one word about it," he said in a clipped tone, "I don't see how you could draw any conclusions."

"I don't need to speak to you. I've seen the real reason with my own eyes."

"What do you mean?"

"I mean you obviously have feelings for Genevieve Montrose!"

He pulled back. "What?"

She scoffed. "Don't pretend you don't know what I'm talking about."

"You mean because she was friendly toward me?"

"She was more than friendly, and you had no problem with it."

He shook his head. "Genevieve is the daughter of my mentor. I've had dinner in their home a few times. We're friends. That's all."

"Well, friends don't grab hold of each other or share a kiss!"

A flash of anger sparked in his eyes. "I didn't kiss her!"

Charlotte spun away, her heart pounding, and pulled an apron from the line.

"Don't turn your back on me!" Ian strode around to face her.

She glared at him. "Don't tell me what to do!"

He closed his eyes, obviously trying to rein in his temper. "Genevieve is outgoing and freely expresses herself, but there is nothing more between us."

Charlotte shook her head. "I don't believe you. I know what I saw, and I'll not be fooled again!"

The muscles in his jaw rippled, and he straightened to his full height. "I'm telling the truth, Charlotte."

She grabbed the last dress from the line and strode toward the house. She could never trust or love a man who was not totally faithful. Misleading her was one thing; lying about it took his betrayal to a whole new level.

Ian's senses reeled as Charlotte disappeared through the back door. Why wouldn't she believe him? He had considered calling on Genevieve, but that was months ago, before he'd met Charlotte. His stomach swirled, and sweat broke out on his forehead. Had Charlotte truly just ended their courtship?

He stomped across the farmyard and headed for the barn. Charlotte was wrong to make assumptions and call him a liar. If that was what she thought of him, then she could just go to Longdale and make a new life for herself. He would accept the professor's offer and leave for Egypt with nothing holding him back. He'd dance with Genevieve by moonlight and take part in his first real dig.

He shoved open the barn door and trudged down the center aisle. He'd come home and worked hard for the last four months, and he'd done it all without encouragement or appreciation from his father. It was time to focus on fulfilling his own dreams and travel to Egypt—even if it meant disappointing his family and leaving Charlotte behind.

He grabbed a pitchfork and speared a pile of dirty hay, expecting to feel relieved now that he'd settled the issue in his mind, but the longed-for peace didn't come. Instead, images of Charlotte, her eyes glittering with hurt and distrust, filled his mind.

He clenched his jaw, determined to erase those images and all thoughts of her. But how could he? She had become a part of him, and dislodging her felt like ripping out a piece of his own heart.

Twenty

2012

Gwen walked into the great hall and looked up at the ceiling. A drop splashed on her arm, and she repositioned a bucket under the leak. Her spirits sagged as she glanced at the other containers they had placed around the hall to catch the rainwater.

She and David had stayed up half the night, setting out pots and buckets and emptying them as the storm blew through. After three, the wind and rain slowed, and they went up to their rooms to get a few hours of sleep before breakfast. Now they were back at the task, trying to save the beautiful hardwood floor from permanent damage.

Lilly walked into the hall, followed by Mrs. G., who pulled a rolling bucket and mop. Outside, the steady rain continued. "We simply must find a way to fix the roof!" Lilly exclaimed. "That has to be done before we start any other renovations."

Mrs. G. squeezed out the mop and glanced at Gwen. "It's a good thing you and David realized what was happening and rolled up the carpets."

She smiled, remembering how she and David had worked together to protect the house through the storm. It had made her almost feel as if she was part of the family—as if she had a true stake in preserving Longdale. Of course, that wasn't true, but it had been a wonderful feeling, especially when David had looked at her with shining eyes and said he couldn't have done it without her. She released a soft sigh as the memory faded. Who would've imagined rolling up rugs and running for buckets could be so romantic?

"Gwen, would you move that pail to the side?" Mrs. G.'s words brought Gwen back to the moment, and she shifted the metal pail out of the way.

Mrs. G. passed the mop over the damp floor with careful light swipes. "I'll call my husband and ask him to come and help take the carpets downstairs. We can hang them up to dry in the laundry room."

"I hope they aren't too wet." Lilly looked up at the ceiling.

"They're just a bit damp," Gwen said. "David and I got them out of the way as soon as we discovered the leaks."

"That's a relief. I'm so glad you were up when that storm started. What time was it, dear?"

"Just after eleven." The timing had given them a few special moments together on the terrace beforehand. The growing connection between them was undeniable. At one point, his gaze had lingered, and she thought he wanted to kiss her. But then the rain had started, the moment was broken, and they'd run inside.

Maybe they hadn't shared a kiss, but they were getting closer to crossing that bridge. She was sure of it. Her heart warmed with a surprising sense of delight. She was ready. David was an honest, caring, and sincere man, and her heart was drawn toward his more each day.

The front door opened, bringing a gust of cold air and shower of raindrops. David hustled inside and quickly closed the door. He wore a plaid cap, a dripping-wet, dark green raincoat, and knee-high wellies. He wiped his feet on the entry rug, then stepped onto the black-and-white tile.

"Stay right there," Lilly called. "I'll get you a towel."

David tossed his cap onto the bench, slipped off his raincoat, and hung it on the doorknob to drip off. Then he pulled off his boots and crossed the hall toward them in stocking feet.

Lilly shook her head. "Mrs. G., can you take care of that?"

"I'm on the way." She hauled the bucket across the room toward the front door to clean up the drips.

David wore a serious expression as he approached Lilly and Gwen. "A big limb blew off the oak tree and landed on the roof." He pointed up. "Right above us. That's why we have all these new leaks."

"Oh dear." Lilly gazed at the ceiling. "Is it still up there?"

David nodded. "It's caught on the slate tiles."

Lilly rubbed her upper arms, looking as though she was chilled at the thought. "How will we get it down? And what about the roof? It must be repaired as soon as possible."

"I called a roofer to come and give us an estimate. He should be here around noon if the rain stops. Maybe he'll help me pull down the limb."

"There is a ladder in the gardener's toolroom," Lilly continued. "What else do you need?"

"Some rope and a power saw to cut it up once it's down." He swiped his hand down his damp face.

Gwen's heart clenched. Hauling a tree limb off the roof sounded like a daunting job. "Maybe I can help."

David glanced her way. "Thanks, Gwen, but I wouldn't want you climbing up on the roof. The slate is slick and dangerous."

She didn't like the idea of climbing up there either, but she hated to think of him tackling the job alone. Hopefully, the roofer would help him. "When the branches are on the ground, I can cut and stack wood with you."

He grinned. "I'll take you up on that." But then his grin faded, and he shook his head. "On second thought, I don't want to slow down your work on the appraisals."

She grimaced. "Right." She'd rather go outside and help David, but he had a point. She'd already taken some time off to visit Elizabeth Monroe and search online for information about her father. The sooner she finished her work, the sooner they would have the funds they needed to repair the roof and start the renovations.

"Oh no." Lilly pointed to the right, where a small puddle had formed at the foot of the stairs. "I'm afraid we have another leak."

Gwen and David exchanged a glance, and she could read the discouragement in his eyes. "I'll grab a bucket." She hurried across the room, following Mrs. G., who toted the mop.

With a worried frown, David scanned the high arched ceiling. Gwen's heart ached as she watched him. All his plans to renovate Longdale would have to be put on hold until he solved this new problem. But it would probably be terribly expensive to repair or replace a slate roof, even if they only did a portion of the house.

She had to find some way to help him get the funds he needed sooner rather than later. If she had the money, she'd gladly loan it to him, but she was still paying off student loans.

An idea struck, and she straightened. She might not have the money, but she knew someone who did.

David glared at the huge oak limb lying on the drive. Shredded leaves and tangled branches littered the front lawn. It would take hours, if not days, to clean up the mess. The roofer and his assistant had helped him get the limb off the roof, but it was difficult to feel grateful when he was still trying to recover from hearing the estimate for repairing the roof. Insurance would cover a portion of the cost, but his grandfather's policy had a high deductible for storm damage.

He kicked at the gravel drive and sent a few small stones flying, then glanced up at the cloud-covered sky. "I don't understand, Lord. I thought You wanted me to help my grandmother save Longdale, but I'm hitting one roadblock after another. What am I doing wrong?" He waited, hoping for new insight or clear direction. But his thoughts seemed as tangled as the broken limbs on the lawn around him.

The houseboat plan had flopped. The renovations were on hold until they received the funds from the auction, and that was at least two months away. Now, a good portion of that money would have to go toward replacing the roof. It could be patched, but that would put them at risk for more leaks in the future. They needed to totally replace the slate tiles on the east side of the house.

He huffed, grabbed a branch, and threw it toward the mounting pile. He'd promised his grandmother he would save Longdale. Was he aiming too high? Maybe it was time to face the harsh reality that not every historic home could be saved. Sometimes the cost was unreasonable . . . but how could he tell his grandmother it was time to give up her home?

Pain radiated through his chest. That news would be like a knife to her heart. He couldn't do it. Somehow, he had to find a way to finance these repairs before there was more damage done to the house.

The front door opened, and Gwen stepped outside. She wore a gentle smile as she walked down the steps and crossed the drive toward him. She glanced at the tumbled mass of branches and slowed. "Wow, that limb is huge."

"Yeah, it's heavy too. It took three of us to pull it down." He glanced at the broken end of the branch, trying to gauge the diameter.

She touched his arm. "I have some good news."

He turned toward her. "What?"

A matching pair of dimples appeared in her cheeks as she

smiled. "I spoke to a potential investor today, and he's very interested in hearing more about your plans for Longdale."

He stared at her. "An investor?"

"Yes. He'd like you to give him a call to discuss the idea."

He blinked. "Who is it?"

Her eyes glowed with a touch of mischief. "My grandfather, Lionel Morris."

David sucked in a breath. "Your grandfather . . . wants to invest in Longdale?"

She nodded. "He and your grandmother have been friends for years, and he has an interest in historic preservation. I thought it would be worth a call."

"Has he ever been to Longdale?"

"No, but when I told him about your plans, he was intrigued and wanted to know more."

"Wow . . . I don't know what to say."

"My grandfather is a wealthy man with a deep respect for historic architecture. If you give him a good presentation, I think you can name your price."

His eyebrows rose.

She held up her hand. "I know what you're thinking. I wasn't convinced at first, but now that I've had time to get to know you and your grandmother and learn more about Longdale, I think it's a good plan—and a worthy investment."

His throat tightened. Finding an investor was remarkable, but knowing Gwen believed in him and shared his vision for Longdale meant even more. He stepped forward and enfolded her in a hug. "Thank you," he whispered. Closing his eyes, he pulled in a deep breath. Her hair smelled like lavender, and she fit perfectly in his arms.

She wrapped her arms around him, holding him with equal strength. "You're welcome." Her voice sounded hushed with emotion.

He held her for a few seconds, silently thanking the Lord for this unexpected answer to his prayers. Then he slowly leaned back. A sense of wonder stole through him as he searched her face. "Gwen Morris, you are . . . an amazing woman."

Her smile bloomed, lighting up her eyes. "So are you." She laughed, and her cheeks turned pink. "I mean you're an amazing man."

He shook his head, and love for her swelled in his chest. She was beautiful and so good to him. His gaze traced the soft curves of her cheeks and gentle dip of her nose. The desire to kiss her and show her how much he cared raced through him. But once he did, the deal would be sealed. There would be no turning back for him. Was he ready to make that commitment?

Assurance flew straight to his heart. The time was right. He was ready, and from the look in her eyes, so was she.

He lifted his hand to her cheek. Their gazes locked as the invitation and acceptance passed between them. Her eyes drifted closed, and she tipped her face up toward his. He leaned down and found her lips were soft and sweet. She returned the kiss with equal passion, and a flow of warmth and joy spread through him.

Their kiss lasted only a few seconds, but the power of it rocked him to the core. He leaned back and looked into her eyes. "I'll say it again, Gwen Morris, you are an amazing woman."

She leaned in with a soft sigh and rested her head against his chest.

Gwen scrolled down the list of auction items on her iPad. She and Lilly had made good progress that morning, despite the pounding and clattering of the roofers. As they moved through the room, Lilly often asked Gwen to tell her more about the artist or designer of an item. She wanted to understand the history and value of each piece before she decided whether it should be added to the list for the auction.

Gwen enjoyed sharing that information with Lilly. She understood how much Lilly loved her home. It had to be daunting to part with so many possessions that had been in her husband's family for generations, even if it did mean the funds from their sale would save Longdale.

A loud bang and a shout sounded above, and Gwen gasped.

Lilly shot a startled glance toward the ceiling. "Goodness, I hope they don't fall through!"

Gwen followed Lilly's gaze. "I don't think we need to worry. David says they're the best in the district."

Lilly cocked her silver brows. "The steep angle of our roof makes the job especially dangerous. I hope they're licensed and insured."

"I'm sure they are. He said they wear safety harnesses."

"That's good to know." Lilly glanced at her watch. "I need to take a short break to speak to Mrs. G. about dinner plans. I'll be back in a few minutes." She walked out of the library.

Gwen crossed toward the window and looked out. David stood on the front drive. At breakfast, he'd told her he planned to spend some time outside that morning to keep an eye on the men as they stripped off the old slate. He wanted to make sure they didn't damage the landscaping in the process.

She smiled, appreciation for him warming her heart. He knew how much his grandmother valued Longdale, and his commitment to protecting and preserving it made her admire him even more.

A week had passed since the storm had blown through and sent the huge oak limb crashing into the roof. Since then, they'd shared many lingering smiles, some meaningful hugs, and a few more toe-tingling kisses. David had been attentive and thoughtful as she continued her work, making her hopeful his attention was more than just fleeting attraction.

David had made his video presentation to her grandfather three days after the storm. She'd listened out of view of the camera and been so proud of the way he'd handled her grandfather's many questions. After an hour's discussion, her grandfather had agreed to invest an amount that had sent a rush of relief through Gwen. The funds came through two days later, and David had set remodeling plans in motion.

Gwen glanced around the library. She and Lilly had a few more items to discuss in this room. The only other rooms Lilly wanted to look through were storage rooms downstairs. When that was done, the list for the second auction would be complete. She would need to finish the research for the appraisals and call for the team to come and pack all the pieces for shipment to London. But after that . . . her work would be done, and her time at Longdale would come to an end.

Would she and David stay in touch through calls and texts after she returned to London? Would he come and visit her? He hadn't said anything about the future. She bit her lip and glanced out the window once more. David crossed the grass and spoke to one of the roofers.

He seemed to truly care about her, but how could she be certain? She pushed that thought aside. They still had time. She shouldn't worry. Surely he would want to continue their relationship when she left Longdale . . . wouldn't he?

But a vine of worry wove around her heart. David seemed sincere, but he hadn't made any promises. Every day she offered him more of her heart. Could she trust him, or was she headed for heartache again?

Lilly walked in, carrying her cell phone. She held the phone to the side and whispered, "It's Elizabeth Monroe. She's asking to come by for a visit, and she'd like to bring her daughter, Carol. Shall we say tomorrow afternoon at three?"

Gwen's heartbeat thudded in her ears. "Three sounds fine, as long as they don't mind weaving their way around the roofers."

Lilly smiled. "I'll give them fair warning." She lifted the phone to her ear and offered the invitation.

A shiver of anticipation raced down Gwen's back. Tomorrow she would meet her father's sister and spend more time with her grandmother. Perhaps she should think of some questions she could ask to learn more about her father. But would the answers bring her comfort and healing, or would they add to her pain and make her wish she hadn't asked?

Gwen's stomach did a nervous dance as she walked with her Aunt Carol and Grandmother Elizabeth through Longdale's great hall. She hoped their visit would help her learn more about her father and build a stronger sense of connection to his family, but she couldn't help feeling anxious.

Lilly looked over her shoulder and smiled. "The roofers are done for the day, so I thought we'd have tea outside on the terrace."

"That would be nice," Elizabeth said as she glanced around. She and her daughter seemed a bit in awe of the house as they traveled through the long gallery toward the terrace.

Gwen glanced at David, and they exchanged a smile. Having him there sent a wave of reassurance through her and boosted her confidence. He opened the French doors, and they all stepped outside.

"Please have a seat." Lilly motioned toward the table that had been set with beautiful floral china and a silver tea service.

"Allow me." David stepped forward and pulled out chairs for Elizabeth and Carol. Then he seated Gwen and Lilly across from them and took the chair at the end.

"We're so glad you could come today." Lilly poured the tea and offered the first cup to Elizabeth.

Elizabeth accepted it with a smile. "Thank you for having us. Your home is beautiful."

Lilly offered the second cup to Carol. "Longdale is a treasure, but it's also a responsibility. I'm grateful my grandson is overseeing the renovations we hope will preserve it for many years to come." Affection shone in her eyes as she looked at David.

Elizabeth leaned to the left to study the view beyond Lilly. "Your gardens look lovely. If there's time later, I'd enjoy a tour."

Lilly nodded, looking pleased. "I'd be glad to show you the gardens. They are my husband's design. He loved working out there." She sighed. "These days, a gardener comes once a week and takes care of it for me. But I still like walking there in warm weather to see what's blooming and to cut a bouquet."

Gwen stirred sugar into her tea and studied her Aunt Carol. She looked about fifty, but it was hard to tell her exact age. Her light brown hair was pulled back in a ponytail at the base of her neck, secured by a rubber band. She wore no makeup, and her suntanned arms and freckled face made Gwen suspect she spent a good deal of time outdoors at the farm.

Carol seemed to sense Gwen's gaze and turned toward her. "Mother said you weren't told anything about Landon while you were growing up. Is that true?"

Gwen's hand stilled. "My parents separated before I was born, and my mother didn't speak of him often. But I knew they were married in Keswick. When I came to the area, I hoped I might find him or his family."

Carol grimaced as though she'd tasted something sour. "Unfortunately, Landon doesn't want to be found by you or anyone else."

Elizabeth gave her daughter a look. "Carol, that's not kind."

"Well, it's true." Pink infused her cheeks beneath her freckles. "Landon has his issues, but that is no excuse for the way he cut himself off from us. How could he be so thoughtless? We have no way to contact him. He doesn't even know Father passed away." Her eyes turned misty, and she looked away.

Gwen shifted in her chair, trying to think of something to say. She glanced at David, and he returned a puzzled look.

Lilly cleared her throat. "Elizabeth, I understand there may be a family connection between the Monroes and my husband's family."

Elizabeth nodded. "Gwen mentioned that when she visited. I remember hearing something about it from my husband's mother, but I don't recall the details. Gwen said you have an old journal that might tell us more about that connection."

Lilly smiled. "Yes, the journal is quite remarkable. When I read Charlotte's entries, it made me feel like I was stepping back in time."

Carol brushed a tear from her cheek and faced them again. "I'd like to see it."

"Of course. We'd be glad to show you." Lilly turned to Gwen. "Would you mind bringing it out for us, dear?"

Gwen nodded and rose. "I'll be right back." She'd brought the journal down to the library that morning in anticipation of her grandmother and aunt's visit. She quickly retrieved it and returned to the terrace. They all turned to watch as she approached the table, her aunt's gaze focused on the journal.

Gwen placed it on the table between her aunt and grandmother. "The journal dates from 1912, before Charlotte Harper came to live at Longdale."

Elizabeth gently ran her hand over the leather cover. "You can tell it's very old." She carefully opened the journal, and Carol scooted her chair closer.

Elizabeth turned to Carol. "I think we have an old Bible that lists some of my husband's family. I'll see if I can find it and look through the names to see if a Harper or Benderly married into the Monroe family at some point."

Gwen returned to her chair and watched their expressions as they turned the pages and skimmed some of the early entries. Her thoughts drifted back through all she'd read about Charlotte and her family. What heartache they'd faced, yet what courage they'd shown in the face of it all. She'd only read about half the journal, and she was eager to read the rest. The entries that mentioned Charlotte's mother, Rose, had been especially meaningful to Gwen.

Charlotte might have lost her father and been deeply hurt by his painful choices, but she and her mother had grown closer as her mother modeled forgiveness and showed Charlotte how to make peace with the burden she carried.

Their relationship reflected Gwen's feelings for her own mother. How grateful she was for all her mother had taught her over the years. Oh, how she missed her mum. But she had good memories and meaningful lessons her mum had passed on that she could treasure in her heart.

If only her mother were here, she could talk to Elizabeth and Carol and resolve some of her past hurts, but that was impossible. It was up to Gwen to bridge the gulf her parents' separation had created in their family. A new sense of determination coursed through her. She would do what she could to find a way forward.

Elizabeth looked up. "Does Charlotte mention the Monroe family or Valley View Farm?"

Her question brought Gwen back to the moment, and she focused on her grandmother. "The Storey family lived at Valley View when Charlotte visited. She describes the beauty of the farm in several passages."

Elizabeth smiled. "That's good to know. My husband loved Valley View so much." Tears gathered in her eyes, and she shook her head. "I'm sorry. I don't mean to be emotional."

Lilly reached across and laid her hand over Elizabeth's. "I understand. Love for one's family and home creates a special bond between a husband and wife. My husband's love for Longdale has been passed on to me, and I'm passing it to my grandson." She smiled at David.

He returned a loving look. "And one day I'll pass it on to my family." His gaze shifted to Gwen. "That's the way it should be."

She met his gaze with a tremulous smile. David's love for Longdale and his skills and vision would protect and preserve his family's home for years to come. Her heart stirred with longing to see it come to pass . . . and perhaps share that future with him.

David clicked off his phone, stepped around piles of broken slate tiles, and strode into the house. He made a quick search of the main floor, looking for his grandmother and Gwen, then he remembered they were working downstairs that morning. He doubted they'd find anything valuable in that old storage room, but it was kind of Gwen to indulge his grandmother and help her look through everything stored there.

From what he could tell when he'd checked earlier, most of the old items wouldn't be worth sending to London for the auction. If his grandmother wanted to clear out the room, he'd have to hire someone to haul those boxes away and donate it all to a charity shop.

He crossed the great hall, his thoughts returning to the possibilities raised during the recent phone call with Max. It seemed the owner of an old manor house near Leeds was desperate to sell, and Max thought it had great potential. He wanted David to go with him to view the property and see what it would take to convert it into a hotel or multi-unit flats. If the price was right, it was the kind of project that could yield a good return and help build his reputation.

He hustled down the steps, grateful Max wasn't holding the houseboat debacle against him. But as he rounded the landing, he thought of all that was happening at Longdale. The roofers would probably complete their work in two or three days. The contractor had called again that morning, asking when they could start taking down the walls to create his grandmother's private quarters. It might not be the best time for him to be away. But he didn't want to let Max down. He'd make a quick trip to Leeds and be back in time to oversee the work at Longdale.

He reached the bottom of the steps and heard his grandmother's voice coming from down the hall. "Oh, look at these lovely old baskets. Arthur and I used to pack a picnic dinner in one of these and take it down to the lake for a romantic evening by the water." Her voice carried a wistful note.

He smiled, glad his grandmother had someone to listen as she reminisced about those happy times.

"I've noticed the way you and David have grown closer," his grandmother continued. "Is there a romance blooming between you two?"

David's eyebrows rose, and he stopped a few meters from the door.

Gwen laughed softly. "I'm not exactly sure what David has in mind."

"But you're fond of him, aren't you?"

He leaned forward, ignoring a stab of guilt for eavesdropping.

"I've never met anyone quite like him," Gwen said softly.

"Maybe you should pack a picnic dinner and invite David to share it with you by the lake. There's nothing more romantic than watching the sunset over the mountains and seeing those beautiful colors reflected in the water."

His heartbeat kicked up a notch. That was a great idea.

"Perhaps." Silence ticked by for a few seconds, then Gwen said, "We should get back to work and see if we can finish going through these boxes before dinner."

His smile faded. It didn't sound like Gwen was in favor of the picnic idea.

Lilly sighed. "I do hope you'll keep my suggestion in mind.

259

David is a fine young man, and I'm not just saying that because he is my grandson. You two are a good match."

He waited for her reply, but all he heard was a rustling sound, like someone opening a box.

He took a step back. Why didn't Gwen sound more enthusiastic about their relationship? Maybe she just didn't want to explain her feelings to his grandmother. Yes, that must be it.

But his chest tightened. He and Gwen hadn't talked about where their relationship was going. He should be the one to lead the way with that conversation. He tensed as he imagined telling her how he felt and what he hoped was ahead for them. They'd only known each other for a few weeks. Was he moving too fast? He didn't want to scare her off. What if he declared himself, and she didn't feel the same way?

He shook his head and quietly walked back down the hall. He needed to think this through and pray about it before he initiated that conversation. Maybe he would wait until he got back from Leeds. That would give him time to be sure he was headed in the right direction.

Twenty-One

1912

Charlotte held Alice's hand as they followed Mum up Long-dale's broad oak staircase. A grandfather clock on the landing ticked off the time, while thick red carpet on the stairs quieted their steps. The scent of beeswax and lemon oil hung in the air, no doubt from the highly polished clock and woodwork.

"Do you think Grandfather will be glad to see us?" Alice's innocent, inquisitive look tugged at Charlotte's heart.

Mum glanced over her shoulder. "I hope so, but he may be in pain from his injuries, so we must be patient and not expect too much."

Alice nodded. "I understand."

Did she? They hadn't told Alice the details of their previous visit, only that Grandfather had not invited them to stay at Longdale. But Alice was quite perceptive for a twelve-year-old. She seemed to realize there were unresolved issues between Mum and Grandfather that had burdened Mum and kept them away from Longdale.

At the top of the stairs, they turned left, and Mum knocked on the first door. She sent Charlotte a quick glance just before the door opened.

"Yes?" An older woman wearing a neat black dress and a prim expression looked out at them. A silver chatelaine with several keys hung at her waist.

"I'm Rose Harper, Mr. Benderly's daughter, and these are his granddaughters, Charlotte and Alice."

"I'm Mrs. Chapman, the housekeeper. Come in. He is expecting you." The woman opened the door wider so they could enter, then she walked out of the room and closed the door.

Charlotte quickly scanned the large, dimly lit bedroom. Heavy navy-blue drapes hung over three tall windows. A dark mahogany chest and large wardrobe stood between the windows. To the right, Grandfather lay in a huge bed, propped up by several pillows. Dark bed-curtains, matching those at the windows, hung at the four corner posts.

A tall, middle-aged man with thinning red hair stood at the side of the bed, holding Grandfather's wrist, and consulting his watch.

"Ah, Rose, you've come." Grandfather looked up at the man. "Doctor Powell, would you hand me my glasses on the nightstand?"

The doctor opened the glasses and passed them to Grandfather. He put them on with one hand. His other arm rested in a sling tied around his neck. "I see you've brought the girls."

"Yes. You met Charlotte on our last visit, and this is Alice."

Her sister smiled and gave a slight curtsy. "I'm pleased to meet you, Grandfather."

His gray eyebrows rose. "You are, are you?"

"Yes, sir. I've heard many stories about you and Longdale."

Charlotte squeezed Alice's hand. Her sister shot her a questioning look.

From a shadowed corner, Mr. Donovan rose from a chair and stepped forward. "Hello, ladies."

"Mr. Donovan." Mum smiled, looking surprised and pleased.

"It's good to see you." She glanced at Grandfather, obviously curious about Mr. Donovan's presence.

"Mr. Donovan has visited me each day since my fall."

"Oh." Mum's gaze darted from Mr. Donovan to Grandfather. "When did you fall?"

"Five days ago." He winced as he shifted on the pillows.

"How did it happen?" Mum asked.

"I was in too much of a hurry going down the stairs, and now I must pay the price."

"I'm sorry." Mum's voice softened. "We would've come sooner if we'd known."

Grandfather lifted his good hand. "I wouldn't have been ready." He glanced at Mr. Donovan, looking as if he hoped the reverend would continue the conversation.

Mr. Donovan turned to her mum. "Your father and I have had several conversations, and I believe he has something important he would like to say."

"What is it, Father?"

Grandfather pulled in a deep breath and blew it out. "I regret many of the things I said during your last visit." His chin quivered slightly, and he glanced toward the window. "After I read your letter, I was . . . disturbed, or as Mr. Donovan would say, I was convicted. But I didn't want to reconsider my position or let go of those offenses." He sighed and looked back at Mum. "But then I fell and had time to think."

Mum pressed her lips together, obviously holding back her emotions.

"Mr. Donovan reminded me that one of Satan's chief schemes is to convince us we have a right to hold on to our grievances. He wants to destroy relationships and keep people apart. But we can defeat him by letting go of offenses and forgiving others as the Lord has forgiven us."

Mum stared at Grandfather, looking uncertain what to say.

Mr. Donovan stepped forward. "Your father has shown true

wisdom in his desire to forgive and rebuild connections with you and his grandchildren."

"That's wonderful. I'm so glad." Mum took hold of Grandfather's hand. "Thank you, Father. That means the world to me."

The old man's eyes glistened. "It's been a long time coming, but . . . welcome home, Rose."

Her mum bent forward and gently hugged Grandfather. He closed his eyes and patted her back with his good hand.

Tears stung Charlotte's eyes. What a gift! Grandfather's change of heart seemed sincere, and it had opened the door to restore relationships, renew hope, and provide a home for her family.

Ian trudged across the hillside and called Bryn. The dog quickly responded, circling the sheep and driving them toward the drystone wall and far gate.

A stiff breeze rushed past, carrying the scent of rain. He scanned the heavy clouds flying eastward. The threatening sky seemed a perfect reflection of his dark mood. Three days had passed since Charlotte had left the farm and moved to Longdale, and he'd not heard one word from her.

He stifled a growl and strode toward the gate. "Come by!" he shouted to the dog.

Bryn raced around the flock, bringing them closer. The ewes with lambs were the most resistant to being herded. He supposed it was their protective instinct that made them wary and unruly. He hustled back, stretched out his staff, and guided two ewes and their lambs back toward the others. Bryn circled the sheep again, and the flock poured through the open gate. After the last ewe trotted into the adjoining field, Ian closed the gate behind them.

With a weary sigh, he set off down the hill, Bryn at his side.

That morning, when he'd risen from bed, he'd determined to telegram the professor, confirm his decision, and prepare to set sail for Egypt. But his mother had spoken to him before he left the house to do his chores. Misty-eyed, she'd given him her blessing to go, saying they would trust the Lord to somehow carry them through the summer. Her tears and gentle words had stung his conscience. Doubts had continued to assail him as he went through his morning routine, and he couldn't seem to reason them away.

He might never receive another offer of an expense-paid trip to Egypt, but he couldn't turn his back on his family and break his word to stay through the summer. Even though he and his father were often at odds, generations of his family had invested their lives in this farm. If he left his family now, the burden they carried would be too great. It was time he put aside his own desires and did what was best for his family.

Closing his eyes, he groaned and released the dream of going to Egypt that summer. He would send that telegram to the professor, but it would say he had decided to stay and help his family.

Charlotte's image rose in his mind again, as it did so many times each day, and the ache returned to his chest. There was more weighing him down than making his final decision about Egypt.

He reached the bottom of the hill, leaned against the dry-stone wall, and rested his arms on top. Lifting his eyes toward the mountains, he scanned their rugged beauty. Shades of green, brown, and purple blended across the face of the fells. That view usually made him feel steady and grounded, but not today.

The words he and Charlotte had exchanged the day she left came rushing back, bringing a storm of conflicting emotions. She had misjudged him and made unfair allegations. He'd tried to explain, but she had refused to listen. Why was she being so stubborn and unreasonable?

Why was she afraid? Did she really think he would lie and betray her?

"Ian!" Milly ran down the path toward him, her face flushed and strands of her hair flying loose from her braid.

He jogged toward her. "What's wrong?"

"It's Dad! I walked into the barn and found him collapsed on the floor!"

Panic shot through Ian. "What happened?"

"I don't know. Mum and I managed to rouse him, and we got him into the house."

"Shall I go for the doctor?"

Milly gulped in a breath. "Mrs. Wallace was visiting Mum. She rode back to the village to get the doctor."

He turned and ran down the path toward the house, his thoughts racing ahead. When he reached the house, he jerked open the door and dashed inside. "Mum?" His voice rang out in the empty kitchen.

Mum walked in, her face pale and her expression grave. "Where's Dad?"

"He's resting in our room."

Ian crossed toward her. "Can you tell what's wrong?"

She shook her head. "We had a hard time waking him, and he's weak. It could be his heart. I don't know." Tears filled her eyes. She lifted her hand to cover her mouth and stifle a sob.

His throat tightened, and he gathered her in for a hug. "Everything will be all right. We'll get through this together."

She sniffed and held on tight. "I don't know how I'll manage without you, son."

"Don't worry. I'm not going anywhere."

Mum stepped back. "But what about your trip to Egypt?"

He shook his head. "Someone else can fill that position. I'm needed here. I'd already decided to stay."

Mum sniffed. "Oh, thank you, Ian. I'm so grateful."

Warmth and assurance filled him, and he placed his arm around his mum's shoulders. "The Lord will take care of us."

She pulled a handkerchief from her apron pocket and dabbed her nose. "Yes, He will. Go see your father."

He nodded, then steeled himself and walked into his parents' bedroom. His dad lay on the bed with his eyes closed. The fearful thought that he might be too late raced through Ian's mind. Then his dad's chest rose and fell, and relief washed over him.

"Dad, are you awake?"

His eyes fluttered open, and he met Ian's gaze. "Son, is that you? Come closer."

Ian pulled a wooden chair over next to the bed and took a seat. "How are you feeling?"

"Not too good." His voice sounded weak, but his breathing was steady.

"What happened out in the barn?"

"I was checking on that ewe with the twin lambs, and suddenly I felt woozy. The next thing I know, your mum and Milly were helping me into the house."

"Do you have pain anywhere?"

His forehead wrinkled. "No. I just feel spent, like an old rag." His chin wobbled, and he turned his face toward the wall.

Ian gripped his dad's hand. "The doctor is on the way. I'm sure he'll know what's wrong and fix you up good as new."

"What if he can't? How will I run this farm?" His dad's voice came out a rough whisper.

"We'll take care of things until you're back on your feet."

"*If* I get back on my feet."

"You will. You're strong. You've got years of life ahead of you."

Dad slowly turned and looked his way. "I've been hard on you, Ian, harder than I should've been."

Ian clenched his jaw, pressing down his emotions. It was

true, but he didn't want to upset his dad by agreeing. "Don't worry about that now."

"I want you to listen to me." He paused and waited for Ian to meet his gaze. "If you want to go to Egypt, then you should go. We'll find some way to manage things without you."

Ian shook his head. "I'm not leaving."

His dad searched his face. "Truly? You're staying on?"

"I wrestled with it for a time, but I've made my decision. I'll stay through the summer. And I want you to know that was my plan before . . . this happened."

His dad slowly nodded. "Why are you doing it, son? I thought your mind was set on going with that professor."

Ian tightened his hold on his dad's hand. "This farm is our heritage. And our family means more to me than any trip to Egypt ever could."

Tears shimmered in his father's eyes. "I'm grateful, Ian, and I'm proud of you."

"Thanks, Dad." Ian had to force the words past his tight throat. The gap between them finally seemed to be narrowing. If only it hadn't taken a serious event like his father collapsing in the barn to prompt the change. He closed his eyes, and holding tight to his father's hand, he prayed for him.

Charlotte wiggled her sore toes in her shoes, hoping for some relief. She'd been on her feet almost continually since nine that morning, serving the stream of customers who had come through the bookshop on opening day.

She had manned the counter, while Mr. Matterly greeted people and helped those who were looking for particular titles. His face glowed as he engaged them in conversation and discussed favorite books and the upcoming Keswick Convention.

Charlotte counted out change to Mr. Walters, a tall gentleman who had purchased two travel books about Switzerland. "These look interesting. Are you planning a trip?"

He smiled as he slipped the change into his pocket. "Yes, my wife and I will be celebrating our twenty-fifth wedding anniversary in August with a trip to Bern and the surrounding area."

"That sounds lovely." Charlotte recalled photos she'd seen of the Alps and the beautiful countryside. "Have you been to Switzerland before?"

"No, but we've been looking forward to this trip for quite some time. It seems like a fitting way to celebrate so many happy years together."

Thoughts of Ian rushed in, and her heart clenched. She forced a smile and passed Mr. Walters his books. "I hope you and your wife enjoy your holiday."

"Thank you." He returned a smile, then glanced around the store. "You have a very nice selection. I'm sure I'll be back, and I'll bring my wife next time."

"We'd be happy to meet her."

He tipped his hat and started for the door.

Charlotte released a wistful sigh. Twenty-five years of love and devotion was worthy of a special trip. Her parents would have been married twenty-five years next June if her father hadn't died. Would their marriage have lasted that long, or would he have left them for E. M. by that time?

Charlotte shook her head. Mr. Walters's happy marriage seemed to be the exception rather than the rule. Love didn't always last. Sometimes it led to betrayal and heartache.

She didn't want to remember her father's betrayal or dwell on Ian's deception, but they seemed impossible to forget. How could she banish the memories of her sunset walks with Ian, or their strolls through the fields? And what about their picnic on the island, their times with the lambs, and the rain-swept kiss they'd shared?

She lifted her hand to her heart. It had only been one week

since she'd confronted Ian and left the farm, but the passing days hadn't eased her distress or quieted her painful questions.

Exploring her grandfather's home and the estate gardens had distracted her for short periods of time. Conversations with Grandfather and quiet evenings with her mum and Alice had helped some. But when she was alone, her thoughts always returned to Ian.

He hadn't tried to contact her, which added to her hurt. Had he already left Valley View as he prepared for his trip to Egypt? At that moment, was he enjoying a cozy conversation—or more—with Genevieve Montrose? Her heart plunged, and tears stung her eyes.

She had to stop thinking of him!

The bell over the shop's front door rang. Charlotte looked up and stiffened.

Ian crossed the shop toward her, determination in his stride. "Hello, Charlotte."

She gave a brief nod. "Good day, sir. How can I help you?"

His serious look softened. "I'm not here to buy a book." He glanced around and lowered his voice. "Can we step outside? I'd like to speak to you in private."

She moved to the left and straightened a stack of books. "I'm sorry. I can't leave the shop."

"You're closing soon. Let me give you a ride home."

"I don't need a ride. My grandfather sends a carriage for me."

A look of impatience flickered across his face. "Surely you can tell the driver he's not needed and send him back."

"I could, but I won't." She sent him a pointed look, then stepped out from behind the counter and started toward Mr. Matterly.

Ian followed her across the shop. "Charlotte, please. I want to explain things."

She turned and faced him. "I believe you've already done that."

His eyebrows dipped. He glanced around the shop, then

looked back at her. "I know you're upset with me, but if you'd only listen, I think we can straighten out this misunderstanding."

"There is no misunderstanding. I know what I saw with my own eyes."

He shook his head and started to reply but stopped as Mr. Matterly approached.

"Is everything all right?" The bookshop owner's worried gaze shifted from Charlotte to Ian.

"Everything is fine." Charlotte lifted her chin. "Ian was just leaving."

His gaze pierced hers. "Very well. If that's what you want." He turned and started for the door. Halfway, he stopped and looked over his shoulder. "I thought you'd want to know my father had a heart attack. He's still with us, but this has been a very difficult time for our family."

Her breath caught, and she forced out her next words. "I'm sorry. Please tell your mother and sister I'll pray for him . . . and all the family."

Ian gave a curt nod, then strode out of the shop.

Her throat clogged as she watched him go.

Mr. Matterly studied her with a concerned look. "That is very serious news about Mr. Storey."

"Yes, it is." Her voice trembled.

"Is that the only reason you're upset?"

She sniffed, still shaken by the news of Mr. Storey's heart attack.

"Have you and Ian had a falling out?" he asked gently.

She crossed her arms, debating her answer. She didn't want to tarnish Ian's reputation, but she could use some fatherly advice. "I'm afraid Ian is not the man I thought he was."

Mr. Matterly frowned. "What do you mean?"

"He made me believe he cared for me, but I've learned that's not true."

"I'm surprised to hear you say that." Mr. Matterly glanced

toward the door, then returned his gaze to Charlotte. "He always seemed attentive and sincere. I had the impression you two were quite close."

"So did I, but I discovered he is involved with a woman at Oxford, the daughter of one of his professors. Last week, she visited their farm, and when I saw how they acted toward each other, I knew his declarations to me meant nothing."

"Are you certain about this, Charlotte?"

She bit her lip. Events with her father had taught her men didn't always tell the truth. Her father's lies and betrayal had cut her to the heart, and Ian's deception was sending her down that same hurtful path. There was no room for any other explanation. Honesty and trust were sacred, and Ian's lies had broken her trust and her heart.

She focused on Mr. Matterly. "Yes, I'm certain. Ian is not the man I thought he was."

Ian strode through the stone gateway and paced down the gravel path between the church and graveyard. Sunshine warmed his shoulders, but it did little to ease his frustration.

Why wouldn't Charlotte listen? He'd humbled himself and come to make amends, but she'd refused to believe him—again! He huffed out a breath and lifted his face to the sky.

"I don't understand it. What am I supposed to do now?"

"I'm not sure, but I'm willing to listen."

Ian spun around, and heat flooded his face.

Concern lit Mr. Donovan's eyes as he approached. "Are you all right, Ian?"

He sighed and shook his head. "Not really."

"I was just going for a stroll." Mr. Donovan motioned toward the path leading away from the church. "Would you like to join me?"

Ian nodded and fell into step beside the reverend, thankful for the distraction. Maybe a walk would help clear his head.

"I hope your father is improving?"

"He seems a bit stronger. But the doctor ordered him to stay in bed, and that's proving to be a trial for him."

Mr. Donovan nodded. "I'm sure that is difficult. I'll pay him another visit soon."

"Thank you. I know he and Mum would appreciate it."

They walked on, following the path through the village that led toward the River Greta.

"Is something else troubling you?"

Ian stuffed his hands in his pockets. "How is it you always seem to know when that's the case?"

"I suppose it comes from years of serving the Lord and caring for His flock." He grew more serious. "So . . . what's on your mind?"

Ian walked on, debating how to answer. He didn't want to blame Charlotte, but how else could he explain the predicament? "Charlotte misunderstood . . . a certain situation, and now she won't speak to me. And since she and her mother and sister have moved to Longdale, there's no convenient opportunity to straighten out things between us."

"What was the misunderstanding?"

"Last Friday, one of my professors from Oxford came to the farm to offer me a position on an archaeology team going to Egypt. His daughter, Genevieve, came along. During the conversation, she took my hand and later, when they were leaving, she kissed my cheek. Just from that, Charlotte assumed I was secretly courting Genevieve."

Matthew clasped his hands behind his back. "I see."

"Genevieve has always been friendly. I think she was trying to persuade me to go along with them on the trip. Perhaps I should've stopped her, but I was so caught up in the offer from her father, I was caught off guard."

Matthew gave a thoughtful nod. "Have you considered how it appeared to Charlotte?"

Ian frowned. "I tried to explain there was nothing to it, but she thinks I'm lying. She wouldn't listen." He couldn't keep the irritation from his voice.

Mr. Donovan slowed and looked his way. "Are you aware of the burden she carries concerning her father?"

"You mean the love letters she found after his death?"

"Yes. Charlotte was deeply wounded by her father's deception. Think how she must have felt when she discovered he was not the loving husband and father she believed him to be."

"I know that was difficult for her."

"Yes, very difficult. And her faith was anchored by her relationship with her father. When he failed to live up to what he taught, she experienced a crisis of belief. And to protect her mother and siblings, she continues to carry the painful secret of her father's betrayal."

Mr. Donovan stopped as they reached the center of the stone bridge arching over the river. "Do you see how those experiences might cause her to view the situation with you and Genevieve in a different light?"

Ian gazed downstream, pondering the reverend's words. "You think she compares me to her father, and that's why she doesn't believe me."

"I think she is fearful of experiencing another betrayal, so that makes her cautious and protective of her heart."

Ian rubbed his chin, replaying Mr. Donovan's words as he considered Charlotte's response.

"When someone's reactions to a situation seem out of proportion, it usually points back to some previous experience, some hurt they are still carrying."

"I see what you're saying. Everything that happened with her father might make it harder for her to believe me." He'd never wanted to hurt Charlotte or cause her to doubt his feelings for her, but that was what he'd done by not considering how her past might impact their present relationship.

"Exactly. Any hint of deception would be reason enough for her to pull away."

"So, what am I to do? I went to the bookshop and tried to talk to her, but she refused to have a conversation."

Mr. Donovan gazed down at the water for a few moments, then looked back at Ian. "You might try writing to her. If you do, I wouldn't bother trying to explain or justify your actions. If I were you, I'd just apologize and tell her you understand that what happened with the professor's daughter hurt her feelings." He clasped his hands together. "But it may take more than a letter to win her back."

Ian studied Mr. Donovan's face.

"She wants to see you stand by your word and to believe she can trust you. And that will take time."

"It doesn't seem fair that I must be the one to—"

"Ian, life and love are not always fair. The servant leader must be the first to apologize, the first to do what's needed to show they are sincere and worthy of restoring the relationship. Remember, the Lord said we are to be peacemakers and do our part."

Ian gazed past the river to the hills beyond and turned Mr. Donovan's words over in his mind. Writing to Charlotte and hoping for a positive response didn't seem like the easy reconciliation he'd hoped for. He wasn't even sure a letter would be the best approach. He would have to pray for patience and ask for opportunities to prove he was a man of his word.

Charlotte adjusted her hold on the handle of the wicker basket as she approached the Storeys' front door. She glanced over her shoulder at the carriage waiting at the bottom of the long drive. She had asked the driver to stop there so she could walk up the hill and have a few moments to collect her thoughts before she arrived at the house.

What would she say if Ian answered the door? Responses rushed through her mind, and she closed her eyes. *Please, Lord, I want them to know we're concerned for Mr. Storey, but I don't want to have an awkward conversation with Ian.*

Summoning her courage, she lifted her chin and knocked on the door.

Moments later, the door opened. Milly looked out. "Charlotte, I'm so happy to see you. Please, come in."

"Thank you. We heard about your father's illness and wanted to bring this basket."

"That's very kind of you." Milly accepted the basket, moved aside the cloth napkin, and looked underneath.

"Our cook thought the chicken soup might help your father regain his strength. And there is also bread, cheese, and strawberry jam."

"It looks wonderful. Thank you, Charlotte, and please thank your mum and the cook. Can you stay for tea?"

Charlotte looked past Milly's shoulder toward the kitchen. "Will anyone else be joining us?"

"No. Dad is resting in his room, and Mum is with him. Ian is out in the fields, checking on the sheep. I don't expect him back for some time."

Charlotte released a breath. "I'd be happy to stay. Thank you."

"Good. I've missed you." Milly walked into the kitchen and filled the teakettle.

Charlotte took a seat at the kitchen table. She glanced around, remembering the meals and conversations she'd enjoyed with the Storey family, and the secret smiles she'd exchanged with Ian. She pushed that thought away and turned to Milly. "How is your father?"

Milly placed the kettle on the stove. "He's improving, and he's strong enough to resent having to stay in his room and rest, but not strong enough to do his usual work around the farm."

Charlotte's stomach tightened. "What will you do when Ian leaves for Egypt? How will you manage?"

Milly looked over her shoulder. "He's not going."

"Not going?" Charlotte stared at her friend. "Because of your father's illness?"

"No, he made the decision before Dad fell ill."

"But . . . he seemed so set on it when the professor was here." Memories of Genevieve clutching his arm and urging him to join them paraded through Charlotte's mind.

"I know he seriously considered it, but the need here is greater." Milly brought two mugs of tea to the table. She sent Charlotte a questioning look. "I thought you'd be happy Ian decided to stay."

Charlotte shifted in her chair. "I'm surprised to hear it."

Milly stirred sugar into her tea. "I thought he would've told you about his decision. Has something happened between you and Ian?"

Charlotte took a sip of tea, debating her reply. Even though Milly was Ian's sister, she was a trusted friend. Perhaps she would offer some comfort or encouragement. "Ian and I did not part well."

"Oh no. What happened?"

"I saw the way he and Genevieve . . . well, it seemed quite clear they have feelings for each other."

Milly frowned. "Ian and Genevieve?"

"Yes. She kissed him before she and her father left."

"She did seem well acquainted with him, but I thought that was because of his connection to her father."

"It seemed much more than that to me."

"He's never said a word about Genevieve, either before or after that visit, but he has often spoken of you."

Charlotte straightened. "He has?"

"Yes, and I've seen the way he watches you when you enter the room. I know he cares for you, Charlotte. I thought you would be announcing your courtship soon."

Charlotte's heart clenched. "That's what I thought as well . . . but when Genevieve was here and I saw them together, I knew there had to be an understanding between them."

"Have you asked Ian about it?"

"We spoke before I left for Longdale, and he denied it."

Milly reached across the table and covered Charlotte's hand. "If he says there is nothing between them, why would you doubt him?"

Charlotte slipped her hand away. "I've seen the cost of blind trust and the dreadful price of betrayal."

Sympathy filled Milly's eyes. "Oh, Charlotte. I didn't know you'd suffered a broken heart."

"Not in that way." She hesitated, then said quietly, "My father was unfaithful to my mother."

Confusion crossed Milly's face. "But your mother always speaks so highly of him."

"Please don't say anything about it. She doesn't know the truth." Charlotte wrapped her hands around her mug, but the warmth did little to comfort her. "After his death, I discovered a packet of love letters. I only read two of them, but it was enough to know he had broken his vows to my mother and deceived us all."

"How dreadful. I'm so sorry." Milly shook her head, sorrow lining her face. "I'm sure that makes it hard to trust, but don't let what happened with your father ruin your chance for happiness with Ian."

A tremor passed through Charlotte, and her hands suddenly felt clammy. Was she misjudging Ian . . . or was she wisely guarding her heart? How could she be sure she was seeing things clearly and making the right choice?

Twenty-Two

2012

The sun was just peeking over the mountains when Gwen walked down the garden path toward the misty lake. She hoped taking an early morning walk would give her time to settle her heart and mind. Something was going on with David, but she wasn't sure what it could be.

Last night at dinner, when she'd told him she'd finished listing all the items for the auction, she thought he would be thrilled, but it barely seemed to register. Later, after Lilly went to bed, they'd gone into the library and sat on the couch by the fireplace. She'd anticipated a cozy conversation and maybe even a romantic kiss to end the evening, but David had been all business. He'd explained more about the call from Max and what this new project in Leeds could mean for him and his company.

She listened carefully and could tell he was excited about teaming up with Max and taking on a new venture. But when she asked him how long he would be away, and he said maybe a day or two, or possibly a week, her spirit plummeted. What if she finished before he returned? Did he think she would still be here when he got back?

He hadn't asked her what she thought about him going to

Leeds, so she'd kept her disappointment to herself. Now she regretted that choice. If they were going to move forward in their relationship, she needed to be honest and tell him how she felt and what she wanted.

But she didn't want to hold him back or seem clingy. Would he feel pressured if she pushed for a conversation to define their relationship? Did he want to continue seeing her when her work was done, or was this just a passing attraction that he could easily dismiss?

She made a frustrated noise in her throat and picked up her pace. This was crazy. They just needed to talk and work this out.

Her phone buzzed in her pocket, and she pulled it out. Elizabeth's name appeared on the screen, and she lifted the phone to her ear. "Good morning."

"I hope I didn't wake you." Her voice sounded tight and strained.

"No, I've been up for a while. Is everything okay?"

"I had a call from a hospital in Glasgow. Landon checked in as a patient there, and he asked them to let me know."

Gwen stopped on the path. "Is he going to be all right? What happened?"

"I'm not sure. I got the call about nine o'clock last night, and they didn't give me any details. I'll call the hospital this morning and see if I can learn more."

Her thoughts spun as she tried to think of what it might mean. "Please let me know what they say."

"Of course, dear. I thought you'd want to know. It is hard to hear he is in the hospital, but at least he is somewhere they can give him good care . . . and hopefully help him get well."

Hot tears burned Gwen's eyes. "Yes, of course."

"Try not to worry. I'll make some calls and see what I can learn."

"Thank you."

Gwen ended the call and stared out at the lake through blurry eyes. Her father must be seriously ill to have checked himself in to the hospital and asked them to call Elizabeth. Was this illness caused by his drinking problem, or did he have some other serious health issue? She sniffed and wiped a tear from her cheek.

Lord, You know exactly what's wrong with my father and what kind of care he needs to get well. Please watch over him and heal him. Thank You that he reached out to Elizabeth. That's a miracle. I'm not sure how I can help. Please make it clear and show me what You want me to do.

She jogged up the hill, crossed the terrace, and ran into the house with one thought in mind.

She had to find David.

David tucked his iPad into his suitcase and folded his sweater over the top. He glanced around the room, looking for anything else he needed to pack. He grabbed another pair of socks and a shirt from the drawer and tossed them into the suitcase.

Just after seven that morning, Max had called and asked David to meet him at the manor house near Leeds at eleven. That was the only time they could view the property before the owner left for a two-week holiday. The drive would take at least two hours. He needed to leave by eight thirty at the latest.

Frowning, he checked his watch and pulled the suitcase zipper closed. He had a few minutes to grab a quick breakfast, then he had to get on the road. He rolled his suitcase down the hall and grabbed the handle to carry it down the steps.

Gwen dashed into the great hall, calling his name.

His heart jerked. "I'm here," he answered as he hustled down the stairs.

She crossed to the base of the stairway and looked up. Her face was pale, and tears laced her lower lashes. "My father is in a hospital in Glasgow."

He met her at the bottom. "Your father?"

"Yes." She sniffed. "Elizabeth just called. She said the hospital contacted her last night."

"Is he ill, or was he in an accident?"

"I don't know. They didn't give her any details. She said she'll call them this morning and try to find out what's going on." She pressed her lips together and blinked a few times.

He set down his suitcase and pulled her in for a hug. "I'm sorry," he whispered into her hair.

She wrapped her arms around him and held on tight.

He closed his eyes, wishing he could carry the pain for her. Footsteps sounded on the stairs, and he looked up.

Lilly came down the stairs. "Oh dear. What's wrong?"

Gwen relayed what she'd learned from Elizabeth.

Concern filled Lilly's eyes. "That sounds serious, but at least you know where he is and that he's being treated for . . . whatever is wrong."

Gwen nodded, still blinking away tears.

Lilly motioned to the left. "Let's have breakfast. That's the first order of the day, then we'll decide what's next." His grandmother slipped her arm around Gwen's back and guided her toward the dining room.

David followed them to the sideboard and served himself breakfast. But the clash in his conscience stole his appetite. How could he leave when Gwen was dealing with this news? But if he stayed at Longdale, Max would be put out. Plus, any financial gain the project could bring his company would be lost.

He glanced at his grandmother. She seemed intent on comforting and supporting Gwen. Maybe that was enough. He'd be back in a day or two, and he could call and stay in touch while he was away.

Lilly placed her napkin on her lap. "David, will you pray for Gwen's father and thank the Lord for the meal?"

He bowed his head and pulled in a deep breath to calm his

racing thoughts. "Father, thank You for this new day and for the food You provide. We pray for Gwen's father and ask You to comfort him and give him healing and strength. Help those caring for him to have clear understanding of the situation and develop a good treatment plan. Please help Gwen trust You as she waits to learn more. We know You will do what is best for him and for Gwen. We pray this in Jesus's name. Amen."

Gwen lifted her head and looked his way. Her eyes shimmered and seemed to reflect a calmer spirit. "Thank you."

He nodded and buttered his toast, wishing he had more time to talk to her. But the clock was ticking, and Max would be waiting for him in Leeds.

Gwen stared out the library window without seeing. She tried to merge the image of her father in the photo taken on his wedding day with a man lying in a hospital bed in Glasgow, but it was no use. She couldn't imagine it, let alone understand what was happening.

The sound of footsteps crossing the gravel drive reached her, and her vision cleared. David walked toward his car. He tossed his suitcase into the back seat, climbed in on the driver's side, and drove down the hill.

She sighed as his car disappeared around the bend, and rubbed her forehead. He needed to go to Leeds. This was an important meeting and a chance for David to redeem himself after the failure of the houseboat plan. She understood that, but why did it have to be today?

She glanced at her watch, then slowly walked back to the desk where her open laptop waited. Somehow, she had to pull herself together, focus on the appraisals, and get some work done while she waited to hear from Elizabeth.

Setting her jaw, she lowered herself into the chair. Lilly and

David needed the funds from the auction, and that wouldn't come through until she finished her work. She clicked on the list and looked at the next item, a set of silver candlesticks from the dining room.

Ten minutes later, her phone buzzed in her pocket. She rose, pulled out the phone, and answered.

"Gwen, it's Elizabeth." Her voice sounded calmer than it had during the earlier call. "I just spoke to Landon's doctor."

"What did they say?"

"Your father has diabetes and heart issues, and he had an episode last night with his sugar levels. But it sounds as though they are getting things under control this morning with medication."

Gwen pulled in a shaky breath. "So, he's going to be okay?"

"Yes, I believe so. I asked to speak to him, but the nurse said he was sleeping. She suggested I call back this afternoon."

Gwen gripped the phone tighter. "When you talk to him, will you tell him about meeting me?"

Elizabeth hesitated. "Would you like me to?"

"Yes. I think it would be best if it comes from you, especially since he's in the hospital."

"Okay. I'll see how he's doing, and if the time is right, I'll explain things."

"Do you think he'll want to meet me?"

A few seconds ticked by before she answered. "I hope so. But whatever he decides, I'm very grateful to have another granddaughter in my life. You're a delightful young woman, Gwen. And if Landon is thinking clearly, I'm sure he'll be very happy to meet you."

Gwen swallowed hard.

"I'll call him around one, and then call you after."

"Thank you. I appreciate it." They said good-bye, and Gwen ended the call.

She sank into the chair and blew out a slow, deep breath. Her father was going to recover. Her grandmother would break the news and let him know about her. Would he want her to come to Glasgow? What would she say when she met him?

She closed her eyes, a prayer rising from her heart. *Thank You for opening the door for me to connect with my father. Please prepare him for this news. Help me know how to handle his response, whatever it will be. I'm grateful, Lord, so grateful.*

Lilly rolled a tea cart into the library. "Would you like to take a break for lunch?"

Gwen smiled. "That's kind of you to bring it in here."

"I knew you were hard at work, but I thought you must be hungry. It's almost one."

Gwen closed her computer and pushed it aside. She pulled over a chair for Lilly, on the opposite side of the desk, and they sat down together.

Gwen took a few bites of the spinach and chicken salad, then pushed it around with her fork.

"Try the lemon poppyseed bread. It's one of Mrs. G.'s specialties."

Gwen took a small bite of the sweet bread. How could she eat when, at that very moment, her grandmother might be telling her father about her?

Lilly looked across at Gwen's plate. "You've barely touched your food."

Gwen sighed. "I'm sorry. I can't stop wondering what my father will say when he hears he has a daughter he never knew existed."

Lilly sent her a gentle smile, reached across the desk, and patted her hand. "If he has any sense, he'll thank the good Lord for the unexpected gift."

Gwen tried to return a smile, but tears flooded her eyes. "What if he doesn't want to see me?"

"Let's cross that bridge when we come to it. There's no sense in worrying about something that hasn't happened."

Gwen blew out a breath, releasing some of the tension. "You're right. We've prayed about it. Now I need to trust the Lord to work it out in the best way possible."

Lilly's smile spread wider. "That's the Gwen I know. Try to eat a little more. You need your strength for whatever is ahead."

Gwen took a few more bites and gave Lilly an update on the appraisals. "It should only take a few more days to finish. I'm going to call and arrange a time for the team to come and pack everything."

Lilly's gaze traveled around the room. "It will be bittersweet to see it all go, but I'm sure it's for the best."

Gwen's phone buzzed. Her heart leaped, and she shot a glance at Lilly.

"Go ahead, dear. I'll clear these things away."

"Thanks." Gwen rose and answered.

"Hello, Gwen. It's Elizabeth again. I spoke to your father."

"How is he?"

"He's tired, but they're giving him good care. He's already feeling much better."

Relief poured through her. "Did you . . . tell him about me?"

"Yes, I did. He was surprised to hear you were looking for him, and he was quite emotional when I told him you'd like to meet him."

Confusion swirled through Gwen. "He knew about me?"

"Yes, dear. He knew."

"But he never tried to contact me. I don't understand."

Elizabeth sighed. "I think you should let him explain."

"He wants to see me?"

"I think a phone call is best at this point. That will help ease the situation for you both. Then you can talk about a time to meet—perhaps here, at the farm, after he's released from the hospital."

"That sounds good." She paced a few steps and looked out the window, but the view blurred before her eyes. "He wants to talk to me?"

"Yes, dear. He's expecting your call."

She gulped. "If you'll tell me how to reach him, I'll phone him."

Elizbeth relayed the phone number, and Gwen jotted it down. "I think talking to you will help him heal."

Tears burned her eyes. Would it be healing for her as well? She thanked Elizabeth, ended the call, and quickly tapped in David's number. It rang three times, and David's recorded voice came on, asking her to leave a message.

She hesitated, wishing she could talk to him, but she had no other option. "Hi, it's Gwen. My dad is doing okay. It was something with his diabetes that sent him to the hospital. Elizabeth told him about me, and I'm going to call him. I just wanted you to know. If you get this message, would you pray for me and call me? Thanks." She waited, wondering if she should end the call with an endearment, but decided against it. "Okay. Talk to you later."

David felt his phone vibrate in his pants pocket, and he shifted in his chair. He and Max were in the middle of an important discussion with Mr. Harold Smithers, the elderly owner of Greystone Manor. This would not be a good time to take a call. He'd have to let it go to voicemail and listen to the message later.

But what if it was Gwen?

"David, what do you think?"

He shot a glance at Max and silently replayed the conversation to catch up.

"I think there's good potential here, but the renovations will be costly." He had to balance his enthusiasm for the project with the reality of the house's condition. It would take a huge investment to bring this manor house back to life, let alone convert it into an income-producing property.

Max glanced around the room. "Would you say it's more suited to multi-unit flats or a hotel?"

David lifted his gaze to the sitting room's ornate moldings and high ceiling. In the corner, the pale green silk wall covering had come loose and folded down, revealing water stains. He was certain that wasn't the only issue hidden in the walls. Still, it was a beautiful house with some amazing architectural features. Gwen would love it. He tensed, wishing he could check his phone. If it was Gwen, he'd call back later and explain. She'd understand.

He focused on Max. "I think individual units would be the best option. We could probably divide the house into six luxury flats."

A slight smile tugged at the corner of Max's mouth, but he sobered as he turned toward Mr. Smithers. "You have an exceptional home, Mr. Smithers, but converting it into individual units will be very costly. We can only move forward if you're willing to negotiate the purchase price."

Mr. Smithers looked around the room with glassy eyes. "Greystone has been in my family for three generations. You can't expect me to let it go for a pittance."

"No, sir. We do not expect that," Max continued. "We'll work up the numbers and make you a fair offer."

The older man rubbed his chin. "My daughter is coming tonight. I'll discuss it with her and let you know our decision in a few days."

Max's eyebrows rose. "I thought you were hoping for an offer before you leave on holiday."

Mr. Smithers lifted a shaky hand. "I don't like the idea of turning Greystone into flats, but they tell me I have to sell."

David leaned forward. "Who are *they*?"

"My daughter and her husband. She wants me to give up Greystone and live with her . . . but this has been my home for eighty-seven years. I can't imagine giving it away to someone else."

"You wouldn't be giving it away." Max gentled his tone. "We'll offer you a fair price that will make it possible for you to live comfortably the rest of your life and pass on a generous inheritance."

"I know, I know." Mr. Smithers lifted his hand. "That's what they all say."

Max exchanged a surprised glance with David. "You've had other offers to buy Greystone?"

"Of course. They want it for the land so they can demolish the house and build a score of modern homes." He shook his head. "Can you imagine . . . they want to knock it down!"

"That would be a great loss," David said. "Greystone is a remarkable home. It deserves to be given a new life, and we're the team that can do it. We're experienced in historic preservation, and we'd do everything we can to honor Greystone's unique history."

Mr. Smithers sighed. "I hear what you're saying, but I'm not ready to make a decision." He rose, indicating the meeting was over.

David and Max walked outside and stopped on the front walkway. David turned and scanned the front of the three-story house. It was an imposing structure built of dark gray stone with a tower on the left, at least a dozen chimneys, and more windows than he cared to count.

He glanced at Max. "What do we do now?"

"We work the numbers and make him an offer."

"It doesn't sound like he wants to sell."

Max crossed his arms. "He either sells, or the place will fall down around him."

David scanned the neglected lawn and overgrown gardens.

"It could be a beautiful place. It just needs someone willing to make the investment and do the work."

Max clamped his hand on David's shoulder. "We're the right men for that job. I'll see if we can convince the daughter to speak to her father."

David pulled his phone from his pocket as they walked toward Max's car. He'd missed Gwen's call, along with two other messages. He clenched his jaw.

"Let's grab some lunch and do some research so we can make our offer ASAP."

David nodded, but his thoughts carried him back to Longdale and to Gwen.

As soon as he had a break, he'd listen to her message and call her back.

Twenty-Three

1912

Charlotte ran her finger down the list of books Mr. Matterly had asked her to pack for the Keswick Convention. He had chosen a variety of theological titles, as well as missionary biographies and devotional reading.

She glanced at Thomas, the new shop assistant, as he placed books on the shelf. Mr. Matterly had hired Thomas to work at the shop while she and Mr. Matterly spent the week at the convention. She was looking forward to manning the book table, but she also hoped to break away to hear some of the speakers.

Mr. Matterly approached and handed her two more books. "Please put these aside for the convention, and be sure to note their titles on the inventory list."

"I'll take care of it." She jotted down their titles and placed the books in the crate.

"I do hope we've ordered enough books. I haven't attended the convention since '08. And from what I've been told, the number of attendees has grown steadily each year." He scanned the shelves behind the counter and reached for another book. "Let's add this one too."

She took the book and noted the title—*Things As They Are,*

Mission Work in Southern India, by Amy Wilson-Carmichael, Keswick Missionary. She opened the book and thumbed through the pages. A few pages of photos were tucked between the chapters, with images of Asian children and villages with huts and coconut palm trees. A thrill ran through Charlotte. If she had free time between meetings and overseeing the book table, she knew what she would be reading.

The bell above the shop door jingled, and Charlotte looked up. Her mother entered and crossed the shop toward the counter. Surprise rippled through Charlotte. Mum had only come to the shop once before, shortly after they had moved to Longdale.

"Hello, Mum. I didn't expect to see you today."

Mum lowered her voice. "I have some news, and I didn't want to wait until this evening to tell you."

"What is it?"

"Mr. Charles Kingsley paid me a visit this morning. He came representing the convention committee. They want to honor your father with a special award on the second night of the convention."

Charlotte's breath caught. "An award?"

"Yes. Mr. Kingsley spoke very warmly about your father."

Charlotte's gaze darted away. What could she say?

Mum leaned toward her. "I know it might be difficult to be the focus of attention as they speak about your father, but I hope you'll plan to attend with me."

Her stomach clenched. How could she take part in an award ceremony for her father and hide her true feelings? "Mr. Matterly expects me to work at the book table. I'm not sure I can get away."

Mum glanced at the shop owner and lowered her voice. "If you explain the situation, don't you think he could find someone to replace you that evening?"

A dizzy feeling washed over her. "I don't know, Mum."

But Mum continued as if she hadn't heard Charlotte. "I sent

word to Daniel, and he said he'll ask for time off and take the train up on Friday." Mum sent her a hopeful smile. "It will be so good to be there together. Mr. Kingsley asked if you might say a few words."

Charlotte slowly shook her head. "I don't think . . . I can."

Mum's expression faltered. "Well . . . all right. I'll speak to Mr. Donovan. Perhaps he can advise me on what to say and help me practice so I can accept the award."

Charlotte clenched her hands, her panic rising. "I don't understand. Why are they doing this now?"

Mum lifted her shoulders. "Several men on the committee were good friends with your father, and they want to honor him and his impact. You will attend with me, won't you?"

Charlotte closed her eyes, then forced a nod. "If that's what you want."

Mum straightened her jacket and nodded. "I think it will be meaningful for Daniel and Alice—a good memory they can hold on to as they think of your father."

Charlotte swallowed the sick feeling rising from her stomach. She'd carried the secret burden of her father's betrayal all these months. Surely she could continue carrying it through that ceremony to protect her mum and siblings from the shameful truth. But how could she stand by silently while they praised her father for his godly character and faithful devotion when nothing could be further from the truth?

Ian helped Milly climb down from the wagon and glanced at the people walking past them toward the center of town where the Keswick Convention meetings were held.

The guest rooms at their farm were full, and the town buzzed with people who had come from all over England and beyond to hear the speakers, take part in the prayer meetings, listen to missionary reports, and enjoy times of fellowship with like-minded Christians.

Ian tied up the horses, then he adjusted his vest and looked down the street. He turned to Milly. "Look at this crowd. I hope I'll see Charlotte."

"Don't worry, brother. I have a good feeling about tonight." Milly brushed her hand down his lapel and smiled up at him. "We've prayed about it. Now you must trust the Lord and let Him guide you tonight."

Ian nodded, recalling his conversation with Milly after Charlotte's visit to the farm. He was glad Charlotte had brought the basket for their father, but he was sorry he'd missed speaking to her. Perhaps it was for the best. From what Milly had told him, Charlotte had still been upset by Genevieve's visit and doubted his faithfulness. Milly had done her best to convince Charlotte of Ian's true feelings. She said Charlotte seemed to soften, but in the end, Milly was uncertain if Charlotte believed Ian truly cared for her.

Since his talk with Mr. Donovan, Ian could see the situation from Charlotte's perspective. He'd spent time praying and considering how to mend their relationship. Twice he'd tried to write to her, but each time he'd ended up crumpling the letter. Words on a page were not enough. He needed to speak to her in person.

That morning, he'd seen an article in the newspaper about the award they planned to give in honor of her father. The announcement had surprised him. No doubt it had surprised Charlotte as well. But he felt certain she would attend. It would be a difficult experience for her. She needed support, and he intended to be there for her.

He and Milly walked on, melting into the crowd. As they approached the entrance to the main tent, Ian's steps slowed. To the right, four long wooden tables were set up with books on display, and behind the tables stood Mr. Matterly and Charlotte.

His heart surged. "There she is," he whispered.

Milly clasped his arm. "Go ahead and speak to her. Don't worry about me. I'll find myself a seat."

He nodded to Milly, then moved toward the tables.

Charlotte held out a book to an older woman with a large feathered hat. "Is this the book you're looking for?"

The woman squinted and then smiled. "Yes, that's it. Thank you."

Mr. Matterly spotted Ian and stepped up next to Charlotte. He smiled at the woman. "I can take your payment, right down this way." He motioned toward the end of the tables, away from Charlotte.

This was his chance. He stepped forward. "Good evening, Charlotte."

She turned to him, and her eyes widened. "Ian." Her voice sounded a bit unsteady.

"I'm glad to see you," he continued. "Milly told me you came by the farm a few days ago. I'm sorry I missed your visit."

"Yes, I . . . wanted to bring something for your father. How is he?"

"He's improving—not as quickly as we'd hoped—but we're grateful he's still with us. The doctor says he must take it slower and not do as much as he did before."

"I'm glad to hear he is recovering. That's very good news."

He softened his voice and took a step closer. "I read about the award they're giving to honor your father tonight."

Her expression faltered as she glanced away. "Yes."

"I thought you might like the support of a friend who understands."

Her gaze returned to meet his. "Thank you, Ian. That's very kind of you." The warmth in her voice filled him with hope.

"Shall I find two seats for us?"

She glanced toward the tent. "My mum saved me a seat in the front row with my brother and sister." She met his gaze. "Would you like to sit with us if there is an extra seat?"

"Yes, I'd like that." He shot a glance toward the tent. What if this was his only chance to say what needed to be said? "Charlotte . . . before we go in, there are some things I want to say." He motioned to the end of the table, and she followed him there.

He was about to speak when piano music flowed out from the tent, and they both looked toward the entrance.

Charlotte focused on him again, her expression earnest. "I'm listening."

He took a deep breath. "I want to apologize. I know I hurt you by the way I acted when Professor Montrose and Genevieve came to Valley View. I'll not make any more excuses or try to explain it away. I've turned down the trip to Egypt, and I have no intention of seeing Genevieve again. Will you forgive me?"

Charlotte's eyes shimmered, and a soft smile formed on her lips. "Yes, I forgive you."

A wave of relief rushed through him. "I hope you'll believe me when I say my affections for you have never wavered, and they never will."

"Thank you, Ian." She looked down for a moment, then met his gaze once more. "I'm sorry as well. It's taken me some time, but I realize I let what happened with my father overshadow my thoughts and cloud my vision where you were concerned. I should have listened and given you the benefit of the doubt. . . . I should've trusted you."

His chest swelled, and he reached for her hand. "Thank you, Charlotte. I'm so glad to hear you say that. You are the only one for me. I just wish that we—"

Inside the tent, the song leaders called out the number for the first hymn, and a loud chorus of voices rose in song.

Charlotte squeezed his hand. "Mum's waiting. I need to go in."

He nodded. "I understand."

She held tight to his hand. "Come with me and see if you can sit with us."

He nodded and squeezed her hand in return, his hope renewed. He had more to say, but it could wait. This was a huge step forward and a new beginning for them.

The third hymn concluded, and Charlotte took her seat. All around her, skirts rustled, and chairs squeaked as the audience settled in to listen to the evening's speaker. She glanced at Ian and found he was looking her way. They exchanged a smile, and her heart fluttered. Ian's sincere apology had reassured her of his true feelings, and she sensed an even greater closeness with him. Their love and commitment had been tested and found to be true.

He shifted slightly, leaning toward her so his upper arm rested against hers. A comforting warmth flowed through her, making her grateful for his strength and nearness.

She glanced at the program. The award ceremony would follow the second speaker's message. When the time came, she had resolved to wear a look of appreciation for her mother's sake and pretend she was pleased the leaders of the convention had chosen to honor her father. She hoped it would help her mother resolve some of her grief.

The speaker, Mr. Horace Billington, a missionary with the China Inland Mission, was introduced to polite applause. He opened his Bible and began his message. Charlotte's thoughts drifted for a few minutes until Mr. Billington began retelling the parable of the prodigal son. It had always been one of her favorites, and she focused her attention on him.

He gazed out across the audience, and his voice took on the intonation of a skilled storyteller. "When the young man had wasted all the money his father had given him, and all his friends had turned away, the only position he could find was working for a pig farmer. For a young Jewish man, that was a distasteful and humbling job. But he was destitute and hungry—so hungry that he longed to eat the pigs' food.

"Sometimes it takes sinking to our lowest point to see things clearly. Those difficult circumstances were just what that young man needed to come to his senses, and he considered going home. But he was ashamed of what he had done and decided the only way he could return would be to offer himself as a servant, for surely his father would never accept him as a son."

Mr. Billington smiled, his eyes scanning the audience once more. "But he did not know the deep love of his father, nor did he realize his father was praying, watching, and waiting for his return. The young man left that pig farm and set off for home. I am not certain how long the journey took, but when his father saw him coming, he ran down the road with open arms. The father and son embraced, and the son was forgiven and restored.

"The father in this parable is a wonderful reflection of our Heavenly Father. He knows our sins and failures and how far we have wandered from the right road, yet He still loves us and calls us into relationship with Him."

Mr. Billington consulted his notes, then he looked out at the audience again. "Earthly fathers play an important role in our lives. The Bible says they are to provide, protect, and guide their children, but most of all, they are to love them and nurture their faith by their teaching and by their example."

Charlotte's throat tightened. She had deeply admired and respected her father in all those ways until she discovered his faults and failures after his death.

"But earthly fathers don't always live up to our expectations, and we are left with painful memories that may damage our earthly relationships and distort the image of our Heavenly Father."

Charlotte blinked, then stared at Mr. Billington. Did he know what her father had done? Had he prepared this message with her situation in mind? Or had the Lord given him those ideas for her benefit?

"Earthly fathers are human, and no matter how hard they try, they are bound to disappoint us. We have all experienced that to some degree, but the Lord often uses those hurts and disappointments to draw us closer to Him.

"There is only one perfect Father, the Lord of heaven and earth, our Good Shepherd. He will never leave us, nor forsake us. He doesn't change and is totally dependable. He is the one we must look to as our true example of fatherhood."

Tears misted Charlotte's eyes as the truth melted away another layer of pain around her heart. Yes, her earthly father's choices had wounded her, but she had a Heavenly Father who would never betray her. His love was perfect, and He would always be there to protect, lead, and guide.

Ian reached for her hand and gave it a gentle squeeze.

She tightened her hold on his hand, and gratitude filled her heart, bringing with it courage and hope. Her Heavenly Father had heard her heart's cry and met each need on this journey. He'd brought Ian into her life, given her family friends and a home, and He was helping her move toward acceptance and healing.

He was, and would always be, the Father she needed.

Twenty-Four

2012

Gwen sat cross-legged on her bed and stared at the keypad on her phone's screen as her stomach quivered. Lifting her finger, she hovered over the screen, then closed her eyes and breathed out a prayer. *Lord, help me.*

Why did she hesitate? For years she'd dreamed of finding her father and talking to him, but now that it was a possibility, she couldn't seem to cross that bridge. Once she made the call, she couldn't hold on to the image of the father she'd created in her imagination. She would have to face who he truly was and accept whatever relationship he offered . . . or didn't offer.

She clenched her jaw. Knowing the truth was better than not knowing. Holding her breath, she tapped in the number. The phone rang once, twice, three times.

"Hello?"

She gripped the phone tighter. "Hi . . . is this Landon Monroe?"

"Yes, it is." His voice was deep but not strong.

"This is Gwen . . . your daughter."

"Oh, Gwen, it's good to hear your voice. Thank you for calling."

"Of course. I'm sorry to hear you're in the hospital." She forced strength into her words. "How are you doing?"

"It's nothing for you to worry about. I'll be fine."

"Good . . . that's good. I'm glad." She waited, not sure what to say next.

"Mum told me you came to Valley View looking for our family."

"Yes. I met a man in Keswick who had a cane that was carved by your father. I'd seen a similar one in the photo of you and Mum. The man told me how to get to Valley View."

"Ah, so that's how you found Mum and Carol."

"Yes. I drove out there with David—"

"Is that your husband?"

"No. He's . . . a friend. His grandmother, Lilly Benderly, is the owner of Longdale Manor on Derwentwater. I've been doing some art and antique appraisals for them."

"You're an art appraiser?"

"Yes, I work for my grandfather at Hill and Morris in London."

"That's wonderful. I'm glad to hear you have a good career like that."

"Well, I've just been there a little over a year. I was an intern first, then in February I started in as a junior art specialist."

The phone line buzzed quietly for a few seconds. "Gwen . . . Mum told me about what happened to your mother. That must have been very hard for you."

She pressed her lips tight, trying to control her emotions, but tears filled her eyes. "Yes, it was so sudden, and we were very close."

He was quiet again for a few seconds, then he cleared his throat. "I'm glad you had each other. She was a good woman. I know this might be hard for you to believe, but I loved your mother very much."

A tear slipped down Gwen's cheek, and she sniffed.

"Oh no. Have I made you cry? I didn't mean to do that."

"It's okay. I'm glad to know you loved her." She gulped in a breath. "Did you know she was pregnant when you two separated?"

"No, she didn't tell me. I found out two years later, when a friend said she had a baby girl. He told me where she lived, and I went to London, hoping to see her. But when I was near her flat, looking for a place to park, I saw her coming down the street with a man. She was pushing a baby stroller and looked so happy." He sighed. "She didn't see me. I didn't speak to her." He huffed out a laugh, but there was no humor in it. "I was a fool to think she'd wait for me to get my life straightened out."

"I'm not sure who that man was. As far as I know, she never dated anyone."

"She didn't remarry?"

"No. It was always just the two of us."

"All those years she was on her own? Trying to make a living and take care of you?"

"We managed. She had a good job at a gallery in London, and Grandfather helped us."

He paused for a few seconds. "Oh, Gwen, I'm so sorry. I made a lot of bad choices that hurt you and your mother."

Gwen gulped. "She never told me what happened . . . why you two separated."

He sighed. "We were young. We only knew each other for a few months before we married. I was proud and hotheaded, and I drank to try and escape my problems. When I drank, I said and did hurtful things. Jessica warned me I was headed for trouble. Time after time she begged me to get help, but I didn't listen." He stopped and cleared his throat. "Only four months after our wedding, she left."

Gwen's throat burned, and sorrow for her parents stole away her words.

"I was angry. Her leaving sent me into a tailspin. But I don't blame her. She told me she couldn't stay unless I stopped drinking. I had a choice to make, and I made the wrong one."

"I'm so sorry," Gwen whispered.

"None of this is your fault. I'm the one who needs to apologize." His voice sounded choked and sorrowful. "I don't deserve it, but I hope someday you'll find a way to forgive me."

Her eyes burned, and she blinked back more tears. He sounded sincere, but was one heartfelt apology enough to make up for years of pain and separation? "Thank you for telling me more about what happened. I'm feeling a little overwhelmed, and I'll need some time to process all of this."

"I understand. That makes sense." Someone spoke to him in the background, but she couldn't make out the words. "They need to take me for some kind of test. Could we talk again tomorrow?"

"Of course. I'll call tomorrow morning around nine, if that's okay."

"That would be great. Thanks again. It means a lot that you called."

"I'm glad we could connect. I'll talk to you tomorrow." They said good-bye, and she ended the call.

Emotion swirled through her as she leaned back against her pillows and replayed what her father had said about going to London after he'd learned he had a daughter. He'd loved her mum and wanted to be reunited, but he'd felt unworthy to step back into her life when he thought she'd found someone new.

His apology replayed through her mind, along with his request for forgiveness. Something she'd read in Charlotte's journal rose to the surface of her thoughts.

When we choose to forgive others, we are not excusing what they did or saying it was right. We're releasing them into God's hands and allowing Him to deal out justice as He sees fit.

As she pondered that thought, the ache in her chest eased a bit. Forgiveness was not a one-time event—it was a process.

There would be layers to peel back and work through. But she could take the first step the next time she spoke to her father.

David tapped his key card against the lock and rolled his suit-case into his dark hotel room. He flipped on the light, checked his watch, and stifled a groan. It was ten minutes after ten, and he hadn't returned Gwen's call. He rubbed his eyes and sank down in the chair. Maybe she was still up.

He tapped in her number and lifted the phone to his ear. It rang once and went straight to voicemail. He grimaced. Why hadn't he taken five minutes earlier in the day and made the call?

Her recorded voice came on, inviting him to leave a message. The warmth and sincerity in her tone grabbed his heart.

"Hey, Gwen. Sorry I didn't get back to you sooner. It's been a crazy day. We met with the owner of Greystone, then we worked on the numbers and met with his daughter this evening to make our offer. It's an amazing property. I know you'd love it. We don't have a deal yet. We're still in negotiations. Max wants me to stay in town and keep working on the plans while we wait to hear back from the owner."

He loosened his tie and leaned back in the chair. "I hope the call to your dad went well. Let's connect tomorrow." He rubbed his eyes again. Man, he was tired. "Good night, Gwen."

The next morning, Gwen got up early, dressed in shorts and a T-shirt, and walked out to the terrace. She scanned the view of the peaceful garden and lake, then set off down the path for her walk. Only a few wispy clouds floated overhead in an intensely blue sky.

Her conversation with her father replayed through her mind as she passed through the garden, and a smile rose from her heart. The prayer she'd offered so many times had finally been answered. She'd found her father, and he'd been glad to talk to her. That didn't change the fact he and her mum shared a painful history, but he'd been honest and taken the responsibility for his part. He'd answered her questions, and she'd heard the sincere sorrow in his voice.

She thought through the series of events that had led to that phone call and shook her head. There was no way it could be a coincidence. God had brought them together, and she was eager to continue their conversation and see where it would lead.

Her thoughts shifted to David's phone message, and her smile faded. His voice had sounded so flat, as though he wasn't interested in anything except his new deal with Max.

Didn't he understand how important this was to her? She'd waited her entire lifetime to talk to her father. But David hadn't cared enough to return her call until after she'd gone to bed. How could she not feel hurt?

She pushed those confusing thoughts away and picked up her pace. There had to be a reasonable explanation. She needed to believe the best about him. That's what you did when you cared about someone. And she did care about him . . . she just wasn't sure he felt the same. Maybe she was expecting more out of their relationship than David wanted to give.

Thirty minutes later, she returned to the house and heard a phone ringing as she entered the great hall. She reached in her pocket but found it empty. She must have set down her phone when she'd tied her shoes before her walk.

"Is that your phone, dear?" Lilly asked as she came down the stairs.

"Yes." Gwen hustled across the hall, snagged it off the settee, and held it up to her ear. "Hello?" Nothing.

Lilly crossed toward her. "Was that David?"

Gwen looked up. "Yes. How did you know?"

Lilly's eyes twinkled. "It's not even eight o'clock. Who else would call you this early in the morning?"

Gwen smiled. "I'll call him back and see you in the dining room in a minute."

"Don't hurry on my account. Enjoy your call." Lilly walked away.

Gwen quickly tapped David's number and put it on speaker mode. It rang three times, then switched to his message. She frowned. That was odd. He'd just called her. Why didn't he answer? She sighed and slipped her phone into her pocket. She'd try again after she spoke to her father.

As soon as she finished breakfast, Gwen walked into the library and phoned her father. She settled on the couch as he answered.

"Good morning. This is Gwen." She injected cheerfulness into her voice.

"Hello, Gwen. How are you?" Her father's words came slower today.

"I'm fine. How are you feeling?"

"Oh . . . I'm a bit tired, but that's to be expected when they wake you up every few hours through the night." He gave a little chuckle. "So, I wanted you to know they're talking about releasing me tomorrow or the next day, depending on my bloodwork. Mum invited me to stay with her at Valley View for a time, and I agreed. I was thinking, if you're still in the area, you might come for a visit. I'd like a chance to see you and talk in person."

Her heart leaped. "I'd like that too."

"Good. I'll let you know when I'm released, and we can arrange a time."

"That would be great." She pulled in a deep breath. "I've been thinking about what you asked me yesterday . . . about forgiveness."

"Yes?"

"It reminded me of something in an old journal I've been reading."

"An old journal?"

"I'll tell you about that some other time. But what I wanted to say is . . . I forgive you."

He was silent for a few seconds, then cleared his throat. "Thank you, Gwen. That's great . . . more than I deserve. I've been carrying a load of guilt and regret all these years. I tried to numb that pain by drinking. But that only made things worse." He paused. "About a year ago, I met a man who helped me get into a program. I've been going to meetings and working the steps. I've been sober for eight months."

"Wow, that's great. I'm so happy for you."

"It's one day at a time, as they say. But I've been asking God for strength, and He's getting me through."

Her heart swelled. "I'm so glad to hear that. I've come back to my faith recently."

"That's good. I've been praying for you. I'll keep it up."

"Thank you." She swallowed hard. What a gift to know her father prayed for her. "David and his grandmother, Lilly, both have a strong faith. It's been helpful to see the way they live out what they believe in their daily lives. It's not just a Sunday-going-to-church kind of faith. It's the real thing."

"I'm glad you have friends like that."

"Yes, me too." Her voice softened. "Especially David."

"It sounds like he might be more than just a friend. If that's the case, maybe you'd like to bring him to Valley View when you come so I can meet him."

She smiled at the protective note in his voice. "He is someone special. And I'd love for you to meet him."

"I'll look forward to it." He was quiet for a moment. "Gwen, I want you to know even though I haven't been in your life, I've always loved you. And deep down, I held on to the hope that we'd meet one day."

She smiled. "I've hoped for that too."

He chuckled again. "Then we've both had a special hope and prayer answered."

David reviewed the day's events as he rode the hotel lift to the eighth floor. He and Max had been in back-to-back meetings since nine that morning. They finally reached an agreement on the sale price for Greystone Manor around noon. Max was eager to get the ball rolling while he and David were both in town. They'd grabbed a quick lunch, then drove all over Leeds to see builders, an architect, a solicitor, and the agent representing Mr. Smithers. Max wanted to get into Greystone Manor with the architect, take some measurements, and begin sketching out the renovation plan.

David had called Gwen first thing that morning, but she hadn't answered. He'd missed her return call when he was in the shower. The second time she called, they were in the final stages of the negotiation. Max had frowned at him when his phone rang, but he'd stepped out of the meeting to answer. She sounded happy about the conversations with her father and had just started sharing what he'd said when Max leaned out the door and waved him back into the meeting. He apologized to Gwen and promised to call her later.

But he'd gone straight from one meeting to the next and then to dinner with Max and two of Max's female friends. He'd been a bit uncomfortable with the situation, but he'd focused on the meal and tried to make the best of it.

The lift doors slid open, and he stepped out. His promise to call Gwen pricked his conscience. He checked his watch and blew out a deep breath. It was late. She was probably in bed already. He considered texting, but he didn't want a buzzing notification to wake her if she was already asleep. He'd call her in the morning.

Back in his room, he kicked off his shoes and loosened his tie, but he couldn't dismiss the nagging feeling that he'd let Gwen down. Why hadn't he made time for another call? Was he more concerned about Max's opinion than doing what was right by Gwen?

He grimaced. It was true he'd always admired Max. He was single and totally focused on his work. He lived, ate, and breathed his next venture. But as far as David could tell, he had no interest in faith or in lasting relationships. When David was with him, some of that intense focus pulled him in and influenced him in ways that were probably not the best.

He bowed his head. *I'm sorry, Lord. I worked hard today, but I got caught up in this project and lost my focus. I should've made time to connect with Gwen. Help me be on guard to make better choices tomorrow. Thank You for Your forgiveness and grace. I need it every day in so many ways.*

Twenty-Five

1912

Charlotte consulted the conference program and shifted in her chair. They'd sung three hymns and heard a stirring message from Mrs. Hildebrand, a missionary from India. It was time for the award presentation that would honor her father. Closing her eyes, she pulled in a slow deep breath and sent off a silent prayer for strength.

Mr. Kingsley walked toward the podium, and two other members of the committee joined him. "Tonight, we want to remember and honor Mr. Henry Harper, a respected leader and devoted follower of the Lord Jesus Christ. He spoke at the convention several times and inspired us with skillful teaching and knowledge of the Scriptures. Mr. Harper passed away in February while speaking at the Higher Life Conference in London. He has gone on to his reward, but he is sincerely missed by us all.

"His wife, Mrs. Rose Harper, his son, Daniel, and his daughters, Charlotte and Alice, are with us this evening. Please welcome Mrs. Rose Harper."

Mum rose, walked forward, and shook hands with the three men. Mr. Kingsley offered her a small wooden plaque. She accepted it and quietly thanked the men. They returned to their seats on stage.

Mum stepped up to the podium and faced the audience with a brave smile. "Thank you for honoring my husband in this special way. My family and I are grateful." Tears glittered in her eyes, but her voice remained steady. "We hope as you think of him, you will remember the focus of his messages, which was to be devoted to God and pursue His highest calling in our thoughts and actions. May that message remain in your hearts and minds in the years to come. Thank you very much."

The audience clapped as she descended the steps from the stage and returned to her seat. A final prayer was offered, and the meeting concluded.

As Charlotte stood, she felt as if a weight had been lifted from her shoulders. They had made it through the award ceremony. She glanced at her mum and was glad to see she looked more relaxed and relieved as well. Several people came forward to greet her mum.

Ian rose beside Charlotte and turned toward her. Smiling, he took her hand. "Your mum needs you now. I'll let you go. May I give you a ride to church tomorrow morning?"

She returned his smile. "Yes, please. I'd like that very much."

Affection glowed in his eyes. "I'll see you at ten. Good night, Charlotte." He squeezed her hand, tipped his cap, and set off down the aisle.

Those who had gathered around shared a kind word or recalled hearing her father speak at a previous convention or in London. When the crowd finally thinned, Charlotte picked up her sweater and program from her chair. As she turned toward Mum, a blond woman slowly approached.

She looked to be in her thirties and wore a light blue dress. As she came closer, she lifted a handkerchief to wipe her eyes. "Mrs. Harper?"

Mum turned to her. "Yes?"

"I'm . . . Eliza Mumford."

The woman's cheeks appeared blotched, and tears filled her eyes again. She looked slightly familiar, but Charlotte couldn't recall meeting her.

Eliza sniffed. "I wanted to say . . . I'm terribly sorry." Her voice shook with emotion. "Henry and I . . . well, we were—"

Mum's eyes flashed, and she stretched out her hand. "Just one moment." She turned to Charlotte and Daniel. "Please take Alice outside. I'll join you in a few moments." Her face had gone pale, but her tone was firm.

Charlotte glanced at Eliza, and recognition jolted through her. Eliza was the woman who had rushed forward when her father collapsed in London. She'd sobbed and called him Henry.

Her stomach dropped. Eliza Mumford was E. M. . . . her father's mistress and the author of the love letters.

Charlotte steeled herself and turned to Daniel. "You go with Alice. I'm staying with Mum."

"It's all right, Charlotte," Mum added. "You can go."

She met Mum's gaze. "I want to stay."

Mum studied her a moment, then nodded.

Her brother looked from Charlotte to Mum, questions in his eyes, but he placed his hand on Alice's shoulder and guided her toward the exit.

Eliza wiped her cheeks again. "I don't want to hurt or embarrass you, but I have to tell you the truth." She kept her voice low so that only Mum and Charlotte could hear. "Henry and I had been . . . meeting secretly for almost two years." Her chin quivered, and her throat convulsed before she could continue. "I'm truly sorry. I . . . I never should've become involved with him. I know it was wrong."

Mum pulled in a deep breath and straightened her shoulders, but she did not seem shocked by the confession. She nodded to Eliza. "Go on."

"I never intended it to go that far. We met here three years ago. I was grieving the loss of my husband, and he offered comfort and counsel. We exchanged letters, and eventually . . . became more involved." She shook her head. "I knew he was married and had a family. That should've stopped me, but I was lonely and longing for someone to make me feel alive again. That was foolish and reckless. I know that now, and I'm sorry, so very sorry." She lifted her hand to her mouth, and her shoulders shook as she lowered her head and wept.

A few seconds passed, then Mum stepped forward and laid her hand on Eliza's arm.

Eliza looked up.

"I'm sorry for the loss of your husband and the heartache you've been through," Mum said softly.

That brought on another round of shoulder-shaking sobs. Mum slipped her arms around Eliza and embraced her.

Tears burned Charlotte's eyes. How could her mum look past her own hurt and comfort the very person who had taken so much from her? She had always admired her mum's faith and trust in God, but her willingness to comfort Eliza left her speechless.

Mr. Donovan walked down the aisle toward them, concern lining his face. He glanced at Charlotte. "What happened?" he asked in a hushed voice.

Charlotte leaned toward him. "That is the woman who was involved with my father."

Mr. Donovan lowered his head and his lips moved in silent prayer. A few seconds later, he stepped forward and gently touched Mum's shoulder.

Mum looked up. She stepped back but kept her hand on Eliza's arm. "Eliza, there is someone I'd like you to meet."

Eliza sniffed and blotted her face with her handkerchief.

"This is the Reverend Matthew Donovan from St. John's Church." She turned to Mr. Donovan. "This is Eliza Mumford. She . . . knew my husband."

An understanding look passed between Mr. Donovan and Mum, then he nodded to Eliza. "I'm pleased to meet you. I hope you'll join us tomorrow for our worship service."

Eliza pulled in a shaky breath. "I'm not sure I'm staying in town. I only came to speak to Mrs. Harper."

Mum turned to Eliza. "Thank you for coming. That took a great deal of courage. Now that you've spoken to me, I hope you will take it to the Lord, accept His forgiveness, and move on with your life."

"That is . . . very generous of you. Thank you." She nodded slowly and walked toward the exit, clutching the handkerchief to her mouth.

Mum lifted her hand to her heart. "My goodness. I knew this day might come, but I didn't expect it to be tonight."

Charlotte's mouth fell open. "You knew about Eliza's involvement with Father?"

Mum released a heavy sigh and sent Charlotte a sympathetic look. "Your father changed a great deal in the last few years. I wasn't certain, but I suspected he might be involved with someone else. After he collapsed and was in the hospital, he confessed and asked my forgiveness. I was stunned and unable to answer him at the time." Emotion rippled across her face. "Then he slipped into unconsciousness and there was no way to say our final words."

"Oh, Mum." Charlotte stepped forward and hugged her mum, then pulled back to study her mum's face. "All this time you knew what he'd done, but you said nothing."

Tenderness filled Mum's eyes. "I know how much you loved your father. I didn't want to take away those good memories."

Charlotte shook her head. "I discovered a packet of letters from Eliza when I was clearing out Father's desk."

Mum gasped. "Why didn't you tell me?"

"I didn't want to hurt you or Daniel or Alice." Charlotte shook her head. "So many times I wanted to tell you, but I felt torn. I knew you were deeply grieving, and I didn't want to add to your sorrow."

Mum reached for her hand. "I'm sorry, Charlotte. That's not the kind of burden a daughter should have to carry for her parents."

Mr. Donovan gently touched Mum's arm. "I believe bringing this into the light will offer healing to you both, and for Daniel and Alice, when the time is right."

Mum nodded. "Yes, we ought to tell Daniel. I wouldn't want him to hear it from someone else." She clasped her hands together. "But I don't think it's the right time to tell Alice. I'll wait until she's older."

Mr. Donovan offered a small smile. "I'm proud of you, Rose. You handled a very difficult situation with much grace and kindness."

Her mum's cheeks flushed, and she smiled. "Thank you. I credit your wise counsel for helping me prepare for that encounter."

He lowered his chin in humble acceptance of her words, then looked at her again. "Not many women would've been able to do what you did for Eliza Mumford."

"I could see she was sincere, and I remembered what you told me about forgiving my father and how it would free me."

His eyes glowed. "Well done, Rose."

Charlotte glanced from Mum to Mr. Donovan. They obviously shared a growing respect for each other. Was there also a hint of affection? It was a surprising thought, but not an unpleasant one. Her mum was a wise and caring woman. She deserved to find happiness and companionship in the second half of her life, with a good man like Mr. Donovan.

He held out his arm. "Let me escort you to your carriage."

Mum took it with a smile, then linked her other arm through Charlotte's, and they walked out of the tent and into the moonlit night, accompanied by the crickets' serenade.

On Sunday morning, Ian arrived at Longdale just before ten. Charlotte met him at the door, and he helped her into the wagon for the ride to church. The rest of the family, including Grandfather, rode in the carriage ahead of them. Charlotte wasn't the least bit embarrassed to sit beside Ian on the front bench of the farm wagon. She sent him a warm smile, tucked her arm through his, and enjoyed the ride into town.

The pews at St. John's were nearly filled when they arrived for the morning worship service. Charlotte and Ian, along with her family, found seats in the second pew from the front. Charlotte enjoyed hearing Ian's warm and rich voice as they sang the first hymn, and she joined in with a grateful heart.

Mum's face glowed as she listened to Mr. Donovan deliver his message from the book of Philippians. Grandfather sat stiffly and didn't seem quite as pleased, but Charlotte was glad he had agreed to attend.

Following the service, they all returned to Longdale and shared a delicious meal of roast chicken, rice, and vegetables from the estate's kitchen garden. It was Ian's first invitation to join the family there. Charlotte smiled as she watched him meet the challenge with confidence, good manners, and polite conversation.

After lunch, Mum suggested they move out to the terrace. She and Charlotte helped Grandfather settle in a large wicker chair that gave him a view of the gardens and Derwentwater. Daniel challenged Ian, Charlotte, and Alice to a game of croquet. Laughter and teasing filled the air as they sent the balls rolling across the lawn. Alice outscored them all. Daniel scooped her up and carried her across the lawn, and they all joined in with her laughter.

Ian leaned down and whispered, "Can you slip away for a walk?"

A shiver of delight traveled down her arms. "Yes, I'd like that."

He took her hand, and they set off down the winding path through the garden. At the bottom of the hill, they passed Grandfather's boathouse and walked out on the dock.

They stopped at the end, and Charlotte looked out across the lake. The deep blue water rippled and sparkled in the afternoon sunlight, and a light breeze cooled her face. The mountains, or fells, as Ian always called them, were painted deep shades of brown, green, and purple—rugged and beautiful in stark contrast with the brilliant blue sky.

"I'd never seen such beauty until I came here."

Ian nodded. "It's a gift we must treasure and protect." He slipped his arms around her, drawing her close in front of him.

She leaned back against him, happy and secure in his strength and love. "Thank you."

"For what?"

"For not giving up on me through this hard season of grief and challenges."

He sighed into her hair. "I'm sorry it took me so long to understand what you needed from me."

She smiled. "I think I needed time to understand it myself." She looked up and met his gaze. "Your example of commitment to your family and trust in the Lord have meant more to me than I can say."

His tender gaze met hers. "And you, my dear, have won my heart."

"Have I, truly?"

"Yes." He released his hold on her. "Let's sit down. There's more I want to say."

Pleasant warmth filled her as he took her hand. They sat on the edge of the dock and dangled their feet over the side, well above the water.

"I want you to know what I've been thinking about the future and hear your thoughts."

She smiled. "I like the sound of that."

"I have only one more term at Oxford. I'd like to return in the autumn and finish my degree."

Her heart dropped, and she couldn't hide her disappointment.

He squeezed her hand. "I'll only be away for a few months. Then I want to come back and manage Valley View."

She waited, hoping he might say where she fit into the plan. When he didn't, she asked, "So, you're not going to pursue a career in archaeology?"

"Not right now. I'll try to keep up with the research, and if the opportunity arises, I might return to it in the future. But my family needs me here, and more importantly, you're here. And wherever you are, that's where I want to be."

She leaned against his shoulder. "I'd go with you to Egypt if you wanted to pursue archaeology there."

"That's a tempting offer, but I think this is the best place for us to live and raise a family."

She turned to him. "A family? What are you saying?"

He shifted to face her and took both her hands in his. "I'm saying . . . I love you, Charlotte, very much. I can't imagine spending my life with anyone else. And I promise no one will work harder to make you happy or cherish you more than I do. Will you make me a happy man and say you'll marry me?"

Joy bubbled up from her heart. "Oh, Ian! Yes, I'll marry you!"

He laughed and hugged her close. "Good, because I can't see a way forward without you."

She rested her head against his chest, comforted by the strong beat of his heart and warmth of his embrace. He was a good man—not a perfect man, but he would be a wise and devoted husband and father. And together they would look to their Father in heaven to lead and guide them toward a life that would honor Him and bring them great joy.

Twenty-Six

2012

Gwen's phone buzzed in her pocket as she walked down the stairs. She pulled it out, hoping to see David's name, but it was Elizabeth Monroe. She pushed off her disappointment and answered the call as she entered Longdale's library.

"Good morning, Gwen," Elizabeth said cheerfully. "I spoke to Landon last night. I can tell your calls have meant a great deal to him."

"I'm glad to hear it. They've been helpful for me as well. He explained some things I've wanted to understand for years."

"I glad you're willing to give him a chance to get to know you. It has given him hope and motivation to get stronger."

Gwen's heart lifted. "I know he's eager to leave the hospital and go to Valley View. He invited me to come and see him there, and to bring David."

"Good. Of course you're both always welcome."

"Any word on when he might be released from the hospital?"

"Soon, I hope. It will be so good to have him here with us." She paused for a moment. "I have something else to tell you. I was cleaning up the guest room, getting it ready for Landon, and I found that old Bible I've been looking for. It has a record of all the births, marriages, and deaths in our family, going back more than one hundred years."

"Oh?"

"And I found Charlotte Harper's name listed."

Gwen sucked in a breath. "Really?"

"Yes. It says she married Ian Storey in July of 1913. That would've been the year before the First World War."

Gwen bit her lip. "I wonder if Ian served in the war and survived."

"Apparently, he did. It says he lived until 1976."

"Good. I'm glad they had all those years together. Does it list their children?"

"Yes. They had three sons, Stephen, Robert, and Miles, and a daughter, Louise."

"Oh, that's wonderful."

"I'm so glad you found Charlotte's journal. Now we know she and Ian are the connection between the families at Longdale and those at Valley View."

Gwen's smile spread wider. "And that means I'm related to Charlotte!"

"That's right. Charlotte is your great-great-grandmother."

Gwen sat back in the chair. Not only was she Charlotte's great-great-granddaughter, she shared a heritage with the families who had lived at Longdale and Valley View.

"Gwen?"

She blinked. "Yes, I'm here. I'm just trying to understand all the connections and what that means."

Elizabeth chuckled. "It is quite a puzzle, but now that you see how the pieces fit, I hope you'll find Charlotte's journal even more meaningful."

Gwen's throat tightened. "It's a treasure."

"Do you think you could copy the entries? I'd like to read them and share them with my daughters."

"Of course." Her thoughts traveled back through what she'd

read, bits of stories and insightful comments Charlotte had written. "I'll work on that right away."

"Thank you, dear. I think it will be meaningful to them."

They spoke for a few more minutes about gathering the family at Valley View when Landon was settled and ready for a visit. Gwen thanked Elizabeth and ended the call.

She slipped the phone into her pocket and gazed toward the window, still processing her connection to Charlotte. Her great-great-grandmother had lived at Longdale for a time. She'd walked through these rooms and strolled in the garden. She'd found healing and restoration during her time in the Lake District, and it seemed she'd also found love.

There were still a few entries Gwen hadn't read yet. She'd saved those, not wanting Charlotte's story to end. But now felt like the right time to read her final entries, then take what she'd learned from Charlotte and write her own story.

She hustled up the stairs and walked down the hall to her room. Sunshine poured through the window as she settled on the bed and opened the journal to the final few pages.

We shared our happy news with my family and then Ian's. We were concerned that Ian's father or my grandfather might not be pleased, but both shook Ian's hand and congratulated us. We are relieved and look forward to making our wedding plans, though they will have to wait until Ian finishes his studies at Oxford.

I've learned so much these last few months. My heart has been sorely tested through the painful revelation of my father's betrayal. That showed me my faith had been built on the unstable foundation of my relationship with him. Now I see I must place my hope in my Heavenly Father and find my security in Him alone. He is the only perfect Father, the one who will always be faithful and true. That gives me a new foundation for my faith as well as hope for my future and the courage to take this next step with Ian.

Ah, Ian . . . I can't help smiling as I think of him and all the sweet and loving words he said to me today. I feel like dancing on the rooftop and singing a song to celebrate this special day. He wants to marry me and build a home and family together. I'm so happy and relieved he has chosen to honor his heritage and continue overseeing his farm and flock and caring for his father, mother, and sister. I will gladly join him in that commitment and look forward to many happy years at Valley View Farm.

Most of all, I'm thankful for the kindness and love of my Heavenly Father—my Good Shepherd, whose heart is true and whose love never fails.

Gwen walked through the gallery with Lilly, her gaze traveling from the empty spaces on the wall to the missing pieces of furniture. Their absence hit her in a strange way—almost as if this was her own home, and she was grieving their loss.

When she reached the doorway, Gwen slowed and looked back. "Would you like me to help you rehang the paintings you're keeping and rearrange the furniture?"

Lilly sent her a tender look. "No, dear. You have enough to do with overseeing the men who are packing up everything."

"They should be done soon. I'll be free to help you after that."

Lilly glanced back at the gallery. "Not today. I think it will take time for me to adjust to all the changes. And with the renovations David has planned, he may want to put some things in storage."

At the mention of his name, pain squeezed Gwen's heart. David was still in Leeds, working on plans for Greystone Manor with Max. His last few calls had been brief and businesslike. He hadn't even called yesterday. David was obviously not a phone guy. She tried to push down her hurt and disappointment, but she couldn't deny feeling disconnected. Was he purposely trying to distance himself from her?

She focused on Lilly again. "Let me know if you change your mind. I'd be glad to help."

"Thank you, dear. What time are you going to Valley View to see your father?"

"Tomorrow afternoon—if he's released from the hospital today. He said he'd call and let me know." She checked her watch, surprised to see it was already after ten. She would give him a call as soon as the team finished packing the items in the library.

"I'm sure you're looking forward to that visit." Lilly sent one last look around the room. "I think I'll go down to see Mrs. G. and have tea with her. Let me know when they take that last load to the lorry. I'd like to thank them for the wonderful job they've done and see them off."

Gwen nodded. "I'll let you know."

"Thank you, dear, for everything." Lilly squeezed her hand, then walked toward the back stairs.

Gwen stepped outside to the terrace and leaned against the balustrade, weariness coming over her. She'd stayed up late each night to finish the appraisals. When she contacted the shipment team, she'd been pleased to learn they had a cancelation and could come right away.

Less than twenty-four hours later, they arrived with a larger team than she expected. They worked quickly and packed all the items on the list, except those in the great hall and library, the first day. They expected to finish packing the items in those last two rooms before lunch. When they drove away, her official work at Longdale would be finished. She planned to stay on, at Lilly's invitation, to spend a few days visiting her father.

She had talked to him on the phone each day, and he'd kept her up-to-date on his recovery and relayed the doctor's encouraging reports. She told him about her school years, her university studies, and work at Hill and Morris. He explained his struggles in his second marriage that led to the divorce. He and his second wife were not able to have children. Knowing Gwen was his only child, and how he had not been there for her, added to his regrets. She reminded him that was in the past and the Lord had given them a chance to build a new future together.

She smiled, touched again by the memory of his hesitant and vulnerable invitation to meet him in person at Valley View. Soon she would see him, give him a big hug, and tell him how grateful she was to have him in her life.

"Gwen?" James, the leader of the shipment team, stepped out onto the terrace. "We're packing up the last two paintings in the library."

Her phone buzzed in her pocket. "Thank you, James. I'll be right in." She pulled out her phone, read Elizabeth's name on the screen, and tapped it.

"Gwen . . . I'm so sorry." Elizabeth's voice choked off.

Gwen's heart seized. "What's wrong?"

"The hospital called a few minutes ago. . . . Landon had a stroke this morning."

Gwen gasped. "Oh no!"

"They tried to revive him . . . but . . . he didn't survive." Her voice broke.

Gwen's head spun, and she gripped the balustrade. This couldn't be happening. He couldn't die. She'd just found him. "But he sounded fine yesterday. We made plans to meet at Valley View." Her voice rose to a panicked pitch. "I don't understand. The doctor said he was going to be all right."

"I know, I know." Elizabeth's voice shuddered. "I didn't expect this . . . and just when he was making such positive changes in his life. Oh, it just seems so unfair."

Hot tears burned trails down Gwen's cheeks. "I can't believe it. I would've gone up to Glasgow if I'd know this was going to happen."

"I know, dear. I wish you two could've met in person." Elizabeth sniffed and cleared her throat. "I want you to know your calls were the highlight of his day. Several times he told me how proud and impressed he was with all you've accomplished. He said you have a very loving heart, and he was so grateful you were willing to forgive him for being absent from your life all those years."

Gwen's throat swelled, and another round of tears overflowed.

Elizbeth heaved a heavy sigh. "We're not planning a funeral. Landon wanted to donate his body to science. When the time comes, the girls and I will spread his ashes at the farm up on the fells he loved. You're welcome to join us if you'd like. But we won't be offended if you'd rather not."

"Please let me know," she said softly.

"Of course, dear. I'll let you go. I need to make a few more calls."

"Good-bye," Gwen whispered, then she clicked off the phone and sank down on the terrace. Raising her knees, she lowered her head and wept for the father she was just learning to love.

David lifted his hand to shade his eyes and scanned the façade of Greystone Manor. Max and the architect stood to his left, waiting for his reply. "I think we should bring out the front terrace about three meters and then lengthen the roof to match. That will give the front a more balanced appearance."

The architect nodded and jotted the info into his notebook.

David's phone vibrated in his pocket. He pulled it out and read the screen.

Max rolled his eyes. "David, can that wait?"

"It's my grandmother. I need to answer." He turned away and lifted the phone to his ear. "Hello."

"Oh, David, something terrible has happened." Breathless panic filled her voice.

A slash of fear cut through him. "What's wrong?"

"Gwen's father had a stroke this morning and he . . . passed away. She's terribly upset. She's upstairs now, packing her suitcase. She says she's going back to London with those men who are taking everything to town for the auction."

A strange buzzing filled his head. "Gwen's leaving?"

"Yes. I tried to convince her to stay, but she's distressed and not thinking clearly. I hate to see her go off like this, carrying such a load of grief. She needs to be with friends, not sitting in her London flat."

A surge of energy shot through him. "Don't let her leave. I'm on my way." He clicked off the phone and spun around. "Family emergency. I need to go."

Max blinked. "You're leaving?"

"Yes." He started across the lawn.

"But what about this project?" Irritation filled Max's voice.

"Call me. I'll be available by phone." He stuffed his cell into his pants pocket and jogged the rest of the way to the car. Gwen was family. She needed him. He was not going to let her down this time.

With his thoughts darting from one dreadful outcome to the next, he made the trip back to Longdale in less than two hours and roared up the drive. The shipping team's lorry was gone.

He jerked out his keys and dashed into the house. "Gwen? Nana?" He strode through the entrance hall and into the library. He scanned the room, and his spirit plummeted.

His grandmother sat alone by the fireplace with her shoulders slumped. "I'm sorry, David. She's gone."

He crossed the room and knelt in front of her chair. "Tell me what happened."

Lilly relayed the details, explaining how happy Gwen had been after each phone call with her father. "Then, this morning, I was on my way to check on the men who were packing up things in the library when she came into the great hall in tears." She shook her head. "Gwen said her father had a stroke and couldn't be revived. It was such shocking news. They were going to release him today. She'd planned to go to Valley View to meet him tomorrow."

David shook his head. "What a terrible blow."

"Yes, it's dreadful. She just talked to him yesterday."

"But why did she leave? I don't understand."

Lilly sent him a pointed look. "She said her work was done, and she didn't have any reason to stay."

Those words hit him like a blow to the chest. "No reason to stay?"

"That's what she said." She leaned forward, her expression intense. "I thought you cared for her . . . but Gwen said she doesn't know what you have in mind."

He groaned and rose. "I should've made sure she knew how I felt."

Lilly pulled out a handkerchief and dabbed at her eyes. "That would've been helpful."

He lifted his hand and pinched the bridge of his nose. His last few phone calls to Gwen had not gone well. He hated talking on the phone. But that lack of connection had sent the wrong message. When Gwen faced devastating news, she'd fled rather than turn to him for comfort. He shook his head, disgusted with himself.

"Well . . . are you going to call her and straighten this out?"

He grimaced at the thought of another phone call. "No. I'm going to London." He swung around.

Lilly grabbed his arm and pointed to the mantel clock. "Look at the time. Even if you leave right now, you won't get there until after nine. Why not wait until morning? Get an early start, then you'll have plenty of time to find her and make things right." She narrowed her eyes. "And I do hope you will be clear about your feelings for her and your intentions."

He straightened his shoulders. "I will."

She rose, her serious expression easing into a gentle smile. "I know you have a good heart, David. I think Gwen knows it too.

You must be honest and make sure she knows how important she is to you." She opened her arms. "Now, I could use a hug."

He stepped forward and embraced her. "Thank you, Nana. I'm sorry you had to deal with all this on your own."

"It was a difficult day, but the Lord was with me. He always sees me through."

David kissed her cheek, grateful for her honesty and wisdom. She was right. The Lord was with them. He would carry them through these difficult days.

Twenty-Seven

2012

The lift doors slid open, and Gwen stepped into the third-floor offices of Hill and Morris. She wrinkled her nose at the scent of floral air freshener. It smelled nothing like the clean, fresh scent of Longdale's gardens.

MaryAnn looked up from behind the reception desk and offered a smile. "Good morning, Gwen."

Gwen nodded. "Morning."

"Nice to have you back."

"Thank you." She continued down the hall and glanced through Charlene's open door.

Charlene looked out. "Welcome back, Gwen."

"Thanks." Gwen didn't offer the expected "it's good to be back" because that wasn't true. London felt crowded and noisy after more than a month at Longdale. The city was hot, and she'd been stuck in the tube for more than an hour last night for some unknown reason. It was almost ten thirty when she finally tugged her suitcase through the door of her flat. Her roommate was already in bed, so she sank into a chair and stared out the dark windows until close to midnight.

"I looked through most of the appraisals," Charlene said. "Good work. I'm sure Mr. Morris will be pleased."

"Thanks. I hope he'll approve."

Charlene nodded. "He has high expectations, but he knows this business better than anyone else." She paused, then said, "Let's do lunch sometime."

Gwen forced a smile, but she didn't reply to the lunch invitation. That was Charlene's way of saying she was ready to put Gwen's mistake with the Hassam painting behind them.

Feeling weary and heartsore, she continued down the hall, determined to talk to her grandfather and learn if he approved of her work at Longdale. Mrs. Huntington was not in her usual seat, so Gwen knocked on her grandfather's closed door, and he called for her to come in.

She pulled in a deep breath and entered his office.

He looked up from behind his desk, and his silver eyebrows rose. "Gwen, I didn't expect to see you today. I thought you were staying at Longdale until next week."

She looked down a moment, then met his gaze. "My plans changed."

He motioned to the chair. "Have a seat."

She slid into the chair facing his desk. "Have you looked through the appraisals?"

"Some. They seem . . . acceptable."

Gwen's stomach tensed. "Is there a problem?"

"No, but it took you quite a bit longer than I expected."

She sat up taller, ready to do battle. "I had to evaluate more than one hundred fifty pieces. You told me to be thorough and take as long as I needed. That's what I did."

He lifted his hand. "There's no need to get upset. I think your appraisals are in line with what I expected."

She released a deep breath. "Good."

"Longdale sounds like an impressive home. I appreciate the

investment suggestion. David Bradford seems to have a solid plan for the estate."

She gripped the arms of the chair, trying to steel herself against her reaction to his name. "Yes . . . it's a good plan."

All that had happened with David and her father poured through her mind. She'd gone to Keswick determined to prove herself. It seemed she'd accomplished that goal, but it felt hollow as she considered all she'd gained and lost in the last month. With David's departure and her father's death, her hopes had faded, and grief had carved more empty places in her heart.

Her grandfather frowned. "Gwen, what is it? You don't seem to be yourself."

She shivered and met her grandfather's gaze. "I found my father. We spoke on the phone, and we were scheduled to meet in person today, but . . . he died yesterday morning."

"Landon Monroe is dead?"

She clenched her jaw. "Yes. He had a stroke. It was totally unexpected." Tears filled her eyes.

"I can see you're upset. But it's probably for the best. The man had serious issues. Look how he treated your mother— deserting her when she was pregnant and never taking any interest in what happened to you. His choices and behavior were disgraceful."

She steeled herself. "No, Grandfather. There's more to the story, and I'm glad I got to hear his explanation of what happened."

"His explanation?" He glared at her. "There is no excuse for what he did to your mother."

"You can't place all the blame on him. She never told him she was pregnant. He had no idea. And she was the one who chose to leave."

"A woman doesn't leave her husband for no reason! He turned to drink. That's what destroyed their marriage."

"He had a drinking problem, but he got help. He changed."

Her grandfather lifted his hand. "That's enough! I won't listen to you make excuses for that man and dishonor your mother's memory. She devoted her life to raising you and giving you a secure and stable home. He did nothing! How can you even speak to someone like that?"

Pain twisted her chest, and she shook her head. "Why do you insist I hate one and love the other? Can't I love them both?"

His face hardened. "No, you can't." He turned back to the paperwork in front of him. "I have nothing more to say. You should go."

Stung, she rose and walked out of his office. Pain vibrated through every nerve as she walked back to her office, closed the door, and sank down in her chair.

Lowering her head, she rested her elbows on the desk and covered her stinging eyes. *Lord, I don't know what to do with all this heartache. It feels like no one cares or understands what I'm going through. I know that's not true. You care, but I feel so alone in all this. Help me. Please, help me.*

She replayed her grandfather's words, and the grief flooded in again. What he'd said about her mother was true. She had made tremendous sacrifices to give Gwen a good life. She never lacked love, encouragement, or support. If only her mum were still alive, and Gwen could talk to her.

If her mum had known Landon went through treatment and then came to London, hoping to be reunited, would she have forgiven him and let him back into their lives? If she had learned the truth before she died, could she have released the heartache she'd carried all those years and forgiven him?

What could she do with all her *if onlys*?

An idea filtered through her mind, and she lifted her head. She was supposed to meet her roommate for lunch. Instead, she texted Lindsey, gave her a brief explanation, and asked to have lunch together another day. Then she grabbed her purse and headed out the door.

Forty minutes later, she walked through the gates of Rose Hill Cemetery and made her way down the shady path. A few birds chirped in the trees overhead, and a soft breeze carried the scent of freshly mowed grass. Some people thought cemeteries were creepy, but she'd always found this small, parklike cemetery a sacred, peaceful place.

Her mother's grave was in the northeast corner, next to her grandmother's.

Gwen leaned down and traced the words on her mother's stone. *Jessica Eileen Morris, September 6, 1965–April 3, 2010. Beloved Mother and Daughter.*

It said nothing about her being a beloved wife. Grandfather didn't believe that was true and never would've added those words. It seemed he had hardened his heart for years and wore his hatred for Gwen's father like a badge of honor.

She sighed and sat down on the grass. "Mum, so much has happened, I don't know where to start." She closed her eyes, knowing her mother wasn't really there, but wishing, somehow, her words would reach her in heaven.

She opened her eyes and brushed her hand across the soft grass. "I met Dad . . . not in person, but we talked on the phone. I understand now why you didn't want to tell me much about him until I was older. He had a hard life, and he made some bad choices. But he changed. He's not the same man he was when you were married. He admitted what he did was wrong and said he was sorry for hurting us. He asked for my forgiveness. I had to think about that, but later I told him I forgave him."

Passages from Charlotte's journal floated through her mind, giving her an anchor in the rising waves of emotion. "I've learned forgiveness is just as much for my benefit as it is for the other person. It's like giving up my right to hurt someone back and letting God handle the justice of the situation as He thinks best."

She looked up, and flashes of sunshine and blue sky filtered through the leaves, sending shifting shadows over her in a gentle, soothing dance. "Dad said he loved me, and he always hoped we'd meet one day." She smiled through her tears, cherishing those words in her heart. "We had some good talks—really good. We were supposed to meet today at Valley View. I so wish that could've happened. It's hard to believe I missed seeing him by only one day."

She blew out a ragged breath. "But I know he's healed and free of pain now. Maybe you two will meet in heaven, and all the old hurts and misunderstandings will be forgiven and forgotten."

That was a comforting thought. Neither of her parents had lived a perfect life. But they both had faith in Jesus and believed He would welcome them home to heaven. Remembering the promise of eternal life didn't make her miss them less, but it did ease that lost, hopeless feeling that weighed her down.

She folded her arms on her knees, then rested her head on her arms. Closing her eyes, she tried to imagine what it would be like to see her parents in heaven. No image formed, and she released a sigh. That was a mystery. She would have to be content to wait and see how it would unfold. Her parents were safe and happy there, and she would be with them one day. . . . That was enough for now.

Her thoughts drifted back to Longdale. What serendipity to learn she had a spot on Longdale's family tree and a connection to the people and life in the Lake District. She pictured the lovely old manor house perched on the hill above Derwentwater. Its remarkable architecture and rich history had touched her in a way she'd never expected. The beauty of the lake, the gardens, and the mountains had been food for her soul. Even though she'd only been there for a few weeks, it had felt very much like home.

As much as she missed Longdale, she missed David more. She opened her eyes and glanced at her mother's gravestone again. "I met someone in Keswick. His name is David." Her thoughts spun back through the special times they'd shared and the hope that had bloomed in her heart as they'd grown closer. "He's a visionary, and he works incredibly hard to see those visions become reality. He's saving his grandmother's estate by converting her home into a luxury hotel." She smiled, remembering how they had pored over the plans and found ways to preserve some of Longdale's beautiful architectural elements. "With his knowledge of construction and my background in art and antiques, I thought we made a great team."

"So did I." The familiar voice came from behind her.

She gasped and looked over her shoulder.

David stood a few feet away. He tilted his head, silently asking permission to join her.

She pulled in a shaky breath and rose. "How did you find me?"

He walked toward her. "I went to your flat and met your roommate. She said she thought you'd be here."

"You came all the way from Leeds?"

"No, I came from Longdale. Nana called yesterday and told me about your father." His voice softened. "I'm sorry, Gwen. I know what it's like to lose a parent, and in your case, you'd just found him."

Her throat tightened. "Yes," she whispered.

"Nana said you were leaving, so I raced back, but you'd already left."

She studied his face, not quite sure of his meaning. "So . . . why are you here?"

"I know I've made a huge mess of this whole thing." His Adam's apple bobbed in his throat, and a sheen of moisture glistened in his eyes. "I got so caught up in my work that I lost sight of what's most important. I hate that I let you down and that I was out of touch when you needed me the most."

She blinked back her tears. "It's been such a hard time. And I didn't know what to think when your calls were so . . . short."

He sighed, regret reflected in his eyes. "I'm so sorry. I should've talked to you about our relationship rather than expecting you to read my mind."

"It has been pretty confusing."

He nodded and took her hand. "I hope you'll forgive me, and we can work this out because . . . I love you."

Her heart melted, and she stepped toward him. "You love me?"

"Yes, I do."

"That's good, because I love you too."

He huffed out a laugh. "Well, that's a relief." He pulled her close and hugged her.

She slid her arms around his waist and closed her eyes, leaning in. She could hardly believe he'd come all the way to London. It was so unexpected—such an amazing gift.

He kissed the top of her head. "I know how much you wanted to see your father. I'm sorry that didn't happen."

She sniffed and pulled back. "I told him about you. He wanted to meet you."

"You told him about me?"

She nodded. "I did."

He gently ran his hand down the side of her cheek. "I would've been honored to meet your father."

Her heart warmed, but then questions flooded her mind. "What are we going to do now? How can this work when I live in London, and you live in Manchester?"

"I've got an idea."

She laughed softly. "You always do."

His eyes gleamed. "Of course."

"Go on. What's your idea?"

"This might sound a little crazy, but what if I offered you a position with my company?"

"A position?"

He nodded. "Your knowledge and skills would be a perfect fit. You could stay on at Longdale and help plan the details for remodeling the interior, using the artwork and furniture we have and buying what we need for the guest rooms. And I could definitely use your help with the Greystone Manor project."

Her heart expanded. "Really? You want us to work together?"

"I know that's asking a lot for you to give up your position at Hill and Morris, especially since you work with your grandfather, but as you said, we do make a great team."

"So . . . you're talking about a business relationship?"

He placed his hands on her upper arms. "Yes, but I want more than that. I want us to go through the seasons together and learn all we can about each other with the goal of moving toward marriage."

Her eyes widened.

"I'm not asking you to decide right now. I just want you to know I'm serious about our relationship. I want us to have time together so I can show you I'm committed. What do you say?"

She rose up on her toes. "I say . . . yes! I'd love to work with you and see what the Lord has for us in the future."

His eyes danced as he leaned down and sealed the deal with a kiss. She drank in the sweetness of his affection and returned the same, showing him how much she loved him and how grateful she was for his love.

Six Months Later

Gwen grimaced and adjusted her hold on the trunk of the eight-foot fir tree she and David had cut down and carried back to Longdale Manor. The branches prickled her arms, and a strong evergreen scent filled her nose. "I thought you said this tree wasn't heavy."

David grunted as he followed her up the main staircase, carrying the bushy lower section of Lilly's Christmas tree. "It's more awkward than heavy."

Gwen huffed out a laugh. "That's easy for you to say!"

He looked up at her with a teasing grin. "Come on, Morris. We can do this."

Lilly stepped out of her newly renovated rooms at the end of the east wing. "Oh my goodness! That tree is huge! I'll hold the door." She slipped inside and pulled her door open as wide as it would go.

After two tries, they stuffed the tree through, leaving a shower of needles on Lilly's new carpet. She'd been amused by their struggles and clapped when they finally pulled it inside.

"Bring it right over here by the window." Lilly hurried across the room to where she'd placed the tree stand. "Then we'll be able to see the lights from outside."

David slowly lowered the tree and maneuvered the trunk into the stand, then he knelt to secure it in place. "Is it straight?" he called from between the lower branches.

"A little to the left." Lilly motioned with her hand, though Gwen doubted David could see anything through the thick branches.

He patiently adjusted the tree until Lilly gave her approval.

Gwen smiled, love for him overflowing her heart. What a man. He'd spent more than two hours searching for the right tree, cutting it down, and carrying it back to the house. And he'd done it all to make his grandmother happy.

David crawled out from under the tree and joined Gwen and Lilly. He brushed off his hands and turned to his grandmother. "Well, Nana, what do you think?"

"Oh, David, it's the most beautiful tree I've ever seen—so full and lush. Where did you find it?"

"Up on the north ridge."

"Thank you, dear." She turned to Gwen. "Thank you both. That must have been quite a feat to bring it all the way up here."

David slipped his arm around Lilly's shoulder. "We're glad

to do it for you, Nana. Gwen had a bit of a struggle, but we made it." He grinned and sent Gwen a teasing wink.

"I'll have you know I carried my end the entire way."

Lilly chuckled. "You two make a good team."

"That we do." David slipped his other arm around Gwen's shoulder.

She snuggled up next to him and released a contented sigh.

"I brought out the boxes of lights and ornaments." Lilly motioned toward the stack on the floor by the window. "David, why don't you get started with the lights? Gwen, I could use your help in the kitchen. Let's make some hot chocolate to enjoy while we decorate the tree."

She agreed and followed Lilly toward her beautiful new kitchen. When she reached the doorway, she looked over her shoulder and found David watching her with an endearing look. "I'll be right back," she called.

"I hope so." He grinned and winked again.

She laughed softly and continued into the kitchen. These last few months at Longdale had been some of the happiest of her life. She'd spent the first few days cleaning and painting the old groundskeeper's cottage, with David's help, then she settled in there. After that, she'd worked alongside David on the renovations at Longdale and Greystone Manor.

David had encouraged her to take on independent appraisal projects. She'd done a few, but most of her days were spent with Lilly and David and their small circle of friends.

Her grandfather had not taken her resignation well. But in November, he'd accepted their invitation and come to Longdale to check on the progress of the renovations. She and her grandfather had a private discussion, and he'd finally come to terms with her decision. When it was time for him to leave, she'd given him a hug and promised to stay in touch. He'd remained stiff and stoic, but at least he'd come, and that was a start.

Lilly hummed a Christmas carol as she placed three mugs on a wooden tray. "Would you put these marshmallows in a bowl?"

"Sure." Gwen cut open the bag and filled a small bowl. "Anything else?"

Lilly glanced around the room, then turned to Gwen. "That's everything. Would you take in the tray? I think it's a bit heavy for me."

"Of course." Gwen added the bowl of marshmallows and lifted the tray.

"Oh, I forgot the gingerbread!" Lilly hustled across the room and took a paper-wrapped square from the cupboard. "I brought this home from Grasmere yesterday."

Gwen smiled, looking forward to that spicy sweet treat.

"You go ahead, dear. I'll be along in a minute."

Gwen carried the tray into the sitting room, and her steps stalled. All the lights had been turned off, and several candles had been lit around the room.

David stood beside the tree, watching her. His eyes shone in the candlelight and reflected something mysterious.

"What's going on?"

He stepped forward, took the tray from her hands, and placed it on the coffee table.

"David?"

He knelt on one knee in front of her, held out a small black velvet box, and looked up with tender vulnerability in his expression.

Her heartbeat surged, and she lifted her hand to her mouth.

"Gwen, from the first day we met, I knew you were special. I had a feeling you were going to change my life for the better, and I was right. Every day since then, I've fallen more and more in love with you. If you're willing, I'd like to spend the rest of my life loving you and building a home and life with you." He paused for a second, then said, "So what I'm asking is . . . will you marry me?"

"Yes, of course I'll marry you!" Joy spiraled through her as she reached for him, and they stepped into each other's arms. Oh, how she loved this man. What an amazing gift he was to her.

He held her close, and they swayed in time to the silent love song playing in both their hearts, a song she was sure would play on for the rest of their lives.

"Oh, wait." He stepped back and opened the box. "I have a ring for you."

She laughed softly and held out her left hand. The diamonds sparkled in the glow from the candle's flame as he slid the beautiful ring on her finger. "Oh, it's perfect. Thank you, David. I love it, but I love you more." She rose on tiptoe and kissed him as her heart overflowed with gratefulness.

A door squeaked, and a soft voice came from the kitchen. "Did she say yes?"

Gwen started to step back, but David chuckled and kept his arms around her. "She did!" he called as they both turned toward Lilly.

The kitchen door swung open, and Lilly strode out. "Oh, I'm so happy! You two are meant to be together. That's what I said from the beginning. I can always sense a special connection like that."

Gwen laughed and hugged Lilly. "Thank you for believing in us and bringing us together."

"Well, I did have a small part in that. But I'd say it was the good Lord above who made this match."

David sent Gwen a broad smile and slipped his arm around her shoulder. "You're right about that, Nana. I'd say Gwen is heaven-sent."

"Oh, I almost forgot." Lilly crossed to the table beside her favorite chair. "I found something I wanted to show you." She opened Charlotte's journal and carefully turned the pages.

Gwen and David crossed the room and joined her.

Lilly took out an old photograph and turned to Gwen. "Can you guess who this is?"

Gwen accepted the photo and studied the young couple. The woman was dressed in a white bridal gown and held a trailing bouquet of flowers. Her dark hair was parted in the middle and tucked under a long lace veil. Her expression was unsmiling but serene. The tall man standing close beside her looked tanned and handsome. He wore a dark suit and serious expression, but proud light shown in his eyes. The sepia tone gave Gwen a clue the photo was taken in the late nineteenth or early twentieth century.

David leaned closer. "Look, he's holding a shepherd's staff."

Gwen's gaze darted to the shadowy left side of the photo and leaned closer. "Yes, he is."

David glanced her way. "Do you think it's some kind of Lake District wedding tradition?"

"We'll have to ask Elizabeth. Maybe you'll need to carry your grandfather's staff on our wedding day."

He grinned. "That would be unique."

Gwen turned to Lilly. "This has to be Charlotte and Ian."

Lilly nodded. "That's right. Their names and wedding date are written on the back. I found it today when I was going through some old photos in the archive room."

Gwen studied Charlotte's image once more as waves of memories washed over her. Getting to know Charlotte through her journal had been like developing a friendship that reached across time. She'd gained so much comfort and insight from what Charlotte had learned and written. Those were timeless gifts that she would always treasure.

David turned to her. "You mentioned naming our guest rooms instead of numbering them. Maybe we should name one after Charlotte and Ian."

"That's a wonderful idea. We could frame this photo and hang it in that room. Maybe I could copy some passages from her journal and have those framed as well. That way her words would live on."

"That's a lovely idea," Lilly said. "And it's the perfect way to honor our family history."

Gwen carefully turned the pages in the journal. "I know one passage I'd like to frame." She found it near the end and read it aloud, "'Time is fleeting, the days fade fast. Treasure faith and family, only they will last.'"

David glanced at Gwen. "I didn't know Charlotte was a poet."

"It's the only passage like that." Gwen's gaze darted to the top of the journal page. "She wrote it just after she attended the Keswick Convention in the summer of 1912."

Lilly stepped closer and gazed down at the journal. "Charlotte was wise beyond her years. We should all take those words to heart."

David nodded, then slipped one arm around Gwen and the other around Lilly, drawing them both closer. "I couldn't agree more."

Gwen leaned her head against David's shoulder, comforted by his strong arm around her and his heartfelt proposal. She would hold on to all she'd learned from Charlotte, nurture her rekindled faith, and focus on building a strong and healthy marriage and family with David. With those as her foundation and him by her side, their future was certain to be bright with hope and promise.

Author's Note

Dear Reader,

I hope you enjoyed reading *The Legacy of Longdale Manor* and taking a literary visit to England's beautiful Lake District. I was privileged to visit many of the places mentioned in this story a few years ago with my dear friend and fellow author Cathy Gohlke. Sailing across Lake Windermere and visiting Beatrix Potter's Hill Top Farm are two of my favorite memories from that trip. We loved sampling the delicious gingerbread in Grasmere and watching shepherds overseeing their flocks of sheep. I was captivated by the natural beauty of the lakes, mountains, and countryside. I loved wandering the streets and visiting shops in several charming villages. I wanted to set a story there, and when these characters came to mind, I knew the Lake District would be the perfect place for them to come and find what they were seeking.

The rich Christian heritage of the Lake District, with the many beautiful churches and the Keswick Convention—which continues today—also stirred my imagination. I like my characters to meet people who live out their faith in practical ways, people who can help them see how God's love and truth can guide them through the challenges they face. Creating Lilly to help Gwen and Pastor Donovan to help Charlotte, Rose, and

Ian gave me the opportunity to show how comfort and wisdom can be passed on to those the Lord brings into our lives.

The themes of fatherhood, forgiveness, and holding on to your faith through painful times are important to me, and I hope they shine through in this story. The first seed for this story came to me as I read the heartbreaking news story of a religious leader's moral failure. I wondered how his wife and children were dealing with those painful revelations, and how it would impact their faith. When I researched the history of the Keswick Convention, I learned that the first keynote speaker they invited had to cancel because of a similar issue coming to light. That brought the ideas together, and I set out to help my characters learn how to strengthen their faith while going through painful times.

England's Lake District is a wonderful vacation destination. I hope you'll be able to visit one day! It's an amazing place where you can enjoy God's creation and renew your spirit. If you'd like an armchair visit to the Lake District, take a look at my Pinterest board for this story, where you'll see character inspiration photos and lots of beautiful images of the story's setting (pinterest.com/carrieturansky/the-legacy-of-longdale-manor/).

If you enjoyed *The Legacy of Longdale Manor* and you're looking for more novels set in England in the early 1900s that are filled with family drama, romance, and inspiration, I hope you'll visit my website, carrieturansky.com, and peruse my other novels.

Until next time . . . blessings and happy reading!

Carrie

Acknowledgments

I am very grateful for all those who have given me their support and encouragement and provided information in the process of writing this book. Without your help, it never would've been possible! I'd like to say thank you to the following people:

My husband, Scott, who always provides great feedback and constant encouragement when I talk about my characters, the plot, the editing process, and what's happening next. Your love and support have allowed me to follow my dreams and write the books of my heart. I will be forever grateful for you and our love and partnership in life!

Steve Laube, my literary agent, for his patience, guidance, and wise counsel. You have been a great advocate who has represented me well. I feel very blessed to be your client, and I appreciate you!

Jessica Sharpe, Jennifer Veilleux, Bethany Lenderink—my gifted editors—who helped me shape the story and then polish it so readers will be able to truly enjoy it. I so appreciate your thoughtful questions, insight, and gracious way of collaborating!

Kathleen Lynch of Black Kat Designs for the lovely cover and for allowing me to offer suggestions and then working those into the design. I love how you captured the heroine, the setting, and the feeling of the story!

Raela Schoenherr, Karen Steele, Anne Van Solkema, Rachael Betz, and all the marketing and publicity team at Bethany House for bringing me into the family, promoting my books, and offering me this opportunity to share my stories with readers.

Cathy Gohlke, who traveled with me to the Lake District and brainstormed ideas for stories based on that lovely setting. Your friendship, prayers, and encouragement are a priceless gift to me!

Cher Gatto, Terri MacAdoo, Stacy Ladyman, and all the ACFW NY/NJ group for your friendship, encouragement, and support. More adventures await us on this journey!

My dear readers, especially those who are members of Carrie's Reading Friends Facebook Group, who offer their kind reviews and help me promote each book. I'm blessed to have such a supportive circle of friends! Your thoughtful posts and encouraging emails keep me going!

Most of all, I thank my Lord and Savior, Jesus Christ, for His great love, wonderful grace, and faithful provision. I am grateful for the gifts and talents You have given me, and I hope to always use them in ways that bless You and bring You honor and glory.

Discussion Questions

1. As the story opens, Gwen learns she has made a major mistake that tarnishes her reputation at work and with her grandfather. She determines to do whatever is needed to regain her grandfather's trust. What lessons did Gwen learn from making that mistake?

2. David's goal was to help his grandmother save Longdale, but he ran into several problems as he worked toward that goal. What were those problems, and how did he overcome them? What did you notice about the way David went after his goals? How did that impact his relationship with Gwen?

3. Gwen and David did not get off to a good start in their relationship. What were the issues that came up for them early in the story, and how did they work through those? Have you ever learned that your first impression of someone was not correct?

4. Gwen grew up without a father in her life. How did this impact her? What did she gain by connecting with her father? Fathers play an important role in our lives. What is one lesson you learned from your father?

5. Charlotte's journal entries had a great impact on Gwen. What were some of the lessons she learned from Charlotte, and how did they help her resolve the issues she

was facing? Have you ever kept a journal or read someone else's journal?

6. Charlotte deeply admired her father, but after his death, she learned he had been carrying on a secret affair. Throughout the story, she struggled with hurt, confusion, and bitterness. How did she work through those feelings? Who helped her, and what did they do to guide and comfort her?

7. Ian was torn between staying at Valley View and working with his family, or returning to Oxford and pursuing an archaeology career. What was drawing him toward archaeology, and what was pulling him to stay at Valley View? What did you think of his decision at the end of the book?

8. Forgiveness is a theme woven through both the contemporary and historical plots. What made forgiveness difficult for Charlotte? What made it a challenge for Ian? How did the need for forgiveness touch Gwen's and David's lives? Did their journeys toward forgiveness motivate you to think about the need to offer forgiveness to someone in your life?

9. The setting for the book is England's beautiful Lake District in the northwest section of the country. Have you read any other books or seen any movies set in that area? Did the descriptions motivate you to want to learn more, look up a map, or even plan a visit? What would you like to see if you went to the Lake District?

10. The role of fathers and the fatherhood of God are important themes in this story. What stood out to you about the fathers in this story? How can a relationship with God help meet needs that our human fathers might not have met?

CARRIE TURANSKY has loved reading since she first visited the library as a young child and checked out a tall stack of picture books. Her love for writing began when she penned her first novel at age twelve. She is now the award-winning author of twenty-two inspirational romance novels and novellas.

Carrie and her husband, Scott—who is a pastor, author, and speaker—have been married for forty-five years and make their home in New Jersey. They often travel together on ministry trips and to visit their five adult children and eleven grandchildren. Carrie is active in the women's ministry at her church, and she enjoys leading women's Bible studies and mentoring younger women. When she's not writing, she enjoys working in her flower gardens, walking around the lake near their home, and cooking healthy meals for family and friends.

She loves to connect with reading friends through her website, carrieturansky.com, and via Facebook, Instagram, and Pinterest.

Carrie Turansky

@carrieturansky

@carrieturansky

Sign Up for
Carrie's Newsletter

Keep up to date with Carrie's latest news on book releases and events by signing up for her email list at the link below.

FOLLOW CARRIE ON SOCIAL MEDIA

Carrie Turansky   @carrieturansky   @carrieturansky

CarrieTuransky.com